Heir

OMAERA PLAYFAIR CHRONICLES

BOOK 1

NATALIE SLOAN

Editing: Bound for Perfection Editing

Cover Design: EmCat Designs

DON'T FORGET

Be sure to sign up for my newsletter to stay up to date on new releases, deals and more.

Sign up here —> https://nataliesloan.com/contact-me/

Become a Patreon Patron to get short stories, secondary character stories, favorite character update stories, exclusive cover reveals, exclusive excerpts from WIPs and more!

Support here —> https://patreon.com/authorwhitleycox

A few other books by Whitley Cox

The

Single Dads of Seattle

Grab book 1 here

https://books2read.com/HBTSD-SDS

*

The Quick Billionaires

Grab book 1 here

Quick & Dirty

https://books2read.com/QDirty-QBS

*

The Harty Boys

Grab book 1 here

Hard Hart

https://books2read.com/HH-HB

*

The Young Sisters

Grab book 1 here

Not Over You

https://books2read.com/not-over-you

*

Doctor Smug

https://books2read.com/DoctorSmug

*

Hot Dad

https://books2read.com/Hot-Dad

*

Snowed In & Set Up

https://books2read.com/SISU

*

Love to Hate You

https://books2read.com/Love2HateYou

For the woman who secretly dreams a naked bear shifter would just rock up to her front door
and claim to be her fated mate.
Same, girl, same. Let's be friends.

Contents

CHAPTER ONE

OMAERA PLAYFAIR

Chase City, Washington, US

"Four of a kind," I said, placing my cards down on the worn felt table in the underground wine cellar. I kept my face neutral because even though I was doing a little touchdown victory dance in my head, I wasn't a sore winner on the outside. But I also knew that nobody at that table had a better hand than my four of a kind. Four queens and ten of spades.

Groans echoed around the table, as well as from some spectators who were betting on me *not* winning.

Not a wise move.

This filly races to win.

The dealer, Damon, nodded and I scooped my winning chips forward, already coming up with at least five ways I intended to spend my winnings tonight. First and foremost, though? A Greek pizza with feta and extra Kalamata olives for me and my best friend, Gemma, who stood behind me telling off some guy who was making noise about me cheating.

Fuck him.

I was no cheat.

I didn't even count cards.

I just had this deep-seated intuition about the other players that not even I could explain. I knew when they had a crappy hand. I knew when they were bluffing, and I knew when I needed to fold. Of course, I read their tells; but it was more than that too. It was almost like I read their minds. I read their energy, their indecision, their confusion, their confidence. I felt their emotions like they were my own.

And by leaning into this . . . *talent,* for lack of a better word, I won nearly every game I played. To the point where players came from all over the country—and from other countries—to try to beat me.

I wasn't banned from places like Vegas and Monaco, but if I went, I probably would be. But I didn't give two shits about those glitzy idiot-magnet type places anyway. I liked the local underground circuit better. It was more my style.

"She's cheating," the loud, obnoxious, and slightly drunk guy continued to say to Gemma. "She has to be. No *girl* can be that good. She's counting cards. Or she's—"

"Just a girl that kicked your friend's ass?" Gemma retorted.

I snickered and gave Gemma's bare knee a loving little pinch. As always, she wore a short skirt with a schoolgirl pleat, even though it was black and leather. Her combat boots hid her black socks decorated with little hot pink cats. Her hot pink crop top covered by a dark denim bolo jacket completed her "I don't give a fuck" look.

"Buy in for this next game is five grand," Damon announced. "We'll begin in fifteen minutes."

Gemma leaned down. "Are we sticking around for another game, or heading out?"

"What would you rather?" I asked, indifferent to whether we stayed or left. I knew I'd win the next game. I could read the over-confidence and hesitation of every person letting the dealer know they were in. Easy marks. The next game would be child's play.

She yawned. "I do have an early morning shift at the coffee shop tomorrow."

I shrugged. "Then let's go. Just make sure you order the pizza from Mario's on Fifth this time, not Mario's on Douglas. They scrimped on the olives last time."

Gem nodded and pulled out her phone.

I stood up, preparing to take my chips to cash in.

"What? Is the big baby girl leaving now?" taunted a square-headed man with a thick Eastern European accent. He had a buzz cut and one lazy eye. Or maybe it was a glass eye. He'd just finished paying his buy-in to the dealer. "Afraid to play against real men?"

I grinned at him. "Yep. That's exactly it. You terrify me and I'd rather cut my losses and go home with some money."

He wasn't expecting that kind of response. When people around him chuckled, he quickly caught on that I was fluent in sarcasm and every syllable I said dripped in it. His face went red and his nostrils flared, reminding me of a bull stomping the dirt and preparing to impale the matador.

"You making fun of me, Big Baby Girl?"

I shook my head. "Nope."

"Because it sounded like you were making fun of me. Nobody makes fun of Ivan Novák."

I glanced around. "Who's Ivan Novák? Is he here? I'll be sure not to make fun of him."

The man surged to his feet and pointed at himself with a thick sausage finger. "I am Ivan Novák and you are making fun of me."

"You're Ivan Novák?" I asked, continuing to play dumb and enjoying the chuckles of entertained spectators around me.

"I am."

"Oh shit! Well, I will be sure not to make fun of you then."

His brows bunched and his face scrunched. Then one of his minions, or lackies, or whatever leaned over and whispered something into his ear. His face flushed red again, and he glared at me like he wanted to rip my head clean from my body. "You *are* making fun of me."

With her arms full of the overflow of chips I couldn't carry myself, Gemma whispered in my ear, "Maybe you should leave him alone. He's getting a little scary. Do you see the vein sticking out in his forehead?"

I did see it. But I was a button-pusher by nature, and something about this guy just irked me. And it wasn't the fact that he called me *Big Baby Girl* either. I mean, yeah, that was annoying as fuck, but it was the way he'd come into the wine cellar with his entourage, barking orders and leering at the waitresses. Then I saw him reach out and grab one girl, Danielle's, ass. She giggled and smiled at him. Because what else could she do in a place with so many criminals and dwellers of the city's seedy underbelly? The tips were good. She needed this job to pay for medical school.

I made a point of getting to know all the staff at all the venues I frequented. They were human too, and deserved kindness and respect. And Danielle was in her second year of med school and drowning in student loan debt.

So she put up with the handsy guests because she knew she had a better life coming to her and her son soon.

"Is Big Baby Girl going to stay, or what?" Ivan asked. "Or is it her beddy-by time? Run home to your mommy, Big Baby Girl. Waa! Waa! Waa!"

"Don't bite," Gemma gritted.

Too late.

"My mother's dead," I deadpanned, keeping my gaze locked with Ivan's as I put down enough chips to buy in for the next game.

Gemma sighed behind me. "Shit."

As I expected, I kicked Ivan's ass at the table. And every other player there too.

The rest of them weren't happy about it, but they weren't sore losers either. They knew what they were getting into in the high-stakes underground poker world. They knew the risk.

I was well known. Famous in certain circles.

But Ivan wasn't happy about his loss and he made sure everyone in that entire wine cellar knew about it. "She is a cheater," he said as I scooped up my winning chips and the dealer collected the cards.

Damon huffed out his nose. "Mr. Novák, we have had many poker and card professionals come and assess Ms. Playfair and we can assure you, she doesn't cheat. Nor does she count cards. She plays fairly and by the rules. I know it's difficult to lose, but you must understand, we take this very seriously as well."

Ivan wasn't having it though. He reached beneath the table and flipped over the whole thing, sending nearly all of my chips flying in every direction.

Security was on him like rats on a brick of gouda, hauling him out. It took three security guards though. Ivan's minions went without a fight, following after their cursing leader who kicked and screamed like a toddler being drug away for nap time.

With a weary sigh, I dropped to a crouch, along with several other people, and began scooping up my chips. I'm sure they wouldn't all be accounted for. A few someones would pocket a chip or two. Whatever. Gemma and I would make sure we grabbed more than enough to cover rent for our loft, rent for Aunt Delia's place, and groceries for the next few months.

Unlike Gemma, who liked to bare her pale midriff whenever she could, I preferred baggier clothes, at least when I played poker. An oversized men's T-shirt was my top choice as it allowed me to scoop all my chips into it like a kangaroo pouch and carry it over to cash in. When I wasn't working, I was happy to sport a crop top now and then.

I made sure to tip Damon before I made my way through the crowd. Conversations echoed around me like comforting white noise as I went to cash in my winnings. I spotted Danielle and gently grabbed her elbow, making sure it was not the arm carrying the tray of empty glasses. "Here," I said, placing a yellow thousand-dollar chip into her free hand. "Thanks for all the club sodas tonight. Your kid deserves to go to music camp. Now you can send him."

She blinked big doe eyes at me. "M-Ms Playfair, I can't."

"You'd better," I said, giving her a wink before walking away.

We reached the cashier, and Gemma and I both dumped the chips on the table in front of him.

Enzo sighed. "Gonna take me a minute, Omaera."

"I know, Enzo. All good."

He went to work calculating my chips while I leaned back against the table.

My belly grumbled. "Have you placed the order for the pizza yet?" I asked Gemma.

She shook her head. "I was going to, then you decided to play another game." She yawned and checked her phone. "Crap. I need to be up in like six hours for work."

"Call in sick. I'll pay your wages for what you'd make tomorrow. Hang out with me, your bestie who you love and would do anything for, including playing hooky at work."

Gemma snorted. "Unlike you, who hates people—"

"I don't hate people. I'm just very selective about who I bring into my inner circle of trust. *Most* people suck, but not all. Marty doesn't suck. Right, Enzo? You're a stand-up man. A wonderful father, husband, and cashier."

Enzo merely smiled. He was too busy counting my chips.

Gemma rolled her pretty hazel-green eyes. "Okay, but unlike you, who hates the grind that doesn't involve cards in your hand and chips on the table, I actually like my job. I like my co-workers and the mindlessness that is making the Karen's of the world their double-shot, no foam, two-pump, hazelnut lattes."

I snorted. "That sounds disgusting."

"The order, or the job?"

"Both."

It was Gemma's turn to snort. "You will survive the day without me. You always do."

Pouting, I simply said, "Order the pizza, but order two. I'm starving. And we'll pick them up on our way. I promise to have you home so you can get a solid five hours of sleep."

"Gee, thanks," she said, rolling her eyes.

I smiled and fiddled with the rose-gold hoop piercing in my right nostril.

"All right, Ms. Playfair, your total winnings for the night are," I turned to face Enzo, "fifteen thousand, six hundred."

Gemma sucked in a breath, like she was sucking through a straw, as Enzo proceeded to count the bills out in front of me.

Once he was done, I smiled at him. "Pull out a hundred for yourself, my friend."

"Thank you very much." He pocketed a Benjamin, then handed me my wads of cash after wrapping them up nicely with a rubber band.

I pulled out the child's diaper I kept in my purse and made sure to stash the cash in there. It was safer. People were less likely to steal a diaper they thought was dirty. I mean, yeah, they could take my whole purse, but they'd have to fight me for it. And I carried a switchblade and mace, and Gemma was a badass bitch who knew Krav Maga like a second language.

"I hope you're calling yourselves a cab tonight," Enzo said. "Walking the streets of Chase City with that much money isn't safe."

"We'll call a cab from the pizza joint, Enzo. It's all good." I linked my arm with Gemma's and we turned to go, my belly rumbling again at the thought of pizza.

We climbed the stairs, arm-in-arm, and were nearly on the dark and empty street when thunder boomed like it was right overhead and a bolt of lightning, so bright and so vivid, cracked out of the sky and hit me square in the chest.

All I heard was Gemma scream before everything around me went dark and quiet.

All I thought was, this can't be how I end. I didn't even get to eat my pizza first.

All hail Omaera Playfair, Queen of the Realm!

My chest hurt.

My body buzzed like I'd just been tasered or electrocuted or both.

My eyelids were too heavy to lift so I just stayed in the darkness.

A moan bubbled up from my chest, and my throat burned.

Oh god. If she dies, I'll kill myself. I can't lose my best friend. I can't. Gemma sounded far away, almost in a tunnel. Her warm hand gripped mine. *Wake up. Wake up, dammit!*

I groaned again and stirred.

She let go of my hand and gripped me by the shoulders. "Maer! Maer! You need to wake up. Maer, wake up." She shook me.

"Wh-what happened?"

She sighed. "Thank god. You were hit by fucking lightning!"

I was?

That's right. I was. Coming out of the poker game. Thunder rumbled and then lightning, as if thrown by Zeus himself, came barreling out of the sky, almost like it was aiming for me. Like some kind of homing beacon.

I opened my eyes into thin slits, but the room was too bright so I shut them again. "Wh-where are we?"

"The hospital, obviously. You think I'd just bring you home after you were struck by fucking lightning?"

Did she hit her head too? Fuck. Thank god she's awake. Thank god. I can't lose my sister. My best friend. She's all I have. She's my only family.

Why did Gemma's voice sound different? She spoke to me, then spoke like she was in a tunnel *about* me?

Maybe I did hit my head on the stairs.

"Is she awake?" came a soothing male voice. Curtains were drawn.

"Sort of," Gemma said. "She's speaking, but hasn't opened her eyes."

"That's because the room is too bright," I croaked, my throat raw.

"We can fix that," the man said. "There."

"He dimmed the lights, Maer. Try opening your eyes now." Gemma squeezed my hand, and I tried to pry open my eyes again.

"Hey there, Ms. Playfair. You gave us quite the scare." The doctor was crazy handsome and crazy young. Not as young as me, because there were very few twenty-two-year-old doctors out there, but if he was over thirty, I'd be surprised.

"Is she going to be okay?" Gemma asked.

The doctor shone a light in my eyes and asked me to follow it as he moved it back and forth. I glanced at my arms and I was hooked up to an IV, had a heart rate monitor on my left index finger, and there were a few things stuck to my chest. I was also wearing a hospital gown. "I think so," the doctor said. "To be honest, you're a bit of a medical marvel and incredibly lucky. You were struck by intense lightning and have managed to come out pretty much unscathed. You don't even have any burns."

"When can I go home?"

"We'd like to keep you here for another couple of hours for observation, but then you should be cleared to leave." His smile brought out two deep dimples. And fuck me, he even had one in his chin. Dr. Dimples, M.D.

"Thank you," I croaked.

"Here." Gemma brought a straw to my lips, and I greedily sipped, relishing the way it softened my thick, dry sponge of a tongue.

Dr. Dimples left and pulled the curtain closed again, leaving Gemma and I alone-*ish* in our little slice of the ER.

"Did you hear that?" I asked her when I could speak without razor blades slicing my tonsils.

"Hear what? The code blue?"

I shook my head. "No. When I first woke up, there was this chant. Like a choir, or chorus, or something."

She shook her head, jostling her wild red curls. "No. What did the choir say?"

"All hail Omaera Playfair, Queen of the Realm."

Her hazel-green eyes narrowed. "Seriously? What the hell does that mean?"

"You didn't hear it? And hell if I know."

"I think you hit your head. Maybe I need to have the doctor request a CT scan or something. Maybe you have a brain bleed." She stood up from the stool she was sitting on. "I'm going to go find him. See what he says. Be right back." She disappeared through the curtain.

I felt fine.

No, that's not true. I felt really different, but not in an "I'm going to die any minute from a subdural hematoma" kind of way.

I can't be pregnant. Not again. Please, not again.

Who said that?

Maybe this broken leg will get me out of my math test tomorrow.

What the fuck was going on?

Gemma and the doctor came back through the curtain.

"Tell him what you told me," Gemma said, fear and worry etched across her face, competing with the endless freckles.

Okay, now I was beginning to worry too. I was hearing voices.

Is she going to be okay? Gemma asked, but without moving her mouth.

I gaped at her. "I'm going to be fine."

She blinked at me, stunned.

"What did you hear when you woke up," Dr. Dimples asked.

"You're going to call for a psych consult when I tell you," I said dryly.

He snorted. "Probably not. You were struck by lightning and your friend says you may have hit your head. I think we can hold off on a psych consult for now. Just tell me what you heard."

"All hail Omaera Playfair, Queen of the Realm." I fixed him with a look that said, "Just grab the straight jacket and wheel me to the nearest padded room."

"Have you heard anything else?" he asked, without showing me any emotion or concern.

"Yeah. When Gemma stepped out to get you, I heard someone say, 'I can't be pregnant again.' Then I heard some boy say something about maybe if he broke his leg he wouldn't have to do his math test."

Dr. Dimples gray eyes narrowed. "Well, the patients on either side of you have cases in relation to what you heard. So maybe they were saying them out loud?"

I shook my head. "I don't think so." I glanced at Gemma. "I can hear Gemma too. Like one minute her lips are moving and she's talking to me normally. Then her lips stop moving and I can still hear her talking, only it sounds like she's in a tunnel and far away."

My best friend is losing her mind.

I pointed at Gem. "See! She just said, 'My best friend is losing her mind.'"

"No I didn't," Gemma protested. "I mean, I thought it. But I didn't say it."

I gasped. "Am I reading minds?"

"That's not a real thing," the doctor said. "Let's get you upstairs for a head

CT and double check there's no brain bleed, or a concussion, or anything.

"Okay, so maybe I'm not reading minds. But explain the chorus chanting that I'm *Queen of the Realm.*"

But he wasn't listening to me. He'd already flagged down some other hospital staff member, and they were unlocking the wheels on my bed.

Fear ripped through me, and I reached for Gemma. "I don't want to be losing my mind. I also don't want to read people's minds. People are fucked up."

She nodded and gripped my hand tight. "People are fucked up. I wouldn't want to read their minds either." She snagged the doctor's gaze. "I'm coming with her."

"You can come as far as the CT, but then you'll have to wait outside."

"Fine. But if you put her in a straitjacket or padded room without telling me first, I will unleash all the ginger rage on you."

Dr. Dimples, the orderly, and I all snorted.

I kissed the back of Gemma's hand. "What would I do without you?"

"Don't even talk like that. You just got a little bonk and zap. You're going to be fine."

But I could see in her eyes, and hear in her thoughts, that she was only saying those things to reassure me and keep me calm. She didn't believe I was fine.

And neither did I.

But something told me this was just the beginning of a whole world of fresh problems I was in no way prepared to deal with.

CHAPTER TWO

Prince Zandren Thorne

I bared my teeth and reached for her long dark braid as I continued to pump, the need to come and spill my seed inside her growing hot and frothy in my balls.

"Oh, Zandren," she bleated like a lamb. "Harder."

Seriously? Any harder and I'd put her head right through the fucking wall.

"You're so big."

I smirked and tightened my hold on her braid, giving it to her harder. But not as hard as I could.

I was big, but this chick was just saying what she thought I wanted to hear.

I could have a cub's thumb for a cock and I wouldn't care.

"Oh god, I'm so close."

"That's right, baby," I growled, my other hand on her hipbone as I plowed into her from behind.

I wasn't quite sure where I was. I had followed my nose ten miles, my belly rumbling as the scent of smoked meat pulled me closer, until I stumbled into the rundown tavern.

The bartender, who I was currently balls deep inside, batted her lashes at me and gave me a drink on the house. Then I cleared out a few ruffians who were trying to make her trashy place even trashier. She thanked me for my service with a steak sandwich and her tight cunt.

My balls cinched up tight against my taint as the heat in my belly intensified. "Yes," she cried. "Oh god."

I bared my teeth again, preparing to unleash my release.

The bed strings creaked and groaned beneath my weight. The mattress was cheap and sagged in the middle, and there were some stains and shoddy putty patches on the wall. But I didn't give a shit. I didn't know this chick's story. And I didn't care to.

This was rutting.

Plain and simple

She wanted cock. And I had a cock to give. A simple, straightforward transaction between two consenting adults.

I was seconds away from emptying my balls as the climax built like a motherfucking cyclone in my body. Baring my teeth again, I shut my eyes, but the booming *crack* from above made me open them again just in time to see the bright light crash through from the ceiling, hitting me in the chest like a spear. I knew there was a cat in the room, but it'd been asleep in the corner until then. When the lightning struck, the cat screeched and leaped onto my back.

The bartender—I think her name was Charlie?—screamed.

I roared.

She screamed even louder, probably because my roar was not at all human-like.

I plowed into her harder than ever. So hard she went flying forward, and headfirst through the drywall.

Thank fuck she missed the studs.

And my dick instantly went soft. Like instantly.

Like someone pricked a balloon with a fucking safety pin.

If I didn't know what the lightning strike meant, I sure as fuck knew now.

My mate had come of age.

"What the fuck?" Charlie screamed, her head in the adjacent room. "What happened? Zandren, get me out of here!"

My cock had already slipped out, but I carefully extricated her from the wall, sitting her up on the disheveled bed. She looked stunned, and pissed, but not injured.

My bear growled inside, and I sniffed the air, catching the faintest scent of my mate. She was far away, but not so far that I couldn't smell her. And no matter where in the world she was, I'd find her.

"I gotta go," I said.

"W-what?" Charlie exclaimed. "What the fuck just happened?"

"I . . . Sorry." Then I was out the door, naked, because clothes sucked and only restricted things.

It was past midnight, but bears have excellent night vision. I continued on over the gravel parking lot in my bare feet, heading toward the trees. The window slid open from her second-story bedroom, but I didn't turn around and look. "You motherfucker," she screamed out into the night.

I didn't respond, but an owl off in the distance hooted.

Already, I'd forgotten her name.

The only name that mattered to me now was that of my mate.

After two hundred and thirty-six years alone, I finally had a mate.

I sniffed the air again. Her smell was sweet, but spicy. Floral too. Like lilacs and honeysuckle, with just a pinch of cayenne. Oh, my mate was already a decadent treat I would treasure.

Once I was out of sight of the tavern, I shifted into bear form, dropping to all fours as my spine arched, my hands and feet elongated, and my skull widened. My canine teeth lengthened, and soft, dense fur sprouted out from my skin. I was an eight-hundred-and-thirty-five-pound grizzly bear now and could run faster in this form than my human form. The only bear bigger than me was my father, the King, and he weighed in at nine forty.

Shaking my shaggy head, I took a moment to scratch my back on the trunk of a tree, really getting in good between my butt cheeks. Then I took off at a steady lope until I made it to the river. The wind blew steady and warm from the south, bringing my mate's scent with it.

The closer to her I got, the stronger I could smell her.

It might take me hours, maybe even days, to reach her, but I would.

And when I did, I would make her mine. Together, we would have oodles of cubs and live a wonderful life. Just like my mother and father did with our family.

Spring was my favorite time of year. There was so much to eat. Baby bunnies were tender and a fun little snack. When I couldn't catch one, I dined on fresh shoots of various tubers and plants, some of the many ripening berries, or delicious fish in the stream. I didn't stop to eat much on my journey, but a bear needs to keep up his energy. So I made sure to grab breakfast, lunch, second lunch, snack, dinner, dessert, and a late-night snack on my way. Not too many meals, but just enough to keep me moving.

I ran throughout the day, arriving on the outer limits of Chase City, Washington, just as the wolves off in the mountains behind me started to howl. I knew a lot of wolves. Some were okay, but most were cocky fuckers. Not as slippery or cunning as fox shifters, but damned close. And the way they insisted on living in such giant communities and packs—no fucking thanks.

I wanted a nice den for my mate, our cubs, and myself. Somewhere secluded. Off the grid, perhaps. Where I could keep them all safe and we could just be together as a family.

It was dark, but the lights of the city still blinded me and even though I had incredible night vision, all the zooming cars and flashing street lights fucked with my eyes. I growled and kept to the shadows, meandering carefully under overpasses and sticking to culverts when I could.

News of a bear in the city would bring out the idiot humans with tranquilizer darts. Then I'd be relocated, and it'd take me even longer to reach my mate.

I could shift into human form too, which would be easier. I would, but I moved faster in bear form and had a better sense of smell.

It'd been a while since I'd been to any city.

I fucking hated cities.

I fucking hated people.

Cars too.

The forest was more peaceful, quieter. There was less pollution and destruction too.

Less selfishness and danger.

Being at the top of the food chain, very little scared me. But humans were fearful creatures and if they saw me, they'd bring out their guns—and guns scared me. Too many of my relatives were killed by guns. By hunters out for a trophy, for a bearskin rug, or a stuffed animal to decorate their home.

My mate's scent was strong now, bringing forth a primal growl deep in my chest. I ached to meet her. To claim her and mate with her. What did she look like? What color was her fur? A light tawny brown? Or a deep chestnut like mine? What would our cubs look like?

Maybe she was one of those rare spirit bears—I'd only ever met one in my life—a blonde, almost-white grizzly. Our cubs would be beautiful, no matter what.

Sniffing the air, I turned west, heading toward the ocean. Her scent mixed with the briny, pungent smell of the sea at low tide, along with the damp pavement as it started to rain.

A group of loud men blasting music from a speaker passed by, so I froze and hunkered down in the shrubs. A car drove by, the sizzling sound of its tires on the wet road competing with the men's obnoxious tunes.

The group passed, so I kept moving. My mate was about two miles away now. But the bushes and trees I could hide in grew thinner and thinner. I'd need to shift, soon.

The smell of garbage with three-day-old pizza and half a club sandwich, pulled my attention. My stomach gurgled.

No.

I needed to get to my mate.

Too much time had already passed. She was probably wondering what was taking me so long. I couldn't keep her waiting any longer. I couldn't disappoint her before we even met.

I told my stomach to shut the fuck up and padded through the park until the trees ended and it was just a big open grassy field. A baseball diamond sat at one end, flanked by dugouts and bleachers.

Such a stupid game, baseball.

Humans did such stupid things.

Grizzly ball was much better. Much more dangerous too. We didn't wear helmets, or cups to protect our genitals. We played with bare paws, teeth, and claws out. Humans would shrink in terror if they ever saw a grizzly ball game. I snorted at that thought as I walked beneath the bleachers, stepping on fallen popcorn, queso from nachos and something sticky—probably part of a candy bar. I licked my paw.

Yeah, it was a candy bar. Not a very good one though. I wasn't a fan of Turkish delight. Give me something with honey any day of the week.

After the bleachers, it was nothing but concrete and buildings. I would have to shift.

With a deep sigh of reluctance, I stood up on my hind legs and let my body do its thing.

My toes and fingers shrunk back to human length, my mandible retracted, along with my canines. My spine straightened, and my fur burrowed back beneath my skin.

Now nobody would try to shoot me.

I walked the last mile to my mate until I found myself in some hipster borough, standing on the sidewalk below a warehouse converted into loft apartments. The name of the building was the Reinvention. Ugh.

"Hey!" someone called out to me from up the street. "Put some damn clothes on!"

I glanced down at my naked torso and wriggled my toes on the wet concrete. Then I looked back to the person, whose voice told me it was a woman, a hundred yards down the street and on the other side. "Don't have any."

She shook her head before disappearing into her own building.

Maybe I needed clothes?

But my mate wouldn't care, would she? Shifters didn't give two shits about nudity. The humans were the ones who got their restrictive underwear in a twist over too much skin. They also had no tolerance for the cold though. Such an unevolved species really.

I glanced around until I spotted a still open bodega up the street half a block. Stalking forward while ignoring the pull to return to my mate. I opened the door for the bodega, causing it to jingle. The South Asian man behind the counter gaped at me.

"Clothes?" I growled.

He shook his head.

"Do you have a lost and found or something?"

Nodding in terror, he reached behind the counter, littered with scratch tickets, gum, lighters, and other stupid human shit, and plunked a cardboard box in front of me.

I grunted and rooted through it. Mostly sunglasses, a wallet with nothing in it, a glove, six socks that didn't match, a pair of children's swimming goggles, and a shirt. That would have to do. I pulled out the red, short-sleeve T-shirt and tugged it on. It was a bit tight. Actually, it was really tight and my biceps made the seams pop. It also hit me just below the sternum.

Better than nothing. I nodded at the clerk. "Thanks."

The man hadn't blinked or closed his mouth.

The door jingled when I opened it again and I made my way back down the sidewalk toward the Reinvention.

I waited in the shadows behind a squat bush, hoping that someone might enter the building and I could follow behind them. There appeared to be a buzzer system and since I had no idea what my mate was called, I didn't want to buzz all the residents and wake them up. But I would if I had to.

My patience waned as time ticked by, my bear growling at me to go and claim her. To meet her and start our life.

Finally, a man with a fedora and brown wingtips sauntered past me and turned to climb the stairs for the front door. He hit one of the buzzer numbers and it rang twice before someone answered.

"It's Sam."

"Come on in."

The door clicked, and he yanked it open. I waited two full heartbeats before I leaped up from my spot and raced to catch the door before it shut again. Sam was already on the elevator by the time I got there, wedging my big toe to stop the door from shutting just in the nick of time.

My mate's scent was so strong now, I knew exactly how to find her.

I located the stairwell and went on the hunt.

Not the first floor.

Not the second.

Not the third.

She was on the top floor.

Heaving open the big door for the fourth floor, I paused and sniffed in either direction.

Left.

Her scent was so strong now, I was heady with excitement and desire. How long would we have to wait before we bonded? Before I claimed her as mine and we mated for life? Before we worked on starting a family? I wanted cubs so badly.

I stopped in front of apartment 405 and shut my eyes, pulling her sweet, floral, and spicy scent deep into my lungs. My cock twitched.

Smiling, I knocked on the door.

I'm here, my mate. Sorry it took so long.

There was no answer.

I knocked again.

I could smell her in there. She was with another female too. This one smelled like lavender and cinnamon. Sounds of them shuffling around and whispering had me pressing my ear to the door.

Someone approached. I pulled back, waiting.

It wasn't my mate who approached the door though. It was the female that smelled of lavender and cinnamon.

"Who's there?" she asked.

"I am the other female's mate."

"Her what?"

"Her mate. I am here. I'm sorry it took me so long."

"Like Postmates? We didn't order from you. We ordered Thai directly from the shop. Is this some kind of game, Chakan?"

Who was Chakan?

I did like the idea of Thai food though.

"I am her mate. Her destined companion for life. Could I please come in so we can finally meet and start our life together?"

"Who is it?" asked my mate.

"Some guy claiming he's your mate. Your companion for life. He wants to come in and meet you so you can start your lives together," her voice held equal parts amusement and skepticism.

"How'd a loon like that get into the building? Call security."

"Please do not call security. I wish you no harm. If I could just come in and talk. Allow me to introduce myself."

"No fucking way, weirdo. Go before we call the cops," said my mate's friend.

"Did you not get hit by a bolt of lightning last night?" I asked, confused about why they acted like they didn't know what was going on. "I was hit too."

The lavender and cinnamon scented female left the door, and they whispered together.

"We have mace," my mate announced. "You stay in the hallway."

"Okay."

Both women padded forward and several security bolts unlocked.

"Are you standing back?" my mate asked.

"I am."

Did all mates react this way at first? Why was she so hesitant to meet me?

Not to mention the fact that she chose to live in a city. What was up with that?

I'd have to ask my father if my mother was just as reluctant, or if this was a new thing.

The big metal door creaked open just a crack. "Why are you not wearing any pants!" my mate exclaimed.

I glanced down my body again. "Because I hate clothes."

The door shut again. More whispering.

"Is this some kind of sick fucking joke?" my mate asked.

"Do you stay in human form all the time?" I asked. "Do you like clothes?"

"Human form? I am a human, you lunatic. Go away. Gemma is already calling the cops."

This was not at all how I anticipated our first meeting to go. I figured by now we'd be on a bed of soft leaves and grass, consummating our union.

"Did you not get hit by lightning?" I asked, growing more desperate as time ticked by.

"I did. How do you know that?"

"Because so did I. It means we are Fated Mates. It means you have come of age. You are twenty-two, are you not? Also, happy birthday."

"What the fuck does that all mean? And it's not my fucking birthday, you pantsless psycho."

It wasn't her birthday? That was strange. "I am your Fated Mate. We are meant to be together. The Fates have divined it."

"You're talking a lot of fucking garbage mumbo jumbo for a man who knocked on my door looking like fucking Pooh Bear."

"What is an obviously deranged and needs to be taken for a seventy-two-hour psych hold," my mate's friend said. "He has no pants, and he's talking about you two being destined to be together. And your birthday isn't until October. Definitely a 51-50 situation."

"You watch too many police procedurals," my mate scolded. "He's also talking about getting struck by lightning too. Maybe . . ."

"Maybe what? We let that nutjob into our home? He's clearly off his meds. He needs help."

"We have mace. Go get the taser and the switchblade."

"You're just as crazy as he is for suggesting this." But my mate's friend stomped away, returning a second later. "He is massive. I doubt the blade will stop him from killing us, you know."

"Yeah, but the taser might give us enough time to run away."

"Why do I let you talk me into this shit?"

"I'm going to open the door again," my mate said. "You stay with your bare ass up against the wall, understand?"

"Okay."

"Move so much as a fucking muscle and I'll spray you and we'll call the cops."

"Okay."

The door creaked open again and some kind of fabric was tossed at me. "Put those on too."

I glanced at the heap of gray on the floor and made a face, then glanced back up into the green eyes of my mate. "You told me not to move."

She rolled those beautiful eyes and scoffed. "Put them on, smartass."

I did as I was told. They were way too small for me.

Men's large gray sweatpants, and they clung to my lower half like stretchy ladies' yoga pants. They cropped at my calves too. "Better?" I asked.

"Barely." But she opened the door. "What do you want?"

Holy fuck. She was gorgeous. Even if she wasn't my mate, I'd have found her to be the most beautiful woman I'd ever laid eyes on. And I've lived for centuries. Along with fire and stubbornness, her moss-green eyes held so much wisdom. I knew that I'd never stop learning from her. She had a hoop nose ring on the right side, tight, dark curls, and a slender, but beautiful face with a light brown complexion.

She was absolutely stunning.

I'd hit the fucking jackpot when it came to mates.

"What the fuck are you staring at, Pooh Bear?" she asked.

I blinked. I still didn't understand this "Pooh Bear" reference. Was it from television? I never watched television. "You, my mate," I simply said, bunching my fists at my side to keep myself from reaching for her. She told me not to move.

"You keep calling me that, and I don't know what the fuck that means."

"We are destined to—"

"Yeah, I heard that, but what does it *mean*? Who are you? And who do you think I am?"

I straightened. Crap, I was going about this all wrong. "My apologies." I bowed. "I am Prince Zandren Thorne, of the Pacific Northwest Bear Shifters. What shifter clan are you from?"

Both women's mouths dropped open.

"Yeah, I'm gonna call the police," her friend murmured, pulling out her phone.

But my mate stopped her red-haired friend with the hazel-green eyes. Her gaze shifted to me, curiosity gleaming in her gaze. She didn't look at me with fear the way her friend did. "What happened when the lightning hit you?"

My cheeks grew warm. "I, um . . . well, I hate to admit this—"

Her friend's phone buzzed. "That's the Thai food," she said.

"Crap," my mate muttered. "Fine. Come in. But you stay far away, okay?"

I nodded and followed them inside the spacious, loft-style apartment. Loads of big leafy plants filled the space, making it feel like a jungle. I liked it. It reminded me of a tropical forest. I met a sun bear shifter once who lived in a forest similar to this.

I moved to the far side of the room near the sliding glass doors for the balcony. My mate, wearing loose-fitting jeans, rolled at the cuff, and a black T-shirt with a skull adorned by purple roses on it, went to the other furthest point of the space. She never took her eyes off me, but the longer she watched me, the more her gaze softened. Did she feel the pull too?

A knock at the now closed door pulled away her friend for a moment, then she returned, bringing with her the scent of Thai food. My bear growled and my belly rumbled.

"Did you hear any," my mate paused to gather her words. "Chorus chanting when you woke up?" she finally said.

"Woke up?"

"Did you not black out when you were hit by lightning?"

I shook my head. "No. You did? Are you okay?" I took a half-step toward her, but she lifted the mace and I moved backward again.

"CT said no brain bleed or concussion," her friend said. "But she claims to be hearing people's thoughts."

Shifters didn't hear people's thoughts. The only species that could do anything remotely like that were the demons. And they infiltrated people's thoughts and manipulated them. They could sometimes read their emotions, and if they were powerful enough, they could hear their thoughts—but usually only the extreme ones, like fear.

Was my mate half demon?

"So you didn't hear anything after the lightning struck?" she asked.

I needed to know her name.

"What is your name?" I asked.

Her green eyes formed thin slits as she contemplated telling me. "Omaera," she finally said.

I rolled her name around on my tongue. The perfect name for my perfect mate.

"Omaera," I finally said out loud. "What did you hear?"

She glanced at her friend, who was pulling their food order out of the paper bag. The woman shrugged. "Might as well tell him. This can't get any fucking weirder."

My mate nodded and focused on me again. She took a deep breath and said, "All hail Omaera Playfair, Queen of the Realm."

CHAPTER THREE

LORD DRAK FERRIN

The scent of blood in the air always soothed me. My nanny used to put a pan of it over the fire in my nursery to help me sleep.

I didn't *want* the man in front of me to bleed. I never *liked* hurting people.

But it was what needed to be done.

It was my job.

My cousin, King Howar Volmark, assigned me as head of his royal guard and made me his primary enforcer.

And interrogation was part of it.

I circled behind the man sitting bound to the chair in front of me. His head hung low, chin to chest, and blood seeped out of his nose and left ear. "At this point, unfortunately, it has come down to a swift and merciful death, or a long and painful one. You *will* die. But it is up to you how that happens. Tell us what we want to know, and I will put two fangs into your carotid and make sure you feel nothing but happy memories as you drift off to sleep. Ignore my request and we can keep you here for weeks."

The man groaned.

"Have you ever been bitten by a vampire before?"

The man groaned again.

"Although we are not mind manipulators like demons, when we plunge our fangs into your skin, anywhere, not just the neck, we can unleash an indescribable amount of pain. Or an unearthly amount of pleasure. It is our choice. We can drain you immediately, killing you. Or we can take small sips, for a very long time. Making you weak. So weak you hallucinate and can barely lift your head. You sleep, but we have ways of preventing that too."

I glanced toward the shadows of the mansion dungeon. Voltan, my second in command and also a vampire, smiled, but all I could see was the glowing white of his fangs.

"Why is there a faction of mages hunting vampires?" I demanded. "Our species have lived at peace with one another for over a century now."

"I don't know," the man murmured.

I nodded at Voltan. He came out from the shadows and delivered another painful beating with the baton.

Our bound mage screamed and whimpered.

I nodded again at Voltan and he stepped back into the shadows.

"You're nothing but glorified zombies," my prisoner muffled before coughing up blood. "You're not like us. Not like shifters or demons. You require others to suffer for your survival. And threatening to drain me of my blood is proof." He lifted his head and glared at me. "You're fucking monsters." He spat a big glob of blood and spit at my feet, narrowly missing my loafers.

"Who is at the helm of this?"

He sneered at me. "I don't know."

"You're just a lackey then? Doing the bidding of some unknown leader? While he sits in safety, you're out doing his dirty work, chopping off vampire heads?"

"Not a lackey if I believe in the cause. I'm a soldier, fighting for what I think is right." He coughed up more blood. "Just kill me. You know you want to."

I didn't, actually.

Death was necessary sometimes, but it was never something I enjoyed.

This man would have to die though. Because he couldn't be trusted not to run back to his keeper if we let him go.

With a weary sigh, I circled back behind him, grabbed him by the hair hard enough to make him squawk as I tilted his face to the concrete ceiling, exposing his neck. His pulse thudded hard in his throat. I zeroed in on his throbbing carotid. "You do know that there are *two* species of vampires, right?"

His eyes went wide, and he whimpered again from how tightly I held his greasy brown hair.

"So your simple mind can understand, I will use the more . . . derogatory terms. There are Daywalkers, like Voltan and myself. The King is also one, as are his subjects. Then there are the Nightwalkers, or the Phaceanesh. They are the ones who *need* to feed to survive. The *zombies*, if you will. A sub-species of our more . . . sophisticated kind. I do not *need* to feed to survive. Do I like blood? Of course, but it is not what I require to survive. Perhaps you have been mistaken, hmm?"

His dark eyes darted wildly across my face. "I was told to take out the vile subjects of the King. The zombies. Those that feast on others to live."

"By whom?" I brought my mouth down to his throat and allowed just one of my fangs to drop. It pricked his grimy skin, causing blood to bloom and trickle down the filthy creases of his neck and into the top of his stained, no-longer-white polo shirt.

He cried out in pain.

I dropped the other fang and leaned in to apply pressure to his neck once more, this time leaving a second puncture mark that slowly overflowed with his lifeblood. "I will repeat myself only once, by *whom*?"

He trembled now, utterly afraid that I would be true to my word. This man didn't want to die, despite his cavalier opinion of death a moment ago. His eyes held true fear and the most minute part of me held sympathy for him. He was told to kill the wrong species of vampire—on purpose—but why?

I leaned in, my eyes on his as I opened my mouth, preparing to give him exactly what I said I would: indescribable pain and a slow, excruciating death.

"N-no . . . no. Please! I'll tell you what I know. I promise!" The scent of urine filled the air, and I glanced down at the front of his pants, which he'd noticeably soiled.

Voltan snorted from the shadows.

My grip on the prisoner's hair loosened just a fraction. "Speak."

"I . . . I don't know who is in charge!" His eyes darted wildly across my face and his bottom lip wobbled. "But . . . t-the man who came to me was a demon."

"A demon."

"Y-yes." He nodded emphatically, spit flying as he spoke. "He said his . . . his boss would make me high in his court if I helped them rid the Realm of . . . of your kind."

"And did he say who his *boss* was?

"No."

"And what was his name?"

"Um . . ."

I tightened my grip on his hair again and brought my mouth closer to his neck.

"His name was—"

Crack!

The dark dungeon filled with a blinding white light as lightning crashed down from the ceiling above and straight into my chest, throwing me backward. The prisoner screamed out in pain from where I'd yanked on his hair, but the screaming disappeared, replaced by the ringing in my ears.

I was slumped against the wall, having cracked my head hard on the brick behind me.

Voltan was already crouched in front of me. "Milord, what happened?"

Lilac, honeysuckle, and cayenne filled my nostrils. It was faint, but it was distinct.

Voltan's eyes met mine, and a warmth filled my chest. Like a fool, I smiled.

He smiled too, when he realized what the lightning was about. "She's come of age, Milord. Your mate, she's come of age."

He helped me to my feet. I brushed my tailored suit clean of any dust and nodded. "I must find the King."

"I'll finish up here with the prisoner."

We both turned to face the bound man.

"Oh fuck," Voltan murmured. "You ripped his head clean off."

Unlike a shifter, a vampire's sense of smell isn't much better than a human's—until it comes to his mate. He can smell his mate from across the country. And she *was* across the country.

Voltan sent me on my way to find the King, saying he'd clean up the bloody mess in the dungeon. I felt a little bad that I'd decapitated the man. I didn't intend to.

I found my cousin speaking softly to his five-year-old daughter, Fiorella, in her bedroom. So, not wanting to interrupt father-daughter bonding, or rile up the young princess, I waited until he kissed her goodnight and left her door open just a crack.

"What news do you have from the mage?" King Howar asked me as we walked down the dimly lit hallway of his Upstate New York mansion. He could have lived in a castle in Europe, but he didn't like how drafty they were. He preferred modern and cozy.

I told him what the mage told us. We entered his study, and he poured us each two ounces of scotch, which we took to the big, green velvet chairs in front of the roaring fire.

"And where is he now?"

I glanced down into my glass, swirling the amber liquid around. "He's dead."

"You killed him *before* he told you who he's working for?"

I couldn't look at my cousin.

"Drak?" Howar pulled out his best kingly voice.

"Lightning hit me when I had him by the hair. It threw me against the wall and I took his head off . . . by accident." I glanced up at my cousin and frowned. "I've never had an accident like this before."

But Howar was already on his feet, yanking me to my feet as well so he could wrap me up in an enormous hug. I stood stiffly, arms at my side, in his jovial embrace. I wasn't used to affection from anyone, not even family. Howar had softened since finding a mate and having a daughter though. He'd turned into a hugger since Fiorella was born. "At long last, you finally have a mate! Dear god, we were starting to wonder if she'd ever come of age. If you'd ever get struck. Where is she? What is her scent?"

He released me and I cleared my throat, dropping back into my seat and taking a sip of the scotch. "I don't know where she is, but it's far. Her scent is not strong."

"What is it though?"

"Lilac, honeysuckle, and cayenne."

He smiled, went over to a small box on his desk, and pulled out two cigars. He cut them and put one in his mouth, bringing the other over to me. As happy as I should be right now, I didn't feel quite right celebrating. I'd just killed an informant. Our species was being targeted, and now I had a mate—a vampire—which meant she would have a target on her back too.

Howar lit his cigar, then passed the metal box of matches to me. I waved him off. "Not right now."

Shrugging, he puffed away, all smiles. "Why are you not happier? You're over five hundred years old. It's about time you settled down and started a family. Aren't you dying to know what she's like?"

I was. A hollow ache sat in my chest the longer I was apart from her. I needed to get on a plane ASAP and find her for the pain to stop.

"I'm worried," I finally said. "Someone is after us. After *our* species. And they're rallying troops of rogue mages to kill us. Why?"

"Not just someone though. A demon." He sipped his scotch. "I'll reach out to King Donovar in the morning and see what he knows. I doubt it's him. He's held peace in this realm longer than any other ruler."

"But the informant said that if he helped him, he'd give him a place in his court."

Howar's mouth turned down. "Are you telling me you think Donovar is behind this?"

I shook my head. "He's always rallied for peace. I can't see it being him. Lerris, maybe?"

Howar tilted his head to the side. "I've always been suspicious of the King's brother."

"You're not alone there."

The ache in my sternum intensified until it felt like someone was driving a stake through my heart. I clutched at my chest, wincing.

"That is the Mate's Ache," Howar said, once again on his feet. "Take the jet. Go to her. It will only get worse the longer you are apart. It will weaken you. Being around her is what you need. You gain strength from your bond."

Nodding, I grunted from the now-dull throb of pain between my ribs. Howar was already on his phone, making a call to fire up the jet. "Do you have any idea where she is?"

"West," I said weakly. "Somewhere west."

"Well, sit with the pilots and tell them when she feels close. They'll get you to her." He wrapped an arm around me and helped me outside, where his driver, Alvo, waited with the limo. "Drak has been struck with lightning," he told Alvo. Alvo's pale face lit up. Everyone in the Realm knew what that meant. "Take him to the airstrip. The jet is being fueled. He needs to get to his mate ASAP."

Alvo nodded. "Right away, Your Majesty."

I slid into the back of the limo, but rolled over onto my side, clutching at my chest. Nobody ever told me about the Mate's Ache. I felt like I was having a heart attack. I closed my eyes, envisioning what she might look like. Was her lightning strike as intense? Did she feel the Mate's Ache too?

It was tradition that the female mate waited, and the male came to her. Otherwise, if they both set off in search of each other, it could be a disaster.

Pain scrunched my face. But it wasn't just the pain in my chest, it was the pain of wondering if she was going through the ache too. If she was in as much agony as I was.

I'm coming, my mate. I'm coming.

I arrived in Chase City in the morning, but I was weak.

The pilot had to help me climb down the stairs of the plane to the limo Howar arranged for me.

I was barely able to tell the limo driver where to go, but I rallied, holding onto my mate's scent and giving him directions as best I could.

It was still early—most shops weren't even open yet— when we pulled up in front of a hospital.

This couldn't be right. Why was my mate at a human hospital?

If she was injured during the lightning strike, wouldn't she go to a realm hospital? Our physicians were far better and knew how to treat the maladies of all species.

But this was where her scent was strongest. She was here.

Panic ran rampant through me as the limo driver helped me out. Hospital staff saw how frail I was and someone ran out with a wheelchair. "Sir. Sir, what's wrong?"

"Nothing," I grunted, batting them off. "I need to find her."

"Who?"

These were humans. If I said, "my mate," they'd call for a psych consult.

But I didn't know my mate's name.

"I'll know her when I see her." I also couldn't tell them that I'd know her when I smelled her.

"Sir, let us check you out. You're very pale and seem dehydrated." A firm hand landed on my shoulder, pushing me into the wheelchair,

I'm pale and dehydrated because I'm a vampire.

But I was too weak to argue. The hollow ache in my chest made it difficult to speak, let alone fight. They wheeled me into the hospital, and as soon as I was in the same space as my mate, I grew stronger. She was here. There was no doubt about it now.

They wheeled me to the ER and helped me climb up onto a bed, pulling the curtains around me. "A doctor will be by to see you shortly," said the green-scrub clad orderly.

My nostrils flared, but I waited for him to pull the curtains and leave before I slid off the bed, allowing my nose to do the work for me.

She was here. Somewhere in this hospital.

Was her strength returning too? Did she know I was close?

I poked my head into various rooms, sniffing.

"You are a lucky woman, Ms. Playfair. A lightning strike like that and zero burns, no burst eardrums, respiratory complications." Disbelief colored his tone. "Frankly, it's a miracle. You're very fortunate." I paused at the corner beside a nurse's station in the E.R. My mate was behind curtains, just like I'd been. I still couldn't understand why she was in a human hospital. But at least she was okay. That was what mattered.

"Can I go home then, please? This has been the weirdest day. I just want pizza and my own bed." My mate's voice was beautiful. Strong and assertive.

"I'd like to wait for the psych consult. You hearing voices does raise some concerns."

My mate growled. I smirked. "I'm fine. I was probably just still unconscious. I *did* pass out, you know."

A man with a clipboard, glasses, and big ears approached her curtains, ducking in behind them. "Hello, I'm Dr. Shapiro. I believe a psych consult was requested."

"I'm not a danger to myself or others. Can you legally hold me?" my mate asked, her ire increasing.

"W-well . . . no," Dr. Big Ears stammered. "I just want to ask you a few questions though."

"Well, I don't want to answer them. Discharge me or I'll do it myself. I'm not crazy. You're treating me like I'm crazy. I was struck by motherfucking lightning."

"Ms. Playfair—" started Dr. Big Ears.

"She's not crazy," another female voice said. "Shocked and scared, maybe. But not crazy. I don't think you need to do a psych consult."

"Exactly," my mate said. "So either discharge me, or I'll get up off this bed and do it myself. But I'm not answering any of your stupid-ass psych eval questions. You can shove those up your ass for all I care."

The curtain flew open and the ER doctor, as well as Dr. Big Ears, left with disgruntled looks on their faces.

I zeroed in on the woman sitting up in the bed, animatedly chatting with another woman with a head of wild red curls. But my mate was the one I focused on.

She was stunning.

A head of wild curls herself—only dark brown with streaks of blonde—a hoop piercing in her nose, high cheekbones, and alert moss-green eyes. But it was her smile that had my chest heating up, and that hollow feeling disappearing even more.

Her gaze flicked across to me and she narrowed her eyes.

Did she feel the pull too? Could she smell me?

I took a step forward, drawn by our intense connection. This wasn't where or how I wanted to meet her, but the Fates had plans all on their own. They made me wait over five hundred years for a mate, and now they had me meeting her for the first time in an overcrowded human hospital. It all had to mean something divine.

"There you are, sir. We need to get you back to the exam bed." An arm looped through mine. "I have an IV for you and we'd like to do a blood draw."

I jerked my arm away and growled at the same orderly as before. "Don't touch me."

Several people in the busy ER turned to watch us, including my mate. But she was distracted quickly by her doctor returning, probably with the discharge papers.

"Sir, if you'll just come with me." Now it was a security guard. He was big, and his voice was far deeper than the wimpy orderly.

"I'm fine," I growled again. "I need to see her." I pointed at my mate, but she was already gone from the bed.

Fresh panic swamped me as I scanned the crowded space in search of her or her friend. But they were nowhere to be seen. Her scent was already growing fainter again. The hollow ache was back.

The security guard easily overpowered me now and led me back to the exam bed where they hooked me up to an IV. "No blood draw," I said.

"Sir, we need to determine if you're anemic," said a phlebotomist, there with a kit to perform bloodwork.

I shook my head. "No. Blood. Draw."

If they took my blood, they'd be shocked to find out I didn't have any of the human blood types. My blood was cold, and didn't have any of the similar human properties. What happened after that, I didn't even want to find out.

What I needed to understand was why my mate left. Didn't she know it was me? Didn't she feel the pull? None of this made any sense.

I needed to get out of there. I needed to follow her. I needed to find her.

But she had already gone too far, and just like I had in the limo and on the plane, I blacked out from the agony. My last thought was an image of her and wondering why she left me here alone, without her.

"He needs blood," came a stern, authoritative voice somewhere off in the distance. "Any will do."

"We can't just give him any blood if we don't know his type," said another voice.

"Not to transfuse. He needs to drink it."

Oh no.

I blinked open my eyes to find a familiar face, Raver. "Hey there," he said, all grins. "Heard you finally got struck by lightning."

I groaned. "Where am I?"

"Still in the same stupid human hospital. But they found your wallet, called Howar, who called me. I'm just over in Seattle, so I drove down to check on you. Where's your mate?" He glanced around as if she were just hiding under the bed or something.

"She left."

His dark blue eyes went wide. "She left? Without you."

I groaned again. "We didn't have a chance to meet."

"Ah, and you're experiencing the Mate's Ache. My brother went through something similar when he was struck by lightning. I hear it's just a curse us vampires bear. No other species has to deal with this."

"I need to find her." I made to sit up.

Raver rested a hand on my shoulder and pushed me back down. "I've ordered some blood. It should help you get enough strength that we can find her together."

The curtain pulled back and several doctors stood at the foot of my bed. A few of them looked terrified, others looked disgusted. The one with the most authority spoke up. "I'm afraid we don't give blood to patients to *drink*," she said, trying for calm, but coming across as patronizing. "We'd like to do a blood panel and tox screen to determine how best we can help Mr. Ferrin."

"Lord," Raver said.

"Excuse me?"

"Lord Ferrin. He is nobility."

"My apologies. How best we can help *Lord* Ferrin."

I shook my head. "No blood work."

"We've hooked him up to an IV because he seemed really dehydrated when he came in, but unless we know what substances he's taken or how severe his anemia is, we can't accurately treat him," the head doctor said, addressing Raver.

"He's not anemic," Raver said. "And he's not on drugs."

A few of the baby doctors snorted.

Whatever.

"Get his discharge papers, please. I'll take him to see our private family physician where he will be treated for his underlying condition," Raver said, scratching at his perfectly trimmed, dark blond beard.

"Uh—"

"I said *please*," Raver barked, which caused all of them to snap into action.

I snorted.

He grinned at me, flashing his fangs and letting them drop just a smidge. "I'll be right back. I'm just gonna go see if I can find you a snack." He took off down the hallway, leaving me in the bed behind all the closed curtains. Even though my species of vampires didn't require blood to survive, when we were in pain or injured, there was no better medicine. A few ounces would help me enough to get to my mate without passing out, and Raver knew that.

A moment later, before any doctors returned with my discharge papers, Raver was back. He was all mischievous smiles as he pulled a bag of blood slightly out from under his jacket to show me. "You can have it in the car."

"Theft is a sin," I said blandly.

"I hear the demons throw killer parties in hell, anyway."

The curtain was pulled back to reveal the head doctor again. "All right, *Lord* Ferrin, this is to indicate that you are leaving of your own accord, against medical advice. Please sign here." I signed, glared at all the hospital staff and allowed Raver to help me walk out to the front exit. He wanted to wheel me in a wheelchair, but I adamantly refused.

I did let him run to the parking lot and bring his car around so I didn't have to walk any further than I had to though.

Once we were on the road, he pulled out the blood bag and handed it to me, along with a paper straw. "I even snagged you a straw from the cafeteria."

"My hero," I said dryly, opening the bag, poking in the straw, and taking a long sip.

Instantly, I felt stronger. The ache in my chest was still there, but my head was clearer and so were my senses. I could smell her again and I gave Raver directions, forcing him to weave through traffic like a racecar driver.

"So what does she look like?" he asked me, his eyes focused forward on the dark, wet road. It was nighttime again. How long was I at the hospital?

A small, faint smile pulled at one corner of my mouth. "Perfect," I said softly.

He smirked. "Is it true you can't get hard for anybody but your mate once she's come of age?"

"From everything I've heard, yes. Across all species, I believe. Donovar said that was the case when he met and mated with Callie."

Raver shook his head. "No fucking thanks. I hope it's another couple hundred years before my mate comes of age."

"Left," I grunted.

He took a left. "Is it the same for the females? Do their legs just like *not* open for anyone but their mate?"

I shook my head and sipped my blood bag. "No idea. Another left."

My mate's scent was strong and heady now. We were close. I sat up in my seat, finishing the bag of blood and tossing it onto the floor of Raver's rental car.

We were in an industrial area now, but it was also where I would say those classified as "hipsters" lived. A lot of the warehouses had been renovated and gentrified into quirky apartments. "Here!" I said, pointing to one of the apartments.

Raver threw on the brakes hard enough that I was thrown forward in my seat against the belt. A car behind us honked.

"A little more warning next time," Raver grumbled, pulling over to the curb.

I closed my eyes and pulled in that floral, spicy scent. She was here. My mate.

"You want me to come in?" Raver asked.

I shook my head. "No. I will be fine."

Raver merely nodded at me. We were childhood friends, growing up in the Middle Ages after the collapse of the Roman Empire. He knew me better than anybody and knew that I would want to do this on my own. I could see the glimmer of concern in his eyes though. We'd been through countless wars together, battered, bloodied, bruised, and nearly beheaded. But he'd never seen me with the Mate's Ache.

"I'm gonna grab a hotel and stick around for the night in case you need anything. Just send out the bat signal."

I snorted and rolled my eyes, opening up the car door.

"Go get 'er, tiger."

Shaking my head, I shut the door, adjusted the coat of my black suit and double-checked that my loafers were scuff-free.

I knew her last name. *Playfair.* I scanned the resident list on the buzzer at the front of the building near the door. There wasn't a *Playfair* listed.

She was with a friend at the hospital, but I was too focused on my mate. I never bothered to listen for another name.

I glanced out at the road where Raver sat in his car watching me. Shaking his head, he got out. "Did you forget your lock picking kit back at the mansion?" His tone was ninety-nine percent sarcasm and one-percent humor.

"I did, in fact."

Pulling out a lock pick kit I recognized from many of our *off-the-record* jobs, he made quick work of the front door lock. "Easy peasy, bro." His grin was all cheese.

"Go sleep, Raver."

"Go get your mate."

I was going to do just that.

I stepped into the lobby as Raver headed back to his car.

Lilacs, honeysuckle, and cayenne.

Taking the stairs, I poked my head on every floor, giving a big sniff down every hallway. It wasn't until I reached the top floor that my heart pounded hard against my ribcage.

She was here.

Unit 405.

I buttoned my suit jacket, hoped that my hair was straight, and gently knocked on the door.

"Who is it?" came a curious female voice.

"It is I, Lord Drak Ferrin, your mate," I declared, something akin to butterflies taking flight in my belly.

"You've got to be fucking kidding me," muttered another female voice.

Footsteps that absolutely could not belong to a woman thundered on the other side of the door. Then the door was yanked open by a man nearly seven feet tall, and almost three hundred pounds, who glared at me with brown eyes.

A bear shifter.

And not just any bear shifter. The Prince.

"What the fuck are you going on about?" he growled.

"Zandren," I said cooly, giving His Majesty a slight bow.

He lifted a light brown brow. "Who the fuck are you?"

"Lord Drak Ferrin, cousin of King Howar Volmark."

Zandren's eyes formed thin slits. "What the fuck are you saying? You're her *mate*?"

"My mate is in there. I can smell her. Lightning struck me late last night, and I have spent every moment since then making my way to her."

"The fuck it did," he barked. "*I'm* her mate. Lightning struck *me,* and I smelled her from over a hundred miles away. Could smell your minty ass before you even entered the building. I told them there was a filthy vampire nearby and they should shut their windows."

The two women from the hospital—one of whom was my mate—crept up behind Zandren. Those curious butterflies in my abdomen were back. I was almost at full strength again.

"What are you talking about?" my mate asked, then her eyes went wide. "I recognize you from the hospital earlier today."

I nodded. "I followed your scent there. But they mistook me for someone ill and tried to admit me. I hope you are all right?"

She glanced at her red-haired friend, then up at Zandren. "Been a weird twenty-four hours. So you're like . . . a vampire?" Her hand went to her throat.

I resisted the urge to roll my eyes. "I am, yes. But you need not fear me. I just ate."

Her friend's eyes nearly popped from her skull. "How long until you're hungry again?"

"I should be fine for a while." I glanced down the hallway in each direction. "Might I come in so we can sort things out, please?"

"Fuck that. I don't know what game you're playing, but she's *my* mate," Zandren said, barring the door with his thick, corded arm. "Get lost, *vampire.* Go run away to your dark, dank castle." He growled like a grizzly, but it came across amusing considering his choice of attire. He was dressed ridiculously. His clothes, gray sweatpants and a red T-shirt, were far too tight and too small for him. Certainly not befitting for royalty. Then again, shifters weren't known for their fashion sense or decorum.

My mate rested her small hand on his. "I feel like we need to hear him out." She glanced up at him. "Much like I did with you. Hmm?"

Zandren growled again, but dropped his hand and stomped back into the apartment. "Fucking hate vampires," he muttered. "Can't be trusted. Not one of them."

I sighed. It was known throughout the Realm that vampires and shifters had a very tedious relationship. We were civil with each other, but neither liked the other. Their disdain for us ran deeper than ours for them though, and it dated back to a very bloody war some hundred and twenty years ago.

"You stand over with Zandren," my mate said as I stepped into the apartment, the smell of Thai food wafting up my nostrils. "I don't know what kind of game this is, but we have mace and a taser, and Gemma's ready to call 911. She also knows Krav Maga."

"I've got the nine already punched in," Gemma said. "And don't think I won't throat punch you."

I joined Zandren on the far side of the room, near the sliding glass door to the patio. He stepped to the side, putting more space between us, while also shooting me a look that said he'd rather be gnawing on my dead corpse right now.

Ignoring the bear, I focused on my mate. "Might I know your name, please?" I asked, my body rebelling against any real distance between us now that we were finally together.

"Omaera Playfair," she said. "Who are you?"

"Lord Drak Ferrin." I bowed. "I do not know of the Playfair family. May I inquire about your parents, please?"

"I never met them," she replied with a shrug. "My mother died shortly after I was born and nobody told me who my father was. But let's figure out why you *both* think you're my mate." She dug her fingers into her hair and pinched her eyes closed tight for a moment. "I mean, I'm still freaking the fuck out about all of this. Vampires and shifters? What next? A witch? A werewolf? A freaking mermaid?"

"Werewolves and mermaids do not exist," I said simply. "And we call witches 'mages' in our realm."

Her eyes flashed open. "You're not helping."

"My apologies."

Exhaling, she began to pace. "This . . . this doesn't make sense." Her gaze landed on Zandren and I. "And yet, deep down, it feels like it does."

My heart fluttered.

"I feel this weird, fucked up, unexplainable pull to both of you." She glanced at her friend. "Maybe I should have had that psych consult."

Gemma merely lifted a coppery brow. "This is super fucked up, but . . . you've always been . . ."

Omaera stopped in her tracks, rounding on her friend, hands on her hips. "Been what?"

"Special," Gemma said softly, her gaze full of love. "Like crazy empathetic. Like you don't only put yourself in other people's shoes, but you actually viscerally *feel* what they're feeling." Her smile was small, but encouraging. "It's one of the things I love most about you. You have this hard shell, but deep down, you're gooier than a perfectly golden marshmallow for a s'more."

"I love s'mores," Zandren murmured.

I rolled my eyes.

Omaera's focus returned to us. "I saw you watching me at the hospital and I did feel this strange pull. Like I was supposed to go and talk to you. But I also wanted to get the hell out of there. They thought I was crazy because I was hearing voices."

Voices? What kind of voices? Vampires didn't hear voices.

"I'm still seriously weirded out by all of this," she went on. "But my aunt taught me to always trust my gut, and right now, my gut is telling me you're not here to kill us. And that you're telling the truth and that I'm supposed to . . . I don't know . . . trust you?"

Zandren nodded, as did I.

"I'd never hurt you," he said.

"Nor would I," I echoed.

Zandren growled beside me. I pulled in a deep breath.

There was a knock at the door. "'Ello, 'ello! It's your Fated Mate, my lovely. Here to claim you and burn up the sheets."

My fangs dropped.

Zandren fell to all fours, and thick, light brown fur rippled in and out of his arms and legs as he sniffed the air. "Fire mage," he growled.

I glanced at Omaera. Her eyes were the size of dinner plates and her mouth hung open.

"Another one?" Gemma said. "You've got to be kidding me."

CHAPTER FOUR

MAXAR RANE

Koh Tao, Thailand

Easiest fucking gig of my life.

And no matter what they paid me, no matter what they offered, I kept the mystery alive by never revealing my secret.

"But how do you do it, Mr. Maxar?" they would all ask. "How can you touch the fire like that? How can you manipulate it and swirl it? How can you put it on your tongue and in your hands and not get burned?"

Magic, bitches.

But to the tourists and locals alike, I was an attraction. Dinner entertainment on the beach as they sipped their drinks, dug their toes in the sand and watched me do more than just fire poi or the fire stick.

No, I made fire my bitch.

I wove it and spun it, condensed it, and stretched it like fucking Silly Putty until they tossed millions of Baht into my hat.

I grinned as a Thai woman I'd spent more than a few nights with walked past, serving drinks to some obnoxious tourists. I couldn't even tell where these fuckers were from. One minute I thought it was Texas, the next minute Ireland. They were too fucking drunk to keep their accent straight.

As long as they tipped, I didn't give a shit if they were from the fucking moon.

I winked at Busaba, and she winked back. We had a no-strings thing that suited us both just fine. And I helped keep the more handsy tourists from getting fresh with her.

She walked past me again, after delivering the beverages to her customers, and gave me a sign that two guys at the far end sitting on pillows needed to be watched. I nodded and kept doing my fire magic shit, smiling for my audience as they oohed and aahed.

"Hey, baby! Another drink, stat!" one of the men called out to Busaba. "If you want that tip, you'll hustle those tight Thai buns."

My nostrils flared and my body temperature went from what it was normally at—around two hundred degrees Fahrenheit—to closer to two-fifty.

Busaba nodded at the men and went up to the bar.

"Yo! Fire Boy, show us something cool. Swallow a flame or some shit." They laughed like the morons that they were.

"Oh, you mean like this?" I asked, snapping my fingers and instantly producing a flame.

The crowd went, "Ooh!"

"That's all smoke and mirrors. Do something that nobody can figure out how you're really doing it," the same cocky bastard hollered. I could see in the eyes of many other beach-goers that these two pricks were ruining the evening for everyone.

I smiled at the men and put the flame on the tip of my finger into my mouth. I closed my eyes and blew, and like steam coming out of a kettle, flames burst from my ears.

Applause thundered, echoing off the calm water.

Busaba walked past me and I kept a keen eye. She brought the men their Chang beer, setting the big bottles down on the squat table with a smile. "That's right, baby. Give us a little wiggle." Then the louder one pinched Busaba's ass.

His friend chortled to encourage him. Then they were both laughing.

A red ball of fire flew from my palm like a baseball destined for the strike zone and landed square in the man's bare chest.

He screamed, and his friend dumped his beer on his chest in an attempt to douse it.

It was magic fire. You couldn't put it out like that, You couldn't really put it out, period.

He continued to scream. Then he got up and found a patch of empty, loose sand. He flopped down and rolled back and forth, crying like a little bitch.

People crowded around him, beating him with the pillows they'd been sitting on to snuff out the flames. Casually, slowly, I walked over to where he writhed in pain.

Not only was it a controlled burn, but it wasn't even that fucking hot—the pussy.

I stood over him. "Do we touch women without consent?"

"Huh?" He'd had his eyes shut. His face was pinched into one of unbearable agony.

I crouched down. "Do we touch women without consent?"

His eyes opened, and he focused on me. "N-no."

"Do we bark orders at the waitstaff and act like obnoxious tourists, ruining the vacations of others?"

"N-no."

"Are you going to apologize and tip Busaba handsomely?"

His eyes darted to his friend.

"Dude, you're fucking on fire. Give him whatever he wants."

The man nodded. "Y-yes."

"Do you promise?"

"I promise. I promise. Now put it out."

Rolling my eyes, I slid down to my knees. "No manners with this generation."

"Please!" he screamed.

"That's better." I angled my face over where the flames danced across his chest, pursed my lips like I was about to suck from a straw, and instead, sucked the fire back into my mouth until there was nothing burning left on his chest. Only a first-degree burn—similar to a bad sunburn. "You're going to want to put some aloe on that." I stood up and dusted off my legs.

The roar from the crowd was deafening now, and it followed me all the way up to the thatch-roofed bar where the bartender, Jai, handed me a tall bottle of water. I chugged it.

"Never ceases to amaze me when you do shit like that, Max," Jai said with a laugh. "I don't know how you do it."

"All smoke and mirrors, my friend."

I glanced out at the sky and the endless stars. It would be the full moon party on Ko Pha-Ngan in a few days. I usually went over because the money was good. Twenty thousand people on a beach, and almost all of them were really drunk, or high on psychedelic mushrooms. I could light a match and put it out on my tongue and they'd all think I was a fucking god.

Busaba came over with a drink tray full of empty glasses. Several Thai Baht were tucked safely beneath one big glass. She pulled out a bill. "Thank you."

I held up my hand and shook my head. "I don't charge you for protection. We've had this conversation before. We're friends, Busaba. I'm going to look out for you—free of charge."

She batted her thick lashes at me. "Can I come to your bungalow later then? Thank you properly?"

Jai chuckled.

"Now that's a 'thank you' I can get on board with."

"Hey!" came a familiar, stupid voice. "I don't know what kind of shitty stunt you just pulled, but it wasn't funny." Dum-dum, who I pretended to almost torch, stomped his too-big-to-be-natural—unless he was a shifter—body over to me. "I don't gotta apologize or put up with a puny little shit like you. Making a fool of me like that. You owe *me* an apology."

I loved my life—except for this part.

Taking a deep breath, I exhaled out a big puff of smoke, making him cough and step back. "I don't, actually. Because although you may be bigger than me. I am smarter than you. I am kinder than you. I am older than you. I am

more dangerous than you. Let's just be honest here. I'm just *better* than you."
I stepped toward him, snapping my fingers again to bring up green flames
this time. "The people on this beach just want to sit, have a drink, and enjoy
some cheap—albeit incredible—entertainment. Don't deprive them of that. Sit
down, shut up, and enjoy the show. Or fuck off."

He eyed my green flames with as much caution as curiosity. "What the fuck
are you, dude?"

My smile was nothing short of evil. "I'm your worst fucking—"

Crack!

Lightning flashed through the sky, illuminating the entire beach. A giant,
jagged fork crashed down from the stars and plunged directly into my chest,
knocking me backward onto the sand.

People screamed.

I was still conscious, but rattled, and when I looked up from where I was on
my back, a crowd formed around so tight I couldn't see the sky.

Jai and Busaba pushed their way through, telling everyone to get out of the
way.

Jai crouched down. "Max, my friend, are you okay?"

Busaba's hand landed on my head, but I instantly flinched and shook her off.
Her face turned sad, but she didn't try again.

I knew what that lightning strike meant.

I'd seen it happen to others.

My mate had come of age.

And now, until we mated, to be touched by another woman would cause me
pain. My heart, mind, body, and soul belonged to only one person now. And I
had to get to her. I had to find her.

"Can you get up?" Jai asked. "Or do we need to call the ambulance?"

"I'm fine," I grunted, my mouth tasting like ash. "Just help me up."

Jai offered me his hand and yanked me to my feet, steadying me when I
wobbled a little.

"Look!" A woman from the crowd pointed to the sand I'd landed on. "Glass."

I turned around where, sure enough, the heat from my body and the lightning had melted the sand and turned it into glass.

A kid bent down and picked up the big, oddly shaped, clear piece. "This is so cool." He glanced up at me. "Can I keep it?"

"Fill your boots, kid."

Lilac, honeysuckle, and cayenne filled the breeze that wafted beneath my nose. I turned toward it, inhaling deeper. My mate's scent.

I needed to leave. Now. There wasn't a moment to waste. Nodding at Jai and Busaba, I headed off down the beach.

"Where are you going?" Jai called after me.

"I don't know. But I gotta go," I replied, not looking back. I didn't have time to wait for one of the shuttle boats in the morning. I needed to start moving now.

I woke up my friend, Somchai, who had a boat, and paid him to take me to Koh Samui which had an airport. From there, I caught a flight to Bangkok, following my instincts that my mate was in the States. I didn't know where in the States, so I paid for a flight to LAX, and would go from there. Her scent would lead me to her door. Of that, I was sure.

I arrived at LAX the next evening. As soon as I stepped outside, I could feel her closeness, and her scent was as strong as ever. I needed to head north.

Renting a car and driving would take too long, so I hopped on the next available flight north, which took me to Chase City. It was just south of Seattle and about two-thirds the size. I'd never been, but again, my instincts told me that when I touched down, it wouldn't be too long before I was with my mate.

"Sir, you'll need to bring your seat up and return your tray table," the flight attendant said to the man across the aisle from me. "We're preparing to descend."

"I don't understand the big deal," the guy argued, pulling out one ear bud, and opening one eye to glare at her. "It's another thirty minutes before we're on the ground. I want to be comfortable and I still have stuff in my cup." He put his earbud back into his ear and closed his eyes again, ignoring her.

She touched his shoulder. "Sir—"

He jerked away hard, unintentionally—from my vantage point anyway—swatting her in the breast.

She gasped.

People around gasped too.

"Are you all right?" I asked her, careful not to touch her.

She held her breast against herself with her forearm, her young, tanned face one of fear and confusion. "T-this is only my first week."

I nudged the idiot's elbow. "Apologize to her."

He pulled out his earbud again and glowered at me. "Who the fuck are you?"

"Apologize to her," I repeated. I really fucking hated repeating myself.

"She touched me first."

"And you assaulted her, because you can't control your reflexes, or do as you're asked by airline staff. Apologize to her." I made sure that when he was looking at me, I tossed some freaky flames into my eyes.

His gaze widened, then he glanced up at the flight attendant. "Sorry," he muttered.

"Now, sit up, finish your juice, and put your tray table back in its secured position, like you've been asked," I went on.

Giving me his best death-stare, he did as he was told. The flight attendant hesitantly took his empty cup, mouthed a "thank you" to me, then skittered off down the aisle.

"Well done," said the elderly man beside me. Thankfully, I'd been seated beside men on all my flights. Even an elbow bump with a woman could cause me pain. "Some people can get so belligerent."

I lifted my brows for a moment. "Some people just don't know how to be decent human beings anymore."

I chuckled on the inside. As far as *human beings* went, I knew only a few who were actually decent. Like Jai and Busaba—and maybe this old guy trying to talk to me. But as a whole, the species was weak, selfish, and unevolved.

We landed without a care, and unloaded off the plane, pouring out into the domestic arrivals portion of the terminal. I didn't have any bags with me. I didn't even have any fucking carry-on. Just my phone, my wallet and my passport.

One of the guys I sat next to on the flight from Bangkok to LAX said I was "raw dogging" the flight, as I didn't have earbuds or anything to keep me entertained. He was stunned that I didn't even watch a show or read the SkyMall magazine.

All I did was shrug. I had enough in my mind to keep myself entertained. Thoughts of my mate kept me busy. What was she like? What did she look like? What was her name? Was she a mage too? And if so, what kind of mage?

The fates worked in mysterious ways. Mages were the wildcards of the bunch—in my opinion—and although mages were usually fated to mate other mages, we seemed to have more variety thrown at us than the other species which bonded mostly with themselves. This was probably why there were so many variations of mages: fire, earth, spellcaster, necromancer, healing, psychic and more. We evolved because our genetics were more diverse. Both my parents were mages, but my uncle's Fated Mate was a very nice fox shifter named Gilda. It was just a theory, but one a lot of mages believed. But, who really knew what the fates were up to with their pairing choices?

It was slow moving, funneling off the plane on the jet bridge, but eventually I broke free of the bottleneck and wove my way through the trudgers and saunterers. I needed to get outside. I needed to figure out which direction to go.

It was dark outside now, and raining, but that wouldn't impede her scent.

Taking a deep breath as soon as I stepped through the open doors, I grew woozy from just how strong I could smell her. I wanted to run. I wanted to run to her now; she was so close. I could practically taste her. And I bet she tasted even better than she smelled.

So I ran.

"Hey!" someone behind me called. "You don't want a cab?"

"I'm good," I replied, continuing at a steady jog.

The dark didn't scare me, and the rain felt good as it sizzled and steamed on my skin. And the closer I grew to my mate, the better I felt. The stronger and more confident. The more excited I became.

My legs pumped harder and faster until I was sprinting. Time ceased to exist. I had tunnel vision. I was focused on the beautiful, blurry figure before me, waiting to be claimed. Waiting for our life to begin.

It was close to midnight when I rocked up to a warehouse converted into an apartment building. What a weird part of town. I bet a lot of hipsters lived here. Just from where I stood, I could see a kombucha shop, a butcher shop, two craft breweries, a gluten-free bakery, and a hot yoga studio.

Oh yeah, this was definitely hipsterville.

Hopefully, my mate wasn't a hipster.

Even if she was, I'd love her.

We could overcome that. I could grow to like microbrew beer and for someone as warm-blooded as me, hot yoga would probably be a piece of cake.

I scoured the building for a way in, finally finding an open sliding glass door on a balcony on the second story. The lights were off inside. Chances were whoever lived there kept the door open for fresh air, or they had a cat that came in and out on its own. I parkoured my ass up to the balcony, barely making a sound as I landed over the wrought iron railing, pausing to see if there was any snoring or sounds within.

Wouldn't it be wonderful if *this* was my mate's place? Maybe she left the door open for me?

I crept inside, mindful of where I placed my feet on the floorboards.

A gentle breath in the single bedroom echoed through the high-ceilinged unit.

It wasn't my mate though. Her scent wasn't strong enough in here for it to be her.

I made my way to the front door and, just as quietly as I had been so far, I opened it and stepped out into the hallway, taking a deep inhale to orient myself.

She wasn't on this floor.

I needed to go up.

So up I went, poking my head onto the third floor.

She wasn't there either.

Ah, my lady fair was on the top floor. The top of the castle for the queen of my heart. How utterly fitting.

When I stepped out into the hallway of the fourth floor, I pulled her perfect scent deep into my lungs and headed in the direction my heart tugged me, stopping in front of unit 405.

Lifting my fist, I knocked on the big metal door, eager to meet my mate and start our lives together. Hopefully, she was just as excited to meet me.

CHAPTER FIVE

OMAERA

Three men stood in front of me.

Three gorgeous men.

All of them looked very different, but all of them were beautiful in their own way.

I'd had a dirty dream like this once, but it sure as hell didn't end in their claiming me in whatever paranormal savage rituals they were probably thinking of.

My head hurt, so I sat down on the yellow corduroy couch Gemma refused to let me get rid of, even though we could afford better. Back when we dropped out of college and were flat broke, we found the couch on the side of the road and carried it with us from apartment to apartment. Now that we were flush with cash, I wanted to get us something newer and better, but she said it was a reminder of how far we'd come.

Burying my face in my hands, I let my tight curls fall forward. "So you're telling me that for thousands of years people and," not lifting my head, I waved one hand to encompass all of them, "whatever you guys are, have been coexisting and humans just never knew?" Finally, I glanced up at the vampire, bear shifter, and fire mage. What the hell was a *fire mage* anyway?

All three of them nodded.

"And have you *ever* heard of your *kind* mating with a human before?"

They all shook their heads.

"Then this has to be some kind of a mistake. Because I'd know if I was a shifter, vampire, mage, or something."

"The other species is demons. There is a sub-species of vampire, which we prefer not to speak of," the vampire said with zero inflection in his tone.

"But there are many shifter species," the bear added. "Bears, cats, wolves, foxes, eagles, and dragons."

"Dragons?" Gemma blurted out, sitting in the green velvet armchair, eating her Pad Kee Mao like this was a soap opera and she was very invested in the characters and plot twists. Only this wasn't a television show. This was my damned life. "There are *real* life dragons? Or are you talking like those Komodo dragons? Because that's cool too. But if we're talking Game of Thrones dragons, then I have to see this."

"Those are technically wyverns," the mage said. "Though, I agree, they look cool."

"We do not have wyvern shifters," the vampire added, again with absolutely no inflection in his voice.

"We do have actual fire-breathing dragon shifters though." The mage's eyes widened with excitement. "Their fire is hotter than anything I can conjure. It's why all Realm weaponry is forged by dragon's fire. Only dragons are blade-smiths."

"I know a few," the bear said with a casual lift to his bulky shoulder. He glanced over at the vampire who stood stoically beside him. He sneered and took a full step away, putting more distance between them.

There was no hiding the bear's complete disdain for the vampire. It radiated off of him in near tangible waves.

Both the vampire and bear hadn't been happy when the mage arrived, but they seemed to have settled whatever initial aversion they had toward him, not that the mage seemed to care.

But the bear wanted to tear out the vampire's jugular, and the vampire was well aware of it and keeping his distance.

Squeezing my eyes shut, I pinched the bridge of my nose. "What does this *Fated Mates* thing mean? Do we have to get married?" I opened my eyes and fixed my gaze on all of them standing there. "You all tell me that you followed my scent—" I paused and sniffed my pits for a second. I wasn't rank. "Then rocked up on my doorstep looking like fucking Pooh Bear, Nosferatu in a GQ spread, and . . . I don't even know what to make of you," I said, waving my hand in front of the fire mage. "An open Hawaiian print shirt, flip-flops. And, are those genie pants? What the fuck?"

The fire mage shrugged. "What? They're comfortable. Lots of room for my giant balls." He snickered and glanced sideways at the other two, but they both shook their heads and scoffed.

"They're hideous," Gemma pointed out.

"I am human. I am not *mating* any of you. I choose who I want to sleep with. And it's certainly not three weirdos who *smelled* their way to me. Thanks, but no thanks."

"You *did* say you felt a pull and that you could trust us though. That deep down you're feeling the Bond too," the bear shifter pointed out.

Ugh. Why did he have to be right? Because he was. I did feel an odd pull to all of them. It wasn't just an attraction. It was so much deeper than that. It was physical. It was emotional. Hell, it was in my freaking soul. I felt it everywhere. In my chest, in my belly, and . . . goddamn it, between my legs too.

"Tell them what you told me. What you heard when you woke up after you were struck by lightning," the bear said. I knew their names, but for some reason, referring to them by name just felt like I was accepting the ridiculousness of all of this. By referring to them as what they *were*, I was keeping a boundary. A level of separation.

"All hail Omaera Playfair, Queen of the Realm," I said, trying to sound bored.

The vampire's mouth dropped open and for just a second, I became mesmerized by his long, white fangs.

"Of the *Realm*?" the mage asked. "As in, King Donovar is dead?"

"Who the fuck is King Donovar?" I asked.

But the mage and vampire had already pulled out their phones and wandered away to make some calls.

"May I borrow your phone, please?" the bear asked. "I need to call my dad."

"Where's your phone?" Gemma asked.

"I don't have one. I just kept losing them when I shifted and forgot my clothes."

His sweet and simple honesty, as well as manners, threw me off even more. But for some reason, I found myself standing up from the couch and handing him my phone. Now all three of them were on calls while Gemma and I just sat there like confused idiots.

The vampire was the first to return, his face paler than it already was. He stowed his phone in the inside pocket of his black coat. Then he dropped to one knee in front of me.

The mage returned next, equally somber, and did the same.

Finally, the bear, who grunted as he dropped his enormous frame to one knee.

"My Queen," the vampire began. "I pledge my allegiance to you."

"And I," the mage repeated.

"And I," rumbled the bear.

"What the fuck is going on?" I demanded, surging back to my feet. "Get up. All of you. Get up and get out. This is ridiculous. I'm not your *queen*. I'm not anybody's queen. I'm Omaera Playfair. A human. A h-u-m-a-n. Got it? Sure, I was an orphan. But my aunt, a nice lady by the name of Delia Refera, raised me since I was a baby. I would know if I was some weird . . . *thing*, like you guys."

The mage shook his head. "Not if there was a cloaking spell cast over you."

"What the fuck are you talking about? Get up. All of you. Now."

They rose to their feet again.

"You," the mage cleared his throat, "are the heir to the throne of the Realm. It has been confirmed that King Donovar was killed last night. As he slept. And he must have been your father. Because the moment he died, his power and title transferred to you, eliminating any cloaking spell that may have been cast."

I shook my head. "No fucking way. No."

"What does this mean?" Gemma asked. "Who killed the king? Who killed Maer's dad?"

"He wasn't my dad," I snapped, facing her.

Suddenly my friend fell to the floor, gripping the side of her head and screaming in agony. Blood dripped from her nose.

"What did you do to her?" I demanded, directing my anger at the men who had rushed to Gemma's side along with me.

But when I turned to them, the vampire and bear both dropped to the floor as well, clutching at their temples as blood poured from their nostrils.

"What are you doing to them?" I rounded on the mage now since he wasn't screaming in pain. It had to be him.

He held up his hands in surrender. "It's not me. It's you. You're angry and taking that rage out on their brains. You need to stop or you'll kill them."

"I'm not doing it," I said. "I'm not."

"I can do mind blocks. It's one of the powers mages and demons have in common. It allows us not to be mind controlled by you."

"Mind control?" I left the bear and vampire to their own devices and focused on my best friend, who cried and writhed on the floor, clutching at the sides of her head as blood pooled from her nose onto the carpet. Tears seeped from my eyes as I brought her head into my lap. "I'm sorry, Gem. I'm so sorry. Please make it stop. I'm sorry. I didn't mean to. I love you. You're all I have. You and Aunt Delia. You're all I have. Please don't die. I'm sorry. I'm sorry." I pet her head as the tears from my eyes fell onto her forehead.

Their screaming had become such a white noise that when it stopped, it took me a moment to clue in. I glanced down at Gemma and she blinked up at me. My bottom lip wobbled, and I cradled her harder against my lap. "W-what happened?" she stammered.

The vampire and bear were no longer screaming in pain either.

Despite having just met them, I did feel a significant amount of guilt at not rushing to help them. The pull I felt for all three men was so bizarre and foreign that I wasn't sure what to do with it. I certainly didn't want them to die or be hurt, but Gemma was my person, and right now, she needed to be my priority.

"Demon powers vary," the mage said. "But because you are the heir to the throne, and now the ruler of the Realm, your powers will be the strongest of all demons. However, since you didn't know you were a demon and just came into your powers, you don't know how to control them. Usually, demons have the power of persuasion. They can delve into the minds of others and manipulate them to make decisions that suit the demon.

"They prey on fear and can hear fear thoughts more than any other thoughts. But they can also plant ideas, like telling someone to kill themselves. And when enraged, and in this case not in control of their power, they can cause a person's brain to begin to hemorrhage.

"That's what happened here. Your confusion and anger over everything came to a head. You snapped at your friend and tried to blow up her brain."

I grabbed a pillow from the couch and tucked it under Gemma's head. "I didn't mean to. I would never hurt her."

The mage nodded. "I know that. But you did because you can't control your powers."

"W-what does all this mean?"

"Well, I'm not sure about the *three* Fated Mates, but mating with your mate will help. It will also give your mate some of your powers, and you some of theirs. It will also link your emotions. He'll feel what you're feeling and vice versa. He can help you manage your emotions so you don't try to fry people's brains. You need to learn how to control your powers. That's number one."

I glared at the redheaded man and the way he so cavalierly explained everything. At some point, he'd moved over to the couch and was sitting there, playing with rainbow-colored flames and making them dance across the tops of his fingers.

My eyes fell to the vampire and bear who had picked themselves up off the ground and now sat there, the bottom half of their faces covered in blood.

Fear shone back at me in Gemma's green-hazel eyes. My heart hurt seeing the way she looked at me, like I was some kind of monster. Just like these three.

What is wrong with my friend? Why did she hurt me?

Now I could hear her fear, just as much as I could see it on her face and in her eyes.

Agony filled me. I'd hurt her. I'd hurt one of the only people in the world who loved me.

I was a danger to her now. To all of them.

"I . . . I need some air," I said, heading to the front door and opening it. "I just need to take a walk and sort out my head."

"You can't leave," the vampire said, using a white, embroidered monogram handkerchief to wipe up his face. Because, of course this pompous prick had an embroidered and monogrammed handkerchief.

If she leaves, it'll hurt again.

Dammit, was I hearing his fears now too? What did he mean if I left it would 'hurt again'? I glared at the man as he wiped his face with the handkerchief. He winced. Shit! Was I spit-roasting his gray matter again? "I can do whatever the fuck I want," I said quickly, before opening the door and slamming it shut.

I sprinted down four flights of stairs, then burst out into the cool, May evening. It'd stopped raining, but the smell of rain on flowers and pavement soothed me. Everything would be so fresh, green, and alive tomorrow.

I wasn't sure where I was walking, but I headed down to Fourth Street and took a left.

I'd nearly killed my best friend.

My only friend.

And the way she looked at me was something I'd never forget.

Gemma and I met our first year of college at Chase City University. We moved into dorm rooms on the same floor, right across the hall from each other. She wasn't sure what she wanted to study, but I was set on mathematics. I'd always had a keen mind for numbers. What I would do with a math degree, I wasn't sure, but it was what I wanted.

We bonded on day one and became inseparable after that. She even transferred into a couple of my classes so we could spend more time together. We rarely fought, and even when we did, they were more differences of opinions than actual fights, which we sorted out by talking like adults.

She came from a middle-class family and had one younger brother. Her parents didn't make a ton of money, but what they lacked for in *things*, they made up for in love.

But right before Christmas during our sophomore year, her parents and brother were returning home from a ski trip and died in a car accident, leaving Gemma with no one—but me.

Of course, she inherited everything from her parents' estate, but it wasn't much. It paid off their mortgage, the funeral fees, and for the rest of her sophomore year. But by the second semester of our junior year, she made the tough decision to drop out. Her parents had a fair bit of debt and the remainder of her inheritance went to cover that.

So, I dropped out with her. We'd already been roommates since sophomore year, and I couldn't go to school knowing she wasn't going to be there too. I had a scholarship, but I gave it up so that Gemma and I could be together.

At first, we tried regular jobs, but I knew early on that I wasn't cut out for retail, or any kind of customer service. People suck. They're rude, entitled, and really fucking stupid.

Then I tried bookkeeping, which suited me better, but it was boring.

It wasn't until I was bookkeeping for a bar downtown that I stumbled across the backroom poker games. I observed at first, but even just when observing, I could pinpoint the winners and losers. I could read their emotions. I could intuit their moves.

When I finally saved up enough scratch for a buy-in, I asked my boss if I could play and he said it was my money to lose.

But I didn't lose. I won. Again, and again, and again.

I quit my job as their bookkeeper and started playing as many nights as I could, winning nearly every game. Then we went to Seattle, and Portland, even down to San Franscisco, where we heard about big underground games, and I won a lot there too.

After about six months of playing and winning, I heard about a big underground game in Vancouver. Only, I didn't have a passport, and there wasn't enough time to apply for one. So I went to a friend of a friend and had one made.

Eventually, he roped me into his business of forged documents and IDs. When he decided to move to Los Angeles to pursue a career in acting, he left me his business, clientele, and all of his equipment. But Gemma wasn't comfortable with having something illegal like that in our home, or being part of it at all. So I gave it up.

I didn't need the extra scratch that came from the side hustle, and it kept us both honest and aboveboard. The last thing we needed was some butthurt bozo I beat at poker, getting his thong in a twist and sending the cops after me for some asinine and bogus reason. Because if the cops showed up to search my apartment and found the forgery equipment, then we'd be toast.

I kept coming back to what Gemma said about me earlier.

That I was *special.*

I knew she meant it as more than just a compliment. And the more I thought about it, the more all the unexplainable things in my life started to make sense.

I was rarely ever sick. I could probably count on one hand the number of colds or flus I'd had in my life. And even when Gemma would be bedridden for days, stuffed up and hacking up a lung, I'd be completely fine. I'd always had this intuitiveness when it came to people, too. It was something I used when I played poker. It allowed me to *feel* my opponent's feelings. Play the player, not the cards. However, it also attributed to my general disdain for most people, because I could feel deep down not only their lack of empathy or kindness, but also their stupidity. People were really stupid. Mob mentality was real and I could usually pick out of a crowd those that would follow the crowd like lemmings off a cliff, trampling anybody in their way, and those who would question the crowd, ask to see who was leading, and stop to help those who had fallen.

There weren't a lot of those kinds of people out there.

Then there was growing up with Aunt Delia. She'd always been a bit of an odd duck. Eccentric and charismatic. Her outfits were out there with crazy patterns and designs, and she wore the weirdest earrings and jewelry. She had a full collection of actual animal bone and horn jewelry too. One pendant was the skull of a squirrel. She said it kept away bad energy.

I chalked that talk up to just a kooky old spinster who was Wiccan and weird.

But now . . . now I wasn't so sure it was so much kooky as it was magical. Maybe she was of this realm, as the fire mage predicted.

But then, why didn't she tell me? Why did she keep so much from me?

By the time I stopped walking, I was eight blocks from home, out of the hipster borough and in a part of town I rarely frequented—the club district.

Ugh.

More people.

And worse than that, they were drunk people.

I rarely knew what day of the week it was. I didn't give a shit. Gemma knew, because she liked people more than I did and wanted to work in a coffee shop a couple of shifts a week. So she needed to know what days she was on the schedule.

I guess today was a weekend. Friday maybe? Because the bass from a few clubs clattered the windows of a nearby office building, and the closer I got, the more I could feel it in the ground beneath my black tennis shoes.

The sidewalks were peppered with people out for smokes or vapes, or waiting in line to get into the club. Most bars with a dance floor and DJ didn't close until four in the morning here, so it was still early. A lot of partiers remained at home, pre-drinking or getting their fake eyelashes on to go out.

Although, Gemma had dragged me to a few raves over the years, neither of us were into the club scene. We went once when I turned twenty-one and lasted all of thirty minutes before I insisted that we bounce. There were just too many people and I wanted to punch nearly every single one of them in the throat.

We went to a quiet pub instead, where we gorged ourselves on nachos, cheap shots of tequila, and gave in to the temptation of karaoke, despite how much neither of us can carry a tune.

A sharp pang filled my chest at the thought of her.

I hurt her.

My best, and only, friend in the world, and I hurt her.

I nearly fucking killed her.

Whatever was going on with me, she needed to steer clear, because I was obviously sick or something. I still didn't believe I was some *heir* to a throne I'd never heard of. Or that the three sexy lunatics who knocked on my door were anything but humans who needed to be medicated and committed. They were not my Fated Mates, and I was not a queen.

"Hey, Little Demon," came a rough and smoky voice from down a dark alleyway. "What are you doing out here all by yourself?"

I paused, squinting to see who was speaking.

The orange burn of a cigarette told me where he was, but I couldn't see his face.

How did he know I was a demon? Nobody had ever said that to me before. There were people around, but none so close that I could join their group and pretend I was with them for the whole "safety in numbers" thing.

"What? Too good to talk to someone below your *station*?" he asked.

Station?

"I-I'm sorry, I don't know what you're talking about," I stammered. I continued walking, eager to get out of this place and the unending noise that pounded into my eardrums, threatening to burst them.

I elbowed my way through a drunk and laughing crowd of twenty-somethings, but was pulled back by a rough, powerful hand on my elbow. "I'm talking to you, *Demon*," he growled.

Tingles of fear raced down my arms. I tried to jerk away, but was hauled backward toward a dark doorway just around a tight, narrow corner, and thrown up against a wall.

"I don't know what you're talking about," I repeated as he gripped my wrists, pressing them back against the wet, mossy brick wall. "What do you want with me?"

Finally, from the glow of a streetlamp across the road, I could see his face.

It was pale—too pale, perhaps? And his eyes glowed a startling yellow. Not like he had cirrhosis of the liver, but the irises themselves were a cat-like yellow, and they shone bright and eerie. He ran his nose up along the side of my neck, inhaling deeply. What was this man?

"Demons," he said with so much contempt I actually got a little offended, even though I still didn't believe that I was one. "You think you're the top of the food chain? You think you're better than everyone? You're hunting us. Killing us for sport. Well, how about we turn the tables, hmm?"

"I . . . I don't," I said, hating that I had a quaver to my voice. "I'm not hunting anybody. I don't know what you mean. I don't think I'm better than anybody."

"You all do. You're so confident . . . so cocky. You're out here all alone. Not a guard, not a mate, nothing." He sniffed me again. "You're not even mated." A feral purr rattled in his throat. "Even better."

Pulling his head back just enough so I could see his face a little better, he smiled like the devil himself, and two long fangs descended down past his top lip, nearly touching his bottom lip.

"Just a taste, hmmm?"

Oh, fuck no. Not like this.

I'd already been through hell over the last twenty-four hours. I was not going to have some psycho who cosplayed as a vampire, plunge his teeth into me in some dark doorway.

Mustering all the strength I could, I leaned my head back into the wall and smashed it forward against his, head-butting him hard in the nose.

My ears rung, but not so loud that I couldn't hear his scream.

He released my wrists. "You bitch!" Then he screamed again and fell to the floor, clutching at the sides of his head as blood poured from his nose, just like it had with Gemma, the bear, and the vampire at my house.

I stared at him, frozen in place. Still plastered against the wall, watching as his brain hemorrhaged in front of me and he shrieked and pleaded for his life. But nobody besides me could hear him over the heavy, unrelenting beat of the music.

And then he stopped.

He stopped moving, he stopped screaming, he stopped . . . living.

My hand flew up to cover my mouth before I could start screaming.

Oh god. What did I just do?

I just killed someone. And there were witnesses everywhere. They'd seen him and I go into the dark doorway. They'd find the body and know that I was the one who killed him.

I spun around, determined to pry my feet from the concrete and run. But when I did, I ran smack dab into the brick wall that was the bear's chest, still covered with that ridiculous, red crop top. His hands fell to my shoulders.

I'd never been so glad to not be alone in my life.

He took one look at the man on the ground and nodded, then stepped forward. That's when I saw the vampire and the fire mage behind him.

Gemma wasn't with them though.

The four of us stood there over the body.

"W-what was he?" I stammered.

"Phaceanesh," the vampire sneered. "Nightwalker."

"Best way to deal with the body is to burn it," the mage said, completely unfazed.

The bear nodded.

"What is a *Phaceanesh*?" I asked. "And what do you mean '*burn it*'?"

The mage looked at me like I didn't know what fire was. "I mean, I have to cremate him right now, so nobody finds him. Even though you're the Queen, a murder has been committed and if we don't get rid of the body, there'd be a hearing and . . . trust me, you don't want that drama. Give me thirty seconds and he'll be your favorite Kansas song."

Zandren scrunched his nose in confusion.

The mage rolled his eyes. "Dust in the wind."

I gaped at him. Not only was he cracking jokes, but he spoke like he was telling me to give him thirty seconds to brush his teeth and tie his shoes before we headed out to go grocery shopping. Not half a minute to scorch a body to ash.

"What did I do?" I couldn't peel my eyes away from the lifeless body, the blood still running out of his nose and onto the damp and cracked pavement beneath him.

"You killed him," the vampire said plainly. "He probably deserved it. Phaceanesh are an abomination and troublemakers."

"H-he was going to bite me."

The bear's head snapped my way. "Did he say that?"

I nodded.

"Well then, he should be glad you killed him and I didn't. Because I'd have ripped him into pieces with my paws." He growled low and deep in his big chest before turning to me and cupping my jaw in the gentlest way and the paradox startled me. He was so big and scary, but the genuine concern for me in his eyes hit me in a weird place in my chest. "Are you okay, Little One?" he asked. "Did he hurt you?"

I stepped out of his embrace and shook my head. "I'm fine."

The mage walked over to the body. "Keep watch."

The vampire and bear nodded, then turned to face outward. But I couldn't tear my eyes away as black flames emerged from the mage's palms and he blasted them at the dead body, covering it in nothing but gorgeous ebony fire, unlike anything I'd ever seen before. Just like he said, it took about thirty seconds, then the flames withered out on their own. He put his hands down at his sides and when the last ember died out, there was nothing left but a pile of smoking ash.

My jaw dropped.

"All clear," he announced, returning to me. "Taken care of. Now we need to get you home, my Queen."

"Don't," I said, swatting away his hand when he tried to cup my elbow.

The briefest flash of hurt flickered through his amber eyes, but he stowed it quickly, plastered on an easy-going smile, and shrugged.

"We need to go home," the bear said. "It isn't safe here."

"It's fine," I said. "I've lived in Chase City my entire life. I've walked these streets at night alone hundreds of times. I don't need you."

"You've never walked them as the Queen of the Realm or a demon without a shield, and who can't control her powers," the vampire said in a tone that had so much judgment and almost disbelief that I couldn't understand something so simple. I wanted to punch his chiseled face.

My anger at him must have done something because he winced and blood seeped from his nose.

Guilt swamped me. "I'm sorry."

He blinked a few times. "It's okay."

No, it wasn't. Anytime I got mad now, was I going to kill someone?

I was a walking time bomb.

"You're not safe with me. If you piss me off . . . which we all know you will, I could kill you."

"Then we need to mate," the vampire said. "It will keep us safe."

"Absolutely not. You should just go."

His nostrils flared. "Absolutely not," he mimicked. I growled. "You are my mate. I'm not leaving you."

"Well, then you've got a death wish because I'm going to get pissed and try to broil your brains at some point. You're insufferable. It's inevitable."

His gaze narrowed on me and I did everything I could do not to squirm beneath its intensity. I also really hated what it was doing to my lower belly and between my legs. "You're not being smart about this, Omaera. It's the safest way to protect you and everyone else. To bring you into your full power."

Even though the more I thought about all of this, the more there was less deniability, I still wasn't ready to just accept it all. I was stubborn and a lot had been thrown at me in the last few hours. "I don't believe in any of this shit," I said. "I don't believe in *Fated Mates* or powers. There has to be a scientific explanation for this. Magic isn't real. It's all smoke and mirrors. Illusions and sleight of hand."

"There isn't a magician on this planet that wasn't a mage," the fire mage said. "We make a lot of money fooling humans."

I glared at him, knowing that I could at least get mad at him and not turn his brain into hamburger.

"Please, let us return home so we can figure this out. We don't need to mate right now, but we do need to figure out how much of the Realm knows the King is dead. We also need to find his brother, Lord Lerris." The bear sidled up to me, but he didn't touch me. The man had to be twice my size, at least.

"What kind of a bear are you?" I asked.

"A grizzly."

"And how do you . . . turn into one?"

He smiled in such a sweet way it settled down my building ire almost instantly. "Tomorrow, I can show you. We can go out to the woods and I can show you. It's not safe here though. If people saw . . ."

"Right." I exhaled. "Was Gemma there when you left?"

The mage nodded. "Yes. She seemed fine."

"H-how do I make sure I don't hurt her again?"

The vampire made an impatient noise in his throat, as if to say, "I already told you how. Mate us."

I glowered at him. He just averted his gaze, but I could see him wince a little.

Dammit. I didn't like him, but I didn't want to hurt him. I didn't want to hurt anyone.

"What do we do with the . . . ash?" I pointed to what was left of the Phaceanesh or Nightwalker.

"He'll be washed away with the next rainfall," the mage said. "I doubt anybody will miss him. Serves him right for assaulting a woman. For assaulting the Queen."

"Come on, Little One. Let's get you home."

I glanced up at the bear and the tenderness he looked at me with. "Okay."

Flanked by the mage and bear on either side of me and the vampire behind, we walked back to my apartment. I had no idea what time it was, but just as we reached my front door, it started to rain again.

"Down the drain he goes," the mage said with delight, referring to the Phaceanesh's ashes. "Fish food."

I punched in my code for the door and it clicked open.

"What is your code?" the vampire asked. "So that we may come and go as we need."

I glared at him.

He stared blankly back at me.

"I'm not giving you that," I said.

"Why not? We are your mates. Where you go, we go. And we may need to enter the apartment without you."

"Get a fucking hotel. You're not crashing in my place."

He shook his head. "Not happening. You are not safe without," he cleared his throat and his gaze shifted side to side to take in the bear and mage, reluctance clear on his face, "*us*."

I was too tired to argue with this black-and-white thinking, impeccably dressed, bloodsucking robot. I simply opened the door and let them file in ahead of me.

Even though the elevator said it could accommodate eight adults, it was crowded in there with the bear. He took up space for at least four people, but the way he stood there, just content with a small smile on his face, pulled so strangely at my heartstrings, I took a half-step away.

I wasn't sure what I was going to walk in on when I got home. Would Gemma already be packed up and gone? Did she lock herself in her room and bar the doors? Would there be a pentagram in the middle of the floor, garlic everywhere, and wooden stakes ready to be plunged into my heart?

I absolutely wasn't expecting her to run up and hug me the moment I walked in, that's for sure.

"Oh, I'm so glad you're okay," she said, squeezing me tight, bringing the familiar scent of her lavender shampoo.

"Me?" I squeaked, not hugging her as tight as I would have liked because I just couldn't risk hurting her again. "I'm the one that hurt you. Are *you* okay?"

We pulled away from each other, still hanging on though.

A voice cleared behind us. "Can we come in, please?" the vampire said with impatience.

I was beginning to really not like this guy.

Gemma and I stepped further into our loft, our sanctum sanctorum, as we called it. The bear, mage, and vampire followed, and the door shut.

"I'm okay," Gemma said. "I took a couple of extra-strength Tylenol, but I'm okay. What happened though?"

"She can't control her powers, and her anger triggered one of her powers. It nearly boiled your brain like soup in your skull," the mage said, opening up our fridge and pulling out a sparkling water. He read the flavor, made a face, and put it back. "Eww, strawberry? Do you have any like . . . lime, or something citrus?"

I glared at him for a half-second. "I think there's unflavored club soda in the back of the fridge, and a lemon in the crisper."

He grinned at me and went to work.

"What happened to you?" Gemma asked me, taking my hand. "Are you okay? These three booked it out of here like you were in mortal danger. I've never seen men move that fast if it didn't involve pizza, beer, or a blowjob."

"I could go for some pizza right now," the bear said. "May I borrow your phone again, please?"

"If you don't have pockets for a phone, how do you have pockets for a wallet?" I asked him.

"I know my credit card number, expiration date, and CVC by heart." He held out his meaty palm for my phone. "May I borrow it, please?"

This guy was so freaking polite it was impossible to say "no" to him. I reached into my back pocket and handed it to him.

"Thank you very much." He wandered away, punching the screen with his giant fingers.

Out of the corner of my eye, I could see the mage in my kitchen, cutting up a lemon with a knife. He plunked the thin round slices into the glass with the club soda, then picked up the glass and put it on his left index finger. Suddenly, the water began to bubble and steam. He was boiling it right in front of our very eyes.

"That's cool," Gemma said. "Even if these guys are freaks of nature, that's a cool party trick. He's who you want when you're out camping. No need for a propane stove. Just use the freak's finger."

"That's Mr. Freak," the mage said, taking a sip of his now-bubbling sparkling lemon water.

Gemma snickered.

"We don't camp," I said. "We don't *rough it.*"

Gemma shrugged. "But if we ever did, we could just bring him along to cook up our baked beans straight in the can."

That made me chuckle. She always knew how to bring me out of my funk and make me smile.

The vampire was sulking in the corner, sitting in the green velvet chair, staring at his phone.

I took a deep breath just as the bear returned and handed me my phone.

"Can we start from the beginning, please?"

They all nodded.

"Good. Because even though the three of you are starting to become less scary, don't for one second think that means I'm going to let you all gang bang me so we can swap bodily fluids and powers. I might have had a dream where I was getting tag teamed by three guys, but that was a dream, and this, unfortunately, is real life. And I'm . . . way too freaking small to even consider such a thing."

CHAPTER SIX

ZANDREN

She deserved answers to all of her questions.

She deserved whatever the fuck she wanted.

I couldn't imagine what was going through her head right now, and the need to protect her ran rampant through my body, unlike anything I'd ever felt before.

She wasn't a bear.

She was a demon.

A queen.

And even though she was my mate, she was also the mate of two other men.

A psycho fire mage who was unpredictable, chaotic, and severely unhinged. And a vampire.

That was all I needed right there.

A fucking vampire. I hated vampires. They were calculating, cold, blood-thirsty, and in my opinion, entirely unneeded in the Realm.

I had my work cut out for me with Omaera, but I was ready for the challenge. Maybe she needed to choose one of us and once she mated with one, the Bond with the other two would be severed?

News of King Donovar's death was spreading throughout the Realm, and nobody could find Lord Lerris either. Was he dead too? Or was he in hiding?

One thing was for sure: I didn't want to push my mate. Up until tonight, she believed she was human. So I could only imagine the questions and confusion she had as she came to terms with everything. The last thing she needed was any initial pressure. Even though mating with us would solve a lot of problems, she needed to come to terms with that on her own. She needed to *want* to mate.

The pizza arrived, and we all sat down on the couches and chairs to fill her in.

"How many people are we planning to feed?" my mate's friend, Gemma, asked. "This is what you order for a football team after practice."

I tilted my head at her as I brought the five extra-larges I ordered for myself over to the couch and set them on my lap. "What do you mean? I ordered you guys some too."

She blinked at me. "Are you going to eat *all* of those?"

"Yes?"

She gaped, then shook her head. "Please don't make a mess in our bathroom when you hurl it all up. I just cleaned it this morning."

What did she mean *hurl it all up*? I would probably still be hungry after this and need to order a donair or kebab or something.

Shrugging, I opened the first box and growled as I smiled at all the delicious meats piled high on my pie.

"Firstly," I said, taking a bite of the stringy pizza. "The Realm is the world of our kind. All *non*-human species. And you are the Queen of all the species. You are also the Queen of the demon species. My father is the King of the Shifters."

"And my cousin, King Howar, is the King of the Vampires," Drak added, sitting like he had a stick up his boney ass in the green velvet chair. Oh, how I wished a stake in the heart actually killed vampires like in the movies. Stupid bloodsucking, pale ass, motherfuckers.

"Is there a mage queen or king?" Omaera asked.

Maxar nodded. "Anysa Sadlyn is our Queen."

"And they all know about me now?"

We all nodded.

"Okay . . ."

"You are the Queen because, although the Realm believed King Donovar had no heirs, he apparently did. Whether he knew about you remains a mystery. But when he died, his powers transferred to you. That is the only explanation." Even though he wasn't actually doing anything but talking, the vampire was still pissing me off. I glared at him and growled as I chewed, wishing it was his bones I was crunching and not the delicious all-meat pizza with cheesy crust I ordered.

"How did he die?" she asked.

"He was beheaded," Drak said with no emotion.

I glared at him. Such an emotionless ass.

Omaera paled. "B-beheaded?"

"It's the only way to effectively kill a demon or mage," the vampire went on.

"How do you kill vampires and shifters?" Gemma asked.

"Vampires you can kill in a number of ways," I said, fixing my gaze on the blood sucker across from me. "Brain hemorrhage—obviously. Beheading is always a good option too. Starvation is another."

Drak glared at me.

I flipped him the bird as I held my pizza slice. He merely rolled his eyes.

"What about sunlight?" Gemma asked. "In *Interview with a Vampire* they turned to dust when they were hit with sunlight."

"Nightwalkers will sizzle and be in immense pain in the sun, but they won't die," Drak said. "Daywalkers are fine."

"How do you kill a shifter?" Gemma was just full of questions, while Omaera sat in the corner of the yellow couch, her knees up to her nose, just listening. But she'd already asked her questions and now was just processing. I could practically hear her cogs spinning as she absorbed all this new information.

"Why don't you explain this one," I said to Drak. "Seeing as your kind has killed so many of my kind." I took a big bite.

He blinked at me curiously for a moment, then turned to Omaera and Gemma. "Beheading. Blood loss. Skinning while in shifter form."

"You forgot one more," I growled.

His gaze narrowed at me.

"Killing her cub in front of her," I said, deadpanned.

He blinked at me more, swallowed, then cleared his throat and focused on Omaera again. "And a broken heart."

"Oh my god, that's . . . horrible," Gemma said. "Why are you guys so—"

"The human race is just as terrible to each other, Gem. Don't shame them as monsters," Omaera said softly. "Think of what kind of torture humans have been doing to each other for centuries. Burning at the stake, drawn and quartered, gibbeted, boiling in oil, gas chambers, firing squads, pulled apart by four horse carts, school shootings, killing fields, bombings, tarred and feathered, 9/11, the Holocaust, the genocides in Rwanda and Cambodia—and those are just the tip of the iceberg. Humans are monsters too." Her face held so much sadness, along with contempt for humans. It was a contempt I shared.

Humans were monsters. My mate and I definitely agreed on that.

Gemma nodded. "That's fair. People have done—and continue to do—horrible things to each other."

Omaera's gaze met mine. "Did vampires do that to your mother?"

All I could do was grunt.

Her bottom lip trembled. "I'm sorry." Then a lone tear slid down her cheek, and her next words came out in a quaver. "I'm really, really sorry."

I grunted again and continued to eat my pizza.

"So you're saying she has an uncle?" Gemma asked, glancing at Omaera with excitement. "Dude, you have family."

Omaera swallowed. "Does this mean I could abdicate the throne and give it to him?"

"I've never heard of an abdication in . . . ever," the mage said.

I shook my head. "Neither have I."

The vampire agreed silently.

"But as Queen, I must have some kind of ruling power to change things though, right? Like I can get rid of the whole Fated Mates thing? We should be allowed to *choose* who we want to marry. Not forced into a marriage like some . . . regency piece of property. I'm not a commodity. I'm not a brood mare to just keep popping out baby bears, mages, and vampires." Her eyes went wide.

"Oh god, if we're not the same species, how would that even work? Would our children be abominations? Outcasts? Freaks?"

Chuckling at her adorable panic, I finished my first pizza, put the box on the floor, and opened up the second box. *Mmmm, mushroom and pepperoni.* "Our children would be bear shifters with demon powers. So they'd have the best of both our powers."

"And ours would be demon-mages. The best of both powers. However, not necessarily fire mages. Their specific mage powers would reveal themselves around the age of five." Maxar said.

We all faced Drak, waiting to find out what kind of spawn he and Omaera would produce. The idea of him rutting with her made my skin crawl and the bear inside me wanted nothing more than to pull his jugular out of his neck and use it as a skipping rope.

"We would have vampire children only. For as long as I have been alive, I have never heard of a vampire mating with a demon. And if it has happened, there is no record of a vampire-demon hybrid. So that means the vampire gene would be dominant."

"Why does the demon species rule all the species?" Gemma asked, having gotten up from the couch to grab everyone plates and napkins. Only she, Maxar, and I were eating pizza though.

"It is said that because demons possess the ability of mind manipulation, they are the strongest. They can sit there and do nothing and basically make your brain explode, or convince you to kill yourself. In the past, there were wars over this. Many, many wars," I pointed out. "But King Donovar ruled peacefully. He didn't abuse his power. He held several court meetings with all the rulers and listened to them fairly. He preferred to say that they ruled the Realm together, not beneath him. He was a very beloved king."

Omaera exhaled. "Well, at least my dad wasn't a tyrant who everyone wanted dead." She frowned. "Someone did though. And they succeeded."

"I already have people looking for Lerris," Drak said. "He is the most likely suspect. Since nobody knew about you, he would be next in line for the throne."

"Or someone else killed Donovar with the thought that Lerris would become

King and be easier to manipulate or overthrow?" Maxar added. "That has happened before. Remember the war of 1689 between King Pyrne of the Demons and King Solovan of the Vampires?"

I nodded. "Another reason why we need to keep you safe. Because if whoever killed your father finds out about you, they're going to try to take you out too."

Her moss-green eyes widened. "Take me *out*? What if I just *give* him the throne?"

The vampire, mage, and I exchanged glances with each other.

"Talk to *me*. Not telepathically with each other," Omaera demanded.

"I don't know much about Lord Lerris, but I'm not sure he's someone we *want* as King of the Realm," I said gently. "He's certainly not someone my father said he'd ever like to see in charge."

"King Howar said the same thing."

"As did Queen Anysa's proxy, who I spoke with," Maxar added.

"I . . . I need to talk to my aunt," Omaera finally said, getting up from her little corner of the couch. "She always knows what to do." Her gaze landed on Gemma. "Right? Boy problems. Life problems. Even math problems, she always has the answer."

"Is she back from her trip to Mexico?" Gemma asked.

Omaera nodded. "Yes, she got in two nights ago. I meant to go see her, but . . . well, I was kind of struck by fucking lightning."

"Where is this *Delia*?" I asked, still reconciling with Omaera's mention of *boy problems*. How many *boys* did she have problems with in her past? And, what kind of problems did they cause her? Did I need to hunt them down and teach them a lesson? Drag them into the woods and treat them to an eternal mud bath six feet under?

"Twenty minutes from here," Gemma said, grabbing another piece of pizza. She glanced at her phone. "It's like three in the morning now. We should at least wait for it to be a decent hour before we go knocking on Delia's door."

Omaera chewed on the side of her thumbnail as she paced back and forth along the transition that separated the kitchen from the living room. "Why do I feel like I need to go to her *right* now?"

"Because you're panicking and you need answers," Gemma said. "But waiting a few hours won't change anything. Let her sleep. You should sleep too."

I nodded, and put my second empty pizza box on the floor. "That's a good idea."

Omaera didn't look convinced, though. She seemed agitated—more than what I'd grown used to. Her chest heaved and her gaze shifted erratically back and forth. She growled. "How the hell do any of you expect me to sleep when . . . all of *this* is going on?" She waved her hands at the three of us. "I really feel like I need to go to Delia *right now*. Like once I talk to her, all of this will make sense."

Gemma's face softened. "And I'm sure it will. In. The. Morning. Let her sleep. And you should sleep, too."

Frowning, I stood up, rested my pizza boxes on the coffee table, and went to her. "There isn't anything we can do until morning. Maybe you will find answers in your dreams, remember something else that happened when you woke up after the lightning." With hesitation, I rested my hands on her shoulders, applying just a little bit of pressure. I wanted to jump for joy when she sighed beneath my touch, closed her eyes, and finally nodded.

"Fine," she gritted out. "But I'm in my room *alone*. You three . . . try not to kill each other . . . or do. I don't care."

Gemma pried herself out of her chair and came over to give Omaera a hug. Jealousy rippled through me at how close her friend got to get to her, and yet she barely let me touch her.

Because you're a beastly stranger she doesn't know, who showed up at her house without any pants on.

Right!

I needed to do better.

"What can I do to help?" I asked, and genuinely meaning it.

She appeared exhausted and barely able to keep her eyes open, but there was still a fire there, still a spark that I longed to get to know better. With a weary sigh, she glanced at me. "Figure out how we can get rid of this whole *Fated Mates* bullshit, because it's not fucking happening." Then she trudged toward a closed bedroom door, slipped inside, and didn't come back out.

We all turned our attention to her friend.

"What are you looking at me for?" Gemma asked. "I'm not your Fated Mate. And thank fuck for that." She took a bite of her pizza.

"What was Omaera's upbringing like?" I asked, eager to know as much about my mate as possible, figuring her best friend was the best source for that information.

Gemma eyed us all curiously. "What makes you think I'm going to tell you anything?"

"Because you love her and want what is best for her. And what is best for her is allowing her mates to properly claim her. So that she is protected and cared for," Drak said. His tone was so dry and patronizing. Like he figured all of this was a no-brainer and humans should just understand. I mean it was a no-brainer to me, but to someone who *just* learned about our world, it had to be a lot to take in. Vampires were such robotic, emotionless dicks. And this one was no different. Why couldn't he just disappear?

"We still haven't even addressed the problem that this *human* knows of the Realm," Maxar said, gesturing to Gemma.

"This *human*?" Gemma snapped. "Excuse me?"

I exchanged looks with Drak, then we both glanced at Maxar. "You do what I think you're thinking and Omaera will burn your balls off before she accepts your brand."

"That's your mark?" Gemma asked with a squeak. "You have to *brand* her?"

"She'll enjoy it," he said without missing a beat before turning to me. "I wasn't thinking of killing her. But finding a spellcaster to wipe her memory isn't the worst idea."

Gemma lunged for the mace that sat on the kitchen island. "Nobody is wiping my fucking memory. You got that?"

"You can't wipe Omaera's memory. So wiping her friend's memory would piss off Omaera. Try again," I said, shaking my head at the stupid fire mage. I went back to the couch and dug into my third pizza box.

"Is me knowing about your realm a bad thing?" Gemma asked, still pointing the mace at us. It might piss off a real black bear, but it'd do absolutely nothing to me. I wasn't about to tell her that though. It was better that humans feared us.

They already feared so many things that they didn't know. Their beliefs were wack.

"It is," Drak said, sitting there apathetically with such a punchable face. "Humans are not permitted to know of our world. And if they do learn of it, we either wipe their memories or eliminate them."

"You kill humans who find out about you?" Gemma's voice was high-pitched enough, dogs were probably howling somewhere.

"We try not to," Drak replied. "But as a form of preservation for our world, sometimes it's necessary."

"Well, you're not wiping my memory or killing me. So—"

"No, we're not," I replied, taking a bite of my honey-barbecue chicken pizza. "But you need to swear on . . . whatever is sacred to you, that you won't tell a soul about our world. About what you know and will learn. Humans are . . ."

"Unevolved. Stupid. Terrified. Selfish. And ruled by an antiquated patriarchal ideology that should have died out centuries ago," Maxar said.

Well, he wasn't wrong. But I was planning to be less insulting.

"I won't tell a soul," Gemma said, glaring at Maxar. "Not all of us are unevolved, stupid, selfish, or terrified. I agree with you about the antiquated patriarchal ideology though."

"No, you actually have to swear on something," I said. "Like it will bind your promise, and if you mutter a word, that promise will break and bad things will happen."

Her green-hazel eyes went wide. "Seriously?"

"Seriously," Drak said, his tone as even and dry as a fucking endless desert.

She glanced around the room, still standing there holding the mace. "Okay . . . uh . . . I swear on the graves of my dead parents and dead brother that I will never breathe a word about your realm to any other human. I will never share what I know or use that knowledge to hurt anyone from your realm." She lifted her brows. "We good?"

"What will happen to you if you do?" Drak asked.

"I dunno? I'll join them in their graves?"

A white beam of light flashed through the room, followed by a loud thunderclap.

"What just happened?" the redhead asked, flipping her focus back and forth between all of us.

"You made a magical, solemn vow. Break it, and you'll join your family in their graves," Drak said.

Her mouth dropped open. "Seriously?"

"Why does she not think we're serious about this?" Drak asked. "I don't understand this human."

"This *human*?" she shrieked.

"You went dark with that solemn vow," Maxar said, shaking his head. "You could have done something less fatal, like a five-day rash, or chlamydia. But I mean, at least we know you'll keep your word with death hanging over your head."

The bedroom door opened and Omaera appeared wearing nothing but a plain, ribbed, gray tank top with no bra, and black booty shorts. She also wore a pale purple, silk scarf over her wild curls. "What is going on?"

"I just made a death vow!" Gemma said, panic in her eyes.

"Huh?"

"I made some magical vow not to tell another human about your realm. Otherwise, if I do, I'll go join my parents and Andrew in their graves. Then there was a beam of light and a thunderclap."

Omaera's gaze swung to mine. "Huh?"

"It was either that, wipe her memory, or kill her," Maxar said with a casual shrug.

I hung my head. "There were other options. She didn't have to choose death."

"I didn't know I had other options. I just suggested something, and the magic took over." Gemma approached Omaera. "Dude, I think this shit is real. Something happened. Like I even *feel* different. And if I do say something, does that mean I'll just die and, in spirit, meet them?"

"No. You will literally be transported by magic to their graves. You will be buried alive," Drak said.

Oh, he was not doing *any* of us any favors.

Omaera rounded on him with a harsh glare. "Reverse it."

"Impossible," he said. "She made the vow. Not us."

"She's human. She didn't know what she was doing." Omaera stomped over to Drak and glared down at him. "Reverse. It."

"I. Can't." He pinched his eyes shut and a trickle of blood dripped from his left nostril. I could tell he was in pain. She was doing her mind squeeze thing again, but Drak was trying to fight it.

There were ways where we could block the demon mind fucks—young cubs and vampires alike were trained to do so. But she was so powerful and untrained with those powers that we were powerless against her. The best thing to do was *not* piss her off.

"Maer. Maer, stop." Gemma ran over to her. "You're hurting him. Stop." She placed a hand on Omaera's shoulder and the relief that hit Drak was instant. The pained contortion of his face softened, and he exhaled before reaching into the inside pocket of his suit jacket and pulling out his embroidered and monogrammed handkerchief.

Remorse filled Omaera's eyes. "I . . . I'm sorry."

Drak dabbed at his nose. "It's fine. But I cannot reverse her oath. That is between her and . . . the higher powers."

"Just don't tell anyone and you'll be fine," Maxar said, grabbing another slice of pizza.

"And if she slips up?" Omaera said frantically.

"This is incentive not to. We all have secrets. This just needs to be one of hers." He shrugged and chewed as a little rainbow flame danced along his moving knuckles.

"I'm going to bed. Gem, you should too. No more death oaths allowed." Omaera glared at all three of us. "You three . . . fuck, I don't even know. You'll probably be here when I wake up, I assume. So . . . try not to fucking snore or break anything." Then she stomped back to her bedroom and slammed the door.

Gemma stared at all of us, holding the mace like a gun as she skimmed the perimeter of the room. Then she made her way to her bedroom.

"Are the only bathrooms in their rooms?" Maxar asked. "I need to piss."

I glanced at both of them. "Do either of you know what a *Pooh Bear* is?"

CHAPTER SEVEN

DRAK

Vampires required very little sleep.

Humans needed between six and ten hours a day. Vampires were at full-battery power after two.

The blockhead bear and the unhinged fire mage snored in the living room. I took my phone out onto the balcony, closed the sliding glass door, and called my cousin.

It was already morning in New York, and I knew he'd be up with Fiorella. So I wasn't rude calling him.

But I definitely needed insight. I needed help.

This was not going to plan at all. She refused to mate, so if we were apart for any length of time, I would get the Mate's Ache and lose strength. But I also didn't want to tell her—or any of them about the Mate's Ache. I didn't trust this group of people and wasn't about to expose my weakness or vulnerability to them.

When Omaera left to go for a walk, I was the first to leave and follow her. Her safety was my main concern, but also, the moment she left and the further she got, the more pain I was in.

It was a struggle to keep up with the bear whose strides were twice my own, and the fire mage who never shut up.

I needed a familiar voice. I needed guidance because right now, I didn't know what to do.

My mate was in trouble. She had two other mates, and she refused to mate any of us.

What was I supposed to do?

"Good morning," Howar greeted me to the sound of Fiorella giggling in the background. "How is your new mate?"

"She refuses to bond. Any of us." I educated Howar on the three mates issue last night. "Any news on Lerris's whereabouts?"

"None. We've assembled a council meeting for later today though. It would be prudent for our new queen to attend."

I resisted the urge to laugh. "I will see what I can do to advise her." I highly doubted Omaera would be interested in meeting with the other Realm leaders, considering she still didn't believe, accept or want to be *Queen of the Realm*.

"She hasn't mated any of you yet?" he asked with concern.

"It's been less than twenty-four hours. Is that typical?"

Howar made a noise in his throat. "I mean . . . those that understand what the Mating Bond will give each of you, do it rather quickly. They know that their mate was not selected at random. The Fates do not work like that. We are carefully matched, which is why some have to wait centuries. But since she's only just come into power . . . you may need to give her time."

"How much time? Someone out there killed her father. She's not safe. She needs the Mating Bond to protect her." I dropped my voice down lower. "I need the Mating Bond to stop the Mate's Ache. She left on her own last night and I could barely stand up."

Howar hummed. "Yeah, the longer you let it go on, the worse it will become. It's also going to be rough every time she leaves until then. Another reason why at least vampire mates bond quickly. Neither want to experience that pain or weakness any longer than they have to."

"The bear and mage aren't experiencing any loss of strength," I said with disdain, turning around to glance through the sliding glass door at the heap of muscle and stupidity sprawled out on the floor with his crop top and tight sweatpants. The mage was on the couch, puffs of smoke drifting out of his nose as he slept.

"The mage will be experiencing something different. He won't be able to touch another female without experiencing pain, at least until they mate. And as for the bear, I'm not sure. None of you will ever get aroused by another woman, I know that. The Fates are very strict in their mating rules, and making sure that mates bond."

Turning around, I leaned against the railing of the deck and glanced over, down to the wet, empty street below. It'd rained again, but it wasn't now. "Any more news on the mage I was interrogating?"

"And killed," he said blandly. "Rella, darling, you have jam all over your chin. Bring Daddy a napkin so I can help you." Fiorella made noises of protest. "There we go, Sweet Pea. Much better. Can I have a kiss?" *Muah!* "Thank you. Go find Mommy, she'll help you get dressed."

"I think you should put Raver on as my replacement. We both know he's good. He'll find whoever is ordering the vampire kills probably faster than I would."

Howar made a non-committal noise in his throat. "It's also something I'm going to bring up at the meeting today. See what the others have heard."

Something niggled at the back of my mind. It was what the bear said last night about a way shifters can die.

"Your silence is telling. What is on your mind, besides the obvious dilemma with your mate unwilling to mate, and your rivals?" the King's tone was tinged with mirth, but also concern.

"Is it true that a way to kill a shifter is to kill her cubs in front of her? That she will actually die from heartbreak?" When I confirmed Zandren's statement last night, I was actually unaware of its truth. But I didn't want to come off as ignorant. This was obviously something he knew, and who was I to argue with the hairy brute? I wasn't surprised by his continued disdain for me. The tedious relationship between shifters and vampires was long-standing and well-known. But this bear was pricklier than most, and not afraid to let me know he'd rather have me for lunch than even try to get along.

Howar was silent for a moment. "Yes," he finally said. "I'm grateful that's not a way to kill vampires. And I don't wish that kind of death on anyone. Why?"

"The bear said it. It's apparently how his mother died. Her cub was killed—by a vampire—in front of her, and she died from a broken heart. Do you . . ." I cleared my throat. "Do you know how and when it happened? The bear is King Ryden's son. So it would have been King Ryden's mate."

Again, Howar was quiet.

I didn't like where this was going.

"It was not a good time for shifters and vampires. We were at odds more than we were on good terms. I wasn't the King—my father was—and we both remember what kind of a racist tyrant he was. He hated that demons ruled. Thought shifters were primitive beasts that didn't deserve a seat at the table. That they're no better than dogs. Pets."

"I remember," I said slowly.

"Your father—my uncle—was his head of military, and—"

"Equally brutal, racist, and tyrannical," I finished, my gut spinning with what I hoped to the gods wasn't going to come next.

"I don't really know *what* happened, or who instigated what but, Goliver, your father, killed Ryden's cub—a young female—in front of Ryden's mother, Leida Thorne, Queen of the Shifters. From what I understand, it was in retaliation for something. But because it was more of a cold war than anything else, there was some semblance of an agreement where children would be left out of the war. They weren't coming after vampire children and we weren't going after cubs or pups."

"But my father broke the agreement."

"He did."

"And he killed Zandren's sister and mother." I was going to be sick. I spun around to look back through the glass door again at the sleeping beast spread out on the carpet with his hands tucked behind his head, his legs out long.

"He did," Howar confirmed. "And it started a huge war. Many from both sides died—including your father and my father. That's when I came into power. That's when King Donovar came into power because his father died too." He snorted. "Out with the old and in with the new. I hate to say it, but when Goliver did that, igniting the war, it culled a lot of the bad seeds from both sides. It allowed you, Donovar, and me to step up and change things. To broker peace. Which we've had for a hundred and twenty years now."

No wonder Zandren hated vampires so much. Did he know who was responsible? Did he know it was my father?

"It was tragic, truly," Howar said with sympathy. "But it yielded the best possible outcome."

"I'm not sure Zandren or King Ryden would feel that way."

"King Ryden knows what happened. He knows I'm nothing like my father and that you are nothing like yours. And we all know that Donovar was nothing like Jaxar. I'm hoping that Omaera will rule like her father—not her grandfather."

"If she ends up ruling at all. She's hellbent on abdicating or figuring out a way to *not* rule."

Howar chuckled softly. "The Gods and their fates are stronger than any magic. She is the rightful heir and unless killed or properly challenged, she cannot relinquish her responsibility. If that was an option, I'm sure I would have considered it more than once these last hundred and twenty years."

"She has an aunt not far from here and wishes to go see her today. She is the woman who raised her."

"A human?"

"I think so? But maybe not, since Omaera had a strong cloaking spell cast over her until Donovar was murdered. So perhaps this woman is a mage and never told Omaera."

"Name?"

"Delia Refera."

"I'll do some digging. What do we know about Omaera's mother? Do we know her name?"

"We know nothing at all. Did you know that Donovar was with someone? I didn't think his mate had come of age. That he was still waiting for her."

"That was my understanding too. Poor man, four hundred and forty, and still without a mate."

"Okay, I'll put out feelers and we'll see what we can dig up. The demon world is more elusive and suspicious than all other species combined. So I doubt my inquiries will lead anywhere, but we can try."

"Thank you."

"Hang in there." I could feel his smile through the phone. "She will mate you."

I exhaled and hung my head, the guilt of what my father did to Zandren's mother weighing heavily on my shoulders. "I hope so."

I disconnected my call with the King at the same time Omaera came shuffling out of her bedroom. She still wore the same thing we'd seen her in last night—black booty shorts that barely covered her buttocks, a gray, ribbed tank top and no bra. She also still had the pale purple, silk scarf on her head. She was beautiful.

I watched her for a moment, knowing she may not be able to see me right away with the glare of the rising sun coming in through the big windows and door.

The way she yawned was adorable. The way she padded barefoot into the kitchen and robotically added coffee grounds to the machine, filled up the machine with water, and turned it on—all sweet. Then she opened the fridge and brought out a carton of oat milk before reaching into the cupboard to pull down two, then three, more mugs.

Even though she didn't want us here, she was still courteous enough to caffeinate us.

Her noise in the kitchen roused the bear and mage, and although they moved, neither got up. They both just rolled over, opened their eyes, and watched her. Just like I was watching her.

Were they as transfixed as I was?

Probably. They were her Fated Mates as well.

A quick glance at the bear showed a ridiculously big erection, creating a ten-man tent in his tight sweatpants.

Either Omaera hadn't looked up and noticed them watching her yet, or she was deliberately *not* looking. She continued to putter in the kitchen, preheating the oven to reheat the pizza and putting the leftover Thai food in the microwave.

I'd barely blinked. I was so mesmerized by her that when the sliding glass door opened and Gemma emerged, I grunted and averted my gaze quickly, as if I'd been doing something wrong.

"Ignore me. You all are anyway. I'm just out here to do some morning yoga before I head to work. All three of you are stupidly obvious, and a little obsessed, you know. Watching her like that. And the fucking boner on bear-man. Jesus Christ. You do know Maer is like five-foot-nothing. How is she even going to take that schlong if she ever decides to?"

A legitimate question I had asked as well when the whole three mates thing came about. Zandren was enormous and Omaera was petite. In fact, all three of us were over a foot taller than her, and though I couldn't speak for the mage, I didn't have a Vienna sausage in my trousers.

Gemma set up her yoga mat and began with some head-down poses.

I took that as my cue to return inside.

Zandren was now sitting up with a pillow over his lap. The mage was gone, but the bathroom door—yes, they had a second bathroom, not part of the one that connected their two bedrooms—was closed.

"I'm assuming since you're all sort of human that you drink coffee?" Omaera asked, fixing me with a questioning look. "Unless you drink tea because all obnoxious British aristocrats drink *tea*." She pinched her thumb and forefinger together and put it to the side of her mouth while raising her pinky finger like she was sipping from a china cup.

"I drink both," I stated. "Coffee is fine."

"Black for me, please," Zandren said. "Can't make it too strong."

The bathroom door opened and Maxar stepped out.

"Coffee?" Omaera asked him.

He nodded. "Ten sugars."

We all stared at him with confused looks—even Omaera.

"How have all your teeth not fallen out?" she asked. "That's disgusting."

"I have a fast metabolism," he said. "I burn it off in like twenty minutes. And I brush my teeth and go to the dentist. That's how." He glanced at me. "Who were you on the phone with outside?"

"The King," I replied. "Asked of any news regarding Lerris." I refocused my attention on Omaera. "The High Council has called a meeting for today, and it would be prudent for you to attend."

She shook her head slightly. "Oh would it now? Would it be *prudent*?"

Oh, this little demoness was testing my patience. I needed to keep her happy, though. If she got angry with me, she might try to fry my brain again.

"My apologies, Your Majesty. King Howar, Queen Anysa, and King Ryden are meeting today with their advisors to discuss the situation of King Donovar's death, and your unexpected appearance and rise to power. They also wish to discuss Donovar's murder, and who your mother was. There has been peace in the Realm for one hundred and twenty years. Since your father and King Howar came into power. I'm sure they just want to meet you and ensure that peace will continue."

Her nostrils flared as she stared at me. "And who would be *my* advisor, or advisors? You three?"

"We're not bad choices. But typically, mates don't attend High Council meetings," Maxar said. "Though, with Drak being Howar's guard and Zandren being Ryden's son, and me just being awesome, you've got a good team behind you."

She smirked at his cocky comment about himself and pushed his coffee mug to the edge of the counter so he knew it was ready. He grabbed Zandren's for him as well.

"Or we can help you find a suitable and trustworthy advisor. A demon advisor if you wish," Zandren added, sipping his coffee. "Whatever you need."

From where I stood near the kitchen, I could see her mulling things over. Her features relaxed, but her eyes still remained on high alert. I accepted my coffee mug from her. I didn't take it black, but I also didn't want to rock the boat and ask for cream. In due time. "Howar and I wonder if perhaps your aunt, this *Delia,* is a spellcaster mage. Perhaps she would be a suitable advisor since you've known her your whole life."

Omaera snorted and made a face. "Aunt Delia a mage? No. I'd know if she were one of your . . . *kind*."

But we all shook our heads.

"Not if she was trying to protect you, keep your identity from being revealed," I said. "Raise you as human."

"And why would she do that?" Omaera snapped. "Why not tell me that I'm a demon? Help me with my powers so that when I *come of age*, or my father is killed, I'm not hit with a giant bolt of fucking lightning and nearly killing people by trying to fondue their brains?"

Gemma came back into the apartment. "Who's fondueing brains?"

"I am, because they think Delia is a mage and kept my powers from me." Her hand trembled as she brought her coffee mug to her mouth.

Gemma scoffed, reached the kitchen counter and accepted the mug Omaera pushed toward her. "Yeah, there's no way Auntie D. is a mage or whatever. We'd know."

It was easier for me to remain stoic than it was Zandren or Maxar. They both lifted their brows.

Omaera narrowed her gaze at them. "You think we're that blind to—"

"Magical beings have co-existed with humans for centuries and you just found out last night," Maxar pointed out, albeit gently. "We are experts at hiding who we really are. And if Delia was doing it to protect you, she'd be extra vigilant about secrecy."

"We need to go see her. Get some answers," Omaera said with growing impatience. She turned to her friend. "What time is your shift at the coffee shop?"

Gemma pouted. "It's a double now because I took yesterday off to be with you. Nine to nine, I'm afraid."

Omaera growled. "So I'm stuck with the Three Stooges all day?"

"They're way sexier than the Three Stooges." She sipped her coffee, smiling over the rim of her mug. "Still freaks like the Stooges, but at least they're more fun to look at."

"I'm going to go get dressed," Omaera said with a sigh, taking her mug with her. "You three can . . . shower, eat, or whatever. Just don't make a mess." She disappeared into her bedroom, making sure we all heard that deadbolt flick closed.

"Do me a favor, boys," Gemma said. "Try not to piss her off, okay? Nobody needs flambéed brains, hmm?" She grabbed a yogurt out of the fridge, along with a banana off the counter, then took her breakfast and coffee into her room, shutting the door.

That left the three of us in the living room together again.

The bear, the mage, and me.

"Dibs on the shower," Maxar said, jumping up from where he sat and taking his empty coffee mug to the sink.

I rolled my eyes.

"I need to find some food," Zandren grumbled, finally prying himself off the floor and standing up. "I'll be back." He left out the front door, causing it to rattle the rafters when it slammed shut.

And then there was just me.

I needed food too. That bag of blood last night helped, but I needed actual food now. Preferably something with high iron content so that if Omaera continued to resist mating, at least I'd have some strength. I went to the fridge and opened it up.

Not much to choose from in the way of meat or high-iron veg.

The freezer, on the other hand, yielded a sirloin steak and some frozen spinach. That would work.

I was busy frying up the steak and spinach with some herbs I found in the cupboard when Omaera came out of her room. It was impossible not to stare.

My mate was . . . perfection. Her black skinny jeans had small rips in the knees and she wore a dark gray, very soft-looking, T-shirt with the name of some band I didn't recognize. It fell off her shoulder on one side and all I wanted to do was sink my fangs into that creamy bit of flesh and hear her moan from the pleasure. Her earrings were little silver spikes that stuck out the same amount—about an inch—at the front and back of her lobe. And she had on the same black tennis shoes as last night.

"What the fuck are you looking at?" she snapped, but very little ire colored her tone.

I chose not to respond.

"What are you cooking?"

I glanced down at the cast iron frying pan. "Food?"

She grunted. "No shit, Sherlock. But why steak and spinach?"

"High in iron. It keeps up my strength."

"You mean it keeps you from sucking people's blood?"

Again, I chose not to respond. I didn't *need* blood. Food was just fine. It just had to be iron rich. But in circumstances like last night when I was very weak, blood was better.

"Would you like some?" I asked.

"I don't eat breakfast. I intermittently fast." She poured herself more coffee.

Shrugging, I turned off the stovetop and moved my frying pan over to the cold element. Then I removed the steak to a cutting board so it could rest. My belly grumbled from the smell.

"Do any of you have cars?" she asked. "Because I don't."

"Not that she can't afford one," Gemma said, coming out of her room dressed in dark jeans and a red long-sleeve shirt. "She just chooses to walk or use public transit."

"It's better for the environment," Omaera said, sticking her tongue out at her friend. "And let's not forget that your parents and brother, and my mother, all died in car accidents. So the less we're in those death traps, the better."

Gemma's expression sobered, then she leaned over and kissed Omaera on the cheek. "I know. I didn't mean to tease."

"Have a good day at work, Gem," Omaera's smile wasn't real. She was rallying and putting on a brave face for her friend. "Text me on your lunch break."

Gemma winked and nodded, then she made eye contact with me since I was the only one left in the apartment. "Remember, don't piss her off."

"I'm trying very hard not to," I replied dryly.

Then Gemma was gone, and Omaera and I were all alone.

"Your accent is weird," she said without hesitation.

"I was born in England and lived there for a long time. The dialects and accents changed over the centuries. I moved around, and each region has its own way of speaking. Then I moved to the States one hundred and twenty years ago to help Howar. So it's a mix of all the places I've lived."

"Hm," she huffed, then didn't say anything else.

"I'm sorry that your mother passed away," I said, hoping that didn't cause her to get angry.

Her frown tore at the hollow in my chest. "Thank you. I was only two weeks old, so I don't remember her. But from what Aunt Delia says, she was . . . she was really something special." She cleared her throat and looked around, sipping from her fresh mug of coffee. "Where is the bear?"

"He went out to find food," I answered, deciding that I'd waited long enough and it was time to slice into my steak.

She nodded. "Is controlling my powers something that *you* can help with? Or just the mage? Or do I need to find a demon to help me?"

The fact that she was talking about getting help and control of her powers was a good sign. Did this mean she was accepting her fate as heir to the Realm? Was she also going to accept us as her mates?

It felt safer not to make eye contact with her, so I focused on slicing my steak into thin, even pieces on the diagonal. "I can't unless we've completed the Mate's Bond. I strongly urge you to agree to mate. It will protect all of us."

"And bind us together for life!" she countered, her tone laced with an ire that worried me. "I *just* met you. You realize that? I've never even had a one-night stand, let alone a one-night eternal commitment." I glanced up to find her staring at me with wide eyes. "Wait, am I immortal?"

"Well, you can be killed by decapitation—"

"But if, like nobody does that, then I'm going to live forever, right?"

"That is generally how it works, yes."

"God, you're so backhandedly rude, you know that? The sarcasm and patronization in your tone is exhausting." A small pain in my brain made me wince. I needed to subdue her. If she got angry with me, she could kill me. Even though she was just coming into her powers, there was little doubt in my mind that she wasn't an incredibly powerful demon. Even if she wasn't the Queen, she would still be very powerful. Lethal. She needed to learn to control her powers before she did irreparable damage to someone she cared about—like Gemma.

I stared at her, gritting my molars in reaction to the ache in my head. "My apologies. I didn't think I was being sarcastic or patronizing. I thought I was answering your questions."

She batted her hand like swatting at an invisible fly. "Whatever. So wait, like if I'm a demon and going to live forever, did Aunt Delia—if she's even a mage, which I still doubt—not think I'd start to wonder why I'm living longer than the average tortoise? Also, why are you like a billion years old but only look around forty?"

"A billion years is an exaggeration, right?"

Rolling her eyes, she scoffed. "Of course."

"I am four hundred and forty-one. And we stop aging around the age of forty. So once we hit forty years old, we don't look any older even though we are."

"Well, then that confirms it. Aunt Delia isn't a mage. She looks older than forty."

I was anticipating her saying that. I held up a finger and chose my words and tone very carefully. "However, spellcaster mages can age themselves. They can cast spells to make themselves—or anyone who asks them—to appear older. And some choose to. There are those who wish to age, who wish to grow old and eventually die. Not everyone wants to live forever, and we have ceremonies and protocols around that."

The bathroom door opened, and the mage came out with a towel wrapped low on his waist to reveal a torso of well-defined abs. He was bone-dry and steam flooded out of the bathroom and rose off him like some weird hot spring.

"Did you hotbox my bathroom?" Omaera asked glancing at the foggy space he just emerged from like a creature from some eerie lagoon. "You need to turn the fan on, dude."

Maxar shook his head. "No. The water was cold. This is just what happens when water touches my skin. It steams off."

Omaera frowned and bunched her brows in a cute way. "Hmm."

Rolling my eyes, I exhaled and dove into my steak. "I guess I need to eat, then shower before the bear comes and uses all the hot water."

Speak of the beast, the door opened and in lumbered the shifter. He'd ditched the red crop top and sweatpants and now wore an open flannel shirt and loose-fitting jeans. He was also licking his fingers.

"Where'd you find clothes this early in the morning?" Omaera asked.

Zandren washed his hands in the sink. "I picked the lock at the clothing store down the road with my claw. I'll go to the bank later and take them money when they open. Then I went to the bakery for breakfast." He peeled off his shirt. "But I'm going to take a shower now." Then he plodded his way to the bathroom.

Omaera snorted and shot me a smirk. "Snooze you lose, Fangs."

Oh gods, this was going to be a nightmare. An absolute bloody nightmare.

CHAPTER EIGHT

Maxar

We tolerated each other because we had to.

For her.

If there was one thing and one thing only that the bear, vampire, and I agreed on, it was that we would do anything for Omaera.

We still didn't like the idea of having to share her, or that we would be tied to each other for what could very well be eternity, but the most important thing was protecting the Queen and getting her the answers she needed.

Even if it meant riding the fucking bus to do it.

Good gods, I hated public transit.

I could run faster than the average bus, and most modes of public transit stunk like stale urine, garbage, and bad weed.

But none of us had a vehicle.

Omaera refused to drive because of how her mother died. The bear was a bear without even a fucking phone or wallet; the vampire was rich, powerful, and had a driver; and I just did whatever the fuck I wanted, which usually meant running or hopping on the back of some guy's motorcycle to get where I needed to go.

"Let's just call a cab," I said, as we walked to the subway station that morning, all of us flanking Omaera like she was some popstar and we were her bodyguards.

Because we kind of were. And she was more important than any popstar. She was a fucking queen.

"No," Omaera said. "The subway is fine. I take it every day."

I turned up my nose and rolled my eyes as we made our way down the stairs headed underground.

"It's cold like a cave down here," Zandren commented. "Smells worse than any cave I've ever lived in though."

"Wait, I thought bears shat in the woods," I said with a laugh.

He turned to me and looked me dead in the eye. "We do. But not in our caves." Then he shook his head and scoffed like I'd asked the stupidest question in the world.

We paid and went through the turnstile, slaloming through people. A train whizzed by, its wheels squealing on the track.

"It's well-lit for a cave too," Zandren added. "I prefer my caves darker."

"It's not a fucking cave, dumbass. It's a tunnel." I snapped my fingers at my sides, creating small benign flames to keep myself busy and distracted.

A small child not too far away caught me, his eyes wide, mouth open.

I smiled at him and put one finger to my lips for him to keep it a secret, then I snapped my finger again and produced a rainbow flame. His eyes went even wider, and he whispered, "Wow!"

"This is our train," Omaera said as one came to a stop on the platform. I went to step on when the doors opened, but she grabbed my hand. "Wait for people to unload first." Her eyes asked me if I was just born yesterday. "Patience, sparky."

A rush of pure pleasure raced through me from her touch. It was the first time she'd ever touched me, and it was like coming home. I'd never felt such peace. Such joy or bliss. I knew that no other woman could touch me now without me experiencing pain, at least until Omaera and I mated. But I had no idea how truly wonderful her touch would be. How magical and powerful her skin would be against mine.

And when she removed her hand, it was as if all the light in my life, all the energy in my body, had drained away like water in a sink.

I was bereft and weak for just a blink of a moment, but it was enough to make me dizzy.

"You coming, mage?" Zandren asked after he, Omaera and Drak had stepped onto the train.

Nodding, I stepped on as well and joined them. It was standing room only, and the four of us were drawing a lot of attention. Probably because Zandren was a beast and hadn't bothered to button his shirt, Drak looked like a model for an undertaker magazine, and my fiery red hair and odd clothing choices always made people do a double take. Genie pants were just so fucking comfortable.

But if Omaera wanted me to wear something else, I would.

For her.

The train jerked to start, and we were all jostled. Omaera put her hand out against my chest, to stabilize herself, and that same intense rush of pleasure filled me up to near bursting. I can only describe it as energy, light, heat, and the buildup to the greatest orgasm of my life.

Her hand only lasted there a second before she pulled it back and held onto the pole with just one hand.

I pouted inside, but remained unfazed on the outside.

It was only a fifteen-minute ride on the train before our stop and we all followed Omaera like lost lambs.

I'd always enjoyed the company of women. I'd been with many over the centuries and certainly found them to be the fairer, but stronger, sex. However, I'd never been taken with one, or rendered to a puppy following one around so obediently, like I was with Omaera.

Was it because she was my mate? Was that the only reason?

Or was there more to it?

Was it because she was the Queen?

We'd only ever had kings for as long as I'd been alive. And as far as anyone knew, King Donovar never had a mate. So there was no queen. Yes, the mages had Queen Anysa and she was a wonderful and fair leader, but she was a leader mainly in title only. The true shift of power and reign over all belonged to King Donovar, or in this case, Queen Omaera now.

We emerged back out into daylight, in a new borough of the city. This area of town was much nicer than where Omaera lived. Less hipster-ish and more family friendly. There were supermarkets, drugstores, pet stores, a dog park, an elementary school, and a medical clinic, all within spitting distance of each other. Flowerbeds covered every available non-road or sidewalk area, and baskets teeming with more greenery and petals hung from the ornate, green streetlamps.

"Why don't you live here?" Zandren asked. "It smells better than where you live. And it's nicer."

I snorted. Maybe there was a second thing that we agreed on.

"Because I like the apartment Gemma and I share. It's ours. What's wrong with it?" She glanced up at the bear. "You don't have to stay, you know?"

"Yes, I do," he said plainly. "And it's fine. This place is just nicer. And smells better."

Leave it to the bear to keep it real and honest.

We reached a tall, narrow, yellow house with white shutters, a plum-colored door, and matching plum-hued wide steps up to the porch. It had a white picket fence all the way around and red geraniums in every plant pot and basket.

"If this is where you grew up, why'd you leave?" Zandren asked.

I snorted. He was digging himself a hole, and I was happy to sit back and watch. The vampire hadn't said a damned word since we left the house, but none of us were complaining. He was a big Debbie Downer, and until I caught him scowling, I often forgot he was even there.

"Do bears live with their parents and families for life?" she asked him, opening the gate on the picket fence.

"No," he said plainly.

She raised her brows at him. "So why should humans be different?"

"Because this place is nicer than your place. This place has a yard. It has grass."

She made an impatient noise in her throat and climbed the stairs. "Again, Pooh Bear, you are welcome to leave my apartment at any time. Nobody is forcing you to stay."

I chuckled, but his deep angry growl made me pause. His eyes narrowed, and he sniffed the air, turning his head back and forth.

"What is it, Lassie? Is Timmy in the well?"

But my smile fell the moment he faced me, dead-serious and contemplating shifting. "I smell demons."

"Yeah, me. Apparently," Omaera said, reaching for the doorknob, but Zandren's big hand grabbed her wrist and he pulled her back until she smacked into his chest.

"Not you, Little One. You smell of lilacs, honeysuckle, and cayenne. This is not your scent. But it is the scent of demons."

Her palms were on his chest, and she glanced up at him. "What does that mean?"

"It means someone has been here to visit Delia before us," Drak said, opening the door and stepping into the brightly-lit home with all the stained glass, wainscotting, and old-fashioned-but-recently-repainted crown molding.

I didn't have such a keen sense of smell as the shifter, but I knew what death smelled like.

Drak, Zandren, and I all exchanged looks.

Omaera tried to break free of Zandren. "Why does the house smell like that?"

Now that she was coming into her powers, her sense of smell would intensify too. If she mated Zandren, it would get even stronger.

Zandren held her tight. "Little One, you don't want to go in there."

"Yes, I do," she growled, shoving against him. "Aunt Delia, are you home?"

Drak was already in the house, and he made his way through it, down the hallway toward the kitchen in the back. Zandren stayed with Omaera on the porch. I entered the house as well, checking out the study, the living room, dining room, the one bedroom on the main floor, and the bathroom.

Drak hadn't said anything yet, which meant he hadn't found the body.

We met at the base of the stairs leading to the second floor and took it together.

"Lerris?" I asked.

"Someone looking for Omaera," he said with a dark tone. "More than one, from what I can smell. Both demons."

"This is three stories. There's a basement too."

Drak shook his head as we reached the top of the wide staircase. "No. She's up here. I can smell it."

I swallowed and followed him down the hallway to another bedroom where, sure enough, there was a body of a woman lying on the floor. Blood pooled out of her ears and nose, and onto the tan and sky-blue rug.

The demon had done to Delia what Omaera was involuntarily doing to Drak, Zandren, and Gemma. They'd tortured her for information until her brain hemorrhaged and she died.

"I thought mages could do mind blocks," Drak said, crouching down to close Delia's gray, lifeless eyes.

"We can," I said. "But if they beat her first, which it looks like they did, she'd have been too weak to keep up the block. It takes a lot of energy to block a powerful demon trying to enter your mind. We still don't know if she even was a mage. I don't smell mage in the house. Then again, there are spells to block the scent."

I pointed out the bruises on Delia's weathered face, the cuts on her mouth and through her eyebrows. She'd definitely been beaten.

Gently, I lifted up her striped blue T-shirt to just show her abdomen and there was bruising there too. Probably internally as well. She'd have been in too much pain to maintain the block.

"What are we going to tell Omaera?" I asked.

"The truth," he said with no inflection.

"You need to let me go," Omaera argued with Zandren downstairs. "I need to see her."

"Little One, it's not a good idea," he protested.

"Let. Me. Go." Her feet thundered up the stairs and her wild curls bounced as she entered the room, slightly out of breath. She took one look at her aunt and her hand flew to her mouth as she gasped, her eyes going wide. "Is she?"

"She is dead," Drak said. "I am very sorry."

Omaera rounded on him. "You're sorry?"

"Careful," I said quickly. "You can't get angry. You can't. I know you want to. I know you probably are. But you can't. You're not able to control your powers or rage yet. And you could kill him."

Her nostrils flared, and her chest rose and fell rapidly as a rush of color filled her cheeks. "Who did this to her?"

I shook my head. "All we know is that it smells like demons."

Zandren entered the room and rested his hands on her shoulders. Instantly, she turned into him for comfort and he wrapped her up in his arms, bringing her over to sit on his lap on the bed.

I'd be lying if I said I wasn't jealous as fuck, but I stowed that green monster. We had other things to deal with right now.

"I told you we needed to get to her last night. Nobody listened to me. I could *feel* her fear. I could *feel* her pain. We could have saved her." She sobbed and shook in Zandren's arms, and I ached to go to her too. To relieve more of her agony. To absorb some of her heartache.

Then it hit me!

I snapped my fingers, creating a neon-yellow flame. "Kase Blackwood lives here."

"And who is Kase Blackwood?" Drak asked.

"He's a necromancer mage."

Drak's gaze narrowed and his top lip curled in disdain, but then his gaze shifted to where Omaera sobbed in Zandren's arms. He nodded. "Call him."

I brought out my phone and called Kase. We may not be able to get the answers that we needed from Delia now, but at least we might be able to see the last things she saw right before she was killed. If I couldn't comfort Omaera the way Zandren was, then I could at least get her some answers and help her figure out who killed her aunt.

Normally a nocturnal creature, Kase didn't pick up his phone right away because he was sleeping. But when I told him what I needed and who it was for, he said he'd put on pants and be over in fifteen minutes.

In the meantime, we headed downstairs into Delia's home to see what clues we could uncover. Did the demons who killed her take anything?

Zandren should have been doing his drug-dog sniffing thing, because he had the best sense of smell out of all of us, but he was too busy with Omaera. So it was up to the vampire and me to do the digging.

We found nothing nefarious beyond a few men's-shoe-sized footprints—that didn't match ours—at the back kitchen door.

Not even an open cupboard or drawer.

I made Omaera a cup of tea and brought it to her in the living room, where she sat with Zandren.

"Was Delia an artist?" I asked, taking in all the beautiful floral paintings.

"She was," she said, accepting the tea. "Landscapes and florals, mostly. But occasionally she did commissions for other things. She liked to be cheeky and sneak in a vulva or penis into her flowers whenever she could." She pointed to a purple bearded iris. "What does that remind you of?"

"Very Georgia O'Keeffe," I mused. I turned to Zandren. "I dated her for a while actually. After her husband died, of course. I'm no homewrecker."

Heavy boot steps on the front porch pulled our attention. We'd left the door open to help air out the house. Kase stepped inside. He was a tall, lanky man with black hair, a slightly sunken face, high cheekbones, and a long nose. But his smile was friendly, and his eyes weren't nearly as haunting as one might assume. But like one would assume, he wore all black. Because, of course he did. Anybody associated with death the way a necromancer, or even Drak was, wore black. It was so cliché, it'd be weird if they didn't.

I stifled my snicker at the idea of Drak or Kase rocking up in a Hawaiian print shirt one day. Or a hot-pink tank top.

Kase gave a slight bow to Omaera. "Your Majesty. My condolences."

"Wh-what are you going to do to her?" Omaera asked.

Kase pressed his lips together and nodded. "A necromancer mage is someone who can help those still living understand the last few moments of their loved one's life. I will simply lay my hand on your aunt's forehead and I will capture the last few remaining minutes of her life." His gray eyes turned hesitant. "I must warn you though, in cases like your aunt's where . . . she didn't die peacefully, the last few moments can be difficult to witness."

"For you?" Omaera asked.

He smiled. "I have seen the worst humanity and the magical realm have to offer in my nine hundred and fifty-six years. Not much fazes me now. But for you, I will tell you exactly what I see, and it may be difficult to take."

She clenched her jaw, took a deep breath, and nodded. "I want to know."

"Very well," Kase said. "Come with me, please."

I took him to the body, and Omaera and Zandren followed. Drak was already upstairs, still searching for clues.

Kase frowned when he saw Delia's body. "I know her."

"You know my aunt?" Omaera asked, pushing past Zandren. "How?"

"Not well," Kase said, with a headshake. "We would bump into each other maybe once or twice a month at Fiddleman's Apothecary. She was there for various herbs and ingredients for spells and potions—"

"So she is a mage," Omaera said in awe. Then she turned to me. "She's one of you."

I nodded. "It would seem so. Though, spellcaster mages are more powerful than fire mages. She probably put a very powerful cloaking spell over you when you were born, hiding you from all other realm beings—including your father. Only when he died, and the power transferred to you, Delia's spell was no match for that power."

Omaera's mouth dipped into a tight frown. "I wish I'd known this about her. I wish she'd told me the truth about who she was and who I am."

"I'm sure she had her reasons as to why she didn't," Zandren said softly.

Omaera turned back to Kase. "Tell me more about what you know of her. Tell me everything . . . please."

Kase frowned, his eyes filled with regret. "As I said, I didn't know her well, I'm afraid. We chatted from time to time just about spells she was working on. That kind of thing. I never knew her name, or her mine. But we were friendly." His eyes turned sad even though he smiled. "A lot of people in our world don't like necromancers. They look down on us. Even though so many use us. But Delia treated me like anybody else. She was kind." His smile grew. "And she almost always had dried paint on her forearm or neck or something. I figured she was a painter."

Omaera's bottom lip wobbled. "She loves to paint."

Kase dropped to his knees beside Delia's head and pulled a small, velvet pouch out of his pocket. He placed five crystals, all varying in size and color, around her head. Then from another pouch he sprinkled a weird, yellow dust into his palm, which he then placed in a heap over Delia's heart. The last thing he did was take a small pocket knife, prick his thumb, and draw a very tiny pentagram on Delia's bruised and bloody forehead.

He glanced up at Omaera. "You're sure about this?"

She nodded. "I need to know what she knows. I need to know who did this to her." Her nostrils flared and a fire I'd never seen before flickered in her moss-green eyes.

Drak entered the room and silently stepped off to the side.

Kase's head bobbed, and he turned back to Delia. Then he placed one palm, then the other, over the pentagram on her forehead and closed his eyes.

Even though it was daytime, and sunlight poured in through the bedroom windows, the whole room went pitch black. I couldn't see a thing in front of me.

"Do not be alarmed," Kase said. "Stay silent."

It was probably for the better that there was no light.

I knew necromancers, and I had no problem with them, but I'd never seen one work before. And I could only imagine that Kase was probably making some pretty spooky faces right now. Faces that would scare the shit out of Omaera.

After probably five minutes of pure silence and absolute darkness, it was like the blindfold was removed and the room reappeared. As if nothing happened.

Kase kneeled over the body and when he looked up at us, tears streamed down his face. He looked viscerally shook and his chest heaved as if he'd just sprinted up the stairs.

I went to him and helped him up, guiding him to the end of the bed. "Kase, man, what did you see?"

He swallowed and turned to Omaera. "I am so sorry."

Her chin trembled. "What did you see?"

"The brutality," he whispered. "She didn't deserve that."

"What. Did. You. See?" Omaera asked again.

"Two men. Demons. One with dark hair and dark eyes. A long nose and big ears with hair long enough to cover the ears. He was . . . he was so cruel. And he enjoyed it."

"And the other?" Drak asked.

"I couldn't see his face very well. But he was blond and tall. Fit. His voice was deep and gritty. He did the kicking while the other did the punching and other beatings. They hit her at the same time with the brain frying though."

My gut spun and anger bubbled and frothed in my stomach until flames raced up my throat.

"What did they want from her?" Omaera asked, her voice soft, almost hollow.

"To know where you were," Kase said. Then he looked at the nightstand abruptly. "In her memory there was a photo frame there. Delia glanced at it." His gaze shifted around more. "It's gone."

We all looked around the room—all of us but Omaera.

"What was the photo of?" I asked her.

Omaera's gaze was fixed on her aunt. "Of Gemma and I at the beach last year. It's probably the most recent printed photo Delia has of me."

"So they know what you look like. They're coming," Drak said. "We need to get you into hiding."

Omaera stood up, shaking her head. She wiped away a tear from her cheek. "I'm not hiding from anybody. They killed the only parent I've ever known. The only person who has ever loved me. I'm not hiding. I'm coming for them. And I'm going to kill them."

CHAPTER NINE

OMAERA

"We need to get you into hiding," Drak said again, following me back downstairs. "You're not going off to find whoever did this and kill them. That is reckless and irresponsible. Particularly since you are the Queen."

I glared at the vampire, who'd yet to show me that the smile muscles in his face even worked.

I knew all about resting bitch face, but this Nosferatu-wannabe was taking the sourpuss look to a whole other level.

I couldn't even be bothered to respond. I was too . . . devastated, enraged, broken and confused to even begin to pick a fight with him. I'd probably kill him if I did, and I'd already killed one vampire in the last twenty-four hours. I didn't need to make a habit of it.

I spun around at the bottom of the stairs and faced Kase. "Is part of the necromancer package that you also take care of the body in a respectable and caring way?"

"Pack—" He glanced at Maxar who lifted both brows high and nodded. So Kase nodded as well. "Yes. Yes, of course. It's all part of the necromancer *package*. We see their last moments and do the body moving. Um . . . what would you like me to do with your aunt?"

Well, now *that* was a loaded question. I'm sure she had a will somewhere. Or actually, if she was a human—like I thought she was until a few minutes ago—then I'm sure she would have had a will. Now that I knew she was a spellcaster mage, I didn't know what to think or assume. Maybe she had nothing filed away for the afterlife because she didn't think she'd ever have an afterlife.

How old was she?

Kase said he was nine hundred and fifty-six.

"What do you do with mage bodies?" I addressed Maxar.

"That's usually up to the family. Besides you, did Delia have any family?"

Another loaded question. If she did, I was never introduced to anyone. But again, if these people were immortal, she probably had relatives out there that I'd never met. Did they have a claim to her body?

"I don't know," I whispered, chewing on the side of my thumb. "I . . . don't know anything about her anymore."

"I have a small space in my basement where I can keep her safe until you decide," Kase said. He turned to Zandren. "I will need help removing the body from upstairs though. If you'd be so kind."

Zandren glanced at me. He'd been the big, burly boon of comfort I didn't know I needed until I sorely needed it. And he smelled really good. Like . . . cedar and honey. He really was Pooh Bear—but with abs. So. Many. Abs.

"The meeting with the High Council is soon," Drak said, his phone clutched in his pale hand. "We should go."

"I have other more important things to deal with right now," I said, glaring at him. "Tell the Council that *the Queen* will not be in attendance."

"I do not advise this," he said through, what sounded like, gritted teeth. "They are the other leaders and will feel quite slighted if you snub the first official meeting."

My eyes flared and heat raced up my neck and into my face. "You do not *advise* it? They will feel *slighted*? Guess."

His brows furrowed, and he looked at the other three men in the room before turning back to me. "Guess?"

"Yeah. Guess."

"Guess . . . what?"

"How many fucks I give about whether or not the other leaders feel *slighted.*" My closed-mouth smile was forced and full of disdain. "I'll give you a hint. It rhymes with *hero.*"

Drak cleared his throat and glanced away.

Maxar smirked and snorted.

Zandren's brows hiked up to his hairline, and Kase was looking anywhere but at me or Drak.

"My aunt, the only person on the planet—besides Gemma—who has ever given a real damn about me, is dead," I went on. "Murdered. I'm not *snubbing* their meet and greet. I am dealing with my grief and figuring out who killed her. And furthermore, *Drak*—by the way, could that name be any more on the nose? Drak. Dracula. Seriously? Ugh—I was never consulted about whether or not today even worked for me. I was *told* that there would be a meeting. When last time I checked, *I'm the fucking Queen.* I rule this roost of a goddamned realm—until I can figure out a way to abdicate—and I will fucking tell *them* when and where the meeting will be. Got it? So go back to *your vampire king* and tell him I'm busy." Then I spun around and stomped off to the kitchen before I turned his brains into a poached egg.

I paced the kitchen, desperately trying to engage in some deep box breathing. That didn't work.

Next, I tried the whole "three things calming technique".

Three things that I could see. Okay, I could see my aunt's favorite china teacup with the pansies on it, sitting in the drying rack in the sink. I could see the yellow, potted ranunculus on her kitchen table perfectly trapped in a ray of sunshine bursting through her kitchen window. And I could see an old and batter-splattered picture of Aunt Delia and me dressed up like maidens at the Renaissance Fair, stuck to her fridge by a flower magnet. I'd been about fourteen at the time, and she hand-made both of our dresses. We went all out with our hair and outfits and it'd been one of the most wonderful and fun-filled days of my life. Emotion choked me and I gripped the counter to keep things in check.

Okay, three things I could see weren't enough. I still wanted to kill Drak. I still wanted to scream, and my pulse raced like I'd just sprinted up a mountain.

I needed to keep going.

Three things that I could touch.

I ran my hand over Delia's old, nearly see-through tea towel hanging over the oven handle. The towel with the chickens and pigs on it. I'd bought it for her one year for Christmas. I was probably no more than nine. I didn't have a lot of money when I went shopping, but I did want to get her something. So I bought her a new tea towel. She said she loved it and that it was her favorite. It probably didn't dry so much as a spoon anymore. It was so threadbare, but she refused to part with it or turn it into a rag.

Next, I ran the pad of a finger back and forth a few times over the bumpy and misshapen spoon rest in the middle of the stove. It was green and pink, and supposed to look like a lily pad and flower. I made it in eighth grade art class. It wasn't very good, but I gave it to her for Mother's Day and she once again said it was her favorite. And finally, I stroked the top of the bamboo cutting board she loved to use. I watched her for hours mincing herbs from her garden, or stripping them from their stems and letting them dry. There were thousands of deep, and shallow, slice marks that crisscrossed the wood grain. If I focused hard enough, I could even hear the rhythmic back and forth rocking motion of her ulu knife against the board.

A hot tear slid down my cheek.

And lastly, three things that I could smell. Sometimes I chose to find three things I could hear, but the fact that I could hear Kase and Zandren moving my aunt's body wasn't something I wanted to focus on right now.

I took a deep breath and held it for a moment.

Aunt Delia's house always smelled of lavender. She said it calmed her and it reminded her of when she grew up. Apparently, her grandparents used to run a lavender farm. That was probably all I'd ever heard her speak of her family. Or at least that was all I could remember.

Another deep inhale, and this time I pulled in the smell of lemon.

I smiled at the lemon balm herb growing happily in a pot on her bright windowsill behind the sink.

I broke off a leaf and brought it up to my nose, inhaling deeper than ever.

Aunt Delia always made the most delicious-smelling soaps, shampoos, and creams. And she put lemon balm in her salads too.

One last inhale . . .

But I couldn't do it.

I couldn't breathe. In or out.

I . . . I was choking. My throat seized, and I gripped it.

What . . . what was going on?

I stomped my foot loudly as panic flooded my mind.

I was going to die.

My aunt was just killed, and now it was my turn. Whoever killed her was lying in wait for me. They set a trap. Or they were still here and casting some kind of spell to suffocate me.

My eyes darted around the room in search of . . . something.

I grabbed the teacup in the drying rack and tossed it to the ground so it smashed.

Drak and Maxar raced in, their eyes wide.

"What's the matter?" Maxar asked.

I gripped my throat and pointed.

"She's choking," Drak said. "What did you eat?"

I shook my head.

"You can't breathe?" Maxar asked.

I nodded.

Black spots clouded my vision. I was running out of oxygen. I was going to pass out soon. Then, I was going to die.

"You need to relax," Drak said calmly. Too calmly. "Demons can only be killed by beheading. Even if you black out, you're not going to die. I think you've stumbled upon a spell and it's been activated."

A spell?

One of Delia's spells?

Why would she cast a spell in her own home?

What did I touch that activated it?

"You're going to pass out pretty soon. Then the spell should run its course," Drak said.

I shook my head. Why should I believe him? I was dying. This was it.

Their faces grew fuzzy and my lungs burned.

Who knew I had this much oxygen in my lungs? Then again, I did pull in a pretty deep breath in an effort to calm down. So much for that technique. I'll never inhale deeply again.

You're right. You won't, because you're dying.

"You need to trust me, Omaera," Drak said.

I swayed. I was going to black out now, and the ground looked very close.

"Whoa, whoa. I've gotcha," Maxar said, swooping in and catching me just as my eyes closed, the world faded, and I nearly face planted on the vinyl floor.

"And you didn't detect the spell when you checked out the kitchen?" Drak asked with a stern, accusatory voice. At least, I think it was Drak. I still preferred to call them the vampire, bear, and mage, but using their names just seemed easier. I didn't like that it added a sense of familiarity among us though.

None of this was permanent. None of this was *eternal*.

My eyes were still closed, but I was breathing.

Thank god.

I was on a familiar couch with a familiar smell. Linen, lavender, and . . . cedar?

"I didn't feel any spells in the kitchen," Maxar protested. "I'm not that kind of a mage. I can't intuit all spells. She was a spellcaster, way more powerful than me. She could have blocked her spell with another spell. *Why* she cast a spell in her kitchen that would suffocate someone? I don't fucking know. But don't come down on me just because I couldn't sense it."

A big hand stroked my hair. "You're awake."

I opened my eyes to find the man that smelled like cedar and honey stroking my hair and smiling down at me with concern in his chocolate-colored eyes.

"What happened?"

"Your aunt cast a spell, you triggered it, and it tried to kill you. But because you're a demon, it didn't. You just passed out. The spell ended because it thought you died. And now you're fine again."

I smiled in spite of it all because he was just so matter of fact. I knew I'd always get honesty from this man, no matter what. Even if that honesty hurt.

"Where is her body?"

His full lips pursed for a moment before he gently said, "I helped Kase load her into his vehicle. He will take care of her."

My heart hurt. "You trust him?"

"I do not know him. But I hope I can trust him. You are the Queen. He knows better than to do something stupid."

"Are you always this . . . honest and straightforward?"

He still stroked my hair. "I am who I am. This is me. I will never lie to you, Omaera. And I don't believe in beating around the bush. Facts are best."

"Facts are best." I made to sit up, and he helped me. "What do you do for work?"

His smile was boyish and sweet. "I don't really have to work. I've been alive so long, my investments and the money I made over the centuries are enough. But I used to be a carpenter. A very good one. I still build things when I want to. If you ever want me to build you something, I will."

Why did an offer like that make my heart swell with joy so much? Nobody had ever offered to *build* me something before. I reached for his big hand and placed my palm on his. The difference in size was laughable. His fingertips and the heel of his hand were rough and calloused, but I didn't mind.

"Your hands are so small," he said. "How do you even catch a fish?"

That made me laugh out loud. "Well, I've never been fishing. But if I did, I'd probably use a fishing pole."

He nodded. "Okay, that makes sense. But I'd like to take you to the river and teach you to catch one with your hands . . . or mouth, one day."

I gaped at him. "My mouth?"

He nodded again. "During spawning season, it's easy. The fish are jumping up stream, they literally just jump right into your mouth. It's like gumdrops falling from the sky . . . but not gumdrops and not the sky."

"You're ridiculous."

He smiled. "I'm okay with that when it makes you smile."

My brows bunched. "Wait, does this mean I'll turn into a shifter if we mate?"

He lifted a bulky shoulder. "Maybe?"

"That'd be weird."

"I'd love it."

I smirked and snorted.

Drak and Maxar heard us talking and joined us from where they were arguing in the hallway.

"You're awake," Maxar said, coming over to stand in front of me with relief in his eyes. "Are you okay?"

I swallowed a few times, took some nice big inhales, then bobbed my head. "Everything seems to be working again."

Drak was in the doorway to the living room. "The Council has agreed to move the meeting to tomorrow."

I glared at him. "Oh, have they now? How courteous of them. Considering I nearly died. And my aunt *did* die. Thank them for their immense and overwhelming generosity, *Drak*."

His gaze was level. "You didn't almost die. Demons can only die via beheading."

I growled at him and stood up. "Why did my aunt cast that spell?" I headed back to the kitchen.

"I wouldn't go back in there," Maxar said, following me. They all followed me. "She might have the place booby trapped with spells."

"But *why*?" I asked, returning to the exact spot of the crime and when I started to choke. "I was standing right here. Trying to calm down. I did the 'three things I could see, three things I could touch, and three things I could smell.' I was going to do the 'three things I could hear,' but one of those things was you guys hauling away my aunt's body. So I went with smell. I picked off a leaf of lemon balm here and smelled it. Then I took in another deep inhale and that's when I started to choke."

Maxar joined me in front of the sink. "Do you think there's something here somewhere that your aunt wanted to hide?"

"From me?"

"From someone who would try to hurt you? Maybe she made contingencies. There are spells mages can cast that are activated when they die, in order to protect things that they've been entrusted to keep safe."

"So then, maybe *I* didn't trigger the spell. Maybe one of you did. Zandren, you, and Kase were moving Delia's body. Maxar what were you doing?"

"I was outside looking for clues around the house. All I found were more footprints in the mud around back. I still think Zandren should go sniff around there to see what he can smell."

"Drak?" I asked, facing him. "What were you doing?"

"I was on the phone with the King. On the porch."

I frowned. "Well, neither of you were hit with the spell, nor did anything weird. So it had to be me. But all I did was pick the lemon balm and smell it. I also touched the cutting board and her tea towel."

I shook my head. This didn't make any sense.

What was she trying to protect?

I turned to Maxar. "What other kinds of mages are there? Is there a mage that can come here and figure out all the spells that are still active or idle in the house? If Delia is protecting something, I want to know."

Maxar nodded slowly. "Another spellcaster, most likely." He pulled out his phone. "I'll call Kase and see if he knows anybody in town that could come by."

"I also want to go to that Fiddleman's Apothecary. It's probably a mage that runs that, right? Maybe even a spellcaster mage?"

Slowly, Maxar and Drak both nodded.

Why were they looking at me like that?

Maxar was about to put his phone to his ear, but I stopped him. "I want to know all the different kinds of mages. All of them."

His brows narrowed, but he nodded, put the phone to his ear and stepped out into the hallway.

"What is your plan?" Zandren asked.

"I don't quite know yet," I said. "But I can feel something working itself out. Delia is hiding and protecting something." Then my eyes flew open wide, and I faced Drak. "Where *exactly* was Delia's body when I tossed that cup to the floor and it shattered?"

"They were loading her into Kase's vehicle. Why?"

"Because now I'm wondering if her body leaving her house was what triggered the spell. And *none* of you were in the house when that happened. Then when I threw the cup on the ground, Maxar was back on the porch, right?"

Drak nodded. "And we came right in to you."

"So had you been in here, maybe you'd have been hit with the spell too. So it wasn't that I did something specifically, it was that her dead body was removed from the house. A shield spell of some kind came down over the house and whoever was in it was supposed to suffocate." My mind whirred with ideas, and my heart galloped as each one of those ideas started to make sense and fall into place.

I didn't want to get my hopes up too much, because we hadn't even scratched the surface of what Delia was hiding or why. But, at least I was pretty certain that the spell trigger wasn't me picking at a piece of lemon balm.

Maxar returned. "Kase said that Monjol Fiddleman is a spellcaster."

Hope filled my chest. "Then we need to go see him. Right now." I headed to the front door. "Drak, you stay here until we get back."

"No," he said, with just the slightest hint of desperation in his tone that it made me pause. No, I had to be making that up. He wasn't desperate. He was cooler than a frozen cucumber. "I'm coming with you."

"Why? We don't need all four of us there. And Maxar speaks mage, and Zandren looks like he needs another meal."

"I do," Zandren nodded. "I'm hungry."

"You do know most mages speak English, right?" Maxar said, probably to me, but I wasn't really paying attention.

"See?" I addressed Drak. "You stay here. Guard the place. Bark if anybody tries to steal the newspaper."

"I'm not staying here," he said.

I rolled my eyes and growled which made him wince so I tempered my voice and took a deep breath to calm my quick temper. "I figured when someone nearly dies, and they find their aunt murdered on her carpet, that people are generally nicer to them. Help them. Do as they ask. Or is that just humans? Vampires don't give a shit about someone's loved one dying."

His nostrils flared. "I'm coming. And you didn't nearly die. Demons can only die—"

"By beheading. Yeah, I know. You've said." This . . . man, or whatever he was, was infuriating. But as much as I disliked him, I also didn't want to be responsible for sauteing his brain. So I just said, "whatever", locked the door, and headed down the stairs. "How far is Fiddleman's?" I asked, directing my question to Maxar and actively ignoring Drak.

"Only a couple of blocks," he said, catching up to me and Zandren. "We shouldn't have to take the subway or bus. We can just walk, right?"

I smirked at him. "Yeah, we can just walk."

He dramatically placed the back of his hand over his forehead like some fainting damsel. "Phew."

We arrived at the unassuming little store sandwiched between a sandwich shop and a barbershop. Fiddleman's Apothecary and Herbs.

"I'm going to grab a quick sandwich," Zandren said, ducking into the sandwich shop before I heaved open the door to Fiddleman's, causing the jingle of a sweet-sounding bell.

A dark-skinned man with short, curly black hair and bright blue-gray eyes came out from a storage room to the side. "Hello folks, and how can I help you three today?" He sniffed the air slightly and smiled. "Quite an unlikely trio, I might add."

"You will bow and apologize to your Queen," Drak said with an angry edge of authority to his voice.

The man behind the counter gawked at him. His eyes went wide, then he swiveled his attention to me. "I . . . I'm . . . My apologies. Y-Your Majesty?"

I glared at Drak. "No. Please don't do that. He's being an ass." I shot Drak another look. "Go sit in the corner. You're being a bully."

He didn't move.

I deepened my stare. Then bared my teeth and hissed at him. "Go."

He winced again because my anger was hurting his head. This time I didn't feel too terrible about it. He was such a rude dick, someone needed to keep him accountable and put him in his place. I held his gaze until he heaved a sigh, nodded and finally sulked off.

"I apologize Mr. . . . Fiddleman, I presume?"

He nodded. "Monjol Fiddleman. And I'm so sorry, Your Majesty. But may I ask . . . what are you the queen of?"

I exhaled. "You know my aunt. Delia Refera?"

He nodded. "Your aunt?" Then his eyes widened and his face lit up. "Omaera?"

I forced a smile, though fresh thoughts of my aunt brought me back to reality like a harsh, wet slap to the face. I swallowed past the hard, spikey lump in my throat. "Yes. It would seem . . ." I pinched the bridge of my nose. "It would seem I am some secret lovechild of King Donovar and my mother, Elena Playfair. Elena died when I was an infant, but Donovar was just killed. When he died, I became Queen of well . . . the Realm, I guess? It's been like less than forty-eight hours, so I'm still processing."

I wasn't sure the man was breathing. He just gaped at me with an open mouth and wide eyes. "All I know is that Delia has a niece she adores. She speaks of you often. You make her so proud."

"She was murdered," I said abruptly, ripping off the news like a Band-Aid.

Mr. Fiddleman gasped. "No. Not Delia."

"By demons."

He covered his hand with his mouth. "Oh. Oh no, no, no. This . . . this can't be. I just saw her yesterday."

And I wish I'd seen her yesterday. Maybe I could have prevented this from happening.

I should have gone to her right away after I was struck by lightning. But she wasn't even home. She was away on a trip, and only just arrived home yesterday. I wanted to give her time to unpack and get back to normal.

Now, I wish I'd just come over anyway. And definitely when I felt the need to go to her last night. She taught me to always listen to my gut. And last night my gut told me to go to her.

I'd never *not* listen to my gut again.

Because if I told her what happened, she could have come clean about being a mage and maybe accompanied me home. We could have protected her.

I took a deep breath, shoved down my grief, and did the best I could to suppress my anger—for now. "Mr. Fiddleman, my aunt cast spells all over her house as contingencies for if something happened to her. I activated one today, or we all did, and it suffocated me. We need you to come to her house and see if there are any other spells. She's hiding something. Protecting something. And I need to know what it is. I need to know why as soon as my father was killed and I got his power, my aunt was then hunted down and killed. Kase Blackwood came and we know that two men entered Delia's home, both demons. They beat her and then fried her brain. They also took the most recent photo of me. So we assume they're coming after me next."

The bell chimed at the front door and Zandren ambled in, a foot-long sandwich in his hand and another one tucked under his arm. "I got you one since you haven't eaten anything today." He smiled at me as he took a bite of his own sub.

Blinking, and still trying to make sense of everything he heard, Mr. Fiddleman nodded. "Y-yes, of course." Then he paused. "Who are these three men? If I might ask. Bodyguards?"

"Something like that," I said blandly.

"We're her Fated Mates and she refuses to mate any of us," Drak said from his spot in the corner. "Even though it will help her get control of her powers."

I glared at him. "Quiet in the corner or I'll give you a dunce cap next."

Mr. Fiddleman grabbed his coat and keys and followed us to the door, where he locked up. He kept shaking his head. "I'm just . . . I'm so torn up about Delia.

This is just the most tragic news."

"Do you know if she has any other family?" I asked. "I feel so stupid. This woman raised me since I was two-weeks-old and yet I know nothing about her."

Mr. Fiddleman shook his head. "I'm afraid I don't know."

I shrugged. "I understand."

"You should eat something," Zandren said, handing me the second sandwich he bought. "I wasn't sure what you wanted. So I hope the honey-garlic chicken breast is okay?"

I glanced at him behind me. He was such a paradox.

Anybody who saw him would immediately assume he was a killing machine. Because he probably was. He could probably tear a person in half with his bare hands. While in human form too. And in bear form, I'm sure he could do even worse. And yet, he'd shown me such softness and caring. The genuine concern in his eyes over the fact that I hadn't eaten yet, eased the ache of my tender, tattered heart.

"Just half, please," I said, my belly grumbling. I never ate breakfast. I always waited until at least noon to eat. Sometimes later, like two in the afternoon, if I wasn't hungry at lunchtime.

He nodded, opened up the wrapper for the honey-garlic chicken and handed me a six-inch sandwich. I took a bite as we walked.

"Is it okay?" he asked.

I nodded and looked at him over my shoulder. "It is, thank you."

The relief and genuine happiness that creased his face tugged hard on my heart strings.

We reached my aunt's house in no time and Maxar opened the gate for us to all step through onto the stone walkway.

All of us walked through except Mr. Fiddleman. The hair on the back of my neck lifted, and I paused just before the bottom step.

"What is it?" Maxar asked.

"This house has more spells on it than anywhere I've ever been," he said, in awe, fear, and . . . sadness. He turned to me. "You say she's been your guardian since you were a child?"

"Since I was two weeks old. That's when my mother died. I don't really know how Delia and I are related though. I assume she's like a great aunt or something. So that means my mom was probably a mage too? Or a demon?"

He still hadn't walked through the gate, but rather stared up at the top floor of the house and the small widow's walk coming off the primary bedroom.

Did he see something we couldn't?

"Powerful magic is at play here," he said. "More powerful than me." His cheeks ruddied a little, though it was tough to see from his dark complexion. "I knew she was a spellcaster mage. I just had no idea how powerful. I . . . feel stupid not knowing. Not getting to know her better when I had the chance."

"Did your aunt have a mate?" Maxar added.

I shook my head. "I don't know. Since I've known her, she's never had a . . . lover. But maybe? If she was centuries old, perhaps she did, and he died?"

Mr. Fiddleman nodded. "Yes. She did have a mate. He died in the war between vampires and shifters some hundred and twenty years ago."

A noise rumbled deep and foreboding in Zandren's chest behind me, and I turned to see him glaring death and destruction at Drak. "You mean when vampires broke the code and went after cubs?" he growled.

Mr. Fiddleman nodded. "Yes. He was a psychic mage, and he saw the war coming. But he also saw the good that would come of it. The peace that the new leaders would bring. He was executed for not warning the shifters about what would happen."

Zandren growled even deeper. "He could have. He could have said something and we still would have won the war."

I glanced at Drak, who was staring at the ground, a deep red stain on his cheeks.

"What happens when a mate dies?" I asked.

"The grieving period is long. Painful. But you can get through it." The sadness in his eyes said he wasn't just recounting something he'd read or witnessed. He'd been through it personally. The heavy bob of his throat and the way his mouth remained in a deep frown made my chest ache. Did he love Delia? Did she love him back? Was he grieving more than just the death of a friend and loyal customer? But rather, the death of a woman he'd fallen for, but for whatever reason, couldn't bring himself to admit it to her?

I'd never been a romantic or a bleeding heart, but the idea of Delia and Mr. Fiddleman going through the rest of their lives without a mate, without love or companionship, caused the ache in my chest to get so strong I had to reach out with my free hand and hold on to the post at the bottom of the stair railing.

"Will you be able to tell us what spells are here and how we can either break them or trigger them so that way they can run their course?"

He nodded slowly. "I can try."

Finally, he released his grip on the gate and stepped forward onto the stepping-stone path, following us up the stairs to the porch.

Maxar had explained my theory regarding the triggering of the first spell that suffocated me. Mr. Fiddleman nodded and agreed that it was plausible, and I was probably right.

We allowed him to enter the house first, since he could clearly see and sense things that the rest of us couldn't.

He entered the study and walked over to the desk my aunt spent hours at in the evenings, recording everything she'd done that day in her journal. Most of it was in reference to the different tinctures, salves, and balms she made with her herbs. Which ones worked, which ones didn't. She also recorded some of her recipes—which now that I think of it, were probably potions—and had a running list of all the plants in her garden.

When one leatherbound book was finished, she stored it on the bookshelf, then started another one. The wall of shelves was full of these books. And she always went in the same color pattern. Green, blue, red, brown, black. Always. Every book was dated from when she started it, to the date of the last entry. She could find a recipe in no time due to her impeccable organization and cataloging skills.

Mr. Fiddleman pulled open the top drawer of her desk, waved his hand, muttered some other language under his breath, and a big puff of pink smoke burst from the drawer.

It filled the room, and we all coughed. Maxar ran to the window and opened it, while Zandren headed to the door and began to waft it open and closed.

My mouth filled with the disgusting taste of . . . *blood?*

"What the hell was that?" I asked, gagging a little.

Drak, seemed entirely unaffected. He probably liked the taste, the freak.

Maxar made a similar face to mine, and Zandren showed very little disgust.

"Blood dust," Mr. Fiddleman said. "I managed to remove the toxic part of the spell, but not the dust itself."

"So wait, there was a toxin in that dust?" I asked.

"A paralytic, yes."

"I need water," Maxar said, running to the kitchen.

I took a bite of my sandwich, but that just tasted like the blood dust too. "Great, now it's on my sandwich."

"I'll eat it," Zandren said. "I eat raw, dead animals all the time. Blood doesn't bother me."

Right. He was a bear. Of course he ate raw, dead animals.

With my own appetite sufficiently gone, I handed him the sandwich.

"This drawer contains a key," Mr. Fiddleman said, picking up a large, iron skeleton key that I'd never seen before.

"Where does it go?" I asked.

He made his way over to the bookcase, tapping on the books on the third from the top row, which was way taller than me. He stopped at a blue bound one and pulled it downward from the top.

Click.

We all scanned the study, searching for the source of the *click*. But Mr. Fiddleman seemed to already know and ducked down, then slid to his belly where the baseboard below the bookshelf had popped open an inch. He wiggled it free to reveal a keyhole.

"There's another spell here," he said. "I'm not sure I'll be able to break it, but I'll try to numb its effects as best I can."

"Should . . . should we stand back this time?" Zandren asked, having already finished the rest of my sandwich. "Is there going to be more dust?"

"I have no idea," Mr. Fiddleman said. He waved his hand in front of the keyhole, muttering more words in a language I didn't understand. This time though, he closed his eyes and, with his other hand, gripped a talisman that he wore around his neck.

Nothing happened. No dust, no lightning or trembling of the ground beneath our feet.

I held my breath anyway though, as he carefully slid the key into the keyhole and turned it clockwise a quarter of the way.

A quick glance beside me showed Zandren standing there with a nervous look on his face. He also had his hands protectively covering himself.

He caught me looking. "It's an important part of me. I'd hate for it to get blown off."

I couldn't hide my smirk, but focused back on Mr. Fiddleman. He turned the key another quarter of the way, and that caused a second *click*.

I'd been breathing again, so I held my breath one more time as he pulled the key free and with it, the panel that concealed the keyhole, to reveal a hidden cubby space with documents and folders stacked inside.

Carefully, he reached inside, but as soon as those papers and folders hit the air, they burst into bright blue flames.

Mr. Fiddleman dropped them to the floor before they burned his fingers.

Maxar stepped forward and a bright beam of yellow fire erupted from his palms and onto the blue flames, dousing them until all that remained was smoke.

And ash.

"No," I breathed. "No." My bottom lip trembled, and I sunk to my knees, picking up the still warm ash in my fingers. A gust of wind from the now-open window blew it off of my fingertips and onto the floor.

"I thought you numbed the spell," Drak said, that accusatory tone back in his voice.

"I did," Mr. Fiddleman said. "I stopped the poisonous gas from filling the room. But I couldn't stop the self-destruct spell on the files."

"So that's it?" I asked. "Now we'll never know what secrets Aunt Delia was keeping?"

"I think the secret she was keeping was *you*, Your Majesty," Mr. Fiddleman said. "For whatever reason, your mother came to her for help. And Delia made a vow to protect you. Perhaps your mother requested that you remain hidden from your father. If she was not his mate and your father took a mate and had an heir, you would still be first in line for the throne, and that heir could challenge your legitimacy. Maybe your mother knew the weight of responsibility for the person that wore the crown and didn't want that for you?" He stood up and brushed off his khaki slacks. "I'm just . . . guessing here."

"No. They're good guesses. They make sense. What was my mother though? Is there a way to find that out?"

He glanced around the room. "There are still a lot of spells in here. In this whole house. It would take days for me to break them all."

"I'll pay you whatever you want," I said quickly. "I have money."

He shook his head and held up a hand with long, boney fingers. "I could never accept payment for this. Even if you weren't the Queen. Delia was . . . special."

"You loved her, didn't you?"

Unshed tears shone in his unique blue-gray eyes. "I . . . I should have said something. I should have worked up the courage. She's been coming into my shop for sixty years, and I've loved her for probably fifty-nine of those. She never brought you in because she was shielding you from this world. But she spoke of you so often. I feel like I know you." His smile was sad, but so full of love. "I'll do whatever I can to help you. To help get Delia the justice she deserves."

"Thank you," I whispered.

Drak's phone rang in his pocket, and he took it out to the porch. I glared at his broad back as he went, wishing he'd just go and not come back. I still wasn't on board with this whole *Fated Mates* thing. But at least Zandren and Maxar were proving themselves to be tolerable, if not even a little likeable.

But Drak was just a rude, pompous, bossy ass who—despite his insanely good looks and that smolder I'm sure he'd been perfecting for a few centuries now—could just disappear and go get locked in his coffin for all I cared.

"You don't have to stay here," Mr. Fiddleman said. "I'm sure you have more important places to be right now seeing as you're the new queen. I can keep working on the spells and let you know if I find something."

It wasn't that I didn't trust Mr. Fiddleman, because I did, or at least I wanted to, but I knew that he was grieving Delia as well. I also wanted to be here when he found something. A clue, or a document that didn't self-destruct like the Mission Impossible sunglasses.

"I can stay here with the mage for a bit," Zandren said. "I don't mind."

I blinked at him. "Thank you."

He nodded. "You should eat though. Please go find some food."

Smiling, I nodded. "I will."

"I'm going to go sniff around the house now, see what I can smell." Zandren stepped toward me and cupped my jaw. "Stay safe, Little One. I'll come find you soon." He tucked a strand of my wild, kinky hair behind my ear. It bounced right back out again. He tried again. It bounced back out again. "Even your hair is stubborn," he growled deep in his throat.

A shiver of something strange but wonderful, raced down my spine from his touch and my belly pooled with heat.

With an animalistic grunt, he released my jaw and headed into the kitchen at the same time Drak returned from the porch.

"The High Council has dispatched a demon advisor. She will be at your apartment within the hour. We need to go."

"A demon advisor?" I asked.

"Someone to help you work on taming and controlling your powers," he said. "Isn't that what you want?"

What I wanted was to wake up from this horrible nightmare and pretend the last forty-eight hours never happened.

But I knew that probably wasn't going to happen, so I sighed and nodded. "Right."

"You're okay here, Mr. Fiddleman?"

He was already breaking another spell near the fireplace in the study. We waited for him to wave his hand and mutter the words. He faced me when he finished and bobbed his head. "Yes. I'm okay."

I flashed him a small, quick smile and thanked him once more before Maxar, Drak, and I left.

"Do we have to take the subway again?" Maxar asked with a pout as we headed back in the direction we came. "Even the bus in daylight would be better."

"Whatever," I said, in no mood to argue. I just wanted to go home, flop on my bed, and cry. I needed to cry. I needed to scream.

I needed to kill whoever killed my aunt.

But first, I needed to learn how to control my powers so that when the time finally came to get my revenge, I didn't kill everyone else around me in the process.

CHAPTER TEN

OMAERA

The demon advisor was waiting for us outside my apartment building when we got there.

She was stunning.

And clearly not happy to have been assigned to, what I'm sure she viewed as, "babysitting duty."

She looked more like a dominatrix than a teacher too. And how she wasn't sweating buckets in those tight, black pleather pants, the black leather jacket, and knee-high, black stiletto boots was beyond me. I was looking forward to ditching my jeans the moment I walked into my apartment, and throwing on some booty shorts.

"You're late," she said.

"I'm as on time as public transit allows," I said, leveling my gaze at her. "I'm assuming you're my new demon advisor?" I walked right up to her and held out my hand. "Omaera Playfair."

She didn't take my hand. Rather, she looked me up and down, a sneer growing on her bright-red painted lips. Then she sniffed and her eyes darkened, her sneer growing. "You're human."

"Uh, no I'm not . . . I've fried people's brains. I'm pretty sure I'm a demon."

"You're a *hybrid*." The way she said hybrid was with so much disdain, it was as if the world itself tasted like vomit on her tongue.

Maxar and Drak gaped at me.

"That's never . . . That's impossible," Drak said. "Humans and . . . It's never happened before. We would have smelled human on her."

"It's never been documented," Maxar corrected. "I'm sure it's happened. And we didn't smell human on her, because all we smell is our mate. Her human scent is probably masked by her unique mate scent."

"How?" the demon woman asked. I still didn't even know her fucking name.

"Well," I started, "when two people—demon or otherwise—get urges in their pants, they take off their clothes, mash their genitals together because it feels really good. And then, if they're lucky, fireworks explode in their brains and nether regions. And sometimes a baby results in that. I guess I'm that baby." I faced Maxar, still perplexed and shocked at this new revelation. "My mother was human."

His brows hiked, and he nodded. "That explains why Delia committed her life to protecting you. I'm not sure how your mother knew about Delia's powers, but either way, it kept you alive. A hybrid heir is . . . Oh, the scandal. And if you did have half-siblings, they'd definitely challenge your legitimacy."

"This explains a lot," I said more to myself than anyone else.

"I cannot teach you," the woman said. "You are human. You are not supposed to know of our world. You're an abom—"

"I would reconsider the word you're about to use," Drak said sharply. "She's *half* human, *half* demon, and *full* queen." That pompous, aristocratic tone of his for once made me happy. "And you have yet to address her properly as Her Royal Highness, Your Majesty, or Queen Omaera. It would behoove you to change not only your tone, but your view of *who* you can and cannot teach."

The demon's eyes flared and sparks flickered in her dark brown irises. "She is human."

"So?" Maxar asked.

Even from where he stood next to me, I could feel his body temperature rising. Purple and orange flames flickered and sparked on his fingertips as he clenched and unclenched them at his sides. "Her father was the King. It doesn't matter who her mother was. She is King Donovar's only living heir. He died, now she is Queen."

"Lord Lerris is still alive," the demon woman said flatly.

"And you'd rather have that waste of skin as the leader of the Realm?" Drak asked matching her cool and even tone. "Maybe you're *not* the right teacher or advisor for the Queen."

At that comment, the demon woman's nostrils flared, and she lifted up her chin. "I'm not sure I *can* teach her. I have no idea how the human side of her will react, or if it is even capable of creating a mind block."

"Humans aren't inept, you know," I said, hating that they were having a conversation *about* me right in front of me, as though I weren't there.

All three of them snorted.

My anger flared. But it was enough to draw her attention and curiosity. "For a halfling, you have a lot of power."

I rolled my eyes. "Yeah, because I'm the fucking Queen. Now, are you going to teach me and *advise* me? Or do I need to send you on your merry way with a "fuck you" salute, and find someone else who can help me?"

Her lip twitched, threatening a smile, but it never happened. She exhaled a long, weary sigh. "Let's see what we're working with, I suppose."

"Yeah, I haven't really stepped into the whole queen role yet, but with that attitude, I think you can address me as 'Your Majesty' until further notice." I headed for the front door of my building, smiling when I heard Maxar and Drak snort behind me.

"What's your name?" Maxar asked her. "You know, for bookkeeping purposes?"

That made me laugh. I used my key to open the door and pushed it hard enough that Drak could catch it and let the other two in.

"Raewyn Vade," she said with no inflection in her tone.

"And you live here?" he asked.

"Yes."

We all stepped into the elevator when the door opened. The ride up was tense and quiet. It made me miss Zandren because I feel like he would have easily cut the tension by saying something witty or goofy. Maxar was pretty clever too. I was grateful for him asking Raewyn the questions, because after the way she regarded me as lower than an amoeba because I'm a hybrid, I wanted to fry her brains until they were sunny side up.

The apartment was empty, which I expected since Gemma was still at work.

My belly churned with hunger and I went to the fridge, grabbing an apple and a jar of peanut butter. Were these people my guests? Did I have to offer them tea and coffee and food and stuff?

Earlier that morning, I heated up the pizza and leftover Thai food for them for breakfast. Then Drak stole Gemma's steak out of the freezer while Zandren went to the bakery, and then the sandwich shop. I'm sure he was ordering a pizza to Delia's house right now too.

I also made them coffee this morning.

I had been as much of a hostess to these uninvited guests as I could muster.

But this bitch with the long, dark hair, perfect winged black eyeliner, and crimson lips didn't deserve tap water, in my opinion.

Slicing the apple, I scooped peanut butter onto each side and then took a bite. This was my go-to snack of choice. A complete protein; it got me my fats, my vitamins, and my fiber. Plus, it tasted like my childhood. Whenever I was upset, Aunt Delia would always put on a pot of rooibos tea, and make me apples and peanut butter. Then we'd sit at her kitchen table in the warm sunshine and she'd make me talk until I felt better. Sometimes she never even said anything. I just needed to vent, and by venting, I solved things myself. But I knew she was always there, listening, lending a supportive ear and an even more supportive heart. I never had to question whether or not she'd have my back or be in my corner.

That sudden memory made my chest ache and my throat grow tight. I set the paring knife down as the rush of painful emotions broke through the wall I'd created around my grief, and it all spilled forth in a wave of tears and sobbing.

"What the fuck?" Raewyn said.

But I couldn't give a damn about her. I shook uncontrollably as the realization that I'd never see or speak to Delia again hit me like an eighteen-wheeler on an icy road.

A very warm arm wrapped around my shoulder, then turned me so I crashed face-first into a hard, hot chest. "It's okay," Maxar murmured. "It just hit you, didn't it?"

I nodded and sobbed.

"What happened?" Raewyn asked.

"Her aunt, a spellcaster mage, was murdered today by two demons. We found her in her home. A necromancer came and recounted the last moments of her life where they tortured her," Drak said matter-of-factly.

"Fuck," Raewyn breathed. "Do you know which demons?"

"No."

Maxar rubbed my back as I trembled and sobbed quietly against him. He was so warm, and he smelled faintly like a bonfire, but not in a repelling way. It was comforting. Slowly, my breathing decelerated, and I wasn't sobbing as hard. The tears still fell and that lump at the back of my throat seemed to have doubled in size, but I wasn't shaking anymore and I was able to pull in deeper breaths.

He released his tight hold on me and held me by the shoulders. "You just lost someone really important to you. It's okay not to be . . . yourself right now. If you break down, it's okay. It's kind of expected." I blinked through the tears at him, for the first time really looking into his eyes and how utterly beautiful they were. So many shades of gold, copper, and amber. And the longer I stared, the more those colors seemed to actually swirl around each other. It was hypnotic, but also calming. His smile pulled me out of my pit of despair. "There's my girl."

I smirked. "*Your* girl?"

His smile was so damned boyish and not at all cheeky like I was growing accustomed to. "A guy can hope."

Letting out a stuttered breath from between thinly parted lips, I closed my eyes for a moment. "I can't believe she's just . . . gone."

"It'll take a while to truly sink in," he said gently. "And it will get easier. But right now, understandably, it's raw. So your emotions will be too."

I blinked at him again. "Who have you lost?"

His smile was sad and small. "Too many people to list right now. Let me finish cutting up your apple for you. You go sit with that angry chick over there." He jerked his strong chin toward Raewyn, who sat like she had a stick up her ass, on the edge of the couch. "Nice shirt, by the way." He tugged on the hem. "I love Tough Love and Rough Play. I've seen them in concert six times."

Swallowing, I blotted at my eyes with the sleeve of my T-shirt, smiling meekly at him before I wandered over toward my *advisor*. I sat on the coffee table facing her. "I understand this is probably not a job you wanted. And I hope this isn't taking you away from family or another job, but I could really use your help. I think we got off on the wrong foot, and if you're willing to start over, so am I." Rolling my lips inward, I held out my hand toward her *again*.

She stared at it, blinking long, thick, fake eyelashes.

Her top lip started to curl up, like the idea of even touching me made her want to retch. She glanced sideways at Drak, who stood not too far away glaring at her, with his arms crossed over his chest.

Finally, she exhaled, almost in defeat, and took my hand. "Yes, let's start over."

I was too emotionally drained, too angry, sad, and overwhelmed to take her reluctance personally, even though it totally was. Whatever. She didn't like me, and I didn't like her. But I needed her, and she was my subject. So she had to obey her Queen.

Not going to lie, I kind of liked that power. Not enough to hang onto the crown for any length of time, and certainly not eternity, but the fact that she didn't really have a choice, no matter how much of a racist she was, kind of brought me a sick sense of joy.

"So, what do I do first?" I asked.

Maxar brought over the plate of sliced apples and a bowl of peanut butter.

Smiling, I thanked him, took it, and dove in.

Raewyn watched with more disdain, her sourpuss face and clear impatience only making me take my time even more.

Fuck you, bitch. I hadn't eaten anything all day. Also, my aunt just died, and I'm your goddamned Queen. So deal with it.

She said nothing as I ate my apples and peanut butter. In fact, nobody said anything.

Drak stood there like a wax figurine, his expression neutral and annoying, and Maxar was on his phone at the barstool at the kitchen counter.

Once I finished my snack, I got up and went to the fridge, pulling out a bottle of guava and spirulina kombucha. I drank the whole thing, maintaining eye contact with Raewyn the entire time. Once I put the bottle into the recycling bin, I approached her again. "What do I do first?"

She stood up from the couch. "You lay down."

Nodding, I did as she said.

"Now, close your eyes and relax."

A bit difficult considering how my life was going right now, but I did the best I could.

I was working on deepening my breath and slowing it down when a knife, an actual fucking knife, sliced through the two lobes of my brain. I bolted upright with a scream, clutching at my head. I pulled my hands away, expecting to see blood. But there wasn't anything there.

I faced Raewyn, furious. But unlike when I'd been angry with Drak, Zandren, and Gemma before, causing them to scream in pain and clutch the sides of their head while blood fell from their nose, a big shield slammed down around Raewyn—in her brain not literally—and my anger didn't penetrate. "What did you do to me?"

Her gaze was unwavering. "Next time I do that, I want you to envision that shield you just felt me put up. Literally picture it in your head and stop me."

I glared at her.

"Lay back down," she said with no inflection.

I did as I was told, still shooting lasers at her out of my eyes. Her shield was still up and impenetrable.

Once again, I tried to relax. She came at me this time with an axe, cutting cross-wise through my brain. I envisioned a shield, but it was weak, and it came down too late. The axe was already in my head. My brain throbbed in pain, and when I reached up and touched my upper lip then opened my eyes, blood stained my finger.

"Again," she said.

So we did it again.

And again. And again.

And every time, she tried a different weapon.

And every time, my shields weren't strong enough.

I was exhausted, and blood poured from my nose and ears, all over the light-blue, crushed velvet, pillow sham Gemma bought at a flea market.

"I think that's enough for today," Maxar said.

"No. She needs to learn how to not only block another demon, but block herself and control her emotions," Drak said. "Again."

Goddammit, these men were hot and cold. Maxar was hot and compassionate, and Drak was as cold as a corpse with zero empathy or consideration. I was getting whiplash.

Popping one eye open, I found the coldhearted vampire standing at the end of the couch, staring down at me with so much disapproval in his gaze, I actually wanted to curl up in a little ball and just weep. Weep because I was tired. I was grieving, and I was clearly a shitty demon *and* queen. He was probably standing there watching me, wondering how he could get out of this Fated Mates bullshit too. That he'd been stuck with a dud. A hybrid, halfling dud that couldn't even do what demons did best. "I'm doing the best I can," I croaked.

Barely a flicker of emotion flashed in his eyes. "If you were, you'd mate with us so you could absorb some of our powers and help yourself."

"Dude," Maxar said with disapproval.

But Drak didn't even flinch at his chastising.

I glared at the fanged freak in front of me.

"Interesting," Raewyn said. "You want to kill him."

I shifted my gaze to her. "Yes, but not really."

Maxar chuckled softly.

Keeping my focus on Raewyn, I asked, "Is there anything else you can tell me that will help me? You've literally told me to envision a shield. And I do. But it's not strong enough, and it comes down too late. What else can I do to make this work?"

Her gaze was unwavering, and I'm sure she expected it to be unnerving too, but I refused to allow her to intimidate me.

"That right there," she said after a moment. "That feeling that you're having about me right now, as well as the one you have about the vampire, the feeling that you refuse to let us intimidate you. Lean into that as hard as you can."

"What does that mean?" I really hated that she could read my emotions.

"Just try it. Close your eyes."

Growling, I closed my eyes and focused on how much I really hated this woman. On how much she was treating me like some misfit mutt, when what I really needed was a bit of compassion, support, and understanding. How hard was it to be kind? Was it that much harder than being a bitch?

I channeled all my energy into not letting her intimidate me. Into hating her. Into not letting her into my mind. I threw up the shield. This time, it was stronger. I could just feel it. It was thicker. Heavier. And it took a lot out of me to keep it up. But when the pressure of something coming down on it dug into my mind, I looked up to find a sword bearing down, but unable to break through.

I smiled and thought more about how I hated this woman, but at the same time pitied her. She didn't know me. And that was her loss. She judged me before she even got to know me, before she even gave me a chance. She was nothing more than a racist bitch with attitude and flawless makeup. But as pretty as she was, that didn't make her beautiful. I was awesome, and I pitied her for not giving me a chance and getting to know that awesomeness.

And just when I thought my shield couldn't get any stronger, the pressure of her sword lifted.

My eyes flew open, my chest heaved.

I glanced at Raewyn. Her eyes held a smile, but her mouth was a flat line. "Better."

I knew without having to say anything, that that was as close to a compliment that I was going to get.

"Again," she said. "Only this time you need to try not to fry *my* brain. I'm going to drop my shield and you're going to have the exact same thoughts about me as you did before. Only this time, don't pity me. Just hate me."

Heat raced into my chest and cheeks. I hated that she could read my emotions so easily. How could she do that even with my shield up though? Was the shield just to stop her from frying my brain? Would I need another shield to keep her out of my head?

I sat up and concentrated on this woman. On how full of herself she seemed. On how righteous and better than me she came across. She literally sniffed the air, and then called me a human and an abomination. She was a racist bitch. A self-important snag without any compassion, kindness, or empathy in her heart. If this was what all demon women were like, then no-fucking-thank you.

"Is that all you've got?" she asked with a haughty laugh. "I feel nothing." She glanced at Drak, "Did she try to fry your brain?"

All he did was nod.

"Was it as pathetic as this?"

Her gaze swung to Maxar. "So, like, what is the deal with you guys anyway? Have you ever been with a demon?"

Fury lanced through me, hot and painful, and I growled, my eyes boring into her skull and wrinkle-free forehead.

She screamed and clutched at her head as I brought down my own blade across the two lobes in her skull. Blood poured from her nose, but she pushed back with a medium-strength shield of her own, and opened her eyes. "Good. Now take your anger and compress it into a ball."

"What?"

She winced. "You have to imagine all of this. Take the anger and compress it. Gather it like colored energy and squeeze it into a ball."

She was struggling to keep her shield up. I knew she could easily drop a stronger one and keep me out, but she needed me to learn how to stop my assault on people. I didn't like that I was hurting her. Even though I wasn't fond of her, even though I pitied her, I didn't want to hurt her.

"Stop pitying me. Hate me, you stupid, hybrid bitch. Hate me, but take that hate and that anger and gather it up. If you let it run free, you'll never be able to control it. Collect it. You . . . you have to."

Closing my eyes—

"Don't close your eyes!"

Jesus. Okay.

Opening my eyes, I focused on her face, contorting in pain. Meanwhile, inside my head, I was scooping up all this red, buzzing energy. It was like fog, but also flickering and pulsing lights. I gathered it in my arms, squeezing it into a small ball. But the ball grew with the more red energy I grabbed. Soon it was the size of a basketball and I held it in my hand.

"Good," she said. "Now drop a shield around it. Like a dome. Trap it."

This was all so weird. The fact that I could do all of this in my mind, just imagine it, but it was actually doing something to someone else, was surreal and not something I'm totally sure I believed. But it was happening, so I needed to just go with it. I set the pulsing, red energy, ball of anger on the ground in my mind, then conjured a shield. A transparent one. And dropped it over the ball, containing that rage. Trapping it so that it didn't wreak havoc when I didn't want it to.

I'd closed my eyes again at some point and blinked them open to find Raewyn sitting there on the coffee table, dabbing gently at her nose with a black hand-kerchief. "That wasn't terrible for your first try."

The front door opened and Gemma walked in, her gaze turning curious when she took in my bloody face, Raewyn, and the blood on her face. "Uh . . . hi."

"What are you doing home early?" I asked, standing up and only a little wobbly. I approached her, unsure how to break the news about Aunt Delia.

"What are you talking about? It's nine-thirty. My shift ended at nine."

I glanced at the clock on the stove. "How long were we doing that thing on the couch?" I asked, turning to Maxar.

"Like eight hours," he said.

My eyes nearly popped clean from my skull. That did not feel like eight hours. That felt more like twenty minutes, an hour tops.

"What is going on here?" Gemma asked.

"Raewyn is a demon, and she's teaching me how to block demon mind control while also blocking my own anger so I don't roast brains anymore."

Gemma's gaze flared. "Oh! Well, that's great. I've had a bit of a headache all day and I wondered if it was because you tried to broil my gray matter yesterday."

I pouted. "I'm sorry again."

She shrugged. "It's fine."

Raewyn stood up from her spot on the coffee table. "I will be back tomorrow morning to work on this with you again." She glanced at Gemma, sniffed the air and made a face of disgust, like she'd just smelled five-day-old fish that fell behind the radiator. Then she was gone.

"Well, she seems like someone I can't wait to get to know better," Gemma said sarcastically. She opened the freezer. "Hey, who ate my steak?"

Drak cleared his throat.

I closed the freezer and took Gemma's hand. "We need to talk."

Her hazel-green eyes went wide. "What's wrong now?"

"Just . . . come with me, okay?" I laced our fingers together and took her out to the patio, closing the sliding glass door behind us, but not before shooting Drak a look that said, "Order dinner for Gemma, you steak-stealing dick."

If he was any kind of Fated Mate, he'd know what that look meant and do the right thing.

"Okay, you're freaking me out a little," Gemma said as we took seats on the vinyl lounge chairs where we liked to read with our bikinis and sunhats on, with the tunes blasting. "What did you find out at Delia's?"

I swallowed past my tight throat. My eyes stung and that rush of pure pain filled my chest again. "Um," I started, my bottom lip wobbling. "We . . . went there, hoping to talk to her, and um . . ." I licked my lips.

Gemma's gaze widened again. "And . . . what?"

I glanced down at my lap and reached for her hands lacing our fingers together. I gave her hands a gentle squeeze. She squeezed back to reassure me. Finally, I lifted my head again and breathed out slowly through thinly parted lips as a tear sprinted down my cheek. "She was um . . . she was dead. They . . . they killed her."

Gemma gasped, released my hands and surged to her feet. "Who did?"

"Demons."

"How do you know?"

"Zandren smelled them, and we had a necromancer mage come and he recounted her last few moments alive."

She stepped out from where our legs touched and began to pace, hammering me with questions.

Questions I could barely answer. Questions that I'd asked a thousand times already since finding Delia there on her bedroom floor.

"How did this happen?" she asked, tears now trekking down her face, like they were mine.

"We think they're looking for me. To take me out as heir . . . or something. We don't know. But that picture of you and I at the beach is gone. So they know what I look like."

"But why'd they kill her? I don't understand."

"Because she wouldn't give up my location. Wouldn't tell them what they wanted to know."

"Which was?"

"Who my mother was. And it turns out she was human. I'm half human, half demon, which is apparently so rare that nobody has ever heard of it happening, or at least it's not documented."

"Oh, I'm sure that's not going to go over well with these pureblood loving immortals. I could tell that that femme fatale with the killer eyeliner didn't like me. Is it because I'm human?"

My head bobbed and I sniffed and wiped away a tear. "She doesn't like me either because I'm half human."

"Jesus. Talk about living in the past. Let's be a little more progressive and accepting here, people. Diversity, equity, inclusion."

I reached for her to stop her from continuing to pace. "Gem, I'm sorry."

Her chin quivered. "I'm sorry too. She's your aunt."

"She is an aunt to both of us. She took you in like you were her own after your own parents passed. We both lost someone special today."

"Now all we have is each other." She wrapped her arms around me and I hugged her back just as tight.

Movement in the apartment pulled my attention. Zandren was back, and he had two big paper bags loaded with takeout food. He spotted me on the deck with Gemma and his face lit up like it wasn't nighttime and a ray of sunshine had just burst through the wall and right onto his face. But when he realized that I was telling Gemma about Aunt Delia, his face sobered.

"Are you going to have a funeral?" Gemma asked.

"I'd like to. I'm honestly not even sure I'm her only family. Since Delia was actually a mage and probably centuries old, maybe she has other family somewhere and they have claim to her body and get to decide what to do with it."

Gemma frowned. "Maybe. But I still think she'd trust you to do the right thing. Her favorite flowers, something in the garden. Maybe a celebration of life, rather than a dour event with people wearing black and crying?"

I smirked. "All I own is black."

That made her smile, and she opened the sliding glass door. "That's true. Okay, then make it a goth party. I think Delia would have liked that too."

The scent of Indian food wafted up my nostrils. Zandren was busy unloading all the to-go containers onto the kitchen counter. "I wasn't sure what you'd want, so I just ordered like half the menu."

Another surge of warm, comforting heat filled my chest, and I found myself deliberately sidling up closer to him, pulling in his cedar and honey scent. "Thank you. This was exactly what we needed." I glared at Drak, who'd eaten Gemma's steak and seemed to hold zero guilt about it. "I appreciate you taking care of us, and not just eating our food, but also providing some."

Gemma brought plates down from the cupboard, and soon, we all had chicken methi matar malai, dal turka, shahi paneer, beef rogan josh, navratan korma, three different types of naan bread, samosas, pakoras, and basmati rice. I was stuffed by the time I put my plate in the dishwasher. But I was also really grateful. Grateful that I wasn't alone. That I not only had Gemma, but for the first time since they showed up on my doorstep last night, that the guys were here and helping me figure out who killed Delia and why.

Zandren brought his plate to the dishwasher too, after having had four heaping helpings. "You sure you had enough to eat, Little One?"

"I'm full," I said with a small smile. "But thank you for getting dinner."

"Anything for you." He cupped my chin with his thumb and forefinger. "I hope you know that."

"I'm starting to," I said softly.

Maxar cleared his throat and brought his dishes to the dishwasher too. "So, Teddy, what did you and Kase find out at Delia's house?"

"Teddy?" Zandren asked with a cute cock of his head.

"Teddy Bear." Maxar's grin was cheeky.

Zandren growled. "Kase was able to disable about eight more spells. There are still more around the house, but he couldn't undo them. He said he's going to do some reading tonight on what he thinks the spells entail and will go back tomorrow to try again."

"And did he find anything else after he disabled those spells?" I asked.

Zandren nodded and reached into the back pocket of his jeans. He pulled out a small, weathered photo of a black woman with wild curls just like mine. She was cradling a small, smiling baby. The woman was smiling too. She was beautiful with kind eyes, and pure happiness radiating from her as she stared down at the infant in her arms.

"Is that my mother?" My throat was tight for the millionth time that day.

He nodded. "Yes, we believe it is. And that's you."

"I . . . I've never known what she looked like. Delia said she didn't have any pictures. Why would she lie to me?"

"To protect you," Drak said. "Everything she did was to protect you."

My gaze flicked to him for half a second before I focused back on the photo. I stroked my finger over my mother's face. "How did you and my father meet?" I whispered. "Why did you want me kept a secret from him?"

"Because you're a hybrid mutt," Drak said. "The Realm would never accept a hybrid, halfling heir to the throne. And if word gets around that you are indeed a hybrid, there will be an uprising. People will pick sides. It also opens up the doors for another species leader to step in and challenge for the main throne." His gaze drifted to Zandren. "Doesn't it?"

Zandren cleared his throat. "My father does not want to rule the Realm. I'll assure you of that now."

"Until he realizes his only other option is a mage, a vampire, a hybrid-demon-slash-human, or Lerris Byrche," Drak pointed out. "Then he might start singing a different tune."

"Would you shut up," I snapped at him. "You're nothing but a Negative Nancy and I'm sick of it. Unless you have something nice to say, just keep your fangs closed."

His blue eyes went wide, and he winced at the same time a trickle of blood seeped from his nose. That's when I realized I was trying to sous vide his brain. I quickly gathered all the red, ragey smoke in my mind as fast and as best I could and squished it into a compressed little ball, then I dropped a dome shield over it.

Drak stopped wincing and blinked a few times.

"Sorry," I muttered. "Are you okay?"

He nodded. "Yes. Thank you for stopping it."

Even though it was him, I beamed anyway. Without the dominatrix demon there, I managed to successfully block my own rage from breaking someone's mind. I was getting the hang of it.

That was one tiny victory in a day of colossal failures.

Hopefully, tomorrow would bring forth more answers than questions, and we found ourselves one step closer to finding Delia's killer. At the very least, maybe that demon bitch with the impeccable winged eyeliner would help me get ever better control of my rage and I'd be able to properly get pissed off at Drak without attempting to blanch his brains.

However, if I did blanch his brains, just a little hopefully, I would destroy the annoying asshole portion. Because that side of him was getting old, fast.

CHAPTER ELEVEN

ZANDREN

I probably shouldn't have done it.

In fact, I know I shouldn't have.

But as time ticked by, my affection for the little demon was getting stronger and stronger.

So when she went to bed and locked her door, I waited until I knew she was asleep—until the whole apartment was asleep—then I picked her lock with my claw and just sat on the edge of her bed for a while watching her sleep. She was so peaceful. So beautiful. I also wanted to make sure she was safe. Make sure no nightmares plagued her.

She just had lost her aunt, the only mother-figure she'd ever known, and besides her roommate, the only person in the world who gave a damn about her—until me, that is—and I knew a thing or two about losing a mother. About the devastating toll it took on your heart. How a loss like that rendered you empty and lost, unsure how to put one foot in front of the other and go on when the person who loved you with every ounce of their soul was gone. Because even though their spirit may still be loving and watching over you, when they're gone, you feel that loss of love like your heart has been ripped clean from your chest. It's an ache I'll never forget, and one I wouldn't even wish on my worst enemy.

It was pure torture watching her leave with Maxar and Drak earlier that day, but I knew that she wanted someone to stay behind with Mr. Fiddleman. So I put my own needs aside and thought about what my mate needed.

She was always on my mind. Always first on my mind. Ever since the lightning strike, I thought of nothing more than her—and food.

And she was worth the wait and effort.

Her fire and spirit. Her sass, and the fact that she swore like a sailor, just made me love her more.

I wanted nothing more than for her to accept me as her mate, but I wanted it to be on her own terms. I wanted her to want me. To want a mate. To want the Bond. So if I had to wait a week, a month, a year, or ten years, I would. I'd waited centuries for her already. What was a little longer until she was ready?

It'd been a while since I shifted and my bear ached to scratch up against a tree and really stretch. I closed Omaera's bedroom door silently and crept out of the apartment, out of the building, and then practically sprinted to the nearest wooded area.

Rather than shift while dressed and tear the clothes I'd just acquired, I was mindful enough to undress properly, fold my clothes, and stash them in a bush before I dropped to all fours and shifted.

The stretch of my bones, muscles, and ligaments was always so pleasurable. It was like that first morning stretch, elongating stiff muscles and working them for the first time in a new day.

Once I was back in animal form, I stood up on hind legs and backed up against an enormous fir tree, where I rubbed my butt back and forth a dozen times or more, grunting and growling in pleasure.

Even though I'd gorged myself on Indian food earlier, I was hungry again. So I headed deeper into the trees in search of something. A rabbit or squirrel, perhaps. I'd dined on a house cat or two when desperate, but I tried not to eat domestic animals. But everything was asleep now.

My belly rumbled. I could leave the safety of the trees and venture into the city, like the bakery dumpster I had breakfast at. But then that increased the risk of someone seeing a bear and reporting it.

I'd have to shift back to human form if I wanted food.

I ignored my grumbling belly and wandered around the quiet, dark forest a little longer, just enjoying the fresh, peaty air and the way the dirt and pine needles felt like cushions beneath the pads of my paws.

Yes, a huge part of me ached to get back to Omaera, but I couldn't ignore the bear side of me either. The side that needed wide open spaces and freedom. That needed soil between my toes and the stars above me.

Would she want to live in the city if we mated?

What about the other two bozos?

I still couldn't believe this was my fate. To share a mate with two other men. And not even two other bears, not even two other shifters. But a lunatic fire mage, and a motherfucking vampire, of all people.

The gods were surely testing me. I could see no other explanation.

After an hour of just scratching up against trees, and wandering the woods, I shifted into human form once again, redressed, and headed back toward the hipster village Omaera chose to call home.

Delia's neighborhood was so much nicer, but if this was what my mate wanted, then I'd deal with it.

A kebab shop was open late. So I grabbed three kebabs on my way back, but just as I reached Omaera's building, the wind pulled an unfamiliar and alarming scent my way.

I sniffed harder.

Demon.

Setting the kebabs on a bench near the front door, I crouched down behind a big, flowering bush and waited.

The scent was still there—bergamot and hyacinth.

A growl rumbled through me as the essence grew stronger. Until, peering through the branches of the shrub, I saw a demon with long, black hair, stiletto boots, and red lips click-clacked her way down the sidewalk. She didn't go to the front door, but rather, she stood below the balconies. Below Omaera's fourth-floor balcony.

Her eyes remained laser-focused forward, almost like she was in a trance.

Who was she?

What was she doing?

Was she here to hurt Omaera?

I knew that a demon had come over earlier to help Omaera with her powers, but if this was the same demon, why was she back in the middle of the night?

She couldn't be here to check up on Omaera. Nothing about this said she gave a damn about my mate. If anything, she was here to hurt her.

I stood up from the bush and walked to the front door, grabbing my kebabs from the bench, and making sure she saw me, and that she knew I saw her. "Hello," I said, nodding at her before punching in the code that allowed me inside.

Then it was a full-on sprint. I booked it up the stairs, taking them three, sometimes four at a time. Screaming echoed from Omaera's apartment when I reached the fourth floor. I burst through the door to find Drak and Maxar standing over Gemma in the hallway, who writhed in agony, blood pouring out of her nose. Omaera was still asleep, but caught up in a horrible nightmare, screaming at the top of her lungs and begging for the pain to stop.

"What's going on?" Maxar asked in a panic.

"There's a demon outside, standing below the balcony," I said.

Maxar ran to the balcony, throwing open the sliding glass door. Bright green flames shot from his palms downward. He jumped up on the ledge and then down four stories below. More flashes of green flames. Drak was busy shaking Omaera, trying to wake her up.

Then all the screaming stopped.

Omaera stopped, and Gemma stopped.

Omaera's eyes flew open and the first thing she did was lunge into my arms. "Oh god, you're not dead."

I glanced at Drak, but held onto her tight, stroking her hair. "No, Little One. I'm not dead. I'm right here. I'm safe. You're safe."

She trembled in my arms. "The nightmare was so real. So, so real."

"That's because some demon bitch was down on the ground manipulating your dreams," I said.

Her gaze flew wide. "Raewyn?"

"Dominatrix type? Long, black hair. Spikey boots?"

Omaera nodded, then glanced around the space. "Where's Maxar?"

"He leaped over the balcony and chased her off with fire."

"Over the balcony?" she scrambled out of my arms and out of bed, but paused when she saw Gemma lying lifeless in the hallway covered in blood. She dropped to her knees. "No. No! No, no, no, no, no. I will kill that bitch. I will tear her brain from her skull with my bare hands."

I crouched down beside her and put my finger to Gemma's throat. "There's a pulse." Picking up the petite redhead, I carried her to the living room and gently set her down on the couch, using the hem of my shirt to wipe up some of the blood from her cheeks and lip.

Omaera was bawling as she knelt on the floor beside Gemma. "You have to wake up. You can't do this. You can't leave me. Please."

Pressing her forehead to the side of Gemma's head, she continued to murmur how much she loved her friend. How much she needed her. Gemma's chest rose and fell, so we knew she was breathing. We knew she was alive. It was the brain damage that was of concern.

Gemma made a noise, then another. Then she groaned and stirred.

Omaera popped up and gently shook her friend by the shoulders. "Gem. Gem wake up. You need to wake up, Gemma."

Gemma stirred some more.

"Gemma Frances McNeil, you need to wake up right now!"

Gemma groaned and her pale blonde lashes fluttered a few times before finally opening. "Wh-what happened?"

Just then, the front door burst open and an unruffled Maxar entered, dragging a furious-looking demon woman. She was bound at the hands and around the mouth with magical orange flame ropes that flickered and sparked. She also wore a flame rope around her forehead like a crown. I didn't know a lot of fire mages, but I knew enough that each flame color had a different intensity and purpose. Green and black were the most lethal. Orange, red, and yellow were gentler and more benign. I'd never seen a rope made of fire though.

He dragged her forward and tossed her to the ground where she grunted and glared at him like she was trying her damndest to barbecue his brain. He'd have a block in place, but that didn't mean she wouldn't try it on the rest of us.

The only person that could stop her was Omaera. Demons of higher power could block demons of lower power from trying to mind-control others.

Was Omaera strong enough? Did she even know how?

"I thought my brain was going to explode," Gemma said. "I woke up, and it was worse than when you did it to me. So much worse."

Omaera pressed her forehead to her friend's temple. "I'm so, so sorry you're tangled up in this. I'm so sorry."

Gemma closed her eyes and leaned into Omaera. "But then, all I could smell were flowers and feel joy. When you were leaning against me, willing me not to die, this surge of pleasure and joy whipped through me like a warm wind. The kind that wraps a flowy dress around your legs and causes your hair to fly across your face." She smiled at Omaera. "I could *feel* your love."

Omaera was crying now, but she smiled and laughed through the sobs as Gemma sat up and the two embraced.

They remained that way for a moment, until the demon bitch on the ground grunted, pulling Omaera's attention away. She untangled herself from Gemma and stood up, slowly approaching Raewyn on the ground. Her nostrils flared and green flames danced in her eyes.

She got beside Raewyn's head and crouched down beside her. "Who sent you?"

"She's got a gag," Maxar said. "Do you want me to remove it?"

Omaera nodded. "Please."

He stepped forward and waved his hand over Raewyn's mouth, essentially snuffing out the flames that tied her lips from touching and inhibiting her speech. She squirmed and writhed against her arm restraints though, glaring at all of us.

Why hadn't she tried to fry my brain yet? That was the sole reason why I didn't tear out her jugular when I saw her standing beneath the balconies earlier. She could attack me before I got the jump on her, then she would have had free rein to kill Gemma and torture Omaera.

"I'm going to ask again," Omaera said slowly. "Who sent you?"

Raewyn's lip curled up into an ugly sneer. "Nobody *sent* me. I'm here to do what is right. And that's eliminate an abomination. You're not our queen. You're a disgusting mutant that never should have happened. I'd never bow down to you, and I know a lot of others who won't."

Omaera blinked at her and nodded. "And my friend? Why did you hurt her?"

Raewyn snorted. "The human? One less human in this world is a good thing."

Omaera nodded again. "Right. So, you acted on your own, fully prepared to murder my best friend and torture me. Were you planning to kill me? Why didn't you hurt the vampire?"

"She's not a high-level demon," Maxar said. "She only has the power to manipulate and attack probably two people at a time."

Omaera nodded one more time. "I see."

"What would you have us do with her, my Queen?" Maxar asked. "I'm happy to dispose of the body the same way we did the Phaceanesh who attacked you last night."

She glanced at Maxar, then at Drak and me. "Is there any reason you can think of that she may be of use to us?"

"She's just a liability. She could hurt any one of us at any time," Drak said.

"Why isn't she doing that now?" Omaera asked.

"Oh! That's because I have a restraint on her," Maxar said joyfully. "See the orange rope around her head? That's keeping her from fucking with us."

I'd never heard of that before. He was handy to have around if he could do that.

I was beginning to see his usefulness.

Why the vampire was here and what he contributed to this pack, I still hadn't quite figured out.

"I suggest we eliminate her," Drak said. "She knows where you live. She's clearly not loyal to the crown, and she could run off and tell whomever killed your aunt about your whereabouts."

Omaera looked at him like he'd lost his mind. "Oh, I wasn't implying that we just let her go. No, no. She tried to kill my best friend. This bitch will die. It's just whether she dies *right now*, or we hang on to her because she's of some use. That's the only question I have. Do we keep her and use her, *then* kill her? Or just kill her right now?"

Maxar's grin was big and maniacal. "Just when I thought I couldn't love you more, my Queen . . ." He pressed his hand to his heart. "You show me your sadistic side, and I just . . . oh, baby."

Omaera rolled her eyes.

Drak stepped forward. "She is of no use to us. She won't give anything up. She is a drain on our time and energy. Holding on to her presents us with a risk of her escaping, or breaking free of her shackles and hurting someone."

"Uh . . . there's no way she's breaking free of those ropes," Maxar said, giving Drak a look that said he was offended. "I know what I'm doing. Fuck you very much. Been playing with fire for a few centuries now."

Drak ignored him.

"Then she dies tonight," Omaera said, standing up. She glared down at the demon who still had so much hate and anger in her eyes, even though she was facing death. "Raewyn Vade, I find you guilty of treason, attempted murder, and attempted mutiny. I sentence you to death." Then she spun around, showing the demon her back and returning to Gemma on the couch.

Maxar nodded. "I'll take care of it."

Omaera shook her head. "No. I sentenced her. I should be the one to do it."

Maxar's, Drak's, and my brows all hiked up to our hairlines.

"Normally, the monarch does the sentencing, but not the execution," Drak said.

"Then they are a feckless monarch," Omaera said, wrapping an arm around Gemma. "Death is permanent. It is not a light sentence and should only be made when there is no other option. If I'm going to bear the weight of this crown—until I can give it to someone else—then I'm going to be the one to carry out the sentence. It's only right."

"Maer," Gemma whispered. "You can't come back from this."

"I know," Omaera said, swallowing. "But she tried to kill you." She glared at Raewyn. "She deserves to die."

Maybe I was wrong, but for the briefest of moments, I could have sworn I saw a flicker of respect flash through Raewyn's eyes. Then it was gone, replaced once again by deep-seated loathing and contempt for my mate.

"Would you like a fire sword?" Maxar asked.

"Is that clean and quick?" Omaera asked, still hugging her friend.

Maxar nodded. "It will cauterize as it slices, so there is very little bloodshed. Should be an easy cleanup. I can also just cremate her like I did the Phaceanesh in the alley."

Even though I was no virgin when it came to murder, execution, war, or bloodshed, I would be lying if I said the cavalier way everyone was discussing killing this woman wasn't affecting me in a nauseating way. Yes, she needed to die. But she was still alive right now, listening to this. Hearing how we were going to dispose of her corpse when she was relieved of her head.

I knew I'd be fine, but I worried about Omaera. She was stoic at the moment, only showing her friend affection, but otherwise numb with rage toward the demon. But how would she cope with this later? When the reality of it came crashing down and the image and smell of burning flesh and a fire sword decapitating a woman returned to her in her dreams?

Because they would.

They always did.

Dreams were something not even the most powerful demon could control.

At least not their own.

They could manipulate others' dreams, the way Raewyn had been manipulating Omaera's dreams, but Omaera wouldn't be able to control her own dreams.

"Maybe you shouldn't see this," she said to Gemma. "You don't need to witness this."

"I'm not leaving you," Gemma said.

Omaera's expression turned gentler than I'd ever seen it. "Please, sweetie. Go to your bedroom and close the door. I don't want you to see me like this. I have the guys. They're going to help me. But you don't need to witness this. Please. Go."

Gemma's eyes flicked back and forth across all of our faces, then over to Raewyn. Finally, she nodded and slowly got up from the couch. "You don't have to do this, Maer. You know that, right? One of them can do it."

"She tried to kill you, Gem. And I'm the Queen. A good leader doesn't shy away from the hard stuff. Delia taught me that."

They hugged. Then Gemma went back into her room, closing the door. A moment later, music began to play from inside her bedroom.

"All right, let's get this over with," Omaera said, standing up and taking a deep breath which exited from her chest in a rattling fashion. She went over to Raewyn and glared down at her. "This could have ended so differently. But you're a xenophobic psychopath. And my kingdom has no place for people like you. Hybrids are people too. *Humans* are people too. And we all deserve to live." Her mouth turned down into a frown. "Well, everyone except you." She held out her hand, and Maxar created a long, broad, flaming green sword. The handle was yellow flames so Omaera could hold it, but the blade itself was a bright green, flickering and dancing. Hot and lethal.

"You won't have to swing it very hard," Maxar said. "It will cut through flesh and bone quite easily."

Omaera nodded and glanced at me, equal parts hesitation and fear in her eyes. I stepped forward, reaching for the handle of the sword. "You don't have to do this. You will still be a strong leader if you let someone else take over. You haven't been Queen long. And you're grieving for your aunt. Let me help you, Little One."

My large hand enclosed around her small one, reminding me of our earlier conversation about how I said I wanted to teach her to catch fish with her hands.

"You don't need this weighing on you. She deserves her sentence, but it's not up to you to see it through." My grasp tightened on hers and for a moment. I really thought she would let me do this for her, but she shook her head, flicked me away, raised the sword, and brought it down over the demon's neck, slowly, but with fluidity. Zero hesitation and with the strength of a thousand queens.

Her eyes glowed bright emerald from the reflection of the green flames as the sharp scent of burning flesh filled the air along with smoke.

The demon, to her credit, said nothing. Not a peep. And until the final sinew piece was severed, she glared at Omaera with so much hatred that I knew, beyond any lingering doubt in my mind, that if we'd allowed Raewyn to live, she would have tried and quite possibly succeeded in killing Omaera.

Her racism ran deep and there was no cure for it. No amount of rehabilitation, therapy or otherwise, would heal the demon of her odium toward humans. She needed to be extinguished.

Once the job was done, and her head had been successfully removed from her body, Omaera dropped the sword to the ground and visibly crumbled right before our eyes.

I went to her, sweeping her up into my arms and carrying her to the couch. She was so small and light, it was like carrying a baby deer. She still wore her purple silk scarf over her hair, and the same tank top and booty shorts that she'd slept in last night. Her skin was like satin against my rough palm as I stroked her legs, calming her down.

The first time I ever took a life had me feeling very similar.

I couldn't breathe.

I couldn't calm my mind.

And I kept wondering if there was any other path I could have taken that would have spared the person I killed.

There wasn't.

And there wasn't a different path this time either.

"You did the right thing," I said softly as she leaned against me. I made sure to turn us away from Maxar as he finished up with Raewyn's body, using the same black flames as before to reduce her to ash. "She would have killed you. She would have betrayed the crown and killed Gemma."

Tears trickled down her make-up free face. "Do you think she's killed other humans before?"

"I'd bet my life that she has."

She nodded and exhaled a deep breath through thinly parted lips. "Yeah, I thought so too. Didn't make the decision any easier though."

"If it'd been easy, I'd be worried. A good leader doesn't take serious issues like this lightly. They weigh their options and look for the fairest, most democratic—and humane way—to deal with a situation. You didn't torture her. I'm sure she felt very little pain. But you've spared many human lives now, taking her out of the equation."

"Has your dad had to do things like this?"

I nodded. "On occasion. There is generally a trial. Sometimes it goes up to the High Council, depending on the circumstances."

Her eyes widened.

"But given that you're new to the crown, and this was a very tenuous situation, you made the right call. And we will all stand by you. Nobody—beside others who hate humans—would disagree with your choice of sentence."

"All done," Maxar said. "You can turn around now."

I spun us around on the couch where the psycho fire mage stood with a big Ziploc bag full of gray ash in one hand and broom in the other. He was also smiling like the depraved lunatic that he was. I groaned and cringed. The man got far too much joy out of this.

Omaera's mouth dropped open. "Burn the broom, please."

He nodded and it burst into flames in his hand, falling to the ground in another heap of ash.

"What do you wish to do with her remains?" Drak asked.

Omaera shrugged. "I don't know." She glanced between all of us. "Is this going to set off a stream of events now? Did she have a mate who is going to come seeking revenge? Parents or siblings?"

"She had no mate," Drak said, his phone out. "I just told King Howar what happened. He is deeply sorry for recommending her. She has no mate, and was orphaned as a young demon. No siblings either. She worked as a bartender at an underground realm BDSM club."

"I need to check on Gemma," she said, almost robotically, standing up and heading toward her friend's bedroom door. "I . . ." she sighed and glanced back at all of us. "Thank you for . . . saving us. For taking care of this." Then she knocked on Gemma's door and entered, closing us out.

"So, do we look for a new demon advisor for her?" I asked, standing up and going back to the kitchen where I'd dropped my kebabs. "She needs help harnessing her powers."

Maxar opened the sliding glass door and dumped the demon's ashes over the side of the balcony, allowing it to get swept up in the wind.

"Leave the door open," I said, when he returned into the apartment. "It smells like burning flesh in here."

"I don't mind the smell," he said with a shrug.

"I already have King Howar searching for a replacement advisor," Drak said, still texting on his phone. "There aren't very many demons in the city. Mostly vampires and mages."

"Demons like it hot," Maxar said. "There are lots in the desert and tropical areas. Not so many in the temperate, coastal, and rainforesty places." He glanced at one of my kebabs on the coffee table. "Can I have one?"

I glared at him, then growled, shaking my head. Bears did not share food. Unless it was with our mate or cubs.

He held up his hands in surrender. "Jesus, never mind. Grumpy fucker." He went to the fridge and pulled out some of the leftover Indian food from dinner, then began gnawing on a samosa.

"She needs to meet with the Council," Drak said. "They're unwilling to reschedule again."

"Was the Council this pushy with King Donovar?" Maxar asked. "Or are they trying to dominate the new, naïve queen from the get-go? Make her think she has less power than she really does? Because it seems to me that they're giving her absolutely no room to figure things out, grieve her dead aunt, her old life, or come to terms with the fact that our world exists."

Drak and I exchanged looks. He was King Howar's head guard and enforcer, and I was the shifter Prince. If anybody knew how the High Council operated, it would be us.

It pained me to admit it, but Maxar was right. The High Council was pushing Omaera and trying to manipulate her. And I didn't fucking like it.

"I take it from your silence that I've hit the nail on the head," Maxar said bitterly, his top lip curling up in disdain. Fuck this stupid mage. He was unhinged for sure, and useful when it came to some of the things he could do with fire, but he was also really fucking annoying with how accurate he was about certain things.

Even though my father was the shifter King, I was now loyal to one person and one person only.

My mate.

Her best interest was my one and only priority.

I would kill my father for her.

But rather than resort immediately to patricide, I figured a phone call would be better. Maybe I could talk some sense into him. Perhaps if he knew that the new queen was his daughter-in-law, he might not be so pushy. He might give her time and space to figure out her new role and responsibility to the Realm.

A quick glance at Drak told me he wasn't having the same kind of thoughts about King Howar as I was about my father. He believed that pushing Omaera was what was best for the Realm.

Well, fuck him.

I was going to put Omaera first, no matter what.

Even if it meant killing my own father to do it.

CHAPTER TWELVE

ZANDREN

I waited until morning before I called my father.

He lived in Oregon, so we were in the same time zone, and calling him in the middle of the night would yield the worst possible outcome.

Vampires needed little sleep and kept weird fucking hours. So it was no surprise that King Howar was up when Drak was texting him.

King Ryden was a different story and needed to be handled with caution. Cub paws were the best way to deal with the grumpy, nearly-six-hundred-year-old grizzly. He was best approached after he was well-rested, had had his coffee and breakfast, his morning nap, and was sitting on his porch watching the birds in the birdbath.

When I tried calling him before, I reached his clerk—Fellwin. Fellwin could be trusted implicitly. My father was away dealing with some wolf shifter drama north of Vancouver, Canada, and unable to answer his phone. But Fellwin, of course, had his ear to the ground and knew everything that went on in the Realm. He also handled my father's calendar because the old grizzly couldn't be bothered to do it himself. I asked Fellwin to keep the specifics of Omaera from my father, as I wanted to be the one to break the news. Not only did I now have a mate, but she was half demon and Queen of the Realm. Yeah, that kind of info deserved to come from me, and me alone.

I texted Fellwin to make sure my father was now home and available. I placed the call

when I knew he would be on the porch, with his sudoku puzzle, tea, and scone.

As always, his answer was a grunt.

"Dad," I said.

"Zandren."

"I was struck by lightning."

Silence echoed back at me. I glanced at Maxar's phone since Omaera and Gemma were still asleep in Gemma's room and I didn't want to bother her to ask for her phone.

Then a sob came through.

I glanced at the screen again.

"Oh, son. I'm so happy. Grandcubs. I can't wait."

Who the fuck was this bear?

Ryden Thorne was one of the grumpiest, hard-headed bears I'd ever met. I knew he'd been different before my mother and sister died, but it'd been over a century, so I forgot what a softer side of him was like.

"Yeah . . . it's uh . . . it's a bit complicated." I paced back and forth on the balcony, the sliding door closed. "We haven't mated yet."

"No? What's the matter?"

"Well, she's um . . . she's not a shifter." Among a long list of other things.

"No?" I could feel his terror through the phone. "Don't tell me she's a vampire. Gods no."

"No. No, she's not a vampire."

"Mage? We can deal with that."

"No. Not a mage."

"Ugh. A demon? Well, it's better than a vampire. Is that why you haven't mated yet? She's playing head games?"

"Dad . . . you know King Donovar was killed, right?"

"Yes, and he had an illegitimate heir that we're trying hard to meet with, but she's being a stubborn little demo—No!" The sound of chair legs scraping across the wood porch made me pull the phone from my ear. "Your mate is the new queen?"

"It would appear so."

"But . . . I heard her mate was a vampire."

"That's true . . . And a mage. And me."

"Three mates? But that's . . . that's impossible. That's never happened before."

"Yeah . . . that's what we all said. But it's the truth. We all got struck by lightning. We all feel the connection. The other thing is that she was being shielded by a spellcaster mage who hid her from the Realm until Donovar died. When he died, the spellcaster's magic ended because the Fates' magic is stronger. But we found out last night that her mother wasn't a mage or demon, not a shifter, or even a vampire. She was human, Dad."

"A hybrid?" His disbelief mimicked my own. I was still coming to terms with the idea of half human, half . . . other beings out there. Surely Omaera wasn't the first of her kind?

"Yeah. King Howar dispatched a demon advisor to help Omaera with her powers, and the woman was a true terror. She smelled human on Omaera immediately and treated her like scum. Then she came back last night to try to kill Omaera's human roommate and torture Omaera."

"Son, this is . . . how many people know about her being hybrid?" Caution colored my father's raspy voice. "Does Howar know? What about Anysa?"

"I . . . I don't know. As far as I know, it's just us . . . and now you. Don't make me regret telling you this, Dad." I made sure my threat was clear. My father was deeply devoted and in love with my mother for centuries. He would have eviscerated his own parents for her, and he knew just by my words that I would do the same for my mate. "Don't push her. I don't know if it's you leading this charge to manipulate the new queen, but stop. Two demons just killed her aunt yesterday. The only parent she's ever known. She is grieving. She is trying to come to terms with this new world, her role and the fact that three men showed up on her doorstep claiming to be her Fated Mates. You need to understand that she needs time."

"I always hoped you'd find a love as deep as the one I had for your mother. I'm proud of the mate you've turned into, Son."

A lump formed in my throat, but I couldn't let my emotions cloud the true reason I called him. "Dad, don't push her. If she's not ready to meet the High Council, then give her time."

"When do I get to meet her then? She's family now."

"When she's ready."

"I'll see what I can do. But I'm just one of three on the Council."

"Yeah, but you're the toughest."

His chuckle was gravelly. "Three mates, huh? That can't be easy. Especially for you, with one of them being a vampire."

"He's an asshole too. You know King Howar's head guard? Drak Ferrin?"

More silence.

"Dad?"

"I know him, yes. He's the King's cousin." The bitterness and hate that resonated through the phone had the hair on the back of my neck standing straight up.

"Well, that's the vampire. And the other one is some chaotic, unhinged, fire mage with a penchant for drama and murder."

"Drak Ferrin," he rumbled. "Golliver Ferrin was his father."

I narrowed my gaze, my attention pulled away by the movement inside the apartment. Omaera and Gemma were awake and in the kitchen. "Listen, Dad. Please, do what you can to tame the rest of the Council. She needs some time to adjust. She'll meet with you all when she's ready. But if you push her, she's . . . well, let's just say, I think her being half human hasn't diminished her powers in any way. She may very well be one of the strongest demons to ever live. She just needs to learn how to control her powers before she kills someone."

After mentioning Drak's name, my father's mood shifted, and I could tell he wasn't in any frame of mind to be on the phone. He grunted.

"I'll call you again soon, Dad."

Another grunt.

"Bye."

The line disconnected, and I stared at the screen for a hot minute before I opened the sliding door and stepped inside.

Omaera was staring at her phone. "There's a game tonight at the Black Fox."

Gemma grunted and nodded, filling up the coffee machine with water. "What's the buy-in?"

"A thousand. But there are some high rollers expected to show up. And by high rollers, I mean men with big egos who will hate to lose to a little girl."

Snorting in mirth, Gemma bobbed her head, jostling her red curls. "I only work a five-hour shift today. Ten to three. So it's totally doable."

"What's going on?" I asked, my belly rumbling with the need for food.

"Poker game tonight," Omaera said. "It'll be good to do something normal. The last few days have been insane. I just want to go back to the way things were." Her gaze turned deadly. "You know, *after* we take care of whoever killed Delia."

"Absolutely not," Drak said, looking up from his phone where he sat like an undertaker on the couch. "It's not safe."

Omaera glared at him. "I'm sorry, but I'm not asking for your permission."

"As your mate, I have a say in things that will unnecessarily put you in harm's way," he countered. "And going out to a poker game is absolutely unnecessary. You need to work on controlling your powers. You also have the meeting with the High Council today."

I glanced away, hoping to the Gods that my father reached out to Queen Anysa and King Howar, encouraging them to give Omaera some time to adjust. However, unlike my father, who had a secondary stake in Omaera being treated gently because she was also his daughter-in-law, I was skeptical the Vampire King or Mage Queen would see it the same way.

Drak's phone pinged, and he glanced down at it, the corners of his mouth dropping into a deep frown. "Never mind. They have agreed to wait until you are ready." He fixed his gaze on me, but it remained deadpanned.

Whatever, you stupid bat.

I was looking out for my mate. Full stop. If his allegiance was still to his king, then he was just going to make mating with Omaera that much more challenging and delayed for himself. He needed to make her his first, and only, priority. Just like I was.

"Perfect! No stupid High Council meeting to bring me down before a game." She brought down five mugs from the cupboard, then glared at Drak. "Because I *am* going."

"Then I will escort you," he said.

She laughed humorlessly. "Not fucking happening there, Fangs. I want some space from all of you. I need it. You're smothering me when all I want right now is some time with my best friend. Some time for us to grieve Delia."

Drak's nostrils flared, and he looked like was trying to decide whether to lose his shit—which I would absolutely pay to see—or vomit. He chose to remain quiet. Dammit.

The bathroom door opened and Maxar stepped out, steam rising off his body, which was just covered by a towel around his waist.

"I'm going to find breakfast," I said, heading for the door. "Omaera, would you like to join me?"

She cocked her head to the side for a moment, blinked, glanced at Gemma, who merely shrugged, then she nodded. "Actually, I could use some fresh air. Just let me throw on some pants."

I grinned like a lovesick fool at the fuming vampire.

Maxar was busy getting dressed, not caring two-shits that he'd dropped his towel in front of Gemma and given her a full view of his cock.

I mean, to be fair, nudity didn't bother me either, and I'd rocked up to their apartment with no bottoms. But Gemma didn't seem nearly as unfazed by the naked man though, and went bright red in the cheeks before hiding her eyes.

"Come on, Maxar," Omaera said, coming out of her bedroom in cute black sweatpants and a gray crop top which showed off a hint of a tattoo along her ribcage. "Just because you're fine flashing that thing around doesn't mean others are. Poor Gemma's scarred for life."

"I've seen dicks before," Gemma countered. "Plenty. Hundreds." Then she went even redder in the face. "Okay, maybe not hundreds. But I'm no virgin. I just . . . wasn't expecting to see one over breakfast, that's all. Especially one that I have no intention of riding."

Omaera snorted. "We'll find you a dick to ride."

Gemma shook her head. "You know I'm on a break from guys. They're nothing but trouble."

Omaera kissed her friend on the cheek and glanced at Maxar, Drak, and I. "Don't I know it."

We took the elevator down to the lobby, and I held the door open for her. It was a warm, spring morning and the birds and bees were the soundtrack to our brief jaunt down the sidewalk. I ached to take her hand in mine, but I didn't want to push her.

"So, where are we going for breakfast?" she asked, glancing up at me and causing the sun to perfectly hit the rose gold hoop in her right nostril, making it shine.

"Just over here. There's a great bakery."

"Oh, I love Plummer's Pastries."

I guided her down the alley behind the bakery to their dumpster of day-old baked goods.

She paused when I lifted the lid. "Wait, what's going on?"

"Breakfast," I said.

"You . . . you eat garbage?"

"It's not garbage. It's day-old pastries and bread. It's perfectly fine. And most of it is still in the bags and boxes."

She backed up, shaking her head. "Look, Pooh Bear, I know you're a *bear* and all . . . which I'm still skeptical about because I've never seen you shift. But I'm *not* a bear and I don't eat garbage. I make plenty of money playing poker that I don't need to go dumpster diving for food. Let's just go around the front and buy something from Randy and Josh."

I frowned. If only she knew how much *good* garbage there was out there.

Pick your battles.

Nodding, I closed the lid and together we walked to the front of the bakery and inside, standing in line with all the hipsters who just *had* to have their Earl

Grey scones and their pumpernickel cobs. My eyes threatened to stay fixed to the back of my head I was rolling them so much.

We reached the front counter and Omaera ordered a box of a dozen mixed pastries.

"What are you going to have?" I asked her.

Her mouth dropped open. "Right. Relentless appetite. I forgot. Josh, make that *two* dozen mixed pastries, please."

The young man with the bright-blue hair in a manbun nodded. "You got it, O."

We carried our boxes out into the sunlight. But I wasn't ready to go back to the apartment and share her with anyone yet. I wanted her to get to know me better, and I certainly wanted to get to know her better too.

"Come on," I said, tilting my head to the side. "I want to show you something."

"If it's your dick, I've already seen it. Impressive, but let's leave our pants on. Okay, Pooh Bear?"

"Clothes are just so restrictive. It's hard to find them in my size. And what do I do with them when I shift?"

She snorted. "All valid. But it's still weird." Her brows knitted together. "So do you like legit live in a cave or a den or whatever?"

"Sometimes, yeah. It's actually very nice. Nice and cool in the summer." I led her across the street and down a path toward the park. People were in the field throwing balls for their canine companions, while others with small children pushed them on the swings, or cheered them on when they came down the slide.

I'd need to go deep into the woods with her to avoid running into people.

"You're not taking me into the woods to kill me, are you? Because I'll toast your gray matter right now." The look she gave me was more playful than it was serious. But I knew her well enough now, to know that she also wasn't kidding.

All I did was give her a cheeky smile in return followed by a growl in my throat that seemed to turn her on rather than intimidate her. The sudden flare of her nostrils and the rush of color to her cheeks was all kinds of sexy and had my cock thickening in my pants.

We meandered off the main path into denser woods, blazing a trail of our own. Mosquitos and other bugs buzzed around us and she swatted at a few. I kept a keen eye out for people or other animals. Some people chose to let their dogs off leash, even though this was marked as a strictly on-leash park. The last thing we needed was Fido or Fluffy stumbling upon us.

Once we were well off the trail and hidden from view, as well as any curious off-leash dogs, I set the boxes of pastries down on a stump and started to unfasten my jeans.

"Whoa!" Omaera said, backing up. "Not happening, bro. If you brought me out here to force me into mating you, I will flash fry the contents of your skull and Maxar will burn you to dust with that magic black fire of his."

I paused and cocked my head to the side, shaking my head slightly. "I'm not going to force you to do anything. Ever. I want you to mate with me because you want to. Because you want *me*. But that means you need to get to know all of me."

Her brows narrowed, but she didn't back up anymore. "Okay . . ."

I finished unfastening my jeans and dropped them to the ground. I never wore boxers. I'd also grabbed shoes and socks when I snagged the jeans and shirt, so I ditched those too. Last was the open flannel shirt. I folded everything neatly and put it on the stump next to the pastry boxes, then stepped back and dropped to all fours.

Giving a happy little shake, because it felt so good when I shifted, I let my instincts take over. My face elongated into a snout, my teeth sharpened and descended, my spine, ligaments, and muscles lengthened, and fur sprouted from beneath my skin. It only took about a minute before I was fully in bear form.

I did another big, satisfying stretch, then faced Omaera. Her mouth was open and her eyes wide. I ambled over to her, and she backed up a little, fear in her green gaze.

My tongue flicked out toward her hand.

She reached out timidly, and I licked her fingers.

She giggled.

Such a lovely sound.

I did it again, and she grew bolder and reached out further to pet my head and scratch behind my ears. Her laughter was the most beautiful music I'd ever heard, and as she grew less afraid and scratched me rougher, I stepped closer. But I stepped a little too close and accidentally nudged her hard enough she fell backward on her butt.

I went to her, licking her face as an apology. Only she continued to laugh, looping her arms around my neck so I could haul her up. She sat up, but remained sitting on the cool, pine needle covered earth. I plunked my butt down beside her.

"Can you speak?" she asked.

I shook my head.

"But you understand me?"

I nodded.

"Which form do you prefer? Human or bear?"

A happy rumble tumbled out of my chest.

She laughed. "I suppose it's less frowned upon for bears to eat from a dumpster than humans. And you can run faster, don't need clothes, and it's completely expected and acceptable for you to be grumpy."

She hit the nail on the head.

"Your fur is so soft." She stroked my nose. "This part here is like velvet." I nuzzled her face, loving how affectionate I could be with her in my shifted form. I licked her cheek, and she giggled. "You're doing this because you can get away with it in bear form."

Damn, she was smart.

Her mouth dipped into a deep frown, and she nuzzled me back, closing her eyes. It felt good to be close to her like this. "I'm really sad, Zandren," she whispered, her words coming out quiet and hoarse.

I nuzzled her more.

"I'm also really angry. Delia is dead and all I want to do is find the people who killed her, and hurt them as much as I'm hurting now." Her sniffles tugged painfully at my heart and she wrapped both arms around me and cried terrible, wracking sobs into the fur of my neck. "I don't know who I am anymore."

I brought a big paw up and wrapped it around her, pulling her closer to me. She collapsed against my chest and continued to cry. I hated how good I felt right now when she was so broken. But having my mate trust me like this, having her turn to me for comfort, was a new kind of joy and pleasure I'd never felt before.

Lifting her head from my chest, she glanced up at me, wiping tears from her cheeks. "Are you purring? Do bears purr?"

I bobbed my gigantic head.

Indeed, bears did purr. Usually, it was cubs that purred when they were content after nursing, but adults could too, when they were just that happy.

And even though she was in pain, I was so happy to just be with her like this. To have her accept my bear form and wrap her arms around me, seeking solace.

Her smile was sweet and small. "It sounds like a muscle car idling."

I nudged her gently with my nose, still purring.

Her eyes widened. "If we mate . . . we don't have to do it with you in bear form, do we? Because you're a very handsome bear and all but . . ."

I chuckled inside, which came out like a choppy growl as I shook my head.

She relaxed and petted me again. "Phew. Because I'm cool with you being a shifter—words I never thought I'd say out loud, by the way—but it'd feel way too much like beastiality otherwise."

I snorted and dipped my head so she could better scratch behind my ears.

"Were you disappointed I wasn't a shifter?" she asked, locking eyes with me. The sincerity and worry in her moss-green eyes made me flick my tongue out and lick her salty, tear-covered cheeks. She giggled and swatted me away. "I'm being serious. Were you disappointed?"

I hesitated, which made her eyes widen, but then I shook my head. No, I wasn't disappointed. I was surprised, but one look at her, and I adjusted my expectations and dove head-first into whatever this new future was going to be. She was my mate, regardless of whether she was a bear, a shifter, a vampire, or a demon. But thank the gods, she wasn't a vampire.

I bent my head and nuzzled my snout beneath her chin. She pressed a kiss to the top of my nose. "This has really helped, thank you." Our gazes locked. "My heart hurts a little less, but it's still pretty broken." I moaned in empathy. I knew exactly how she felt. My heart shattered when my mother and sister died. And even though time had passed, and I was better, the pain of losing a parent never completely went away. I could only imagine her pain was compounded because Delia was the only parent she'd ever known.

We sat on the earth for a little longer, her tears falling with abandon on my fur. I let her hug me as hard as she needed. And when the emotions came back and thrashed her once more, she buried her face in my neck and screamed as loud as she could, her fingers tangled up tight in my fur. I didn't mind. I was a big bear and could handle it. If I could take away her pain completely, I would. I'd absorb it, or live with it myself for eternity as long as she was able to live freely without it.

I'm not sure how long we sat there, but I ignored the incessant rumbling of my stomach and let her get it out. I let her cry and scream and feel all the feelings. She tried so hard to be tough. To tell the world she didn't care, but deep down, she cared so much. She cared about her aunt. She cared about Gemma. She really was the perfectly cooked marshmallow ready for a s'more.

The sharp *caw* of a crow overhead pulled her attention. She'd stopped sobbing about fifteen minutes ago and just clung to me, softly weeping and sniffling. She lifted her head, her eyes red-rimmed and wet. I flicked my tongue out and licked her cheeks again, tasting her salty tears. She smiled and laughed through stuttered breaths. "We should get back. And you're probably starving."

I was.

But I didn't care. If she needed me to hold her for ten days and fast while doing it, I would.

"You can shift back if you want." She stood up from the ground and brushed the dirt off her sweatpants. "Thank you for showing me this side of you."

I licked the back of her hand and nuzzled her chest before stepping back and standing up on my hind legs. Slowly, my nose shrunk, my fur receded, and my spine straightened. My muscles, bones, and ligaments all returned to their human size and shape, and I was quickly back in my naked human form.

She blinked at me and smiled. "Now I get why you never want to wear clothes."

Grinning, I reached for my shirt and slid into it. "They're just so restrictive."

"If we mated, would our children be heirs to both the shifters, demons, and the entire realm?"

I loved that she was asking about children. I nodded. "Yes. Our cubs would not only be powerful shifter-demon hybrids—which is incredibly rare, and I'm assuming extremely powerful—but they'd also be heirs to two royal thrones."

"Cubs . . ." she mused. "They'd be like . . . baby bears."

"They would be."

"That's kind of crazy."

I pulled up my jeans and padded over to her on bare feet, feeling comfortable enough to rest my hands on her hips. "Crazy good though?"

"Would I give birth to them in bear form?

I shrugged. "I don't know. I don't think so though."

"Well, find out for me."

I chuckled, loving that she was even talking about us mating and having cubs. I still didn't like that she was saying *if* we mated, not *when* but she'd get there. I could feel our bond growing. Pressing a kiss to her forehead, I said, "I'll ask around." Then I went and grabbed my socks, shoes, and the boxes of pastries, opening up the top box and shoving a bear claw into my mouth, devouring the entire thing in one bite. "You want one?" I asked her with a full mouth.

She smirked and reached into the box, pulling out a powdered sugar donut. "I'm breaking my fast early." She took a bite, which caused powdered sugar to coat her lips and chin.

"Worth it though, right?"

Moaning, she rolled her eyes and nodded as she spoke with a full mouth like I did. "So worth it."

I ached to lick the sugar off her lips, but I wasn't sure we were there yet. We'd already made so many strides today. I needed to let her set the pace. She was grieving, and I didn't want to take advantage.

We headed back down the path we blazed until we hit the main trail, passing a few people jogging or pushing a baby stroller.

I held the boxes in one hand, but my hand closest to hers was free. I glanced down at where our hands swung in tandem. She noticed.

"What's up?" she asked.

"Can I hold your hand?"

Her smile was small and sweet but it made my entire body light up and come to life. She reached for my hand. "Yes."

Nothing could ruin how good my mood was right now. I was smiling like the biggest idiot, but I didn't care.

She giggled. "Your smile is a little creepy it's so big."

"Don't care," I said. "I'm just that happy."

A cold, minty scent wafted up my nostrils just as we turned a corner and Omaera said, "What the fuck is he doing here?"

Well, apparently there *was* something—*nay*, some*one*—that could ruin my mood. I growled as the vampire approached us.

"How'd he know where to find us?" she asked.

"He'll have followed your scent. It's as distinct as a fingerprint and as your mates, we're more in tuned to it."

Now it was her turn to growl. "Well, I don't like it."

Me fucking either.

Drak approached us. "Where have you been?" he demanded. "It's not safe for you to be out here. Not when someone wants you dead."

I glanced down at the idiot-stick dressed all in black on such a warm day. "She's with me, bozo. She's perfectly safe."

"I'm also a demon," Omaera hissed. "You need to back off the whole possessive protector thing. It's not a good look on you."

We all began to walk back toward the street. I handed the boxes to Drak, despite his look of severe displeasure when I did so. Then, for good measure, I reached into the top box and grabbed an old-fashioned glazed.

"King Howar has found you a new advisor," he went on, ignoring her comment.

"Whoopy," Omaera said with a big dramatic eyeroll, followed by an irritated look on her face. "I don't want one. I'll figure it out on my own."

Drak shook his head. "I don't recommend that. You got one lesson from—"

"A psycho killer, *qu'est-ce que c'est?*"

His brows bunched, as did mine.

She looked at us both like we lived under rocks. "The Talking Heads? Do you guys not know anything about pop culture? You're like a trillion years old."

"I don't watch television or listen to music much," Drak said. Neither did I, but I didn't need him thinking we had anything more in common or that we could bond over. Fuck him.

Snorting, I finished the old-fashion glazed, and reached across Omaera to stop Drak, open the box, and pull out a Boston Cream.

"That is why I suggested we *not* meet at your home this time," Drak said. "We meet in a neutral location so the advisor can't ambush you like—"

"The psycho killer did," she finished.

Something niggled at the back of my neck, but I waited until I swallowed my donut and the apartment was in sight. "I'm not sure how much we should advertise Omaera's hybrid status. What if this next advisor feels the same way Raewyn did, and she runs off and tells people? For all we know, Raewyn spilled the beans too."

Drak was quiet until we reached the front door of the apartment. "I will meet with them and vet them ahead of time then. You can hide around the corner and if I deem them trustworthy, you can come out of hiding."

Omaera used her key to open the door. "Or, you go and vet them, I stay home, then you call and let us know. *Or* we just don't meet with another advisor."

He was a pale motherfucker to begin with, but the mention of going without her made the bastard pale even more. What the hell was that about?

"I think it's best if we all go together," he said as we stepped onto the elevator.

"You're so fucking controlling," she said, shaking her head. "It's super annoying. And besides, Raewyn could smell my human side. So what's to say this one won't be any different?"

"That's right," I said plainly. "Maybe we need a mage instead of a demon?"

Drak made a noise of protest in his throat, but otherwise chose to remain quiet until we got back into the apartment.

"I'm going to go shower." Omaera glanced around the apartment. "Where's

Gemma?"

"At work," Maxar said, lounging on the couch with his phone.

"But she didn't start until ten."

His ruddy brows pinned together. "Yeah, and it's noon."

"Noon!" She spun around and faced me. "Did you know we were gone that long?"

I shook my head. Time ceased to exist, or matter, when I was in bear form. Add in the fact that I was in my happy place with my mate, and it felt like it stood still and I never wanted it to end.

She blinked a few times, coming to terms with how long we were gone. "Jeez, time just flew by." Her gaze softened when she looked at me. "But in a really great way."

I grinned like an idiot at her, puffing up my chest just enough for the other two to take notice. I could feel the heat of Maxar's envy, and the death-glare from Drak had me chuckling.

Yeah. Too bad, suckers. The key to this little demon's heart was compassion, patience, and a soft place to land. And I was going to give her all of those things and more because she was my mate, and I was head over paws, madly in love with her.

CHAPTER THIRTEEN

OMAERA

Even though my heart was in shambles, I felt a lot better when I climbed into the shower.

Zandren, in bear form, was a sight to behold.

He was massive, first of all. His paws were enormous, his claws long and sharp, and don't even get me started on those lethal canines of his. And yet, with me, he was a teddy bear. A Pooh Bear.

My Pooh Bear.

He let me cry into his fur, grip it until my knuckles ached, and scream into his neck so loudly that I'm sure people thought there was a murder happening in the woods.

He gave me exactly what I needed when I didn't even know I needed it.

And for some reason, breaking down while he was in bear form was easier than if he'd been in human form. I felt less . . . vulnerable. Even though he could understand me and would remember everything we discussed after he shifted, it just felt safer on my soul.

Then Drak showed up and ruined everything—the fucker.

What the hell was his problem?

Zandren and Maxar had no problem being away from me. But Drak threw a hissy fit whenever I mentioned the two of us being apart. Then he followed Zandren and me into the woods.

Talk about boundary issues.

He also looked worse than I'd ever seen him when he found us on the trail. Normally, he was a pasty-faced robot, and I didn't let his lack of color worry me too much. But when I saw him coming toward us, the man looked near death. That didn't stop me from being pissed off at him, of course. But my continued concern for him lingered on the fringes too. And the fear and concern for my whereabouts, that was clear as day in his mind. It hit me hard in the solar plexus, softening a lot of my ire.

I might joke about wanting him dead, but I didn't actually want the guy to die. Regardless of my general dislike of him, I still felt that infernal, magical pull toward him. It was why, despite what my spiteful brain told me to do—like *not* bring down a mug for his coffee—I did it anyway. Because as much as I fought it, I knew we were Fated Mates. My gut was never wrong, and my gut told me that these three weirdos were . . . mine.

The longer I spent with them, the stronger the pull. The stronger the attraction. I felt it more with Zandren than the other two, but I'm sure I'd feel it just as much with Maxar and Drak, eventually. Well, maybe not Drak, but probably Maxar.

I still wasn't totally on board with the whole bonding or claiming thing, but we'd cross that bridge once we found and dealt with Delia's killers. One thing at a time.

Still wrapped up in a towel after my shower, I sat down to pee and when I wiped, I saw red.

Oh, wonderful. My period was here.

It'd been inconsistent my entire life. I never knew when it was coming. Sometimes I was every twenty-nine days, then I'd go a lovely thirty-seven or forty between. Or, the universe would get drunk and forget, and make my cycle extra short—like twenty-one days. Stupid universe.

Just peachy keen jellybean.

Growling, I dug around under the bathroom sink for my menstrual disc. I'd pre-sanitized after my last period, so it was good to go. These little silicone things were a game changer. Better for the environment, safer than tampons, and they held more blood too.

After I washed my hands, I stepped out of the bathroom into my bedroom.

The loft was a peculiar layout. Even though there were only two bedrooms, there were also two bathrooms. But the one bathroom had two doors, each one opening to a bedroom. The other bathroom was just on its own off the hallway. Gemma and I usually just shared the joining bathroom, but it was nice to have two just in case we got food poisoning.

After I selected my clothes for the day—denim cutoffs, and a black metal-band T-shirt cut into a crop top and that slid off my shoulder. I decided I wanted to let my skin breathe and went makeup free. My hair would take a while to dry if I stayed inside, but if I went out—like I intended to—it would be dry in no time.

I opened my bedroom door to hear the three men arguing.

Ugh! I rolled my eyes and went to the coffeemaker to brew a new batch, since the stuff in the carafe was cold.

As soon as I stepped into the kitchen, Drak stopped what he was doing—which was arguing like a pretentious ass with Zandren—and stood up. "What is going on?"

"I'm making coffee? Would you like some, Bat Boy?"

"No."

"No, *thank you*. For a snooty aristocrat, your manners are trash."

He walked toward me, a feral look in his eyes I'd never seen before. His fangs descended. I backed up until my ass hit the fridge. He crowded me.

Fear ran icy through me and I glanced around his broad frame to see Zandren and Maxar already up off the couch, approaching.

"Wh-what's going on?" I stammered

"He's like possessed or something," Maxar said.

"You're bleeding," Drak said, closing his eyes and taking a deep inhale just inches from my face.

"No, I'm not." I lifted my hands and placed them on his chest—he was cool to the touch—and pushed him away. He didn't budge. "Drak. Move."

He moved all right, but he didn't back up. He dropped to a crouch and pressed his nose to the "V" of my shorts. "You're bleeding here."

Well, that earned him a knee in the face and a kick to the chest. He landed on his ass in the kitchen and I rushed to get away. "You're fucking sick. What the hell is wrong with you?"

He was quick to get back up on his feet, blinking. "I . . . I don't know."

Was he out of the trance now? What the hell was going on?

"Wait a minute," Zandren said. "Are you bleeding?"

"I just got my period, but I don't really call that *bleeding*. I mean, yeah, it is, but it's not like an injury. It just happens once a month, not a big deal."

"But I think it is," Zandren said cautiously. "When a female shifter—a mate—goes into estrus, male shifters lose their minds. All rational thought disappears. Even if we haven't sealed the Mating Bond. If they're mates, they go bonkers. Luckily, females only go into estrus every few years and even then, pregnancy can be rare. It's a way to keep the species from booming."

"So you think because Drak is a vampire, it's the opposite for vampires?" Maxar asked. "He's going bonkers while she's on her period?" He wrinkled his nose. "That's nuts."

Zandren shrugged. "Do you have a better explanation?"

Already, Drak was staring at me again with that savage, lustful look in his eyes. But it wasn't a look that said he wanted to kill me and eat me. It was a look that said he wanted to *eat* me, like in the clit-sucking, orgasm-causing kind of way.

I backed up even more, making my way toward my bedroom. "So what the hell do we do? Chain him to a chair for five to seven days? If he gets free, what's he going to do to me?"

"I make a habit of *not* fraternizing with vampires," Zandren said. "I don't know."

"Me either," Maxar said with disdain. "Freaky blood suckers."

"Not helping," I cried as Drak prowled toward me. Zandren, noticing the fear in my eyes, leaped into action and looped his arms through Drak from behind, restraining him and keeping him in place. But Drak bared his teeth and hissed at Zandren. Then some crazy super-human strength came over him and he tore free of Zandren's grasp by flipping Zandren over his head and onto his back on the floor.

"*Oof*," Zandren said before growling and flipping back to his feet. "What the fuck?"

Maxar quickly conjured a yellow lasso of fire and whipped it around Drak's midsection and arms. He tugged hard, keeping Drak from coming after me. "Omaera, get into your room," he shouted. "Now."

Wide-eyed and terrified, but also intrigued by all of this, I scrambled to open my bedroom door and ran inside, slamming and locking the door. Not that I thought a simple lock would keep a centuries' old vampire from getting in and devouring me if he wanted to.

Grunts and gnashing teeth echoed from the living room as Zandren and Maxar struggled to restrain Drak. What would it take to keep him from coming after me? And if he did get me, what would he do?

Was I just supposed to stay holed up in my room all day? For the next five to seven days? How was this going to work? Couldn't he take a pill or something? If I gave in and let him . . . do what his instincts were telling him to do, would that satiate him? Or would it give him a taste and he'd become more crazed than ever?

Also, how come he had no idea what was happening to him? Did vampires not talk about this with each other? Or was it because I was human?

I had way too many questions, and the three men in my living room could answer zero of them. I needed to find a vampire, a female vampire, and see if she could provide me with some clarity.

There was a Vampire King, right?

Did that mean there was a Vampire Queen? Just because my father—the Demon King—didn't have a mate didn't mean other kings didn't have mates.

I poked my head out the door to see Drak sitting on the kitchen barstool, wrapped in yards and yards of flaming, yellow rope. He struggled against his restraints and gnashed his teeth at Zandren and Maxar. His fangs descended, blue eyes wild.

He discovered me watching, and his pupils dilated, darkening the cobalt of his irises to almost black. His nostrils flared and a primal, savage need took over his angular features. I was . . . mesmerized.

I couldn't look away and a big part of me wanted to give myself to him. To allow him to . . . do what his baser instincts told him to do.

"Omaera," Maxar barked, noticing me. "Back in your room."

"Is there a Vampire Queen?" I asked.

"Yes, Queen Calliope. Why?" Zandren asked.

"Because I want to talk to her. To find out what this *is* exactly. If I'm safe."

Zandren and Maxar exchanged looks for a moment, then eventually Maxar nodded and dug out his phone. He punched in a few things before walking over and handing it to me. "Here."

"You have the Queen on speed dial?" I asked, loathing the streak of jealousy that whipped through me.

"Not the Queen, but this will get you through to her. I had a brief, albeit passionate, dalliance with one of her handmaidens."

More hot jealousy tore through my body.

He smirked. "It was centuries ago. My heart and cock belong only to you now, my Queen."

Glaring at him, and hating that he knew I was jealous, I snatched the phone from his hand and closed my bedroom door.

I hit dial on the number.

It rang four times before someone finally answered.

"Maxar Rane, it's been nearly two hundred years. What a surprise." Her voice was like a kitten's purr and I wanted to rip off her ears and shove them up her butt so she could hear me kicking her ass.

"I'd like to speak with Queen Calliope, please."

She huffed a small laugh. "May I ask who is speaking? Not just anybody gets to speak with the Queen."

"Please tell her that it is Omaera Playfair, Queen of the Realm and daughter of the late Donovar . . ." Shit, what was my father's last name?

Thankfully, I didn't have to figure that out because this handmaiden was tripping over her words to apologize. "Your Majesty. I'm terribly sorry. Yes, one moment. Oh, I'm so sorry."

I smirked. Yeah, that's right. You apologize.

"Hello?" came a much more refined and gentle voice a moment later. "Queen Omaera?"

"Yes. Hello, Your Majesty."

"It is I who should be addressing you as 'Your Majesty'."

"How about you just call me 'Omaera'?"

She laughed softly, the way you would expect a queen to laugh. "And you can call me 'Callie'. How can I help you, Omaera?"

I wandered over to my bed and sat on the end of it, glancing at myself in the full-length mirror on the wall beside my dresser. Exhaling a long sigh, I said, "Do you get your period?"

She was silent for a moment. "Uh-oh."

"I take it you know what's happened?"

"I can guess."

"So you do get your period?"

"Well . . . vampires only get their periods every few years. Much like shifters who only go into heat or estrus every few years, vampires are the same."

"Wait, so you get pregnant *on* your period?"

She made a noise of agreement. "It is the only time a vampire is fertile."

"Sooooo . . . that sends the vampire males into—"

"A psychotic, horny frenzy."

I laughed at her candidness. It was refreshing.

Her laugh was more like a bird's titter. "How do you cope with the bleeding?"

"Like the other four billion women, or whatever, on the planet. With wine, chocolate, a heating pad, Advil, and pimple patches."

"And estrus? How do you deal with that?"

"I mean, I just deal with it. I've been ovulating and menstruating since I was twelve. I'm kind of just used to it. It's crampy once in a while, but not as bad as when I have my period." My eyes went wide. "Wait, does that mean Zandren's going to go batshit bananas when I ovulate?"

"Oh! That's right, you have three mates. Have you mate-bonded with all of them?"

"I've mate-bonded with none of them. I met them like two days ago and things have been rather busy since then. I'm also not in the habit of committing myself to a complete stranger—let alone three—for eternity. Trust issues and all."

"How is Drak?" she asked.

"Psychotic. Feral. A pompous ass with boundary issues who keeps looking at me like a piece of meat he either wants to eat or fuck. If he gets out of his restraints and gets to me, what will happen?"

"He will try to tear off your clothes and mate with you."

"Like rape me?"

"No. There is still a level of humanity within him, though it's very thin. He will just become relentless. When you looked at him, did you not feel different too?"

Now it was my turn to be quiet.

"You did, didn't you? That's how it doesn't turn into rape. It's like he casts a spell on you and you will willingly submit—and enjoy it. And want more of it. You'll want it nearly as badly as he does. You'll let him take you."

Heat pooled in my belly and, if I'm being honest, between my legs.

"After I . . . let him take me, will his desire end?"

"Umm ... more like it will become an unbearable, all-consuming need for both of you. You'll want to lock yourselves in a bedroom for the whole time and not leave for anything. It's actually ..." she sighed, "It's actually really wonderful."

"You mean this is going to happen for all five to seven days every month? Look, I love sex as much as the next sexually liberated woman, but that's ridiculous."

"You bleed every month?"

"Yes?" She was missing the point. I didn't want to be locked up and boned to within an inch of my life once a month for nearly a week. Even if I did enjoy it. And if the same thing was going to happen with Zandren, then that was a large chunk of my life devoted to non-stop magical feral fucking.

"Is that typical for demons?" she asked. "To bleed monthly?"

"I have no idea, but it's typical for humans. You *do* know that my birth mother was human, right? I'm a hybrid."

Fresh silence, and this time, tense as a warren full of rabbits with a fox scrabbling at the front door stretched between us.

"No," she finally whispered. "I did not know you were a hybrid" Calliope's tone was different now. Reserved and a lot less open and friendly.

Did I say something wrong? Was she like that demon I killed yesterday and racist against humans? Worry dripped down the back of my spine like a popsicle melting in the sun. "Callie, is there something wrong?" I asked, nervous as hell.

"It will happen every time you bleed. Once he gets a taste, it won't decrease his appetite. I have to go. Good luck. It was nice to meet you." Then the call disconnected.

I stared at the phone for a moment, my stomach spinning as my pulse picked up tempo in my temples and my mind raced. What did I just do?

Not even thinking about the fact that a horny and possessed Drak was out in my living room, I opened my bedroom door and stepped out. "Did you not tell King Howar that I'm hybrid?" I asked, directing my question to a wild-eyed Drak.

Zandren and Maxar pivoted to me, fear on their faces.

"Did you tell the Queen that you're half human?" Zandren asked panic in his honey-brown eyes.

"Yeah. I thought the other royals knew. Wait, are they racist too?"

Zandren glanced at Maxar, then they both looked at Drak.

The vampire shook his head. "I haven't told anyone. Not even the King."

"So the other royals *are* racist?" I blurted out.

"We don't know. But it's best to be cautious," Maxar said. "Why do you think Queen Calliope went weird after you told her you are half human?"

"She couldn't believe that I bleed every month and asked if that was normal for demons. I told her I have no idea, but it's normal for humans. Then she went quiet and tense, and she couldn't wait to get off the phone with me."

"Oh fuck," Maxar breathed.

"You can't tell anyone else," Zandren said. "Nobody. This has never happened before and we don't know how the Realm is going to react." He went pink in the cheeks. "I have told my father, but I let it be known that if he told a soul, I'd kill him."

My eyes bugged out. "You threatened to kill your father? To kill the King?"

He shrugged, then looked at me like I'd lost my damned mind. "You are my mate, Little One. Nobody else matters now. If anybody touches you, tries to hurt you, I will kill them."

Maxar nodded. "Same here. Nobody else matters anymore, my Queen. You are all that matters to me now. You and any children we may have in the future."

My jaw went slack. I glanced at Drak whose nostrils flared like a bull in the pen ready for the rodeo. His eyes remained fixed on mine, but he nodded in agreement with them.

A tremor of something very strange jangled through me. I knew that Delia and Gemma loved me. That they would jump in front of a train for me. And I would do the same for them.

But to have these men, these strangers vow to kill for me, was oddly beautiful and only drew me to them more. Zandren threatened, and promised, to kill his own father.

"Isn't there some kind of sedative we can give him?" I asked. "Maybe Mr. Fiddleman has one?"

"That's not a bad idea," Zandren said. He glanced at Maxar. "Omaera and I will go visit the apothecary. You stay here with fangs, since your flame ropes are all that are keeping him from tearing us apart to get to Omaera."

Maxar nodded, and Zandren and I headed for the front door.

Drak let out a grunt scream at a surprisingly low register. It also sounded like he was in pain.

I went back into the living room and stepped closer to him.

"Careful," Maxar said. "His strength right now is insane. I'm not sure if my ropes will hold him if you get too close."

"Are you in pain right now?" I asked Drak.

His eyes, although feral, softened as I got closer. He strained against his restraints. "Not right now," he said, his voice hoarse. "But—" He stopped and shook his head. "No."

"What were you going to say?"

He shook his head again, his nostrils still flaring wildly. "Go. I know you don't want me. So go."

I blinked a few times, studying his face and the warring emotions in his eyes. The sincerity behind his last statement combined with that animalistic desire to mate with me. To claim me.

Crap! I'd forgot to ask Calliope if the first time Drak and I had sex it would mean we mated and bonded. If we did it on my period, would that expedite things? I had so many questions and she went and ended the call so abruptly that I didn't have time to ask them all. Now I wasn't even sure if she'd take my call if I tried again.

"We should go," Zandren said from the front door.

Nodding, I joined him and we left, although I felt kind of shitty about abandoning Drak when he was clearly in a lot of pain, even if he refused to admit it.

Zandren and I made it to Fiddleman's in decent time, and the bell chimed sweetly when we opened the door. There were a few people in there, perusing the aisles with baskets full of various herbs and other paranormal paraphernalia, but when Mr. Fiddleman saw us, his eyes lit up. I couldn't tell if it was because he was happy to see us, or worried about what more terrible news we had to deliver in person.

I waited until he was finished with the customer at his counter before stepping forward. "Your Majesty," he said, with a small head bow.

I shook my head. "Omaera, please, Mr. Fiddleman."

He nodded. "I haven't been back to Delia's yet. I planned to go this evening after work though. Yesterday took a lot out of me. My apologies."

"No need to apologize. Please. It took a lot out of everyone."

"How can I help you?" he asked.

I glanced at Zandren before meeting Mr. Fiddleman's piercing blue gaze. "We need to sedate Drak."

The older man nodded. "Okay. May I ask why?"

"She's bleeding," Zandren said. "And he looks wilder than I do when I shift."

Understanding dawned in the spellcaster's eyes, and he nodded. "Ah, I see."

"And humans bleed like this every month, unlike bears and vampires who are fortunate enough to only bleed every few years." I rolled my eyes. "Immortal and they only get PMS and cramping every couple of years. Jesus, how come I didn't get that part passed down from my father?"

"I can compound a pill that will help reduce his drive. But it only lasts for six to eight hours, then will need to be administered again. It will sedate him somewhat, but not completely. Is he locked up right now?"

"Maxar has him restrained," Zandren said. "But the vampire's strength is out of this world at the moment."

The mage's head bobbed. "Yes, it would be."

"But you can help us help Drak?" I asked.

"Yes. Yes, of course. Just give me a moment and I'll put together the spell and convert it into a compounded capsule. Shouldn't take more than ten minutes."

I exhaled in relief. "Thank you."

His smile was small, but kind before he turned around and began pulling various things in jars off his wall of shelves.

Zandren's large hand gripped my elbow gently, and he tugged me away from the counter so we could whisper in the corner without any other patrons hearing. "You need to keep your hybrid status quiet," he said, his voice low. "In fact, I think we need to keep you being the Queen quiet all together."

I narrowed my gaze at him.

His expression softened. "It's for your own safety. I don't care that you're half human. You could be half demon, half hyena, and I'd still be madly in love with you and want to mate with you and have weird looking cubs with you."

I was unable to hide my snort of a laugh.

The corner of his mouth jerked upward just a touch. "But others might not think that way. Others like Raewyn. There is a lot of hatred toward humans in the Realm. A lot. Over the centuries—hell, over the millennia—various kings have tried to cull the human race. But there have always been enough people with common sense who stop them. It hasn't changed though. There are those who think the human race is weak, unevolved, and should have expired long ago. And the idea of having one of them as our Queen will sit poorly with many." His soft brown gaze shifted around the shop, seeing easily over the shelves that made up the aisles to watch the other customers. I couldn't see the customers, but Zandren's expression was wary and his nose sniffed the air, picking up everyone's scents.

"Do you hate humans?" I asked.

His nose wrinkled for a moment. Then he shook his head. "I hate *people*."

I smiled at that. "I hate people too."

His triumphant grin was adorable. "Just another thing we have in common."

That made me smile even wider.

"You know how some people are cat people, and some are dog people?"

I nodded. "I'm not a cat person. It's probably because growing up in Aunt Delia's house, cats terrorized the neighborhood at night. They would fight right below my bedroom window."

He nodded. "Yeah, as much as I don't really care for wolf shifters, non-shifter canines are quite lovely. Very devoted. I'm definitely a dog person."

"Me too."

"The same is for humans. I'm not a human person. Do I want to see cats—or people—eradicated from earth? No. But I wouldn't want one as a pet. Nor would I set out to befriend any. I'm sure there are decent cats out there. Just like there is the odd, decent human—like Gemma. But like ticks, you just never know which one is carrying Lyme disease. So it's better to avoid them all."

"That's a pretty great analogy."

He beamed at my praise, then affectionately cupped my cheek. "We need to protect your human side though. So no more telling anyone about it, okay? We don't know who we can trust."

"Okay," I whispered. "I won't tell any more people that I'm a hybrid. But people like Raewyn, demons will be able to smell it, right?"

He shrugged. "Perhaps. Maybe some shifters and demons will, yes. But we just need to get a handle on your powers and figure out who killed your aunt. Then we can meet with the Council and gauge their reaction."

"How did your father take it? Obviously not well if you had to threaten to kill him?"

Now, he really smiled, and damn if it didn't steal the oxygen straight out of my lungs. "He was so thrilled."

"Seriously?"

"When I told him I was struck by lightning. . . I haven't heard him that excited in over a century. Not since before my mother and sister passed. He's excited about grandcubs."

"I'm sorry. Grandcubs?"

His smile turned boyish. "You've brought up cubs, so . . . he's just excited. No pressure though."

I swallowed. "He's agreed not to tell anyone that I'm . . . you know . . . an abomination?"

He snarled when I said the word, and my heart swelled for this oversized teddy bear. "He knows the strength of the Mate's Bond and how, if anything were to happen to you, I'd tear through an entire army to save and avenge you. It's how he was with my mother. The Bond is deep and strong, and we all know it. The smile and understanding in his voice reassured me that he knows the consequences of a betrayal like that. And he accepts it."

I blinked again. "That's heavy."

With a casual headshake, he frowned. "Not really."

"Can I ask . . . are there same-sex mates? Is the Realm progressive? Are the Fates progressive?"

That made him smile even wider, and I had to reach out and grip a shelf to keep from swooning.

"There are. Yes. The Fates are progressive. They know that they can't force someone to love or bond with just anyone. Our mates are carefully selected. It's why sometimes it takes centuries."

"H-how does it work to have offspring then?"

"We can still procreate when we're not bonded. It's just less likely. So they have to find unbonded donors and cross their fingers. It doesn't happen often, but it does happen, and some of the pregnancies, or surrogacies, take. Otherwise, there is adoption. Again, not common, but it happens. I know a bear shifter couple, two wonderful men, and they adopted a wolf-shifter pup whose parents were both killed by human hunters. She is the light of their life, even if she drives them nuts with her midnight howling."

I giggled. "I'm glad that the Fates are mindful of all kinds of love. I'm still struggling to understand why they thought giving me *three* mates was a good idea though."

"Me too," he grumbled, wrapping an arm around my shoulder and pulling me into his warm, honey-scented embrace. He pressed a kiss to the top of my head.

I glanced up at him, foreign feelings swirling inside of me. Warmth filled my chest and cheeks.

"You're seriously the most beautiful woman I've ever met," he said softly. "And I'm two hundred and thirty-six years old. I've met a lot of women." His smirk was playful and boyish again.

"What were you doing when the lightning hit you?" I asked, getting so wonderfully lost in his soulful eyes. Even though he was in human form right now, I could *see* the bear in him. His eyes didn't change when he shifted, and I liked that.

I wasn't expecting him to go pink in the cheeks from my question, so that just piqued my interest like crazy. He cleared his throat and broke eye contact.

Oh, now I *had* to know.

"What were you doing, Zandren?" I asked mostly serious, but also playful.

"I um . . ." His lips twisted. He still couldn't look at me.

My eyes widened as the lightbulb flicked on. I grinned even though a tight cord of jealousy wrapped around my heart and squeezed. "You were in bed with someone?"

All I got was some sheepish side-eye.

"It's okay, you know? You can tell me. We weren't mates at the time. I never assumed any of you were virgins, and I sure as hell hope you're not expecting me to be." I stared at him until he faced me properly again. "What happened exactly? I'm curious to know how it affected you."

I didn't think his cheeks could get any pinker, but they did. "I went soft," he grumbled. "I'll never be able to get hard for another woman now." There didn't seem to be any regret or frustration with that. All I could sense from him was embarrassment. And as much as that cord of jealousy cinched tightly around my heart, I knew he had no reason to be embarrassed and no way on earth would I ever get upset.

"You were inside her?" I squeaked.

He groaned. "I . . . yeah. Then her cat—fuck, I hate cats—freaked out from the lightning, jumped on my back and I accidentally bucked forward so hard that her head went through the drywall and into the next room." He dropped his head in shame. "It was not my proudest moment."

I burst out laughing and pressed my hand to his hard, well-defined chest. "Oh, Pooh Bear."

More side-eye. "You're not mad?"

"Mad? God, no. We were not fated at the time, but to maintain this vein of honesty, I'll admit to feeling jealous hearing that you were with another woman, even though I have no right to feel that way."

Pride surged through him and he puffed up his chest and grinned down at me. "Jealous? Really?"

Now it was my turn for the side-eye. "That wasn't meant to be an ego stroke."

"Too bad. I'm taking it as one."

I rolled my eyes. "Was she okay after you threw her into the wall?"

"I didn't *throw* her. And to be fair, from a carpenter's standpoint, the walls were as thin as freaking paper and weak. I helped free her, made sure she was of sound mind, then I left."

"You left her without taking her to the hospital?"

"I caught your scent and had to go."

"Zandren."

He was looking sheepish again and glanced up at me from a bowed head with adorable puppy dog eyes. "I just had to get to you."

I exhaled. How could I fault him that badly?

I couldn't.

"Ready," Mr. Fiddleman announced from behind the counter.

I tossed Zandren some more side-eye, but this time it was cheeky and he smiled back as we wandered toward the counter.

"You'll want him to take one capsule four times a day. They last roughly five hours, and if you don't want him to start to go feral again, you'll want to make sure he stays up on his doses. Nothing fancy about them. Take with water, or not. They should start to work within thirty minutes. It won't completely stop his . . . um *desires*, but it will damper them down significantly. You may not need to restrain him, but rather just keep an eye on him. Don't let him be alone with Omaera." He said that last part to Zandren.

Zandren nodded. "I try not to anyway. I hate vampires."

Mr. Fiddleman grunted. "Yes, well, they are an interesting and serious lot, aren't they?"

"Among other things," Zandren said mostly under his breath.

"How many pills are here, Mr. Fiddleman?" I asked.

"Enough for two months' worth, Your Majesty."

"Omaera," I insisted. "Please, call me Omaera."

He stared at me, blinking. "I'll try."

"I so appreciate you doing this," I said, turning my shoulder bag over so that the pouch was right in front of me and I could dig out my wallet. "How much do I owe you?"

The apothecary held up his hand, his gray-blue eyes going wide. "Oh no. I can't charge the Queen. I . . . I could never."

Huffing through my nose, I paused. "Mr. Fiddleman . . ."

He chewed on his lip, then sighed. "When I was at Delia's yesterday, I noticed a small ulu knife in her kitchen. It's the sharpest I've ever seen and in pristine condition. I understand if you say no, but—"

"It's yours," I said. "I have no use for it. Please. If that is what you will accept as payment, then by all means, when you return tonight, take the ulu knife. I think she'd be thrilled to know another spellcaster was making use of it."

He smiled. "Thank you, Your Maj—Omaera." With his long fingers, he slid the brown glass pill bottle across the worn wooden counter to me. "I'll be sure to have more ready for you in two months' time. I have to make small batches as they only have a sixty-day shelf-life."

"I appreciate it."

"And I will make sure to let you know what I uncover at Delia's tonight."

"Again, I so appreciate it."

Zandren leaned forward, fixing the old mage with a serious look. "We also appreciate your discretion regarding Omaera's lineage. At least on her mother's side."

Mr. Fiddleman's eyes widened. "Y-yes. Y-yes, of course. I would n-never breathe a word to anyone. Delia was . . . she meant a great deal to me. I would never do anything to hurt her, or you. Ever. Your secrets are all safe with me."

Zandren nodded. "Good. Then we have nothing to worry about."

Mr. Fiddleman's gaze found mine. "Good luck, Your Maj—Omaera."

I smiled and winked at him. "Thank you, Mr. Fiddleman. We'll chat again, soon." We took a half-step toward the door before I spun around. "There's no magic spell, or pill, or spray, or something that can mask my . . . *other* side, is there? My mother's lineage, I mean?"

It took the old mage a moment to understand what I meant, then his gaze flared before he shook his head and frowned. "Before you . . . *took the throne*," he whispered, "Yes. But not now. No magic performed by me would be strong enough to mask the magic of the Fates. I'm sorry."

I matched his frown. "I had a feeling you were going to say something like that. Thanks anyway."

We bid him farewell once more, then Zandren and I left with our bottle of pills intended to keep Drak from turning into a horny vampire bat.

Though, if I was being perfectly honest, I was kind of intrigued and turned on by the idea of Mr. Super Serious with a stick up his ass, losing his composure and turning into a rabid beast. A small part of me wanted to poke the monster and see what would happen. But a bigger part of me—the smart part of me, not the horny part—knew I needed to give him a wide berth and stay the course.

I needed to figure out who killed my aunt, kill them, and get a handle on my powers.

Easy peasy.

All while keeping a safe distance from the insufferable, sexy vampire who wanted to devour me like a Sunday dinner.

Again, easy peasy for the Queen of the Realm, right?

CHAPTER FOURTEEN

OMAERA

We arrived back at the apartment, and I scuttled off to my bedroom so Zandren and Maxar could give Drak the capsule. Then they waited the appropriate thirty minutes before Zandren knocked on my door. "I think it's safe to come out now."

I nodded and glanced at my phone. Gemma would be home soon.

Stepping into the living room, I glanced at Drak, who was still restrained and sitting on the barstool, wrapped up in flaming rope by the sliding glass door.

I still hadn't had any coffee today and was seriously feeling the caffeine deprivation.

"Here," Zandren said, wandering into the kitchen. "I just made you a fresh batch, since I know we keep pulling you away from your coffee." He poured a healthy amount into a green and tan hand-thrown mug that said, "I'm not a bitch, I just don't like you." Smirking after reading it, he went to the fridge. "Oat milk, right?"

I nodded, all tingly with joy from the simple, yet wonderful, fact that some-one was in my kitchen making me coffee. And that he knew I took oat milk. I'd only had coffee in front of him once. How did he remember?

He poured the perfect amount of creamy oat milk into the coffee, then handed me the mug with the handle out. I gripped it with both hands and leaned against the counter, letting the steam and incredible chocolatey scent of the dark roast fill my nostrils. "Thank you," I said softly. "I really needed this."

His smile was all kinds of youthful and sexy, reminding me more of a teddy bear than a ferocious grizzly. "I know."

My gaze pivoted to Drak, whose nostrils no longer flared like an agitated bull's. "How are you feeling over there, Fangs?"

His gaze was level, irritated, and arrogant. So, normal for him. "Better," he said cooly. "Thank you for going to Fiddleman."

"You're welcome."

Uncertainty creased his face for a moment. "I apologize for my . . . less than civilized behavior earlier. For dropping to my knees and—"

"Apology accepted. Don't mention *that* again, please."

The flush of color to his cheeks was subtle, but noticeable, and he averted his gaze. "Noted."

I hope she's not afraid of me now. I hope she can forgive me. Drak's voice and words drove hard and fast into my mind, and I nearly dropped my mug as my head snapped up and I stared at him.

"What?" he asked, with a knitted brow.

"Did you just . . . did you say something?"

"I said '*noted*.'"

"But nothing else?"

"No."

I wish she could see how badly we need to mate. How mating would help all of this.

"There it is again. You're talking."

He shook his head. "No. I'm not."

I was hearing his fears. Much like I'd heard them when he found Zandren and me in the woods.

"I'm hungry," Zandren said.

"You're always hungry," Maxar countered.

"Yeah. So?"

The front door opened and Gemma walked in, looking as beautiful as ever, despite the events of last night and Raewyn nearly killing her. Guilt still gnawed at my gut with serrated teeth over what nearly happened. And it happened because she was with me. She was my best friend, my roommate, my sister. As much as I didn't want to leave her, maybe it was for the best? At least until I got a handle on my powers and could better protect her.

"What's going on with The Count over there?" Gemma asked, referring to the fire ropes wrapped around Drak. "Did he misbehave and now he's in a magical timeout?"

"You could say that," I murmured, still a little shaken from hearing Drak's thoughts.

Gemma set down her purse and a fabric shopping bag on the counter. She came to me and rubbed my back. "How are you doing?"

I exhaled and leaned my head against hers. "Been better. I'll admit that much. But more importantly, how are you after last night?"

She wrinkled her nose. "I woke up with a migraine."

"Shit."

"But I took some Tylenol and drank a lot of water. Then more water, then took some electrolytes, and even though it's better, the headache is still there."

"Go lay down then. I hate that this happened to you."

She nodded, appearing more exhausted and in pain than when she initially walked in. "I stopped and bought your favorite gelato on my way home. Don't let it melt. Put it in the freezer." She pointed at the shopping bag.

"You're the best," I said, kissing her on the temple before shooing her off to her room.

I followed her and helped her climb into bed. Then I brought her more Tylenol and Advil too, along with some water, and waited until she took the pills. I closed the blinds in her room, grabbed her some earplugs and once she was all tucked into bed, I kissed her forehead and left.

I was nearly at the door when I heard her voice.

I hope I'm okay. I really hope this isn't a sign of my brain slowly bleeding and killing me. I don't want to lose Omaera. I don't want to lose her to those men. To lose her, or die. I don't want to feel like this. I'm scared.

I rushed back to her side. "You're not going to lose me. You're going to be okay."

She stirred. "Hmm?"

Oh, god. I was hearing her fears just like I'd heard Drak's.

I kissed her head again, then slowly left, sicker than ever that my best friend was so scared and all because of me.

The shopping bag was empty when I returned to the kitchen. "Who touched the gelato?" I asked, regretting my accusatory tone.

"I put it in the freezer," Zandren said. "So it didn't melt." He got up from his spot on the couch and approached me, picking up the mug of coffee and handing it to me. "Drink this. It was made with love."

Smirking, I took a sip. Goddammit, it was good. Closing my eyes, I moaned. "Fuck."

The same purring sound as when we were in the woods together rumbled, and I opened my eyes to find Zandren staring down at me, grinning. "You take care of everyone else. Let someone take care of you."

My smile was small and fake as I nodded at him. "I'll try."

"Maxar went out to get dinner. He needed a break from babysitting. But I need you to keep me company so I don't haul off and murder the vampire here. He's making it difficult not to just bite his head off."

"I haven't said a word to you, *shifter*," Drak said with his educated, arrogant tone.

"Yeah, but your face is saying so many things," Zandren countered.

I rolled my eyes. "All right. That's enough." I took another sip of my coffee and moaned again.

"That's the best sound in the world, Little One," Zandren murmured. "At least so far. I'm guessing the noises you make during sex are even better."

My cheeks caught fire, and I glanced anywhere and everywhere but at the big bear staring at me. I cleared my throat. "I um . . . how about we work on some mind power stuff?"

Zandren snickered. "Sure. What did you have in mind?"

"I want to try to infiltrate your thoughts and manipulate you. I also want Drak to piss me off—"

"So you can murder me while I am restrained?" the vampire asked with a scoff.

"No. So I can *not* murder you. I need to practice. So . . . piss me off, Blood Boy."

Gemma slept through dinner.

I checked on her several times, even woke her up to see how she was feeling. She said her head felt better, but she was tired and felt the headache on the fringes. She just wanted to sleep. I put more Tylenol and Advil on her night-stand, along with water and a granola bar, before letting her be for the night.

Maxar went and picked up falafel and shawarma for everyone. So we dined on delicious Middle Eastern cuisine. I locked myself in my room, and Zandren and Maxar released Drak from his restraints long enough for him to eat and use the bathroom.

I waited up for a while, hoping Mr. Fiddleman would call Maxar to let him know any new spells he discovered at my aunt's. But we heard nothing.

I practiced a lot on all three of them. Sending thoughts of persuasion and manipulation into their minds. Nothing nefarious. Though I did *persuade* Drak to bok like a chicken, which was pretty hilarious. He didn't think it was funny, but I didn't care.

True to form, the vampire did a good job pissing me off with just his words and face, but I managed to compartmentalize my rage, shove it in a box, and keep from making his nose bleed or brain hemorrhage. We called that a win.

Maxar took the couch and Zandren asked how we would all feel if he shifted and slept on the balcony. He also asked that we leave the sliding glass door open slightly so he could still hear the coming and going of the house.

We obliged.

Once I was safely locked away in my room again, they released Drak from his restraints, only to tether him to the leg of the love seat so he could sleep reclined, but not get very far.

I waited until midnight when I knew everyone would be asleep before I slipped into a pair of dark jeans, the same crop top as earlier that day, and my black leather jacket. I yanked on my combat boots and let my hair do its thing. Then, like a starved mouse willing to risk the trap to get the cheese, I tiptoed as quiet as ever, opened my bedroom door, and crept across the apartment to the front door.

Nobody in the living room stirred.

I didn't even look in the direction of the couches as I slipped out the front door. Then I took the stairs and was as silent as could be when I burst into the night, free as a bird.

Even though Zandren and I went to the woods that morning, I was feeling so smothered by these mates. They barely knew me and yet, they wouldn't let me be.

I knew there was love there. Zandren said as much. And maybe that's because they felt it the moment the lightning struck, but I was still getting to know them. I was still making sense of everything. Of my role as Queen, of the fact that my father was a demon—the King—my mother was a human, and my aunt was a mage. A dead mage, no less. I was working through my grief as best I could, but it didn't seem like there was any time for that. I could crumble later.

Right now, I had to figure out how to be Queen, how to be a demon, and find the two men who killed Delia.

But for just a few hours, I needed to go back to a time before I was hit by lightning. Before three gorgeous men knocked on my door asking me for forever.

I had my bear spray clutched tight in my palm, a switchblade in the other. Not to mention, I was armed with the demon power of deep-frying brains. I was safe.

Keeping a keen eye out around me, I headed for the bus stop. Even though the subway would be faster, dangerous things happened in tunnels and stairwells. I was already being stupid leaving; I didn't need to be doubly stupid.

Whatever. I could *be* stupid. Twenty-two-year-olds were stupid. My prefrontal cortex wasn't even fully developed. And right now, after everything that happened in the last three days, I deserved not only some time by myself to do what I wanted to do, but I deserved a break from all things magical. I just wanted to go back to a time before shit hit the fan.

It was nearly one o'clock by the time I arrived at Black Fox. It wasn't my first time at this establishment and the bouncer let me in with no fuss. I thanked Roman with a wink and a fifty-dollar tip. I always tipped all the staff very well. Bouncers, bussers, bartenders, servers, the cashier, the dealer. I usually left with at least a grand less in my pocket because I spread the wealth.

But these people worked hard. And tipping them ensured not only excellent service, but if things got dicey—which they had in the past—because some egotistical jackass got his tighty whities in a twist, the staff was quick to jump to my defense and get me the hell out of dodge.

I made my way through the front of the house, which was a lounge, bar, and nightclub. It was a weekday, so things were slow. I said "hello" to the two bartenders—Alex and Felix—waved at the servers who knew me, and winked at the DJ, who waved back as I headed for the spiral staircase at the rear of the room. There was another bouncer there, guarding the velvet rope.

Damien lit up when he saw me. "I was hoping you'd come," he said. "Where's your cute little ginger friend?"

I pouted. "Home with a migraine. I'm flying solo tonight."

He nodded, turning serious again. "I'll let Cane know. Make sure nobody bugs you." He unhooked the rope, and I handed him a fifty, then lifted up onto my tiptoes and kissed his chiseled cheek. "Thanks, Damien. You're the best."

Down, down, down the spiral staircase I went, the pumping sounds of the club music growing fainter the deeper into the earth I stepped.

The poker game was held under the bar in what was at one time a speakeasy during prohibition times. The above ground club was actually an old textile shop.

Laughter filtered up toward me, along with the sound of ice being dumped into glasses. Different music—jazzier stuff—played, and the faint hint of cigar smoke made me cringe. Nobody was allowed to smoke down here, but I knew that smell. I knew who would be at the table.

Ugh!

A few heads turned my way as I entered the room with the big, green felt table set up. I nodded at those who waved my way and said hello, but I didn't stop to speak to anyone. I headed straight for Marty, the cashier. "How's it going, Marty?"

"No complaints, Omaera. How are you?"

"Been a wild three days."

His brows hitched up. "Oh, yeah?"

"Probably not as wild as yours, seeing as you've got brand new twins at home. How are Alyssa and the boys doing?"

He smiled sweetly at the mention of his wife and twin sons. "Rio has decided he doesn't like sleeping at night. And Sam screams if anybody but Alyssa holds him."

"So you're exhausted and yet you're still here?"

He sighed. "Day job doesn't pay enough. Alyssa's job has no maternity leave and she can't bear to leave the kids in daycare."

I frowned and reached into my purse. "Well, I just remembered that I never got you guys a baby gift, so as a belated gift—and if you say no, I'll kick you in the shins—here is a small bump. Hire a nanny or something. Just get some sleep, okay?" I handed him five hundred dollars.

"Omaera, I ca—"

"I said 'I'll kick you in the shins' and I meant it."

He accepted the cash as tears welled up in his eyes. "Thank you."

"Cross your fingers I win big tonight and there'll be more where that came from." I handed him my buy-in, and he exchanged the cash for chips. Then I casually wandered through the crowd to an empty seat at the table.

"Omaera," Cane, the dealer said, purring my name. "I'm glad you made it."

"Me too. How are you, Cane? How's your mother?"

His amber eyes twinkled and crinkled at the corners, creating deep lines in his tan, weathered face. "She's better, thanks. She was on the waitlist for a new hip. They said it would be a year or more, but the fall she took the other day was a blessing in disguise. They got her in right away, gave her a new hip, and she's already up and walking."

"Oh, wow. That is a blessing in disguise. I'm so happy to hear she's doing better. Send her my best, please."

Cane grinned. "Well, she's still a cranky old thing, but she's *less* cranky now that she's not in pain anymore."

I chuckled. "Less cranky is always better."

The seats beside me filled up with other players, and the bell to announce that the game would start in five minutes, chimed.

"Ms. Playfair, can I get you something to drink?" asked Cherise, one of the servers. "Your usual?"

"Please," I said to her.

"Club soda with a splash of blueberry syrup and a wedge of lemon coming right up."

"Thank you."

She brought my drink in record time, and I tipped her handsomely.

"You're a celebrity," came a gravelly voice to my left. "Everybody knows you by name. The help even knows your drink order."

I resisted the urge to roll my eyes. "No. I just play the local circuit and I get to know the staff at the events. They're people too, you know." Lifting my gaze and taking a sip of my drink, I came face to face with an older gentleman. His hair was a deep, rusty red, and that included his thick, bushy mustache. He was probably old enough to be my father—even though my real father was centuries old. And his belly was large and barrel shaped. His eyes were a pale green, almost gray, and the capillaries on his nose had burst, creating red spiderweb like veins. I glanced at the drink in his hand to find it a double of some amber spirit. Probably a very expensive scotch.

His suit was expensive. Dark. And he smelled faintly of peppermint.

He wasn't the cigar smoking jerk I was waiting to see.

He thrust his right hand forward. "Ambrose Charlston."

"Omaera Playfair," I said, taking his sweaty palm in mine.

"What's a little thing like you doing out so late and down here?"

I glanced at him, chomping down hard on the inside of my cheek. "As I said, I play the local circuit. And my size has nothing to do with my ability to play poker. I'm also old enough to be out later than when the streetlights come on."

He huffed and reached inside his suit jacket to tug on his suspenders. "No need to get emotional. It was just a question."

No need to get *emotional*? I wasn't getting emotional. I was getting defensive, but even that was handled without any anger in my tone.

"Let's just play poker, hmm?" I said, as everyone else around the table settled down. There were ten players in total.

Cane gave a quick rundown of the rules as he always did. Then he dealt the cards.

I had an okay first hand. Nothing to get too excited about. Nine of spades and king of diamonds. I quickly calculated the probability of what each player could get, based on my cards being out of the deck.

My odds of winning weren't spectacular, but with that king, they weren't completely terrible either. Sure, the same suit would be nice, but I could work with these two cards.

Slowly, we went around the table and placed our bets. The man to my left with the ginger mustache placed his bet—five hundred.

Already, just based on the way he cleared his throat and popped another peppermint in his mouth, I could tell that he had nothing. He was a bluffer through and through.

The buy-in for this game was five thousand. I bet five hundred to start.

The man to my right bet five as well. Then, it was the cigar-smoking asshole beside him who chuckled like he smoked a pack a day, and pushed six hundred in front of him.

I refused to make eye contact with him, even though I could feel his gaze on me.

The remaining players placed their bets based on their two cards.

Then the dealer burned one card before dealing three cards from the deck face up for the start of the community river.

Three of diamonds. Two of diamonds. Nine of clubs.

Okay.

That nine of clubs with my nine of spades at least puts me in the game with a pair.

I glanced around the table, watching the tells.

When you play poker for a living, you don't look at it like gambling. You view it as the grind, just like every other working stiff out there. This was what I did to pay the bills, buy food, and keep a roof over my head. The goal was to keep the money safe and never leave with less than I showed up with. Win one, big bet an hour and don't get cocky. Quit while you're in the black. Folding is not failing.

I repeated these things to myself several times throughout each game. Even when I wanted to bluff and play my opponent, I knew better than to get too arrogant and risk losing more than I came with. Folding wasn't the end. Folding wasn't failure.

The other thing about playing poker for a living was that you learned a lot about people without ever asking them a single question. Like the man next to the ginger mustache beside me, he was a Nervous Nelly. His nails were gnawed down to the quick. A few Band-Aids on his left said he'd already nibbled those down enough to make them bleed.

The question was: did he nibble when he had something good? Or something bad?

I shouldn't be here. I'm a terrible player. My hand is bad. They're going to take all my money and I won't be able to pay rent. Why did I let Ricky talk me into coming?

Oh, that was interesting.

The man beside him kept flaring his nostrils and fiddling with a chip in his right hand, flipping it back and forth. Then he'd check his cards after five flips, put them down again, smile discreetly, and flip five times once more. I'd played with him before. This meant he had a good hand.

No fearful thoughts filled his mind.

The woman beside him blinked a lot and kept side-eyeing everyone. She also refused to put her cards down. She kept them in her hand as if she'd forget them if she set them down.

I need to fold. I can't afford to lose his money. He said he'd leave me if I kept coming to these games.

I narrowed my gaze in her direction. She caught me looking at her and went pink in the cheeks.

The man beside her was watching me. His features were wolfish. That was the best way to describe him. One eye was a pale blue, the other amber. His brows were bushy and low down over his eyes. He bared his straight, white teeth. "So this is how you win, huh?"

Now it was my turn to blink. "Excuse me?"

He sniffed. "Little demon playing mind games," he whispered. "Manipulating the other players to fold."

I swallowed. No. That wasn't how I played at all.

He smiled diabolically with bared teeth; the canines extended down further, just enough to let me know he wasn't of the human world.

"I don't know what you're talking about."

"I can smell you. Couldn't smell you before tonight. Your spell must have worn off."

I glanced around the table, hoping to God nobody was listening.

Nobody was.

He managed to keep his voice low enough and everyone was in their own little world, calling and betting. The woman with the gambling addiction folded, as did the nail biter. Then it was mustache's turn, and he upped his bet, matching the last raise with another hundred.

My turn now. But I was frazzled by this shifter across from me and hadn't had a chance to study all the other players. Okay, I needed to get my head back in the game. You played the players more than you played the cards, and right now the shifter was doing a damned good job playing me. Everyone knew that if you couldn't spot the sucker at the table in the first thirty minutes, you *were* the sucker. And I sure as hell was not the fucking sucker here.

I had a nine of spades and the king of hearts. My only play at the moment was a pair of nines. And although people won with lesser hands than that one pair, my odds weren't looking good.

I studied what everyone else bet. Three of the ten of us so far had already folded, which left seven in the game.

I pushed another two hundred "in" chips forward.

The man to my right folded. Now there were six left in the game.

The cigar-smoke smelling asshole pushed four hundred "in" chips forward.

The man beside him—the cut-off—bet four as well.

Then it was back to the dealer.

Cane burned another card and placed the fourth card face up in the community row. Eight of clubs.

This didn't help my chances at all.

A few people around the table sighed in frustration. Including the ginger mustache beside me. The chip flipping man with the flaring nostrils smiled, but only for a second, before stowing that grin and slapping on a resting bitch face. But I could already feel that he had nothing. Would he continue bluffing? Risk more money? Or cut his loses and fold? How well did he play the other players?

The small blind—the player right after the dealer, which was another woman—folded. Which meant now the big blind—the person after her—had to start the bet based on the new card in play.

And that just happened to be the shifter. Refusing to take his eyes off me, he bet three hundred, which meant he probably had a pair of some kind—or two—or the makings of a flush with the two and three or the eight and nine.

Blinking lady had already folded, so it was up to nostrils to fold, call, or bet. He folded.

Called it. He would have been a terrible bluffer anyway.

Nail biter had already folded, so then it was mustache's turn.

He hummed and hawed, glanced at his cards three times before finally matching the shifter's bet of three hundred.

I refused to look at the shifter, even though I could feel his eyes burning on me. I increased the bet to three fifty. The man beside me had already folded, which meant it was cigar smoker's turn. He raised the bet to four fifty. I knew he shifted his gaze my way, but I still refused to bite.

I hated this man, and he knew it. He was goading me. Trying to out play me and get in my head.

The cut-off folded as well.

This left just four of us in the game.

The shifter, the mustache man, the cigar smoker, and me.

Cane burned another card, then placed the fifth and final card face up in the river.

It was a king of spades.

Holy fucking shit.

I had two pair.

I didn't react. Gemma and I had worked on killing any of my tells. I had none.

I never reacted when I had good cards or terrible cards.

The shifter went all in, smiling at me as he pushed all his chips into the middle.

Mustache man huffed in frustration and folded, throwing his cards down onto the table with a dramatic flair.

There was nothing I could do besides fold or match his bet, and as much as I didn't want to go all-in and push all my money into the middle on two pairs, I had to.

Lastly, was the cigar smoker.

Like always, he waited the dramatic minute, glancing at his cards several times and swiveling his gaze between myself and the shifter. Finally, with a deep sigh, he pushed all his chips into the center as well.

The room was tense as fuck. Nobody spoke. Breaths were held. Assholes were clenched.

The shifter flipped his cards over first. A two of hearts and a jack of diamonds.

He had two pairs as well.

But my pairs were better.

"Two pair," Cane announced. "Jacks and twos." He smiled when he turned to me. "You're up, Omaera."

With my heart pummeling my ribcage, I flipped my cards over.

The crowd gasped.

"Two pair," Cane said again. "Kings and nines."

A very wolfish growl rumbled across the table from the shifter

"You're up, Mr. Cavendish," Cane said to the man who smelled like cigar smoke.

Mr. Cavendish, also known as Ricky C, a full-of-himself rounder with groupies, fancy cars and, from everything I've heard, a very small dick, flipped over his cards to reveal a three of spades and a jack of hearts. He also had two pairs. But they still weren't as good as mine.

"Two pairs," Cane announced. "Jacks and threes. The pot goes to Omaera with a winning hand of two pairs of kings and nines."

Never wanting to showboat—too much—I smiled and leaned forward, scooping my chips toward me. It was a good and profitable game. This was exactly what I needed to get out of my head, out of my grief and confusion, and make some money as well. I could head home now to the chaos that awaited me.

As I was gathering my chips, the shifter leaned forward. "I'm sure Cane, Marty and Mr. Bello would love to hear how you've been cheating by persuasion and manipulation all these years." His voice was low, growly and laden with threat.

Mr. Bello was the guy who owned the lounge upstairs and ran the games in the basement. It was rumored he had ties to the mob, but he'd never been anything but nice to me. Besides, I played fair, never cheated, and I made sure to tip his staff well. He liked me. And I . . . respected his establishment and choice of enterprise by not getting on his bad side.

"And I'm sure the High Council would love to hear how you're threatening to out another member of the Realm because you're a sore loser," came a very familiar, distinct, and oh-so-pompous voice behind me.

I spun around to find Drak standing there, fuming at not only the shifter, but me as well.

Oh, lovely. The vampire who, despite being old as fuck, couldn't for the immortal life of him understand motherfucking boundaries.

What other wonderful surprises and delights did this night have to offer me?

CHAPTER FIFTEEN

OMAERA

I gaped at Drak. "How the hell did you find me?"

He rolled his blue eyes. "Same way I found you the first time. And the second. And the third."

I whipped back around to face the shifter. He'd gone pale in the face and his eyes grew wide with fear. "Wh-who are you?" he stammered.

I lifted a brow. "None of your business. But King Ryden and King Howar are close personal friends of mine."

His gaze flicked back up to Drak, then to me. He nodded vigorously. "Y-yes, of course. My sincerest apologies." He scrambled out of his seat, the intimidating man with different colored eyes no longer there. What replaced him was a scared puppy with his tail between his legs, who could not get out of there fast enough.

As much as I was irritated at seeing Drak, it was kind of fun to put the run on someone who thought they could threaten me.

It did make me pause and wonder if my demonness was part of the reason why I was so good at poker though. Was Delia's spell strong enough to mask all of my capabilities? Or were some of them too powerful for even her spell and leaked through, like the subconscious power of persuasion? Was I a cheater? A subconscious cheater?

A hand thrust forward. "I suppose congratulations are in order." I glared at the hand with the douchey rings, perfectly manicured nails, and the ace of spades tattoo on the inside of his wrist. How utterly cliché could you get? And he would literally tell anybody who asked, it was because he always had an "ace up his sleeve." *BARF!*

Lifting my gaze, I didn't bother to take Ricky's hand. "Thank you."

After an awkward moment with his hand out and mine *not*, he retracted it back beside him. "So, when are we going to stop playing this cat-and-mouse game, Omaera?"

"I have absolutely no idea what you're talking about. You're a rat, and I'm . . . well, I'm more of a bear person than a cat person."

Drak made a noise behind me. I stowed my smile as best I could.

"We could make a killing doing the rounds, Maer-Maer. You and me, hustling by night, tangled up in the sheets by day. We could go to Vegas and slaughter at the tables. Enter tournaments. Take this to Monaco. I don't know why you stick close to home when there are millions to be made outside the comfort of the Pacific Northwest. You're playing it safe. Too safe."

I rolled my eyes and exhaled. "So many bad ideas to unpack here. I uh . . . no. No thanks, on all of those offers. I make very good money. I don't *need* or *want* more. I'm happy with my life. Besides, you're way too old for me." I also had three way better looking mates at home waiting for me. They might be older than dirt, but at least they didn't smell like cigar smoke and have terrible cliché tattoos or fingers covered in douchey rings.

Ricky scoffed and shook his head. "We always *need* more money. And I'm only thirty-one. How old are you? Also, I like 'em young."

I resisted the urge to vomit from that last comment. I also refused to bite and tell him my age. Too many people were listening to our conversation already. "I'm not like you, Ricky," I finally said. "And thank god for that. Bye now." I made to reach down and grab the hem of my T-shirt since I usually wore a baggy one to games to collect my chips, but realized I was in a crop top. *Ugh.*

"Here," Drak said, removing his suit coat and helping me scoop them off the table.

"This your . . . boyfriend?" Ricky asked, giving Drak a quick up and down once over. "He's definitely older than me. Or is he your bodyguard"

"Something like that," I grumbled. As much as I hated Ricky C., I also didn't want to brûlée his brains. At least not in front of so many people.

Drak looked damned fine in his black, button-up dress shirt and black slacks. Who knew the monochrome bat could be so sexy? He held my winnings in his coat against his chest and growled at Ricky. "Excuse us, please."

Ricky's amber eyes went wide with fright, but he stepped back, flipping his floppy, blond, frat boy hair and allowing Drak and I to move through the crowd toward Marty so I could cash in my winnings.

"Not here, but we are going to have a very serious conversation about your inability to respect boundaries," I murmured, almost under my breath, as we waited for Marty to pay me out.

Drak's gaze remained level with mine, but he didn't say anything.

"Decent haul tonight, Omaera," Marty said, counting out my cash in hundred-dollar bills. "Any big plans for all your winnings?"

"Just rent and food, Marty. You know I'm not a fancy girl." This was the conversation we had every time I played, and Marty was the cashier. It was a running joke between us now.

He chuckled and finished up. I tipped him well like I always did, made sure to tip my server again, as well as Cane, who was already dealing up a new game. "Buy your cranky mom something nice," I said, tapping the dealer on the shoulder and handing him a hundred dollars.

"I sure will," he said with a big grin. "Thanks."

After pulling the baby diaper out of my purse and storing my wads of cash inside it, I gave a jerk of my head toward Drak, indicating he should follow me. We made our way back up the spiral staircase to the lounge.

I tipped Damien on my way out. "Heard you won big," he said.

"And now, I will humbly take my winnings home."

He winked at me.

Drak growled

I rolled my eyes.

I was half way to the front door when a strong, cool hand on my elbow hauled me backward.

"Hey!"

But it was Drak, so I calmed down . . . a little.

He had me in a small, dark, secluded alcove and was pulling me along further. Past the washrooms and toward a closet.

We stopped before we reached the closet door.

"Don't you ever do that again," he said with another growl, his gaze hard to read in the dim light.

I jerked free of his grasp and gave a growl of my own. "I'll do whatever I damn well want to. Not only am I a free woman, but I am *not* your mate. Don't you *ever* tell me what to do again."

He winced a little, which is how I realized I was flash-frying his brain. I quickly pulled back my rage, gathered those thoughts and contained them in my mind. His expression relaxed.

"Why did you follow me? Don't you understand boundaries? Space? The need to be alone?"

"You are in danger," he said. "I *am* your mate, and even though you are unequivocally an enormous pain, it is my duty to protect you."

My heart slammed hard against my ribs, and my chest heaved as my eyes adjusted to the lack of light. And as if truly possessed, something changed inside Drak as I watched. His pupils dilated, his nostrils flared and that same feral look of obsession, of craving from earlier today, flashed in his eyes.

Holy shit! How did I forget about the . . . the blood lust, or whatever we were calling it? The capsule from Mr. Fiddleman was wearing off.

His lips parted and his fangs dropped down as his pulse matched mine, causing the vein in his neck to throb. I licked my lips, unable to peel my eyes away from his.

The man was infuriating. An undeniable pain in my ass. He was pompous and arrogant. Cold and aloof. He didn't care about my feelings or my heart. He wanted to mate because that was what we were supposed to do. He wanted to control me. He wanted to possess me.

And yet, at this very moment, that was all I wanted too.

"I don't like you," I whispered.

"I know."

"You're insufferable."

"You're not exactly a joy to be around either."

That made me smirk.

"What kind of name is Drak anyway?"

"It's my name."

"Were you named after Dracula?"

"Bram Stoker's *Dracula* came out in 1897. I'm much older than that."

Even though we were having a conversation as casually as two people on the bus together, we were both out of breath, unable to peel our eyes away for even a second. My panties flooded, and we were close enough now, with our hips touching, that I could feel his growing arousal.

"So, maybe Dracula was based on you?"

The corner of his mouth tipped up less than an inch. "It was based on Vlad the Impaler. Who died before I was born. Not a nice guy, from what I've been told."

"So maybe it *was* based on you. Hence the name?"

"Are you saying I'm not a nice guy?"

I huffed a laugh. "Maybe you were Vlad the Impaler and you're older than you say you are."

He didn't respond.

Our words were no more than whispers. Sexy whispers between two people who couldn't stand each other, yet neither person wanted to pull away. The longer we stood in that dark hallway, the more I needed to find out exactly what he'd do to me if given the chance.

"You're a control freak," I said, my chest rising and falling faster than ever.

"And you're a brat who takes unnecessary risks."

"You have boundary issues."

"You don't know when to listen to reason."

"I could toast your brain right now."

"Then do it." The way his pupils darkened to absolute midnight was mesmerizing.

Our faces were inches apart now. He had my back against the wall, boxed in by his enormous, broad frame.

I swallowed, and his gaze dropped to my throat. To my neck, and what I'm sure was a plump, juicy vein. "What happens when you bite? Will it turn me into . . . you?"

Another ghost of a smile. "No. Only Phaceanesh turn people, if they can control themselves not to completely drain the person and kill them. My species is only born."

Well, that was a relief.

"You will feel pleasure unlike anything ever before," he added. "When I bite you."

I swallowed again and licked my lips. His gaze followed my tongue and his nostrils flared.

"You need to stop following me."

"No."

No?

Just "no"?

Well, that got my temper flaring again. I tried to shove him away, but he wouldn't budge. The capsule from the spellcaster was wearing off, and he was getting stronger by the second.

Huffing and puffing, I glared up at him. "You're such an asshole."

He didn't say anything.

"I hate you."

He still didn't say anything.

I shoved him again, and an unexpected sob choked out of my throat. "I hate you. Did you hear me?"

His mouth opened and his fangs dropped even lower while at the same time, his gaze turned hooded. He pulled in a deep breath and closed his eyes for just a moment, while at the same time a deep, primitive rumble reverberated in his chest.

"I hate you." My words were more of a whimper than anything now.

He gripped my chin with his finger and thumb, forcing me to look at him. He was a tattered thread away from snapping and going fully feral on me. I could see the crumbling restraint in his eyes. He knew what was happening. We both did. And there was no way to stop it now.

With one more tension-filled look between us, I took a deep breath and leaped up onto his hips at the same time our mouths crashed together. His hands kneaded my ass cheeks as his big body plastered me up against the wall. I had one arm looped around his neck while the other hand fished along the wall for the doorknob to the storage closet. I found it, and thank god, it was unlocked. We tumbled inside, where it was completely dark. Not even a sliver of light seeped in from under the door.

But I didn't fucking care.

His hands were everywhere, but mostly on my jeans, searching for the button and zipper. I was back on my feet and swatted his hand away because I could do it faster myself.

I unbuttoned them and shimmied them down my legs. But those damned combat boots I loved so much took a bit of finessing to get off my feet so I could peel out of my pants.

I ditched my pants and underwear, then scrambled in the dark for the front of his pants, but he pushed me away and dropped to his knees, cupping my ass and hauling me forward. His hands were surprisingly cool. Not icy cold, but cool. Even his lips were cool.

"No," I protested. "I have my period." I tried to shove him away.

"I know," he said, pressing his nose to the top of my mound. "I need to taste you."

"I . . ." Why was I so turned on by the idea of this? What the fuck was wrong with me?

His tongue darted out and flicked my clit. My leg spasmed.

Slowly, my eyes adjusted to the darkness and there actually was a small strip of muted light pouring in from under the door. He guided my right foot up onto an overturned bucket to better expose me.

I loved my menstrual cup, but emptying it could be a messy process, so if I knew I was going to be away from home for any length of time, I put in a tampon instead.

This was one of those occasions.

A gentle tug on the string at the same time he flicked my clit again had me sucking in a sharp breath. "I have to," he said, his voice hoarse with restraint. "I need to."

I needed this too.

God, how I needed it.

"Okay," I breathed, nodding even though I wasn't sure he'd be able to see me.

He tugged again on the string, and the tampon slid out. I'm not sure where he put it, but I'm hoping it was in the garbage or something. I had spare tampons in my purse, so it wasn't like I needed it to get home.

His tongue flicked out again, only this time, instead of hitting my clit, he probed inside of me. Fucking me with that long, skilled muscle. Just like his hands and lips, his tongue was cool, too. It was almost like he'd just brushed his teeth and was going down on me with a cool, minty mouth. My hot-for-him body didn't know how to handle the difference in temperature, yet, I also didn't want it to stop. It tingled and sent icy zaps racing through me until my nipples beaded in my bra and goosebumps broke out along my arms.

I exhaled and ground against him, bucking into his face. His nose hit my clit, and I gasped. The scent of blood and my arousal filled the small closet, suffocating the initial smell of industrial cleaner, but I didn't care. I didn't care about anything, but how fucking hot—and weird—this was. But the weirdness turned me on too.

I'd never been one to get *too* wild in bed. Sure, I dabbled with handcuffs, blindfolds, and I'd even let one guy spank me. But this was a whole new level of kinky I'd never even fathomed.

He moaned in pleasure and that just spurred me on too. I gripped his thick, silky hair, holding him in place as he feasted on me—literally.

Two fingers probed inside of me and pumped, as his lips encircled my clit again and he sucked, sending another cool, refreshing rush through my veins.

I cried out and held onto his hair tighter.

An orgasm unlike anything I'd ever felt before brewed hot and wild in my lower belly. I couldn't think straight. I couldn't think of anything but how badly I wanted Drak. How badly I *needed* him.

He removed his fingers and pushed his tongue back inside me while those same fingers found my clit and rubbed perfect circles.

It wasn't until he withdrew his tongue just enough to flick the hood of my clit with his fang, making me gasp from the sharp snap of pleasure coated in pain, then he dove his tongue back inside and I exploded. I was unprepared for how hard the climax was going to hit me, and I nearly fell off the overturned bucket and into the wall of cleaning supplies behind me. But Drak's free hand shot out and gripped my ass hard, holding me in place so I could finish out my orgasm.

I rode his face with zero shame, tilted my head to the ceiling and let the warmth, and wave after wave of unadulterated bliss, flood me from top to toe and back. A sob broke free of my throat, but I didn't even care. Tears pricked my eyes as my body convulsed with each fresh strike of pleasure.

Drak never stopped.

He never slowed down.

He just kept sinking his tongue into me. Kept rubbing my clit.

He did the whole fang on clit thing again, which just made one orgasm roll into another. I wasn't sure I had the strength to stay standing. But he held me in place with his hand on my ass, his fingers digging into my flesh. Thankfully, I liked that added bit of pain and contact. It just pushed the pleasure all that much higher.

As I began to come down from orgasm number two, he pulled his head away. I couldn't look down at him though. I couldn't see my blood all over his face. As hot as this was, I was grateful for the dark.

He stood up to his full height, unbuckled his pants, and fished out his erection. I might not have been able to look at his face, but I had no problem staring at his cock.

Holy shit.

He reached behind me, gripped my ass, and I leaped up onto his hips again. It took very little effort for him to notch himself properly at my core and slide home. We both moaned as I sunk down, taking every inch of him I could.

His grunts were savage and primal, and that just pitched me to new heights of arousal. I'd never come more than once with any sexual partner, but I already knew I could come again—and possibly, again. Maybe it was that we were Fated Mates, maybe it was some vampire voodoo spell, or the fact that I was bleeding and he was in blood lust. Or maybe the perpetually grumpy vampire was just that good. I had very little brain power to delve into the maybes. So I ignored them, putting them into the back of my brain to entertain later, and instead, I gave over to the moment. To the desire racing through me.

Drak bucked up harder and harder, grunting with each thrust. I bobbed up and down on his waist, using his shoulders for leverage. The way his pubic bone hit my clit just galvanized everything higher, better, and had me chasing orgasm number three at an alarming speed.

I tilted my face to the ceiling again as the pressure in my belly grew hot and tight. I was close, and as hard as I tried to hang on, I couldn't.

I broke again with a sharp, gasping cry and at the same time Drak plunged his fangs into my neck, hurling my entire soul up into the stratosphere as the orgasm of all orgasms threatened to kill me.

Heat radiated out from where his fangs punctured my flesh, creating magical sparkles and tingles I'd never felt before all throughout my body. Usually my clit and core were the epicenter of my climax, but now I had two orgasm nuclei in my body. He removed his fangs and replaced them with his mouth where he sucked, pulling blood from my jugular and once again, feasting on me.

The more he sucked, the harder and stronger my orgasm. I never wanted it to end.

My leg muscles shook around his waist. My toes curled and cramped, and my clit throbbed as his pelvic bone continued to rub against it.

I barely registered his grunts and moans, or that he'd paused his own efforts and was coming. My orgasm was still going. I wasn't going to have a fourth orgasm. I was never going to have any more orgasms after this, because this one was never going to end.

And I was kind of okay with a death like this.

Didn't the French call the orgasm *la petite mort*, anyway? Little death.

Well, this was a big death, and I was on board for it. Kill me now, Bat Boy. I'm going to meet my parents with a smile on my face—and no pants.

He stopped sucking and swept his tongue across the puncture marks as he continued to lose himself inside me, finding his own release.

I didn't think it would happen, but I was both saddened and grateful when the tremors and pleasure receded. There were a few aftershocks, but my toes stopped cramping and I could hear things besides my own thundering heart again.

After a few stuttered breaths, he helped me to my feet. I wobbled instantly, but Drak was there to keep me from keeling over into the mop and bucket.

"I . . . I need to put in a new tampon," I said, still in a daze, as I searched the floor for my dropped purse. I located it, breathing a sigh of relief because my purse also had all my winnings.

I spun around and inserted the new tampon then went on the hunt for my underwear and pants.

I dressed quickly, making sure to keep my back to Drak until I was presentable. I also really didn't want to see his face.

Reality was hitting me like a slap to the face with a wet cloth.

I'd just hate-fucked a vampire who also ate me out while I was on my period. And all of this happened in a bar storage closet. Now we had to leave while his face was covered in my blood.

None of this was good.

"You can turn around now," he said, his aristocratic tone back like it'd never left.

"I don't want to see my blood all over your face."

"It's not."

I whipped around where, sure enough, his face was void of the evidence. "H-how?" I asked.

He pointed to the sink and roll of brown, bathroom paper towels along the far wall.

Nodding, I exhaled in relief. "Let's get out of here."

His head bobbed as well. I poked my head out the door to double-check that the coast was clear before stepping out into the hallway. He followed me, and we beelined it for the front door. The bartenders—Alex and Felix—called my name and said goodbye. I only gave them a cursory wave and smile, keeping my head ducked down until I hit the sidewalk.

Drak stayed a pace behind me as I made my way toward the bus stop.

I was looking more at my feet than in front of me, which was why I ran headfirst into a honey and cedar-scented bare chest.

"Whoa there, Little One," Zandren said, gripping me by the shoulders.

I glanced up at him, my face instantly getting hot. Maxar was behind him.

They both sniffed the air for a moment and their gazes shifted to Drak, darkening like someone had just snuffed out the sun.

"You okay?" Maxar asked. He stepped to the side and addressed Drak. "Would have been nice if you'd let *us* know about your little field trip." His gaze turned more serious, and he focused on me again. "He hasn't taken a capsule in hours . . . did he? Are you okay?"

"We uh . . . we handled things," I said. "But he should probably take one now."

Nodding, Maxar reached into the pocket of his genie pants and pulled out the brown bottle. He dumped one capsule onto his palm and held it out for Drak.

The vampire took it and swallowed without argument.

"You had me worried sick, Little One. Drak's gone, *and* you're gone. I didn't know what happened." Zandren gently cupped my jaw. "Why did you leave?"

My sigh was weary and defeated. The way he was looking at me had me feeling all kinds of guilty. I felt like if I'd told Zandren my need for some space, he would understand, considering how he likes his space and alone time too. Why didn't I trust that he'd understand? Why didn't I confide in him?

"I just needed to be by myself for a little bit," I finally said. "I wanted my old life back, even if just for one night. I went to a poker game. I only played one game, but I won." I lifted up my purse. "Lunch is on me." My humorless chuckle was a meager and unsuccessful attempt to soften the tense moment between the four of us.

Zandren still had my jaw cupped. His brown eyes softened in the harsh glow of the orange streetlamp overhead. "I get that. Please, just tell me you need space next time, so I don't worry." He was hurt, but he was trying hard not to show it.

I nodded. "I will. I promise."

He and Maxar nodded. It was all they really could do. They couldn't punish me. Though, to be honest, I was kind of curious what kind of punishment they could come up with. But more than anything, I wanted them to stop looking at me like I'd betrayed them because I didn't trust them enough to tell them the truth. I didn't trust them because I didn't know them.

No, that wasn't true.

I didn't know them very well, and I was slow to trust in general. But my gut told me I could trust them. And I was beginning to—especially Zandren. Our time in the woods showed me another side of him and I wanted so badly to believe his intentions were good and pure. "I want to go home and check on Gemma," I said, smothering a yawn with my fist. "Did anybody check on her before they followed me?"

All three of them shook their heads.

I rolled my eyes. "You know. She and I are a package deal. So if this whole Fated Mates thing is actually the way our lives are going to go, then Gemma is part of this fucked up quadruple."

"No, she's not," Drak said.

I spun around and glared at him. "Yes. She is. You might not want to fuck her and sink your teeth into her, but she's family. She's *my* family. The only family I have left. So you better start giving a damn about her if you want me to start giving a damn about *you*." Then I stomped off ahead of all of them toward the bus stop, not giving two shits whether they followed me or not.

But, of course they did. And something told me, they always would.

CHAPTER SIXTEEN

DRAK

I knew she wasn't in the house when the Mate's Ache woke me up. My heart felt like it was being ripped in two. Similar to how it felt when she went off to the woods with the bear earlier that day. She just kept leaving me.

So I followed her, knowing exactly what her reaction would be when she discovered me. And she didn't disappoint.

I intended to just stay upstairs in the lounge, expecting the Mate's Ache to be bearable with her downstairs. But the mage's capsule was wearing off and my need to be near her grew more intense than I could stand.

I was careful when I entered the speakeasy and skirted behind people so she wouldn't notice me. She'd never forgive me if my presence affected her game.

I noticed the wolf shifter across from her almost immediately.

He was giving off vibes I didn't like, but I didn't want to say anything and give my presence away. We were also surrounded by humans, and the last thing we needed was the mere mortals finding out a wolf shifter, demon, and vampire were in their midst.

So I stayed quiet and stood behind Omaera toward the back, keeping an eye on her and the shifter.

Pride roared through me when she won. But, of course she would. She was spectacular in every way. Tough as nails and incredibly clever. I was also impressed by how she treated the staff working the speakeasy. She knew everyone by name, was polite, and tipped very well. Unlike the majority of the other players and patrons who treated the staff like *the help* and barked orders at them. A lot didn't use their manners or tip either.

I planned to stay quiet for as long as I could.

I could feel the effects of the capsule wearing off and my need to devour and consume Omaera was making my decision to remain unnoticed more and more difficult. It wasn't until the wolf shifter threatened her that I knew I needed to step in.

Her reaction to me being there was less than welcomed. And I expected that.

But it allowed me to be closer to her. It allowed me to smell her. Feeding the hungry growl of my more primitive side.

I wasn't happy she left the safety of the apartment, but the little demon was quickly demonstrating her fierce independence and resistance to mating any of us. I wished she could see how mating us would help her with her powers and help the Realm. It was the smart and logical thing to do.

But I'd never force her.

None of us would.

The Mating Bond also wouldn't take if done without consent. Not that I would ever force myself on anyone, let alone my Fated Mate.

Which was why I felt nothing but shame as we walked toward the bus stop.

I was unable to hold back my urges, and I took her in that closet. I took *the Queen of the Realm* in a bloody broom closet, for god's sake. I was a stronger man than that. I should have pushed through the desire. I should have risked the Mate's Ache and left before she noticed me.

Maxar had the pills because he said he didn't trust me to not toss them. But I should have demanded that he put at least one in my pocket in the event we were separated and I was alone with Omaera.

I knew she consented, but I still felt awful.

She hated me.

She said as much more than once.

I wasn't an easy man to love; I knew that. But the pain of my mate hating me was a fresh and debilitating kind of agony I wasn't prepared for. Nobody talked about a mate resisting the Bond or the kind of hell it would create. So either this was a new phenomenon, and I was the first vampire whose mate rejected him, or it was so painful nobody spoke of it because they had repressed those haunting memories.

I remained quiet as we waited at the bus stop, caught up in a deep bout of reflection and self-flagellation. How could I do that?

How could I take her like that?

I wanted the first time I was with my mate to be special for her. To be special for both of us. To be something she consented to—and not because she was under my fucked up vampirical hypnosis because of my own feral blood lust. I wanted her to consent because she wanted me. Because she wanted me forever as much as I wanted her forever.

If I could stay away from her, I would.

If I could let her be, I would.

But I couldn't.

The Mate's Ache was too painful. And the longer we went without mating, the harder it would be to be away from her at all. I was grateful for the capsule compounded by the mage. At least I could be civilized while she bled.

I regretted taking her in that closet the way I did. And yet, my body continued to thrum with post-coital bliss. The taste of her lingered on my tongue and lips. I'd never tasted anything—anybody—so sweet. Her blood was like the most decadent nectar, and I couldn't get enough. I could have easily drunk her dry if I didn't stop myself. And it wasn't because I wanted to kill her, it was because she tasted that good. It was because being with my mate, drinking my mate, was as whole as I'd ever felt in my nearly five and a half centuries. I could only imagine that mating with her would feel that much more extraordinary.

But I had to wait.

Until she consented to the Bond. Until she *chose* me.

The bus ride back to her apartment was quiet.

None of us really said anything.

I'm sure Zandren and Maxar knew exactly what happened between us. The way their noses sniffed and wrinkled as soon as we ran into them said they had an idea of what transpired between Omaera and I. I didn't care.

I was just as much her mate as they were.

Maybe there was some jealousy there because I got to be with her first. But there was no bond forged in our union. In my fugue state, I mentally pushed for it—slightly—but I could feel her resisting. The Fates would not allow a non-consensual Mate Bond. As disastrous as the whole Fated Mates thing could be, at least the Fates had done one thing right.

I avoided Zandren's gaze, but I could feel the heat and hate of it burning on my face.

Omaera sat between him and Maxar at the back of the bus. I sat to their left.

Besides a couple of men at the front of the bus heading out on some kind of a night shift in trade uniforms, we were the only passengers. They unloaded before we did, and then it was just us four until we reached our stop a block from Omaera's home.

"Thank you," Omaera called out, the first to get off the bus from the door in the middle of the vehicle. "Have a great night." She waved at the driver, who waved back to her.

I said nothing. Neither did Zandren, nor Maxar.

"Would it kill any of you to be pleasant to other people? To humans?" she asked in frustration. "You know that bus drivers are people too?" She glanced specifically at me. "Or do you just see them as lowly peasants here to serve us?"

I blinked at her. "I . . . no. I don't see them that way."

I caught Maxar's and Zandren's eyes, and they both looked thoroughly chastised.

"If this whole fucked up, quadruple thing is going to work, you three need to trust me more. Give me space and respect my boundaries. And for Christ's sake, be humble, gracious, and polite." Her gaze pivoted back to me. "And I don't mean pompous WASP polite, where all your manners are actually backassward insults. I mean 'please and thank you' said with sincerity."

I swallowed and nodded.

Zandren stared at his feet and murmured, "Okay."

"Yes, my Queen," Maxar whispered.

We followed her to the apartment building, but even I smelled it and I wasn't a fucking shifter.

Zandren stopped in his tracks and dropped to all fours, snarling.

Thank god it was nearly four in the morning and nobody was around to witness such idiocy, but nevertheless, the potent scent of demons in the air had the hair at the nape of my neck standing straight up.

"They were here," Zandren growled, clambering still on all fours and in human form toward the front door. He used the code Omaera gave us to get into the door, then bounded into the lobby.

We hustled after him, taking the stairs because, for some reason they just felt safer than the elevator. I could already tell by the scratches on the carpet on the landing of each floor that Zandren had shifted. And if the scratches didn't give that away, the pile of clothes and shoes on the second floor was proof. I gathered them up and followed Omaera and Maxar.

We reached the fourth floor and the scent of demon was stronger than ever. Normally, I couldn't smell another species, or even other vampires, but this was intensely strong. Like damp fire logs and . . . death. That was the only way I could describe it, and even that didn't sound right.

Panic rolled off Omaera in tenuous waves as we reached the fourth floor and she burst out into the hallway.

The door to unit 405 was already open.

Zandren, still in bear form, stood in the living room, his eyes sad as they zeroed in on Omaera.

Her gaze swiveled to Gemma's bedroom door, which was wide open. She ran into her friend's room, screaming her name. She flicked on the bedroom light, ruffled up the linens on Gemma's bed, then went into the bathroom they shared, through it, and into her own room.

We all knew the truth though.

Gemma wasn't here.

They took her.

With tears streaming down her cheeks, green eyes wide in horror, Omaera returned to us in the living room. "Why?" she asked, shaking her head. "Why'd they take her?"

I shook my head.

"D-Do you think they're going to k-kill her like they did Delia?"

I had to keep myself from going to her. From comforting her. I'd already messed up once, going against my own moral code and touching her when I swore I wouldn't. Now, I had penance to deal with, and no matter how much it hurt, I was going to give her the space she needed.

That didn't stop it from gutting me to the spine when she fell to the ground and wrapped her arms around Zandren's big fury neck.

He moaned like bears do and nuzzled her.

I'd never been so jealous in all my life. And I'd just had sex with her.

But she hated me.

What we did in that cleaning closet was nothing short of animalistic. Savage. I was in a fugue state of lust and she was under some kind of spell I had inadvertently cast on her. If she was of total sound mind, she never would have agreed.

"We have to find her," Omaera said, her words muffled as she pressed her face into Zandren's neck. "What if they hurt her? What if they kill her? She's human. She won't be able to withstand half the torture they delivered to Delia."

"What do you think they want with Gemma?" Maxar asked.

I shook my head and pulled out my phone, dialing the King. "Zandren, you should call your father. Maxar, call Queen Anysa."

"Yeah, because I have her on speed dial and she picks up," Maxar said sarcastically. "I'm not like you two aristocrats. I'm just a fire mage. No royal blood line bubbling in these veins."

I rolled my eyes just as Howar picked up. "New demon advisor should arrive tomorrow. How is our new queen?"

I took the call out on the balcony. "Not good. Her roommate and best friend was just kidnapped. By demons."

"The same that killed her aunt."

"We believe so."

"And this roommate was human?"

"*Is* human," I corrected. Why did he already refer to Gemma as deceased? How odd. "She's Omaera's best friend. We can't just let them have her. They're after Omaera, so they're either using Gemma as bait or—"

"They took her by mistake."

"Gemma was in the picture with Omaera. The one the demons took from Delia's house. So they must have tracked Omaera down here, not realizing that the women are roommates and they just assumed Gemma was Omaera."

Howar hummed a response.

"We don't even know where to begin."

"I'll let Anysa know. She may know of a hunter mage in the area."

"I'll ask Maxar too. We've also met with a spellcaster mage who runs an apothecary, and he seems to have a bead on many of the goings on in the area."

"How are you holding up?" Howar asked. "Callie tells me your mate is bleeding."

"Yes. It's not been easy. We had the spellcaster mage mix up a compound to help with the fugue. But it wears off quickly, so I need to continuously take the capsule every four to six hours, otherwise I become—"

"Irrationally aroused and unbelievably strong."

"To put it delicately."

Howar chuckled. "You just need to mate. Then it will get easier. The Mate's Ache will go, and she'll be more apt and willing to join you in the lust."

I suppressed a groan of regret. "Zandren is calling King Ryden. But please let me know what Anysa says. I have to go."

Howar and I said our goodbyes, then I returned to the apartment. Zandren had shifted back to human form and was indeed on the phone, as was Maxar.

Omaera was on the couch, tucked tight in the corner, hugging her knees and staring blankly ahead, as though in a trance.

All I wanted to do was comfort her.

But I wouldn't touch her again. Not until she asked me to. Not until it was clear that she wanted me to.

Maxar was the first off the phone. "That was Fiddleman. He knows of a hunter mage only half an hour from here. He's going to call him and have him come immediately."

I nodded.

Zandren got off the phone he borrowed from Omaera a moment later. "My father said the entire shifter community is at our disposal. He's dispatching a wolf shifter named Bauer to come help us track."

More nodding from everyone but Omaera. She still stared straight ahead. I wasn't even sure if she was blinking.

Zandren—totally naked—wandered into the kitchen. He put on the kettle, grabbed a mug from the cupboard and, after a little searching, found where the tea was stored. The electric kettle roared as the water heated up.

I stood there like an imp, useless and unable to help in any way.

Zandren—still without clothes—poured the steaming water from the kettle into the mug over the tea bag, then brought the mug to Omaera. "Here."

Jealousy ripped through me as their hands touched when she accepted the mug, her gaze flicking up to his face for just a moment. But the tenderness with which they regarded each other was like a stake through my heart.

"Your clothes are on the counter there," I said, regretting the bitterness in my tone the moment the words came out.

The bear grunted and glanced at the pile of fabric,

What was there to do but wait for reinforcements? Zandren could probably sniff things out to a degree, but he wasn't a hunter mage, and based on how close he sat with Omaera, my guess was he wouldn't leave her side for anything.

One of the few things I agreed with him on.

After about forty minutes, there was a buzz on Omaera's phone. Zandren answered it.

"Bauer Brennan. And Arik Saije," came two very distinct deep voices.

The bear buzzed them up, and we waited.

I'd never met either of these men, but they came recommended. So we had to trust them enough to let them in on some of our secrets.

Less than two minutes later, there was a hard knock at the door.

I needed to make myself useful, so I went and let them in.

Immediately, the shifter looked me up and down, and his top lip curled into a sneer. "What the fuck is a vampire doing here?"

I exhaled in defeat. "My apologies. I know how hated we are."

"We're all her Fated Mates," Maxar said.

Bauer's turquoise-blue eyes widened. "Seriously? Has that ever happened before?"

"Not recorded," I said blandly.

He growled slightly because I spoke again, and stalked into the living room.

The hunter mage—Arik—had alert, brown eyes that scanned the room with quiet assessment. His nose wrinkled a few times. "There were two demons here. Two demons and a human."

Maxar, Zandren, and I nodded. "Yes. We believe the demons are the same two who killed Delia Refera, a spellcaster mage." I'd already grabbed a recent photo of Gemma off the fridge, as well as some of her clothes from her bedroom, and brought them to Arik and Bauer. "Her picture and clothing so you can pick up her scent."

Bauer did no more than grunt. Arik quietly thanked me and accepted the items.

Both men were tall. Nobody was as tall as Zandren, but we all towered over Omaera.

Arik—the hunter mage—was olive skinned with sun-streaked brown hair, pronounced cheekbones and a dimple in his chin. I'd met hunter mages before. In fact, the mage I accidentally beheaded the night the lightning struck was a young, low-power hunter mage. There were all different kinds of mages out there, variations even I'd never encountered.

Did Maxar ever get that list of mages to Omaera like she asked? If so, I would like to take a peek at it sometime. Generally, Realm species kept to themselves for the most part, but one thing I did know about mages was that unlike demons, shifters and vampires who came into full power by the time they reached about twenty-five, mages took longer to gain their full power. The older the mage, the more powerful. So those who were only twenty-five or thirty had weak powers compared to those like Maxar, Monjol Fiddleman and Delia who were centuries old. How old was this hunter mage who came to help? Would he be of any real use? Or was he just the only one available and within driving distance?

"What do we know so far?" Bauer asked, his accent indicative of an East Coast life, probably a long time spent in the Boston area.

"Gemma is human. Twenty-three-years-old—"

"Twenty-two," Omaera corrected, her voice raspy and broken. "Her birthday is in three weeks."

I glanced at her and nodded. "My apologies. Twenty-two. Red hair, fair complexion—"

"Yes, we see all of that in the photo," Bauer snapped. "But why would the demons take her?"

I stowed my initial defensive reaction to his tone. Replying with my own, more educated rhetoric of retaliation would serve nobody. Least of all, Omaera. "My apologies." I gave a slight head bow. "She and Omaera are roommates. We believe they took her for one of two reasons. Either as leverage or bait to draw Omaera out, or simply in error. They *thought* she was Omaera."

Arik nodded.

Bauer shook his head. "Wouldn't they smell she wasn't a demon?"

"You'd think," Arik said. "Who knows how these fuckers work?" He sniffed Gemma's hoodie. "When they realize the human is neither the Queen, nor a demon, what do you think they will do with her?"

"We're hoping they contact us to attempt an exchange," I said. "Killing Gemma will only cause Omaera to go deeper into hiding."

"No, it won't," Omaera said with more fire. "I'm already out for blood after what they did to Delia. This will just make me rain down even more. They killed one of the two people in my life who have ever given a damn about me. And now they've kidnapped the other one. If they kill her, I will burn this fucking earth to the ground to get to them and make them pay." Her gaze landed on me. "And I mean everyone involved. And that goes for those who stand in my way."

Everyone in the room was silent for a moment, processing the gravity of what she just said.

"Well, we need to be proactive," Bauer said. "We can't just sit around hoping they get into contact with us and set up a meeting for an exchange. I doubt they went far. Chances are they'll have taken her somewhere nearby. The longer the transport, the more room for error."

Arik nodded. "I agree. I'm not picking up her scent at the moment, but once I get outside I probably will. Cross your fingers that it doesn't rain. That will make things more challenging."

"The best thing for you to do is stay put," Bauer said, addressing Omaera. "Even though demons can only be killed by beheading, if you're out and about, that puts a target on your back."

"I'd like to know *why* they're coming after you," Arik added. "What exactly is their motive?"

"We speculate it's Lerris Byrche," I said. "King Donovar's brother. Nobody knew Donovar had an heir. So when he died and the power and title were transferred to Omaera and not Lerris, we're assuming he set out to find her and usurp the throne."

"All speculation of course," Bauer said with a harsh glare my way.

"Of course, but it makes sense. Who else would have motive to go after Omaera? And why now?"

"I want to know how they found Delia," Arik said. "It makes me wonder if they're using their own hunter mage?"

I hadn't thought of that. But there were certainly mercenary mages out there. There were mercenary everything. Those whose allegiance wasn't to the crown, but to the highest bidder.

"Does your mother have a grave, Little One?" Zandren asked, his big arm wrapped tightly around Omaera.

She nodded. "Yes. Delia and I visited it often when I was younger. I still go a few times a year though. I haven't been in about four months. Why?"

"Start there," Zandren said.

Bauer and Arik nodded.

"We'll need an address for the gravesite." Bauer pulled out his phone and waited for Omaera to rattle off the address.

"All right," Arik said. "Stay here and wait for further instruction. We won't take long, but we're going to go to the gravesite, Delia's house, and follow any trail we can interpret from here." He leveled his brown gaze on Omaera. "We'll find your friend. I promise."

It wasn't lost on anybody that he didn't say *alive*.

Fresh tears flowed down Omaera's cheeks, and she swallowed. "Thank you," she whispered.

Arik and Bauer nodded, then headed out, leaving Zandren, Maxar, Omaera, and I alone.

"Drink your tea, Little One," Zandren said, picking up the mug from the coffee table and handing it to her. "It'll help."

She sipped it gingerly, the tears still trickling down her cheeks.

"I'm going to make some calls to other mages, see if they know of any mercenary mages and if they might be working with the demons," Maxar said, pulling out his phone. "If there is a mage helping them, I'll burn them to ash myself." He put the phone to his ear and wandered out to the balcony.

I glanced at Omaera, feeling more helpless by the second.

"I um . . . I'm going to make a call too," I said, pulling out my phone. Maybe Raver knew something. He seemed to have his ear to the ground on both nefarious and non-nefarious things. He liked to ride that edge between the wrong side and the right side like a tightrope walker.

And even if Raver knew nothing, I was soothing my own self-loathing by appearing to help.

Right now, there probably wasn't a vampire alive that hated themselves more than I did. And yet, if given the chance to go back and make things right, I'd probably make the same decision all over again. Because my mate was just that sweet and I was already going through withdrawals.

Omaera was a drug. And I was an addict.

An addict who never wanted to quit her, despite how much she hated me.

CHAPTER SEVENTEEN

ZANDREN

My heart ached for Omaera and her pain.

If I could take it away and make it my pain, I would in an instant.

But that wasn't how things worked. Not even if we mated, could I absorb her pain. I would certainly feel it more intensely than I did now, but I wouldn't be able to diminish it or take it on myself.

How were mates supposed to protect each other if we couldn't take away their suffering?

So I did what I could.

I held her.

I made her tea.

I let her cry as hard and as loud as she needed to.

I offered to shift into bear form again if she preferred, but she simply shook her head and snuggled in tighter to my embrace.

At some point, she fell asleep against me, and despite the circumstances, I'd never felt happier or more whole than to have my mate asleep in my arms.

Maxar and Drak were making calls, so it was up to me to protect Omaera.

I carried her to bed and when I went to lay her down, she stirred, blinking open those beautiful, moss-colored eyes. "Lay with me, please," she croaked, reaching for me and wrapping her arms around my neck.

Grunting, I nodded, and she scooted over to the far side of her queen bed. I curled up around her. She fit perfectly against my front, all tucked in, safe.

"What if we're too late?" she asked, her voice raspy.

"We'll find her," I said, squeezing her tighter. "You felt your aunt's pain, right? You knew when she was still alive?"

She nodded, then spun around to face me.

"Can you feel her?" I asked. "Can you feel Gemma?"

Closing her eyes, she took a few deep breaths. All I did was watch her, drinking in her beauty, and not for one second taking for granted how lucky I was to hold her and be her mate. She blinked open those gorgeous eyes, and they flooded with tears. "I can feel her fear. She's alive. But she's terrified."

I bobbed my head and held her tighter. "Hold on to that feeling. As much as it hurts you to feel her fear, at least we know if she is scared, she's still alive."

Omaera swallowed and nodded.

Blinking up at me as one tear fell down her cheek, she cupped my jaw the way I often did with her. I rarely shaved, and my beard was coming in thicker, perhaps slightly unruly too. She stroked the wiry scruff. "I had sex with Drak."

"I know."

"We didn't mate-bond though."

"I know."

"Are you . . . are you upset?"

Staring into her sweet, yet fierce gaze, all I could do was smile, then press a kiss to her forehead. "No, Little One. I'm not upset. Jealous . . . envious, perhaps. But not upset. He is your mate as well. And if it was what you needed at the time, then I am in no position to be upset or judge."

Her face scrunched up. "It . . . it's all so strange. He is insufferable."

I chuckled deep in my chest, jostling us both. "That he is."

"And has some serious boundary issues."

"No argument there."

"And yet, I feel this innate pull toward him."

"It's probably part of the blood lust. But also because you're Fated Mates."

Her hand pressed to my chest. "I feel it with you too. And with Maxar. It's strongest with you though. And unlike with Drak, where I resist it for as long as I can, with you I . . . I want it. I want more of it. You've been nothing but patient and kind. You take care of me like only two other people in my life ever have. I feel safe with you."

"I would lay down my life for you, Little One. I would kill every last soul on earth for you. Just ask." I swallowed. "And the thought of someone hurting you . . ." A deep growl rattled my chest. "I can't even . . ."

Her thumb ran back and forth over the whiskers on my jaw. "You're such a Pooh Bear, but with a murderous streak."

"I only kill when the ones I love are in danger."

"You love me? You barely know me."

"Doesn't matter. What I feel in my soul . . . in my heart is unlike anything I've ever felt before. It's consuming. It's . . . it's like a drug and all I want is more and more. I feel so whole, so complete when I'm with you. Even just lying here beside you fills my heart with immense joy."

Her smile was small but endearingly sweet. "You're everything I've ever wanted in a partner, Prince Zandren Thorne."

"And you're what I've dreamed about for two centuries, Queen Omaera Playfair."

We bowed our heads together until our foreheads met. Our free hands found each other, and we entwined our fingers.

"Are you ever going to kiss me?" she asked, her forehead still against mine.

I smiled. "It's all I've wanted to do since the first moment you called me Pooh Bear."

Tilting our heads in the opposite direction, we pulled our foreheads away just a little, and my lips found hers. The kiss started out sweet, almost timid, but in mere moments, her arms were around my neck and I held her hip and jaw, coaxing her mouth open wider so my tongue could explore.

The flash of lightning that cracked into the room was less dramatic or intense than the one a few days ago, but we both felt it. It was as if it hit me and bounced into her. I hoped that I absorbed most of the shock.

She gasped and broke the kiss, locking eyes with me in wonder. "What just happened?"

"I . . . I think we mate-bonded."

"B-but doesn't that involve sex?"

"I thought so."

"I . . . I haven't had a lot of boyfriends in my life. I don't trust easily. I don't let people in. And even though I don't know what falling in love feels like, I don't think it feels like this." She swallowed and her eyes shifted back and forth across my face. "From everything I've ever watched on television or read in books, falling in love is supposed to feel like this wild roller coaster, sickening but exciting. Consuming."

I wasn't sure where she was going with this, so I kept my expression neutral but open, even though my heart relentlessly battered my ribs in anticipation.

"This doesn't feel like that. With you, I feel seen. I feel known. You take care of me. You anticipate my needs. You don't push, and you respect my boundaries. And although it's all happening lightning fast—" She paused and chuckled at her choice of words. "I don't care. I haven't *fallen* in love with you. I've gently, perfectly, slid into it. Like two puzzle pieces that just . . . fit."

My whole body erupted with joy and I'm sure I was smiling like an idiot.

"When we kissed, all I could think of was . . . I think I could be with this bear forever. If he's shown me who he really is, then I'm okay with forever."

"I'm not perfect," I said. "But you've seen all of me."

"Not the murderous side yet." Her smirk was playful.

"No. Not that side."

"So . . . are we like, really mate-bonded now?"

I shrugged. "It's a first for me too. I didn't even know an emotional bond was a possibility."

"It seems I'm all kinds of firsts in this secret world, hmm?"

Nuzzling her neck, I kissed her. "I kind of like that we bonded this way instead."

She lifted her head. "Really?"

That made me grin again. "Okay, well, I'd be lying if I said I didn't want to have sex." My erection pressing against her hip said as much. "But I'm okay waiting until things settle down. You're my Bonded Mate now. That's what matters."

Nibbling on her lip, she glanced at me. "I do still have my period. And I have a tampon in. But, um . . ."

Smiling like a Cheshire Cat, I caught her wavelength. Wait, was I reading her mind? Was the Bond that fast to start giving me her powers and her mine?

She flipped over to her back and I bent my head, pressing kisses along her neck, down over her cropped shirt, to her belly. I lifted the hem of her shirt slightly to reveal a tattoo of purple roses that looked wet, surrounding a skull inked onto her ribcage. I kissed that too, while I unclasped the button of her jeans and tugged down the zipper.

I pushed my fingers down beneath the elastic of her cotton boyshort panties, beyond the trimmed downy hair until I found her wet center. Her hips bucked as I gathered some of her arousal before dragging my fingers back up to her throbbing clit.

"Kiss me," she whispered. "You're really good at that."

Grinning, I dropped my mouth to hers as I ran wide, rough, concentric circles around her clit.

She moaned into my mouth, and her hips leaped off the bed. My cock strained against my jeans, but I shoved down my own needs. This wasn't about me. This was about Omaera. She needed this.

And any part of her that I could get, I would take and be the most grateful bear in the world. We had a lifetime now. Eventually, we would be together, but at the moment, I needed to take her mind off the pain of Gemma and Delia and help her find a little joy. A little pleasure.

Her arms looped back around my neck and she tugged me down to her, kissing me deeper. Her tongue massaged me, exploring my mouth, pulling growls and rumbles from deep in my chest. My fingers picked up speed on her clit, gathering more of the slick silk from her center as I rubbed her pulsing clit. It swelled beneath my touch and her hip lifts became more erratic. She mewled and whimpered into my mouth, grappling at me, pulling me closer. Her breathing increased and hot puffs from her nose hit my upper lip as she rode my fingers.

I broke the kiss and dropped my mouth to her neck, biting her just hard enough, but not too hard. Not enough to break the skin. I vaguely noticed the small puncture marks from Drak's fangs, but ignored them. This moment was about Omaera and me. Nobody else was welcome.

The moment my teeth pressed against her sweet flesh, her back bowed and she broke with a sharp cry. Her clit throbbed and swelled even more as fresh arousal gushed from her center. I gathered more, continuing to rub circles around the pulsing bud. She gripped my hair and hauled my face away from her neck, capturing my mouth again in another kiss. She bit my bottom lip and tugged before diving back in and sucking on my tongue. I groaned and flicked her clit hood with the nail of my thumb and her leg spasmed. Smiling against her mouth, I did it again. Her leg twitched.

This woman, this demoness, my queen was my everything now.

Her pleasure was my priority. Her life was all that mattered to me.

Her chest heaved and her whimpers into my mouth had my cock pressing harder than ever against my zipper. Once her muscles relaxed and she collapsed back to the bed, I peeled my lips from hers, smoothed the hair away from her face, and kissed her cheek. "My queen. My mate."

Her smile was as sweet and sleepy as could be. "My prince. My mate."

I was stupidly giddy from that comment and it must have come through in my smile.

Grinning, she sat up and rolled me over to my back, straddling me and opening the button and zipper of my jeans. But I was quick to grab her hands and stop her. "No. This isn't . . . I don't expect."

"I know," she said, pulling my pants down so my cock sprang free. "And that's why I am." Then she dropped her head and took my cock in her hot, wet little mouth.

My fingers found her hair, and I held her in place as she ran her tongue up from the base of my shaft to the crown and back, swirling the tip and giving it a playful extra lick.

I groaned and bucked up with my hips, encouraging her to go deeper. To see how far down her throat she could take me. I knew I was big. In all ways. Tall, broad, and with a big cock. Most bear shifters were big. So I'm sure there was some level of trepidation on her part as to how we'd even fit or whether she could even take me.

From everything I'd heard, the Fates didn't fuck around and they intervened when necessary to make sure that no mate was ever *hurt* or unable to be with their mate that way.

But she was raised human, and was half human. So maybe things would take some time and easing in to. Exploring each other the way we were now was A-OK by me though. We had a lifetime together to perfect things. Right now, we were just . . . connecting.

She deep-throated as best she could, but even when I hit her tonsils, there was still another two inches, at least, left outside her mouth.

"Jesus," she said, after she came up for air. "That thing'll never fit inside me."

Chuckling, I cupped her jaw and guided her back down. "The Fates will help."

"I sure as hell hope so. It's like a python." She brought me back into her mouth, using her hand to help stroke and not ignore the base.

I was close in seconds. The sight of my mate's head bobbing in my lap, her hot, wet little mouth surrounding my cock, it was pure perfection. I'd already been close when she came from my fingers, so it took no time at all for me to finish now. My grasp on her hair tightened as the tingles in my lower belly intensified, the warmth spreading higher and lower until my balls cinched up against my taint and I finally let go.

The way the back of her throat hugged and contracted around my crown, swallowing as I came, filling her mouth with my seed, was nothing short of earth-shattering. Maybe it was that she was my mate, but I'd never had an orgasm quite like that. And it just kept going. It spread from my cock and balls down to my toes, causing them to curl. Then up into my arms, my fingers tightening until they locked in her curls, holding her in place. My brain short-circuited and either that was angels singing or a weird ringing in my ears. I growled and huffed with each surge of pleasure until I was spent and boneless. I collapsed, depleted of energy, and all brain cells, against the bed, releasing her hair and letting my arms flop out to the sides.

She released me with a wet *pop,* sitting up and wiping her lips discreetly with the hem of her shirt.

My hand came up, and I stroked her tattoo. "What's the significance of this?" I liked the look of her straddling me like this.

Nibbling on her lip, she glanced down at my thumb on one of the roses. "Delia told me that *Omaera* means rose in my father's language. I Googled and searched for the language, but came up with nothing. But it still brought me comfort to know that one bit of information about him. About where I came from. The skull is because I like skulls, and also because both my parents are dead. Morbid, but whatever."

"It's sexy," I murmured, struggling to keep my eyes open.

She slithered down my body and lay on top of me. My hand cradled her ribcage where the tattoo was. "You're so warm, and surprisingly comfy."

I kissed her crown. "Sleep now, Little One. Nothing we can do but wait."

Pressing a kiss to my chest, she nestled in, and I wrapped my arms around her protectively. "I'm glad we mated."

"Me too."

"I'm still not sure your dick's ever going to fit though."

I chuckled enough to shake us both. "We'll go slow. Remember, we have a lifetime together now. Eternity. No need to rush things."

Her sigh echoed the contentment in my heart. "An eternity . . . I think I'm okay with that."

I was more than okay with it. I was over the fucking moon.

CHAPTER EIGHTEEN

OMAERA

A bear-like snore woke me up. Thick, veiny arms lightly dusted with blond hair wrapped tight around my body, keeping me warm and safe.

My cheek was pressed against Zandren's bare chest, with more soft, blond hair tickling my lip and nose.

Grunting from how much of a furnace he was and how I needed to escape the inferno, I wiggled to get him to release me.

He grunted, snorted, and opened his eyes. "'Mornin'."

"Too hot," I said, panting.

Nodding, he relaxed his arms, and I sat up, straddling him. Then I immediately remember all of last night and leaped off the bed, throwing open the door.

Maxar and Drak were in the living room with coffee, along with Bauer and Arik.

"Fresh pot just made," Maxar said, jerking his chin toward my fancy machine.

I ignored the coffee. "What do we know about Gemma? Do we know where she is? Do we know who took her?"

Zandren came shuffling up behind me, resting hands on my shoulders with affection and protection. He kissed the crown of my head. "Coffee?"

I nodded, and he made his way into the kitchen.

"We visited Elena Playfair's gravesite," Bauer said, remorse in his eyes. "Someone desecrated it."

My eyes nearly popped out of my skull. "What? How?"

"They dug it up. Exhumed her body—then left it there."

My jaw dropped. "Why would they do that? Oh my god. My mother's corpse is just . . ." Anger, sorrow, and disbelief formed a sickening cyclone in my gut until I thought I might be sick.

"Presumably it was a way to figure out how your mother died. And what species she was," Arik added. "Also to get her scent, which will be tied to yours. They will be similar. Just like any children you have will share similar scent markers as you—particularly the females."

"D-do you know when this happened? Before or after Delia was killed?"

"We can't say for certain. But based on the fact that nothing had been done about the grave site, the casket was just laid open and disturbed, I would say it was recent. Last day or two. Maybe three at most."

"Well, I was only just hit by lightning Friday. Delia was killed Saturday, and it's Monday now. So . . ."

"We understand. It's just tough to tell." Arik's expression was grim. "We visited Delia's home as well and just like the gravesite, we scented the demons. They are definitely working with a mercenary hunter mage though. I smelled him too." His face darkened. "I also know him."

"Yarvak?" Maxar asked with disdain.

Arik nodded.

Maxar growled. "Fucker has zero morals. He provides his services to the highest bidder, regardless of whether that bid is from an unscrupulous source or not. He's been on the Council's watch list for a long time."

Arik nodded again, as did Zandren and Drak.

"Yeah, I smelled him at the gravesite," Arik went on. "My guess is they were told by whomever hired them to look into your mother. When they found out she was dead, they exhumed her body to get answers on where to find you, which led them to your aunt—the last person to touch her, I'm assuming. And when

Delia wouldn't give you up, they killed her. But then Yarvak followed the scent trail from your mother and possibly Delia's home, if she had anything left of yours, to your apartment here."

"But Gemma doesn't have my scent, so why'd they take her?" I frowned. "I mean, we *do* share clothes sometimes. And live together. Would that be enough for her to have my scent on her and confuse the hunter mage and demons?"

"Yarvak is a mercenary hunter. Not a kidnapper. Not a murderer. Although he has no morals, he does have a code which he will stand by rigidly. He won't go beyond finding someone. So he'll have told them where to go, but the demons were the ones to do the kidnapping. And they obviously couldn't differentiate. At this point, because they exhumed your mother's body, they knew that you are half human. So they could smell human when they came to the apartment. My guess is that they probably figured your human scent was stronger than your demon scent, which led to them taking Gemma. Who knows how these sadistic fuckers work?" Arik shook his head and exhaled with frustration out of his nostrils.

"Or they took Gemma because Omaera wasn't here and they're using her as bait," Bauer added.

Arik nodded in agreement. "Or that."

"So do we know where they have Gemma?" I asked. "We need to get to her now."

Bauer scratched at his stubbly chin. "We've managed to track her scent to a place across town. An abandoned meatpacking plant."

"I know that place. We've been to raves there before."

They both nodded.

"I could only smell two demons when we were there. More may be on the way. But if the four of you go, and it's just the two demons, it should be manageable."

"The four of us? What about you two?" Were they just going to abandon us when we were this close to getting my friend back? Were they going to abandon their Queen? An uncomfortable rush of helpless fury filled my chest, and I had to quickly lasso it and squeeze, condensing it into a ball and putting a shield over it. Even though she was a xenophobic, murdering bitch, Raewyn's one lesson on containing my anger had proved to be very helpful, more than once.

"I have a code too," Arik said. "I'm a hunter. Period. I find people. I don't fight. I don't kidnap or kill. I also have a mate and kids. I'm not going into battle. I'm sorry."

Bauer nodded. "I have a wife and pups at home. I agreed to help find the human, but unfortunately, I'm not willing to risk my life for one. I won't risk leaving my mate and pups without a mate or father."

"Not even for your Queen?" Drak asked, anger edging his tone.

Both Arik and Bauer made regretful faces, though Bauer still managed to also convey his deep-seated hatred for Drak.

They faced me. Arik bowed his head slightly. "I'm sorry, Your Majesty."

"As am I," Bauer echoed.

I exhaled and nodded, expelling a lot of energy to *not* parboil their brains. "Please take us to the meatpacking plant. Then you may take your leave."

They nodded. We gathered ourselves; I put on better clothes, and even Drak dressed down in less formal and restrictive attire. I wasn't sure when he'd gone out to get clothes, but I also didn't care. He was still in all black, only this time it was black sweatpants and a black hoodie. Maxar was in loose-fitting, black, stretchy pants and a black sweatshirt, while Zandren said he planned to shift when we got there, so color-matching with us wasn't a concern.

Keeping with the theme, I wore all black as well—it was easy since ninety-five percent of my wardrobe was black anyway. I went with yoga leggings and a tight-fitting, but stretchy, black hoodie. I put my combat boots back on and a knit cap over my wild hair, which I tied into a bun at the nape of my neck.

It felt like we were going to rob a bank or knock over a jewelry store.

"I have a minivan," Bauer said. "We can take that."

I froze as the elevator reached ground level. I hadn't been in a passenger car in ages, and the idea of squeezing into a minivan with all this testosterone sat uncomfortably under my skin.

Zandren reached for my hand and gave it a squeeze. "It's the fastest way to her, Little One. I know you're reluctant, but it'll be okay."

His smile was all the reassurance I needed. Or at least that's what I told myself, and I rallied.

For Gemma.

I would do whatever it took to save Gemma.

She was my person.

Well, now I had at least two people. Gemma and Zandren.

I'd get in a car to save Zandren too.

Nodding, I took a deep breath and said, "Okay."

We piled into Bauer's minivan, which had Cheerios on the floor, a sippy cup under the seat and so many children's books shoved into the pockets behind the front seats.

"How many pups do you have?" Maxar asked.

Bauer snorted in mirth as he pushed the start button for the van. "Six. Two are grown though. Four are young pups, and my mate is pregnant with our second set of twins."

"Jesus," Maxar murmured. "That's . . ."

"Dogs for you," Arik finished from the front passenger seat. "Almost as bad as rabbits."

"Fuck off," Bauer said with a grin, as he pulled away from the sidewalk and out into traffic. "We're just lucky."

"And fertile as fuck," Arik added.

I had to work on not holding my breath. Zandren sat beside me, our fingers laced together. Maxar was on the other side of me against the window and Drak was in the back, kept company by his perpetual bad mood. We made sure to give him another capsule before we left and also stashed one in his pocket, just in case we were gone longer than four hours. The last thing we needed on this raid was for him to get distracted with the need to jump my bones again.

What normally would have been a twenty-minute drive across town was closer to forty because of the morning rush hour traffic. I was on pins and needles the closer we got to the warehouse. The area of town was still quite in-dustrial, unlike where my apartment was located, which used to be the industrial district, but was now residential and commercial.

Bauer parked his minivan in front of the meatpacking plant and unrolled his window. Arik did the same.

They both sniffed.

"They're here. So is Gemma," Arik said.

"Can you tell if she's still alive?" I asked, fear ransacking me until my voice and body shook. "I can feel her fear, but . . . I need you to confirm it."

Arik nodded. "I believe she still is. The body *does* smell different when dead. And I don't smell death here."

"Which says a lot, considering it used to be where they packed dead animal meat," Bauer added.

"Good," I breathed, only feeling a modicum better.

"We're going to leave you here," Bauer said.

I nodded. I couldn't really argue with him. I'd been orphaned. That was the last thing I wanted to do to either of these men's children or mates. They agreed to help us, but they also had a code. And I needed to respect that code. Without them, we'd still be searching for Gemma. So at least we knew where she was now.

Maxar, Zandren, Drak, and I piled out of the minivan, thanking the wolf shifter and hunter mage for all their help.

It was a foggy, gray day and rather drizzly, so the fact that we were dressed in black even though it was the morning, wasn't as redundant as I thought it might be.

Zandren sniffed. "I can smell them too." He dropped to all fours and shifted.

I'm not sure I'd ever tire of watching him shift. It was still really new to me, but it was so fascinating to watch that I hoped the novelty never wore off.

He was my big, ferocious Pooh Bear in seconds, instantly nuzzling my side with his muzzle.

"So . . . like what do we do?" I asked, glancing around for signs of people. There wasn't anybody around, but steam rose from various warehouses, indicating that businesses were still running as usual.

Despite my world coming to a full stop when Gemma was kidnapped, the rest of the world kept turning. People kept living their lives, caught up and making the best of their daily grind.

"Well, you put on these first," Maxar said, making four orange flame ropes and waggling his fingers over them like he was enchanting them with some kind of spell. "I figure if putting this rope on Raewyn stopped her from frying our brains, the same principle should apply if *we* wear them. It should stop the demons inside from trying to fondue our gray matter."

"I thought you could block demons?" I asked.

"I can. But we don't know what kind of demons we're dealing with." His expression turned sad. "Delia could block them too, but—"

"Right," I said, not needing him to finish that sentence. But they had beaten her so badly that she didn't have the strength to maintain the block. Then they attacked her and tortured her until they nuked her brain.

Drak cleared his throat. "Why didn't we do this sooner?"

Maxar shot him a look. "I wasn't sure if it would work. I'm happy to leave one *off* your head though, smartass."

The vampire grumbled something and accepted the fire rope, tying it around his head.

I let Maxar place it on my head. Zandren did the same, but his ears kept twitching and it wouldn't stay put. "Is it itchy?" I asked him.

He nodded his big fury head.

I tried tying it tighter, but he growled.

"Try to keep it on," I said. "I'd hate for them to hurt you."

He licked the back of my hand and kept it on as best he could, even though his ears continued to twitch.

We followed my big grizzly around the building as he followed his nose to the back door, then up a flight of metal stairs to a second door on an upper level. He used his claw to pick the lock and carefully opened it so it didn't creak or squeak.

Maxar went in first, followed by Zandren, then myself, and finally Drak.

It was dark inside, but even I could feel the presence of the supernatural. Were these my new powers beginning to take shape, courtesy of my Mate-Bond with Zandren? I could also see better.

Bears had excellent night vision. Did this mean my night vision was superior too?

It felt like my sense of smell was stronger. The air smelled like damp fire logs and . . . death.

Arik said he couldn't smell death—just demons and human—so I took solace that the death smell was simply the makeup of whatever evil demon thought it was okay to steal from a queen.

We crept along the metal grate that made up the second floor. If you hung your head over the railing, you could see down into the ground-level main part of the warehouse. I wasn't going to do that though. If I saw Gemma chained up or hurt, I would lose my shit, and any semblance of our plan would be over.

We let Zandren lead the way, the soft pads of his paws silent on the grate. His breathing was heavy, but quiet enough they probably couldn't hear us.

All the exposed duct work ran below the catwalk where we traipsed. There were a few sets of stairs that led elsewhere, all metal grates and rusty, but Zandren seemed to know exactly where to go, so we just kept following him.

We reached the end of the line, which was the landing for more stairs heading downward.

"What's the plan?" I whispered, even though we'd gone over it in the minivan on the way over. I needed to hear it again.

"You go," Maxar said. "Whoever is there needs to think that you came alone. As far as we know, they don't know you have mates, or that you're aware of your powers. They could be banking on your human side being dominant."

"This is all speculation, of course," Drak said.

"Of course it is, but we have nothing better to go on right now," Maxar snapped while still whispering. "Everything is speculation. For all we know, it could be King Howar or Queen Anysa pulling the strings here because they want to usurp the throne from the demons once and for all."

Drak glared at him. "Howar would never."

Zandren snorted like he wasn't so sure.

Maxar shot a skeptical look at Drak. "How well do you know your King?"

"Better than you know your Queen," he retorted.

"Table the pissing match until after we have Gemma safe and I've killed some fucking demons," I said with a hiss, glaring at both of them.

Thankfully, they actually managed to show a little remorse.

"A hybrid has never been documented. But the idea of a hybrid having a mate—let alone three—is so unfathomable that it's a safe bet they're not going to expect us." Maxar glanced over the railing and down into the main ground level of the warehouse.

"Unless Gemma told them," Drak followed up.

Maxar nodded. "Here's hoping she didn't."

Zandren rumbled next to me, and I turned to him. He licked my hand, then my face. "I'll be safe," I said, kissing his snout. "I promise."

I glanced at Drak and Maxar. "I'm going to go rescue my friend."

They both nodded, then watched as I took the long metal stairs down to the main level. I never looked back because I knew they had my six. I couldn't take my eyes off my twelve though. Demons, at least the only other one I'd met, were as slippery as they came. So I needed to expect the unexpected and keep my wits about me.

I reached the main level, taking in the old, wooden pallets strewn about, along with some thick, blue packing plastic. I glanced over at the metal scraps, old brown blood smears on the concrete floor, and the hooks and chains hanging from a long metal rod that ran nearly half the length of the space, supported by thick iron posts secured to the floor. I'd never seen the place in the daylight, let alone without a DJ booth, flashing lights, and people dressed in crazy clothes and glow sticks dancing to the beat of the music with a plethora of psychedelics in their system.

I had to assume that they just tarped over some of this stuff, or moved it out of the way when they hosted a rave in here. But maybe they just set up the DJ booth and stage to block the permanent structures?

"Hello?" I called out, my voice echoing up to the rafters. "Gemma?"

Silence.

"It's Omaera Playfair, Queen of the Realm. Illegitimate daughter of King Donovar and Elena Playfair. I'm assuming I'm the person you're looking for, and you either took my best friend by mistake or as bait. A mistake either way, but you've gotten what you wanted. I'm here."

I swallowed and tuned into my surroundings, listening for even the faintest sound of breathing.

Gemma was here. I could feel her. I could feel her fear. I sniffed the air and relaxed just a little. Lavender and cinnamon.

"I highly suggest you bring out my friend—unharmed. You don't want to see me when I'm angry."

A deep, raspy chuckle made the hair on my arms and the back of my neck stand straight up. A cold drop of fear played leapfrog down my vertebrae, and I spun around. Where was the sound was coming from.

"Stupid girl," said the same voice. "Stupid little girl. Stupid little *human*."

"*Half* human." I corrected. "At least I'm not a coward, hiding in the shadows. I'm here, aren't I? I'm here to get my friend and take her home."

Slowly, from behind a corner that led to a hallway, he appeared, sauntering with his ego leading the way. I'm not sure what, or who, I was expecting, but this man wasn't it. He was . . . ordinary. Handsome-*ish*, in fact. Tall, muscular with blue-hazel eyes and thick, dark brown hair. His features were chiseled, with a strong chin and high cheekbones, and his swagger was practiced and confident. *Too* confident. A four-inch, pink, puffy scar ran up the right side of his jaw, and he would have looked even better if he'd hidden his thin lips with some facial hair.

His chuckle grated on my few remaining nerves, and when he looked me up and down, sneering like I was no more than dog shit on his shoe, I knew then and there that only one of us was going to walk away from this encounter alive.

"Where is Gemma?" I asked, determined not to let my voice crack.

"You mean the *human*?" he asked, curling his thin top lip up in disgust. "Why do you even care?"

"Because she's my best friend and I love her. And not all humans are bad. Just like not all demons are bad, present company excluded."

He chuckled some more, and I gnashed my molars together at the irritating sound. "I knew my brother took a human whore. We all slum it at some point in our lives. I just never expected it to result in a . . . *child*."

Even though they'd all speculated that the culprit was my uncle, I was still flabbergasted that it was true. He caught me off guard and my mouth opened, but no sound came out.

I gathered my wits quickly though. This was just like a poker game.

I needed to keep my face neutral. Kill my tells. Play the player. There was only one sucker here and it sure as hell wasn't me.

"Yes, well, their union *did* result in a child. The rightful heir to the throne of the Realm. Let me ask. *Uncle, dear,* how did my father die?"

His smile was serpentine, and I resisted the urge to squirm. I didn't have a lot of fears in life, but snakes and cars were at the very top. God, I hoped there weren't any snake shifters.

"Sir. Sir," came a petulant voice from the same direction Lerris had come from. Then a slimy demon with beady eyes, ears too big for his head and greasy, dark hair appeared, reminding me of a ferret that fell into a vat of oil. He took one look at me and sneered.

"What?" Lerris barked.

"She's not alone, sir."

Lerris's eyes found mine, panic in his gaze.

I smirked. "You think I'd be stupid enough to come alone?"

He doused his initial fear and smiled with feigned confidence. "Let me guess, you brought your little human friends with you?"

"Nope."

"What's that on your head?"

I lifted my brows. "Just something my mate made me."

Now, I really had his attention. His henchman's too. "M-mate?" he stammered. "That's not possible."

"No? Then why do I have one?" I tapped my chin. "No, wait. I don't have one."

Relief creased his features.

"I have *three.*"

Lerris shook his head vehemently. "Impossible. You're lying. You're a filthy, disgusting human and a liar. No hybrid has ever been recorded. So for the Fates to give you a mate, let alone three . . . you're lying."

I shrugged. "Maybe. Maybe not."

He tried to infiltrate my mind, but Maxar's fire crown was doing its job. I could feel Lerris trying to manipulate me and burn my brain, but it wasn't working.

When he realized it wasn't working, he roared with fury.

I fought back, harnessing all the anger and fear I had over losing Delia, over never meeting my parents, over losing Gemma, and this new, fucked up world I was part of, and I blasted him hard right back.

He wasn't prepared for it and crumpled to the ground with a scream.

But he was a strong, old demon. So he rallied quickly and shot back to his feet.

A scream from the side drew my attention. That's when I saw Maxar, wrapping Lerris's henchman in a rope of fire and binding his hands and feet, then gagging him.

I smiled at Maxar, then quickly pivoted back to face Lerris. "Where is Gemma?"

Still thinking he had the upper hand, my demonic uncle grinned, reminding me so much of The Joker. "The throne belongs to me. I am the rightful heir to the Realm. Not you. Not some disgusting, abomination, half-breed."

A sharp scream from down the hallway where they both originated diverted my attention. Gemma. Her fear slammed into my brain and I could almost feel the pain and terror as if it were happening to me.

Ignoring Lerris, I took off in that direction, weaving through the narrow corridor and into what had probably once been an office and staff locker rooms. There were bathrooms here too. I knew that. We used those during the raves.

"Gemma!" I called out. "Gem!"

Another harsh, pained scream.

Was Lerris torturing her from where he was in the main part of the warehouse. Could he project his power that far away without looking at his target?

Raewyn was able to do it to you and Gemma. So obviously it's possible.

Right!

That motherfucker. He really deserved to die. And not swiftly the way Raewyn did.

Slowly. Painfully. And I was going to enjoy it.

"Gemma!" I cried out, the panic and guilt hitting me in nauseating waves. I clutched my stomach and choked on a sob. How could we leave her alone in the apartment? How could the guys not have checked on her before they followed me like imprinted little ducklings?

I tried various doors, but they were all locked.

A third, terrified, agonizing shriek juddered my soul.

"Gemma!"

Drak appeared, slightly out of breath. "Did you find her?"

"No! She's screaming, but I can't figure out where she is."

"Maxar said it's Lerris who took her?"

I nodded. "And killed Delia. And my father."

His eyes widened.

"He's out in the main part of the plant. Go. Detain him. I need to find Gemma."

Drak nodded and took off in the direction I came.

I kept trying doors.

More and more screaming.

Where was she?

The hallway was never ending. I grunted and growled, wishing for Zandren's strength so I could just tear down the doors. She had to be behind one of them. I just couldn't get in to her.

I ran back out to the main part of the warehouse only to see Zandren charge Lerris, teeth bared and ready to destroy. But as he charged him, his flame crown fell off, and that was enough of a window for the worst to happen.

I watched it like it was in slow motion.

The moment Zandren's eyes changed. His target, his mission, his alliance was distorted. Lerris had his mind now, and rather than tear it to shreds, he was going to use my mate as a weapon. A weapon against us.

Maxar was there, throwing flames at Lerris. He landed quite a few good hits. Scorch marks covered my uncle's clothes, and he had to pat out flames a few times. But when the last batch of black flames whizzed out of Maxar's hands, Zandren spun around and charged Maxar, roaring and shoving him to the ground, standing on top of him. He slashed at his shirt with his sharp claws. Maxar screamed out in pain.

I ran up, crying, "Zandren! Zandren, stop! You're hurting him."

I glanced over to find Drak in a hand-to-hand battle with Lerris. He kept baring his teeth, his fangs dropped, and he searched for an opening to lunge forward and bite. But Lerris evaded him well.

One of them would land a sharp blow, knocking down the other, then the other would retaliate with just as much precision and force. They were matched for strength and agility.

I couldn't worry about them right now though. I had to trust that Drak had this. My focus was on stopping Zandren from killing Maxar. I threw myself over Maxar's body. "Please," I sobbed. "Please stop. You don't want to do this."

I braced for the swipe of his claws against my back, but they never came.

Glancing up, I found him sitting back on his rear, staring at me with a confused head tilt.

He even gave a cute little whimper.

"He can't hurt you because you've mated," Maxar wheezed beneath me. "You're the only thing keeping him from killing me. Lerris has manipulated his mind and made him believe that we're the enemy."

Lerris landed a harsh blow to Drak, sending him flying across the warehouse and into the wall. That pulled Zandren's attention, and the murderous look returned to the bear's eyes. He bounded forward with a devastating growl, head-butted Drak, then opened his mouth wide and took a huge bite of the vampire's thigh. Drak bellowed out in pain.

I screamed. "No!"

Lerris clambered back up to standing and laughed. "You've only mated with the bear. If you'd mated all of them the bear wouldn't attack the other two. Stupid girl."

"And where's your mate?" I asked. "Hiding from you, I'm sure."

"She hasn't come of age yet," he said, brushing debris off his black pants as he walked toward where I still lay across Maxar's body. He removed my flame halo and sharp shards of pain speared my brain.

"Ahh," I cried, closing my eyes and visualizing pushing him out and slamming down a shield. The pain receded. It was working.

"You have powers," he said, surprised.

"I am half demon, and also the Queen," I said, slightly breathless.

"Not for long." Stepping over to a small table I hadn't noticed until now, he pulled a sword from a sheath, then walked back toward us. "Do you know what this is?"

"Your dildo?"

Fury flickered back at me in his eyes. "Disgusting child. It is Moloch's Sacrifice."

"And I'm supposed to know who that is?"

He scoffed and shook his head. "All the more reason the throne should be mine." He lifted it high in the air, preparing to behead me. I couldn't risk Maxar getting hurt any more than he already was, and I wasn't sure if Drak was even still alive.

No. He was alive. I could feel his energy. Even if we hadn't bonded, I could still feel our connection. Still feel the pull . . . and also his fear. He wasn't dead, but he was hurt and scared.

"Zandren!" I cried out, hoping that he'd come to me. That he'd leave Drak, see his mate was in trouble and come to my aid before it was too late. "Help!"

The large sword glinted under the harsh glare of the obnoxious fluorescent lights hanging among the exposed duct work.

Was this really how it ended?

Was this really the finale of my story? This man killed my father and my aunt. Was he going to get the hat trick and finish me off too?

I glared at him, funneling all the anger and loneliness, the fear, and betrayal I'd ever felt in my life into a big ball of fire in my mind. Then I brought in all the other emotions too. The love. The joy. The independence and stability Delia gave me. The unwavering friendship and support from Gemma. The pure and utter devotion of my mates, even though they'd just met me. Zandren's love and how with him I felt so seen. So known. I was vulnerable with him, and I was vulnerable with so few people. Gemma and Delia were the only two people who had ever seen me cry until three pushy men showed up on my doorstep, telling me I was theirs and they were mine forever.

I hated the idea. But I also kind of loved it.

The ball of fire grew bigger and bigger. Brighter and brighter. I closed my eyes and, with every last ounce of energy and power I had left, I hurled that ball directly at Lerris.

A startled and pained cry made me open my eyes. Lerris was on the ground, halfway across the warehouse. Drak leaned against the wall, bleeding from his leg, and Zandren was . . . I glanced around.

Where was Zandren?

I carefully climbed off Maxar. "Are you okay?"

He nodded. "I . . . I think so. I'll live."

"Zandren?" I called out. "Where are you?"

"I had to put him out," Drak said, his voice weak.

I ran to him. "You what?"

"I had to. Or he was going to kill me. I had to . . ." Drak was paler than I'd ever seen him, and he could barely keep his eyes open. "I bit him and then I wrapped the flame rope around his head."

I took in Drak's bare head. "Where is he now?"

"He stumbled that way." He pointed. "I had to put him down. I'm sorry."

I glanced in the direction Drak pointed, only to see two big bear paws sprawled out behind the pile of pallets and packing plastic. I ran to Zandren and checked to see if he was breathing. He was. Thank god. Then I ran back to Drak.

"What can I do?"

He opened his eyes, just barely. "I need . . . I need to feed."

"To feed?"

He lifted his brows, then nodded.

Oh!

"Oh . . . uh . . . okay." I double checked that Lerris was still unconscious and Maxar was okay before I and tilted my head to the side to expose my neck. "O-okay."

"A wrist will do," he said weakly.

Swallowing, I pulled up the sleeve of my hoodie to expose my veins. He carefully slid one descended fang into my skin, which hurt less than a vaccination, then pressed his lips to my flesh. In seconds, his complexion regained color, and I watched before my very eyes as his wound began to close up and stop bleeding.

Unlike the first time he bit me when we had sex, this wasn't as pleasurable. It didn't hurt, but I got no ethereal high. No out-of-body experience.

He removed his lips and swept his tongue over the puncture hole to seal it. I helped him stand, and he only hobbled a little as we made our way over to Maxar and helped him sit up. "You need to make another flame crown thing for Drak," I said.

He nodded and used up probably every last bit of energy he had to create one more.

I picked up the thrown sword and held the immense weight in my hand. A rush of pure magic flowed from the handle up into my arm and body, filling my heart with heat and, just like that, the sword wasn't heavy anymore. I spun around to go deliver Lerris his final death blow, to make him pay for all the people he killed, but he was gone.

CHAPTER NINETEEN

OMAERA

Another cry in Gemma's voice down the hall had us all running.

The sword was now an extension of me and I held it out in front as I made my way down the hallway. Maxar and Drak hobbled behind me as best they could.

A door was open, and another scream shook my bones.

I ran in to find Lerris standing over Gemma as she writhed on the floor, blood flowing out of her nose and ears. She clutched at the side of her head. Blood seeped from the corners of her eyes and it looked as though she'd raked her nails repeatedly down her face. Everything was battered and bloody.

Rage filled every corner of my body and just as I prepared to charge forward and take off Lerris's head, thunder cracked through the room like a sonic boom, shoving my uncle hard against the far wall, his head hitting the brick with a deafening *crack*. Maxar and Drak were thrown too.

Only I remained standing.

I ran to Gemma, brushing the hair off her face. "Gem. Oh Gemma! I'm so sorry."

"He's getting away," Drak said pointing at Lerris, who was scrambling to stand up and open the exit door right next to him.

I wanted to kill him. But my friend was more important. My mates and their injuries were more important. This wasn't the end of my war with Lerris. But for now, it was the end of the battle. I needed to care for my soldiers, take them home to heal.

Lerris and I locked eyes. Triumph mixed with pain flickered back at me. "Those powers aren't yours, you mongrel. You can't hide from me. I'm the true king and the whole realm knows it."

Then he limped out the exit, the slam of the door making the whole room shake.

I shook Gemma by the shoulders. "Gem. Gemma, you need to wake up."

Her eyes were closed, but she was breathing.

"Help!" I demanded, looking to Maxar and Drak.

They scrambled up from where they were on the floor and made their way over.

"What do I do?

Maxar kneeled down beside Gemma, hovering his palms above her body and allowing little yellow and purple flames to flicker out. Some of the cuts on her face began to heal.

"That's all I can do," he said, extinguishing the flames. "I don't have powers to heal her anymore. I don't have enough energy to cauterize anymore. I'm sorry."

"It's enough for now," I said. "Stay with her . . . please."

They nodded, and I ran back to find Zandren.

How did Drak put him down with a bite? Did he have different kinds of bites? Did he have a poison in his fangs like a snake that paralyzed people?

I reached my big bear and fell to the floor beside him. "Zandren." I shook him gently. "Zandren, you need to wake up now." Resting my hand on his head, I bent low and pressed my forehead to his. "Please wake up. Please."

"My fangs have a paralytic in them," came Drak's voice behind me.

Didn't I *just* ask them to stay with Gemma? I spun around prepared to give him hell, but he had Gemma in his arms and Maxar was behind him. My expression softened.

"It's voluntary," he went on. "It's why I could bite you and not cause your limbs to stop working. But I bit Zandren and injected the paralytic, so he stumbled away and then stopped moving. It'll wear off though."

"When?" I asked, stroking his fur.

"I gave him a big dose because he's huge, so a few hours."

"Gemma needs medical attention now."

Drak nodded and gently set Gemma down beside Drak.

"We need to get out of here. We're sitting ducks," Maxar said, glancing around. He appeared mostly healed, but his tattered shirt from Zandren's claws hung like scraps of torn fabric off his ripped abdomen.

He was right. Lerris could dispatch an army to finish the job. We needed to leave. We also couldn't go back to the apartment. He knew where we lived. It wasn't safe anymore. Nowhere was safe.

Drak was on his phone. "Yeah, and we'll need a safe house too." He nodded. "'Kay. Thanks, Raver." He hung up. "Our ride is on his way."

Because Bauer and Arik left us, Drak promised to take care of our getaway vehicle. Hopefully, the driver would be strong enough to help lift Zandren.

In less than five minutes, Drak's phone buzzed and he went to let in this *Raver*.

Another vampire, of course. And between the two of them, and Maxar, they managed to drag Zandren's body outside, where they then rolled him up a ramp made of the pallets and into the back of a big, cube van. We nestled Gemma beside him, and I ordered them to take us to the hospital.

"What are we going to do about *that* thing?" Maxar asked, pointing at Lerris's henchman, who was still bound, his eyes wide with fear.

I glanced at the fire mage. "No loose ends. Lerris—and possibly this fool—killed my father and my aunt."

Maxar grinned. "Shall I make him suffer, my Queen?"

I hummed for a moment; the henchman made a noise of protest against his gag.

"We need to get going," I finally said. "Make it quick."

Maxar nodded. "As you wish, my Queen." Black fire shot from his palms and there was just a quick scream of protest around the gag before the henchman's body burst into flame, crumbling to ash a moment later. The acrid smell of burned flesh hung in the air, making bile coat the back of my tongue.

"To the hospital," I said suppressing the urge to gag and getting comfortable between my best friend and my bear-shifter mate, in the back of the cube van.

"Too risky," Raver said, holding onto the door of the van. "There's a healing mage—equivalent, if not superior, to your human doctors—not far from here."

"Gemma's human," I protested, stroking my friend's hair.

"The healing mage will still be able to help her," Maxar said. "It'd be tough to explain some of her injuries to a human doctor."

"Fine," I exhaled, glancing down at Gemma. "Let's go then."

Raver nodded and shut the door, leaving Gemma, Zandren, Maxar, and me in the back, while he and Drak took the two seats in the front.

"She's going to be okay," Maxar said, wincing from pain as he held his abdomen, which was seeping blood from where Zandren had clawed him. He funneled some flames against the gashes to cauterize the wounds.

I glanced at him, pure, unadulterated rage bubbling up in my belly. "She better be. I'm already on the warpath. You don't want to see me when I have nothing left to lose."

We arrived at the healing mage's house about two hours later. Raver said he could have taken us to a closer one, but he wanted to take us out of immediate harm. And since Zandren was still paralyzed and unconscious, and Gemma was also unconscious but alive, I reluctantly agreed.

The healing mage lived out in the middle of nowhere, surrounded by trees, with a river running below a small hill at the rear of the yard. Birds chirped and squirrels tittered like the world wasn't going to total shit as we unloaded from the van.

We left Zandren in the vehicle, since there was no use moving him, and Raver carried Gemma into the house.

"Your Majesty," greeted a comely woman with bright white hair, sharp blue eyes, and twin dimples, as we arrived at her front door. She bowed her head. "It is an honor to meet you." Her expression turned sad. "I'm so sorry about Delia. I knew her well, and she was so kind. Truly tragic."

I pressed my lips together and nodded curtly. "Thank you."

She ushered us inside and motioned for Raver to set Gemma down on a hospital bed inside what appeared to be a proper infirmary. Western medical equipment along with a whole wall of herbs, poultices, and other medicinal plants took up half the room, while four beds took up the other.

"We'll be safe at Melissima's," Raver said. "She's on the right side of all of this."

Melissima nodded and pulled on some latex gloves. I tugged close a chair, settling beside Gemma, and held her hand. Tears spilled down my face as I took in all the dried blood covering her. This was because of me. I'd never not feel this guilt. Never not try to make it right and keep her safe.

"She will be okay," Melissima said, resting a gloved hand on my shoulder. "I can feel her energy. Feel her fight. She is tired. She is weak, but she isn't ready to leave this world yet."

I choked on a sob as more tears fell. "Thank you."

"You go get some rest. I need time with the patient. There is hot water in the kettle in the kitchen."

"I don't want to leave her."

"I understand, but I need my entire magical focus to be on her. If you are here, you will absorb some of my energy and focus. She is human, you are not. I am not. Anything I practice will default to you, as we are of the Realm. I need you in another room so my magic can only go into her."

"She'll be okay," Maxar said, resting a hand on my other shoulder. "We're just going to go to the adjacent room."

I kissed the back of Gemma's hand and reluctantly stood up, following Maxar, Drak, and Raver out to the living room.

Maxar went into the kitchen and found tea bags. He filled up four mugs, bringing them to everyone. When he pulled his hand away to give me my mug, that's when I caught a glimpse of just how badly Zandren's claws had scored him. He wasn't bleeding anymore, but I saw muscle and bone. And oh, god, was that . . . was that part of his liver?

I sprang up from my seat. "You need to go see Melissima. I can see your bones."

"I'll heal," he said with a wince before sitting down in the last empty seat at Melissima's kitchen table. "She needs to funnel all her magic into Gemma. If she has any left, she can take a crack at me."

A roar from outside had the three men lurching to their feet.

Zandren.

I raced out the front door, nearly tripping over a sprinting chicken in the yard, before I made it to the back of the van.

Zandren had shifted back to human form and was stirring, trying to sit up. I crawled into the van. "Easy. Easy."

He blinked open those soft, brown eyes that I loved. "W-what happened?"

"You tried to kill us," Maxar said. He pointed to his abdomen.

Zandren blinked. "I did that?"

I ran my hand affectionately over his bare thigh. "Lerris took control of your mind when the flame crown fell off. He turned you against us. Well, everyone but me."

Guilt filled his eyes. "Who else did I hurt?"

"Nearly bit off my leg," Drak said deadpanned.

Zandren shrugged. "You probably deserved it."

"Drak bit you and injected a paralytic into your body so you'd stop attacking everyone at Lerris's behest," I said.

"Did you at least get Lerris?"

We all exchanged looks.

"He uh . . . he got away," Maxar said.

"But we'll find him," I replied. "Now that we know it's him and what he's after, he can't hide forever. And we won't hide forever. Just enough for everyone to get strong again."

Raver's expression turned sad. "I wonder if he's behind the vampire killings?" He glanced at Drak. "Didn't the mage you captured say that a demon approached him and promised him a high position in his master's court?"

"Vampire killings?" I asked, taking Zandren's hand in mine and giving it a big squeeze. What were they talking about?

Raver nodded. "Someone is coming after vampires. Killing them with zero provocation or remorse. Women. Children. Families. Nobody is safe."

My eyes widened. "That Phaceanesh, the one I killed in the alley, he said something about being hunted."

"You never said anything about that before," Drak said, his tone accusatory.

"I've been a little busy," I shot back, shooting a harsh glare his way before refocusing on the other three men again. "He said *'you're hunting us. Killing us for sport'.* But he was referring specifically to demons. Then he said something about turning the tables, which I assume meant that he was going to kill a demon. I must have completely forgotten about it until now."

"It was a traumatic night for you, Little One," Zandren said softly. "A lot happened. It's understandable."

I smiled at him, then turned back to Drak and Raver. "How long has this been going on?"

Drak pressed his lips together for a moment in thought. "It's been happening for probably the last six months, but in the last month it's gotten more frequent. Near daily reports of murders or attempted murders. A lot of vampires are going into hiding." Drak's expression was dour. "I was torturing a rogue hunter mage for information when I was struck by lightning."

I swallowed. Torturing?

Could he see my demeanor change when he mentioned his vocation?

"He was caught trying to sneak into a vampire family's home. Said there is a reward for every vampire head you bring in. At first, we thought he meant the Phaceanesh, but either he misunderstood, or all vampires are being targeted." Drak glanced at Raver. "After I was struck by lightning, I recommended to King Howar that Raver take up the position I once held, figuring out who is behind this."

"And you think it's Lerris?" I asked.

"We don't know. But it makes sense. If Lerris killed Donovar, he expected to have a court of his own. So to make promises like the one he made the mage isn't unfounded." Drak focused on Raver. "Do you know the name of the henchman Maxar torched?"

Raver shook his head. "No. But I'll find out. Once I know you're all safe in hiding, I'm heading back to New York to meet with the King. Then I'm going to go hunting."

Zandren stood up, and I helped his naked ass climb down out of the cube van.

"Melissima has some clothes in here that'll fit you," Raver said, leading the way back into the house. "You're not the first bear she's hosted."

Zandren grunted. "Don't really care about clothes."

"The rest of us would prefer not to have a staring contest with your one-eyed snake, thank you very much," Maxar said dryly.

Zandren merely grunted again.

Raver ducked into a back room, returning a moment later with a stack of clothes. After some trial and error, Zandren settled on gray sweatpants that actually fit, and a yellow T-shirt that he looked like he was going to Hulk out of any second.

The men all sat down at the table, and after I made Zandren some tea and brought it to him, I went to grab a spare stool from the island to sit on, but he snagged me around the waist and hauled me into his lap, kissing the nape of my neck. "I'm sorry if I hurt you, Little One."

"I was the only one you didn't hurt," I said, settling into him, grateful for his sturdy presence and warmth behind me.

Drak and Raver exchanged looks, but they stowed them as soon as they caught me watching.

My brain hurt from how many questions cannoned around inside of it. And one that wouldn't leave me alone was: what was the thunderclap all about?

"You okay?" Zandren asked, rubbing my thigh.

I shook my head. "No. Not at all."

He kissed my shoulder.

"What do you think that big thunderclap was all about?" I asked, addressing Maxar and Drak, since Zandren was unconscious and in a different part of the warehouse when it happened. "The one that happened right before Lerris escaped."

Drak lifted one shoulder and shook his head.

"I think it was more of your powers gaining strength," Maxar said. "As we've seen, when you're enraged that's when things get *intense*. That's when your powers are strongest. And you were not only terrified for Gemma, but also livid with Lerris. I think it was just . . . for lack of a better term, you reaching the next level of your abilities."

Drak and Raver both nodded. Zandren grunted behind me and rubbed my thigh affectionately.

"Yeah . . . I guess that makes sense."

"Scared the shit out of Lerris, so it worked," Maxar said in an attempt to make me feel better.

I gave him a meek smile of appreciation.

"So now what?" he asked. "Lerris isn't going to stop. He basically said as much. He wants the throne. Someone out there is paying for vampire heads, and for all we know there could be an uprising in the making when the Realm finds out a hybrid is our new queen. Just because we're all cool with Omaera being half human and we welcome the diversity in the gene pool, doesn't mean everyone is going to just take this new regime lying down."

"Particularly because not only is she half human, but any offspring resulting in her mating with anyone of us, will be a human-demon hybrid with another species," Zandren added. "That's three species. Unheard of as far as I know. And we all know how," he cleared his throat, "*pure* some people prefer their species to remain."

Maxar, Drak and Raver all made faces of disgust.

"Such outdated views," Raver said with a headshake. "Diversity is the spice of life. I'd be perfectly fine if my mate turned out to be a mage or demon."

It was lost on nobody that he didn't say *shifter* as well. Zandren made a faint, low growl in his chest, but it was soft enough that I was probably the only one to hear it.

"It means we need to prepare for battle," Drak said cooly. "It's coming, whether we like it or not. Everyone will choose a side."

They all turned to me.

I lifted my brows and pivoted on Zandren's lap so I was sitting sideways and could see him, as well as the other three. "Then I guess this means war. We fight for freedom. We fight for peace, and . . ." I glanced at the sword Lerris had nearly beheaded me with, where it sat in the middle of the table "we fight for vengeance."

Preorder Book 2 Here —> https://books2read.com/OPC-Pain

SNEAK PEEK

PAIN

BOOK 2

THE OMAERA PLAYFAIR CHRONICLES

Preorder Book 2 Here – https://books2read.com/OPC-Pain

CHAPTER ONE

Drak

The longer Omaera put off our mating, the more and more painful the Mate's Ache was going to get. Howar said as much, but even if he hadn't, I was experiencing the agony firsthand.

Raver and I stepped outside to take a call with Howar and let him know what went down with Lerris. He didn't seem nearly as shocked as I expected him to be.

Even though we all speculated that it was Lerris behind the killing of Delia Refera, Omaera's aunt, I knew Omaera was still surprised that it was the truth. We'd all been surprised.

But Howar remained alarmingly calm.

Even Raver and I glanced at each other when the vampire king simply said, "Hmmm. Yes."

"Any news on the vampire killings?" Raver asked. "I needed to get Drak and his mate into hiding, but I am at your disposable, Your Majesty."

"Nothing new," Howar said. "It has been quiet over the last few days—thankfully. I would still like you here, though, Raver. With Drak on the West Coast and with a mate to court, I need a new head of security."

"Of course, Your Majesty."

"How goes the courting, Drak?" Howar asked, directing his question to me. "Is she still bleeding?"

I cleared my throat. "It's uh … it's a slow process. She is very … strongly opinionated and stubborn."

"Have you told her about the Mate's Ache?"

"I have not."

The king scoffed. "You're too noble for your own good. Tell her. Maybe then she'll feel guilty about putting you in constant pain and agree to bond with you."

The last thing I wanted was for Omaera to mate me because she pitied me. Our relationship was already contentious enough without adding a pity bond to it.

I clutched at my chest as a sharp pain speared between my ribs. Raver's dark blue eyes went wide with concern. I shook my head to dismiss him. Omaera was no long in the house and she was moving further away from me. Far enough away that my body didn't like it.

"Talk some sense into him before you get here, Raver," the king said blandly. "Or tell her about the Mate's Ache yourself if Drak has too much decency or whatever to do it. They need to mate or soon she won't even be able to be in a different room before he's writhing on the floor in pain."

Raver's brows rose as he appealed to me to heed the king.

I gritted my teeth and shook my head stiffly. Not going to happen.

"Let me know when you're back in the city and I'll organize a flight for you," Howar said to Raver. "And send me the coordinates of the safe house they're at so I can keep tabs on my stubborn cousin and our new queen."

"I will," Raver replied.

"Good good. I'm glad all are well. It's too bad Lerris got away, but we'll put out a realm-wide BOLO for him. He won't be able to hide for long."

I could merely grunt now. The pain from Omaera's growing distance was so bad.

"Chat soon, Your Majesty," Raver said.

"All right. Goodbye."

Raver hung up his phone and turned to me. "What's wrong?"

"She's ... she's not in the house," I said with a grimace, turning back toward the healer mage, Melissima's house, which was where we were staying.

Raver's eyes went from concerned to panicked and he left me standing next to the box truck he brought us all there in, and ran back into the house. I stumbled after him.

"Where is she?" he asked. "Where is the bear?"

I grunted when a new rush of pain filled my chest. "They've left together. Not too far. I'd probably pass out from the pain if they actually left. And she would never leave her friend in the infirmary." I collapsed into the plush black velvet cushions of Melissima's couch. "They're ... they're probably on a walk in the woods."

Raver frowned. "You really should tell her about the Mate's Ache. I hate seeing you like this."

I shut my eyes when a headache joined the chest pain. "No. We're at odds more than we're not. She doesn't like me. She's said as much. Telling her about the Mate's Ache would only force her to betray her true feelings. When ... *if* we mate, I want it to be because she truly wants to."

"And if that takes a hundred years?" Raver asked.

I peeled one eye open, my vision slightly fuzzy from the pain. "Then it takes a hundred years."

Raver shook his head and made a noise of disagreement in his throat. "I've always known you to be a stubborn son of a bitch, but this is taking it to a whole other level. You're being stupid, now."

"Don't you think I *want* to mate her?" I gritted out. "And I tell her that we should all the time."

"But *why* do you tell her? Because it's for the good of the realm or because it will stop your suffering?"

I didn't say anything, and I closed my eye.

"Yeah, I figured. Like I said, *stupid.*"

The infirmary door beyond Melissima's kitchen opened and the platinum-blonde mage with the flowy dress beneath her surgical smock trailed behind her like a patchwork train. "Where is the queen?" she asked, her sharp blue eyes scanning her home.

"I believe she and the bear have gone for a walk," Raver said. "How is the human?"

"She will live," Melissima said, removing her surgical smock and shoving it into a whicker hamper next to her dishwasher. "It will take a long time for her to heal from all of her injuries, but she will live. It is her mental injuries that have me the most concerned."

"Mental how?" came a voice from the hallway just before the dark redheaded fire mage with a psychotic streak emerged, knuckling sleep out of his eye. "You know that if Gemma isn't okay, Omaera will never forgive herself."

"Yes, I can feel the love Gemma has for the queen and the love the queen has for the human. However, I do fear that although she will recover ..."

I opened my eyes to focus on the healer mage.

Her gaze turned more serious than ever. "She will never be the same person she once was. It's too soon to say what parts of her brain were damaged from the repeated torture and attacks. There is a lot of swelling and once the herbal poultice I mixed up for her reduces the swelling, I'll be able to better discern what parts were damaged."

Maxar pulled out a chair for the table to sit down, but the healer mage stopped him with a dainty hand on his arm. "I would like to check out your injuries, too, Maxar. If I may? I have time now."

He winced when she touched him forcing her to cock her head in curiosity and pull her fingers away.

"But do you have the energy?" he asked. "Or should you be reserving what you have in case Gemma takes a turn?"

Her mouth dipped in concern for a moment before she shook her head. "I have done all I can for the human right now. All we can do at this point is wait. Wait and hope."

We all exchanged pensive looks before I was forced to close my eyes again.

"All right, then," Maxar said. "Where would you like to examine me?"

"The spare room where you were resting should be fine. I don't want you in the infirmary with Gemma otherwise it would cause some of my healing powers that I left with her to transfer to you since you are of our realm and she is not."

"Whatever you say," Maxar said. "Meet you in there."

"I just need to grab a few things," Melissima said.

I didn't bother to open my eyes, but I felt the shift in air pressure and knew she approached. Her cool hand on my forehead confirmed it. "You are experiencing the Mate's Ache." It wasn't a question.

I popped open the same single eye as before. "What do you know of the Mate's Ache?"

"I know all that ails those of our realm. It is my job."

"He won't mate with her," Raver said. "He's being stupid."

I growled, and my other eye opened, too. "It's not that I *won't*. It's that she doesn't want to. She *won't*."

"Have you told her of the Mate's Ache?" Melissima asked.

"The answer is *no*," Raver said. "And there's no sense berating him about it. He's trying to be all noble and shit and wait until she *wants* him. Right now, they're more enemies than lovers in this enemies to lovers romance trope."

Melissima's eyes widened.

Raver scoffed, looking mighty pleased with himself. "What? I pay attention to things. And I happen to know that the enemies to lovers trope is a fan favorite in both books and movies. It's a classic. A tale as old as time. But this idiot is stubborn and determined to play the wounded hero for a hundred years if he has to."

I glared at my best friend.

He gave me a smug look back.

"I can make you a tea that will help manage the pain. It won't take it away, and drugs like morphine and codeine won't work. But it'll dull the ache enough that you can function."

"Man, they just keep pumping you with drugs, don't they?" Raver asked. "Aren't you also a taking drug for your blood lust because your mate bleeds every month?"

Melissima's eyes went even wider. "When was the last time you took your medication for that?"

I couldn't remember. I took it right before we left to go find Lerris and get Gemma back, but ... that was hours ago. I put a spare capsule in my pocket if we ended up getting delayed, but I didn't have the whole bottle.

Melissima clicked her tongue. "I see. Well, I'm no spellcaster mage, but I do have the means to make you a similar compound to what I'm sure was made for you before. For now, though, stay away from Omaera. I'm going to go deal with Maxar, then I'll return and brew you the tea and make the compound."

"Thank you," I croaked.

"You're an idiot," Raver repeated.

I glared at him. "Water," I said with a groan. "Be useful and get me a water so I can take my remaining pill."

Rolling his eyes, he complied, returning from the kitchen a moment later. I reached into the inside of my jacket pocket and pulled out the capsule made by Mr. Fiddleman, the spellcaster mage. I wasn't feeling the blood lust, but then again, maybe it was because Omaera was far enough away?

I didn't want to risk it.

Locking eyes with my oldest friend, I shoved down the pain so it wouldn't cloud my thoughts. "Do me a favor, Rave?"

He grunted and lifted his thick, dark brows. "Hmm?"

"Don't give Howar the real coordinates to here, okay?"

Raver's eyes darkened and turned serious. "Okay. But why?"

I shook my head and closed my eyes again, barely able to stay awake from how bad the pain was now. "Just don't."

Preorder Book 2 Here – https://books2read.com/OPC-Pain

If you've enjoyed this book, please consider leaving a review wherever you purchased it. It really does make a difference and helps an independent author like me.

Thank you again.

Xoxo

Natalie Sloan

ACKNOWLEDGMENTS

There are so many people to thank who help along the way. Publishing a book is definitely not a solo mission, that's for sure.

Thank you to my new editor Vanessa at Bound for Perfection. It means so much that you enjoyed this book and you did a tremendous job editing.

Thank you to Danielle Young, your suggestions (especially regarding our favorite Pooh Bear) on my plot were so helpful.

Megan J. Parker-Squiers from EmCat Designs, your covers are awesome. I love these covers so much, you outdid yourself.

Author Ember Leigh, my author bestie, I love our bitch fests—they keep me sane.

My fabulous assistant, Megan MacPhail of Kiss My Smut, what would I do without you? You are amazing and I SO appreciate all your hard work, beautiful graphics and that you also beta-read this one for me. Thank you!!!

My parents, in-laws and brother, thank you for your unwavering support. The Small Human and the Tiny Human, you are the beats and beasts of my heart, the reason I breathe and the reason I drink. I love you both to infinity and beyond. And lastly, of course, the husband. You are my forever, my other half, the one who keeps me grounded and the only person I have honestly never grown sick of even when we did that six-month backpacking trip and spent every single day together. I never tired of you. Never needed a break. You are my person. I love you.

ABOUT THE AUTHOR

Natalie Sloan is the mother of two gorgeous, wild little girls, and married to her high school sweetheart. She's traveled the world, taught abroad, and now she and her scientist husband with their kids, dog and rabbit call Nanaimo, BC home. She loves writing filthy romance that tugs at your heart strings until you think they might snap, with cantankerous heroes and steel-spined heroines.

Make sure you subscriber to her newsletter to stay up to date on all things reverse harem.
Sign up HERE —> https://nataliesloan.com/contact-me/

OTHER BOOKS BY NATALIE SLOAN

Light the Fire
Revolution Inferno Series
Book 1

https://books2read.com/light-the-fire

Stoke the Flames
Revolution Inferno Series
Book 2

https://books2read.com/stoke-the-flames

Burn it Down
Revolution Inferno Series
Book 3

https://books2read.com/burn-it-down

OTHER BOOKS BY WHITLEY COX

Love, Passion and Power: Part 1
The Dark and Damaged Hearts Series: Book 1

https://books2read.com/LPP1-DDH
Kendra and Justin

Love, Passion and Power: Part 2

The Dark and Damaged Hearts: Book 2

https://books2read.com/LPP2-DDH
Kendra and Justin

Sex, Heat and Hunger: Part 1
The Dark and Damaged Hearts Book 3

https://books2read.com/SHH1-DDH
Emma and James

Sex, Heat and Hunger: Part 2
The Dark and Damaged Hearts Book 4

https://books2read.com/SHH1-DDH
Emma and James

Hot & Filthy: The Honeymoon
The Dark and Damaged Hearts Book 4.5

https://books2read.com/HF-DDH
Emma and James

True, Deep and Forever: Part 1
The Dark and Damaged Hearts Book 5

https://books2read.com/TDF1-DDH
Amy and Garrett

True, Deep and Forever: Part 2
The Dark and Damaged Hearts Book 6

https://books2read.com/TDF2-DDH

Amy and Garrett

Hard, Fast and Madly: Part 1

The Dark and Damaged Hearts Series Book 7

https://books2read.com/HFM1-DDH

Freya and Jacob

Hard, Fast and Madly: Part 2

The Dark and Damaged Hearts Series Book 8

https://books2read.com/HFM1-DDH

Freya and Jacob

Quick & Dirty

Book 1, A Quick Billionaires Novel

https://books2read.com/QDirty-QBS

Parker and Tate

Quick & Easy

Book 2, A Quick Billionaires Novella

https://books2read.com/QEasy-QBS

Heather and Gavin

Quick & Reckless

Book 3, A Quick Billionaires Novel

https://books2read.com/QReckless-QBS

Silver and Warren

Quick & Dangerous
Book 4, A Quick Billionaires Novel
https://books2read.com/QDangerous-QBS
Skyler and Roberto

Quick & Snowy
The Quick Billionaires, Book 5

https://books2read.com/QSnowy-QBS
Brier and Barnes

Doctor Smug

https://books2read.com/DoctorSmug
Daisy and Riley

Hot Dad

https://books2read.com/Hot-Dad
Harper and Sam

Snowed In & Set Up

https://books2read.com/SISU
Amber, Will, Juniper, Hunter, Rowen, Austin

Love to Hate You

https://books2read.com/Love2HateYou
Alex and Eli

Lust Abroad

https://books2read.com/Lust-Abroad
Piper and Derrick

Hired by the Single Dad

https://books2read.com/HBTSD-SDS
The Single Dads of Seattle, Book 1
Tori and Mark

Dancing with the Single Dad

https://books2read.com/DWTSD-SDS
The Single Dads of Seattle, Book 2
Violet and Adam

Saved by the Single Dad

https://books2read.com/SBTSD-SDS
The Single Dads of Seattle, Book 3
Paige and Mitch

Living with the Single Dad

https://books2read.com/LWTSD-SDS
The Single Dads of Seattle, Book 4
Isobel and Aaron

Christmas with the Single Dad

https://books2read.com/CWTSD-SDS

The Single Dads of Seattle, Book 5

Aurora and Zak

New Year's with the Single Dad

https://books2read.com/NYWTSD-SDS

The Single Dads of Seattle, Book 6

Zara and Emmett

Valentine's with the Single Dad

https://books2read.com/VWTSD-SDS

The Single Dads of Seattle, Book 7

Lowenna and Mason

Neighbors with the Single Dad

https://books2read.com/NWTSD-SDS

The Single Dads of Seattle, Book 8

Eva and Scott

Flirting with the Single Dad

https://books2read.com/FWTSD-SDS

The Single Dads of Seattle, Book 9

Tessa and Atlas

Falling for the Single Dad

https://books2read.com/FFTSD-SDS

The Single Dads of Seattle, Book 10
Liam and Richelle

Hot for Teacher

https://books2read.com/HFT-SMS
The Single Moms of Seattle, Book1
Celeste and Max

Hot for a Cop

https://books2read.com/HFAC-SMS
The Single Moms of Seattle, Book 2
Lauren and Isaac

Hot for the Handyman

https://books2read.com/HTHM-SMS
The Single Moms of Seattle, Book 3
Bianca and Jack

Mr. Gray Sweatpants
A Single Moms of Seattle spin-off book

https://books2read.com/MrGraySweatpants
Casey and Leo

Hard Hart

https://books2read.com/HH-HB
The Harty Boys, Book 1

Krista and Brock

Lost Hart
The Harty Boys, Book 2

https://books2read.com/LH-HB
Stacey and Chase

Torn Hart
The Harty Boys, Book 3

https://books2read.com/THART-HB
Lydia and Rex

Dark Hart
The Harty Boys, Book 4

https://books2read.com/DH-HB
Pasha and Heath

Full Hart
The Harty Boys, Book 5

https://books2read.com/FH-HB
A Harty Boys Family Christmas
Joy and Grant

Not Over You
A Young Sisters Novel

https://books2read.com/not-over-you

Rayma and Jordan

Snowed in with the Rancher

A Young Sisters Novel

https://books2read.com/snowed-in-rancher

Triss and Asher

Second Chance with the Rancher

A Young Sisters Novel

https://books2read.com/second-chance-rancher

Mieka and Nate

Done with You

A Young Sisters Novel

https://books2read.com/done-with-you

Oona and Aiden

The Bastard Heir

Winter Harbor Heroes, Book 1

Co-written with Ember Leigh

https://books2read.com/the-bastard-heir

Harlow and Callum

The Asshole Heir

Winter Harbor Heroes, Book 2

Co-written with Ember Leigh

https://books2read.com/the-asshole-heir

Amaya and Carson

The Rebel Heir
Winter Harbor Heroes, Book 3
Co-written with Ember Leigh

https://books2read.com/the-rebel-heir
Lily and Colton

The Matchmaking Heirs
First Winter Harbor Christmas
Winter Harbor Heroes, Book 4
Co-written with Ember Leigh

https://books2read.com/the-matchmaking-heirs
Callum, Harlow, Carson, Amaya, Colton, Lily

Rescued by the Single Dad
The Single Dads of San Camanez: The Brew Brothers
Book 1

https://books2read.com/RBTSD-BB-SDSC
Brooke and Clint

Summer with the Single Dad
The Single Dads of San Camanez: The Brew Brothers
Book 2

https://books2read.com/SWTSD-BB-SDSC

Justine and Bennett

FIND ME HERE

Website: nataliesloan.com

Email: authornataliesloan@gmail.com

Instagram: @authornataliesloan

Facebook Page: https://www.facebook.com/authornataliesloan

Exclusive Facebook Reader Group: www.facebook.com/groups/natalies-loanrhreaderroom

Bookbub: https://www.bookbub.com/authors/natalie-sloan

Subscribe to my newsletter HERE: https://nataliesloan.com/contact-me/

Printed in Great Britain
by Amazon